THE BIG ALPHA IN TOWN

**Also by
Eve Langlais, Milly Taiden, and Kate Baxter**

Thanks Fur Last Night

THE BIG ALPHA IN TOWN

Eve Langlais   Milly Taiden   Kate Baxter

 St. Martin's Griffin ≈ New York

THE BIG ALPHA IN TOWN. Copyright © 2018 by St. Martin's Press. Bearing His Name. Copyright © 2018 by Eve Langlais. Owned by the Lion. Copyright © 2018 by Milly Taiden. No Need Fur Love. Copyright © 2018 by Kate Baxter.

All rights reserved. Printed in the United States of America. For information, address St. Martin's Press, 175 Fifth Avenue, New York, N.Y. 10010.

www.stmartins.com

The Library of Congress Cataloging-in-Publication Data is available upon request.

ISBN 978-1-250-18048-3 (trade paperback)
ISBN 978-1-250-18049-0 (ebook)

Our books may be purchased in bulk for promotional, educational, or business use. Please contact your local bookseller or the Macmillan Corporate and Premium Sales Department at 1-800-221-7945, extension 5442, or by email at MacmillanSpecialMarkets@macmillan.com.

First Edition: May 2018

10 9 8 7 6 5 4 3 2 1

CONTENTS

Bearing His Name by Eve Langlais   1

Owned by the Lion by Milly Taiden   143

No Need Fur Love by Kate Baxter   263

THE BIG ALPHA IN TOWN

BEARING HIS NAME

Eve Langlais

CHAPTER 1

"I need you to find a woman for me," Ark said as he slid into the booth across from his cousin.

"Have you tried calling an escort agency?"

"Not that kind of a woman. A specific woman."

"Then perhaps you should look into online dating."

"I don't think I'll find her there because the woman I'm looking for is supposedly pregnant with my kid."

That caused a bit of choking on Stavros's part and smirking on Ark's.

"What the fuck is wrong with you announcing shit like that while a man is eating." Stavros set down his sandwich and took a swig of his iced tea. "How could you forget to cover your *péos*?" His cousin lapsed into some Greek slang. "What's the first thing we taught you if you're going to play with the ladies?"

And by "we" his cousin meant Ark's well-meaning brothers, cousins, and uncles. They all had advice to give a teenage boy—some of it made sense, like *Watch for skin before you zip.* Other stuff was a little more obscure, such as Uncle Dimi's *Just don't do it.* Don't do *what* was never exactly explained.

"I always cover it. But accidents happen." None that Ark recalled having, but he certainly had to wonder, given the card he'd received. "I got this in the mail." Ark slid over a sealed plastic bag to his cousin. As soon as he'd lifted himself off the floor and realized it contained no address or name, he'd preserved it.

The bag remained untouched as Stavros ignored it. Instead, he used both hands to bring the sandwich—a hefty beast layered with thin slices of roast beef, a thick slice of provolone, caramelized onions, a bit of salad dabbed with balsamic, a smear of mustard over a butter-toasted Panini bun—to his mouth. It looked delicious.

Want some. His mouth watered as Stavros took a bite and chewed slowly while holding half of the sandwich—which left another half.

So hungry. Ark grabbed it, avoiding the slap by his cousin as he made off with it like a bandit. He licked it and cast a sly eye at his cousin.

Stavros grimaced. "You didn't have to do that. I was going to offer it to you. I want to save room for the pie."

Ah yes, the famous sweet and salty honey pie that many a bear indulged in when in the neighborhood.

Drool. He debated ordering two pieces as he savored his bites of the sandwich. Some might wonder that he could think of food at a time like this. His bombshell still sat on the table. But he wasn't too worried. First off, he didn't quite believe the note, and second, his cousin would take care of it when he was ready. This was how Stavros worked. Slow and steady. Until he came after you. Then he struck with lightning speed.

I have the coolest family. Ark seriously did. Between his own brothers and his cousins, plus add in his uncles and his father, family gatherings often devolved into wrestling matches. Outside of course. No one dared start something in the house since the incident with his *yiayia*'s favorite vase.

The glued and jagged pieces sat on the mantel, a reminder of the great wooden spoon incident of 1997.

They ate their sandwiches and demolished the fries before Stavros wiped his fingers on a napkin and said, "Now you may explain what is in the bag. And what you need me for."

"I got a card in the mail."

"The mail?" His cousin arched a brow.

"Yes, mail as in sent in an envelope with a stamp and an address."

"Your address?"

"Yes, my fucking address. How else would I have gotten it?" Ark stabbed a finger at the baggie, pointing at his address, handwritten in block letters on the envelope.

"What's the letter say?"

"It's a card. Blue on the front and there's a picture of a stork carrying a baby wrapped in a blanket in its beak. Inside the card . . ." Inside was the sucker punch.

Congrats, Asshole.
It's a boy.
The woman you never called back

His cousin arched a disbelieving brow. "An anonymous card arrives in the mail and you believe it?"

A frown pulled at his brow. "Not entirely, but then again, why would she lie?"

"Why indeed says the poor little rich bear who drives a Lexus."

"Because it's a very well equipped vehicle."

"So is a moderately priced Camry."

"But it's not as pretty." Nothing wrong with a man stroking his car lovingly every time he parked it in the garage.

"Neither is your mug, but apparently women still manage to find it attractive, hence why you manage to get pussy. And now that pussy is claiming you left a present behind."

"*Claiming* because I'd say there's a strong possibility I didn't." Because Ark was so very careful about these things.

"A DNA test will quickly determine the truth."

"And if she's not lying?"

"Then you do the right thing. Or I'll shoot you."

Better his cousin shoot him quickly before his mother stripped the hide from his body. "So here's the problem. She didn't leave a name or address."

"I know." His cousin turned the baggie over in his hands, checking out the postage marks on the envelope.

"What do you mean 'you know'?"

"I know because you weren't the only one to get a card." His cousin reached into his coat and withdrew a handful of colored envelopes, tossing them onto the table. "Guess what's in these?"

Ark noted the same block lettering on the outside, and he could just imagine the card on the inside. "How many?"

"Seven now that I know of."

"Why us, though, and why that message?" Ark shook his head. "What was she think—"

"If it is a she. Could be a guy who sent this too. Chances are it's someone who wants to see if any of the boys will crack and then they'll hit with the blackmail."

"You think it's a hoax? If it is, then it's not a very funny one." His brow creased, and his bear grumbled, not happy at all. "I want to know who sent it." Because for one heart-attack moment he'd truly wondered if he'd impregnated a girl. If that happened, and word got out, he'd find himself tackled to the ground—by his mother—and forced into a wedding—by his grandmother and her sisters—to a stranger with a baby.

Except, according to Stavros, there was probably no baby. And that, for some reason, made him mad—*because babies are cute*. Really cute so long as they belonged to other people.

"What should we do now? We can't let them get away with this," Ark said with a crack of his knuckles. "Bruises, broken bones, castration—"

"You do realize I'm an officer of the law—"

"Currently serving a suspension."

"—and you're talking about assault."

"Aren't we protected by some family law?"

"That only works if we're married. Are you proposing? Do you want us to adopt the imaginary baby you and seven other cousins that we know of are having?"

"You are no fun since you joined the boys in blue." And to think that as children, Stavros had led them in wondrous mischief. Now he arrested them for the same things he used to do. Since when was watering weeds in an alley against the law? Indecent exposure his hairy ass.

Hairy as a bear, not a man.

"I might be an upstanding citizen now"—the statement so incongruous that Ark couldn't help but snicker—"but that doesn't mean I don't have any fun. And how many times has the family found having a cop in the family useful?"

"I haven't. You haven't cleared a single parking ticket yet."

"But I did stop giving them to you in order to meet my quota."

"Let's get back to the card. What should we do next, Mr. By the Book?" Ark rolled his eyes. He also scratched himself. Obeying the law made him feel so dirty.

"We do nothing for the moment. Whoever sent this covered

their tracks well. Mailed the cards via regular postal service in different states. No fingerprints. No address. No name. Nothing."

"So we sit on our paws and wait for a lucky break?"

We could wait in a sunny patch with a bowl of berries to snack on. His bear had definite ideas.

"We need a trail to hunt. I'm figuring the culprit will contact some of you soon and try to take this scam to the next level." Stavros tucked the baggie with his and the other cards inside his jacket. "The others were clean, but just in case, I'll have Johnson run it for prints and see if we get anything."

And if they did, then what?

Shake the hell out of the idiot who'd scared the honey out of him.

I need some golden remedy, stat!

CHAPTER 2

"You did what?" her sister screeched as she paced the room. "I specifically told you I did not want you to get involved."

With her legs sprawled over the edge of the couch, Jade continued to file her nails. "You only told me that because you're an idiot."

Ruby whirled and shook a finger at her. "No, what's idiotic is contacting a group of guys looking to find the one I had sex with once."

"Mind-blowing sex according to you."

"Yes, it was hot and sweaty and fun. But that's all I remember of him."

"Well, he certainly made sure you'd remember him. Or have you forgotten something?" She eyed her sister's protruding belly.

A hand dropped protectively on it. "He didn't do it on purpose. He used a condom. I remember that."

"And yet you can't remember his face."

"It was a Halloween party. It was dark. His costume was hot."

"You were drunk."

"Two drinks is not drunk, just happy. I was in the mood, so I found someone like-minded." Ruby shrugged. "Not all of us are prudes when it comes to sex."

Not a prude, just picky. Jade had issues with intimacy. "He could have at least called you. You gave him your number."

"I wrote it on his hand in lipstick. It probably got smudged."

"Or maybe he never meant to call." Jade knew men. They were fickle.

"Could be." Ruby shrugged. "A shame, though. He was really good at it."

"I can't believe you still lust after him."

"The man truly was a god. I gotta say, for a spur-of-the-moment encounter, he totally rocked my world."

A spur-of-the-moment encounter that left fruit. "What I'd like to understand is how you could not know you were pregnant. Didn't the missed periods clue you in?"

"You know I was never regular with those things. And I just thought I was getting fat because of that awesome pastry store I hit on the way to work every day."

"I can't believe I didn't notice at Christmas. Are you sure you're that far along?"

Ruby nodded. "Doctor says I got knocked up in either October or early November by the size of the baby. And I didn't hook up with anyone for over a month after that party on account of the move."

It still bothered Jade that her sister had kept secrets. They were always so close. "I should have never let you go out west by yourself."

"Not this again." Ruby rolled her eyes. "You can't keep me bubble wrapped forever. It's not that bad. I'm pregnant. Whoop-de-doo. Happens to women all the time."

"It's a lot of responsibility to handle on your own."

"And yet hundreds of thousands of women do it every day. So can I."

"What of the father, though?"

"You mean Zeus?" Ruby's grin widened. "Just think of it. A god impregnated me. And not just any god, the mightiest Greek god of all." Her sister's eyes brightened as something devious struck her. "Ooh, maybe we'll call the baby Hercules."

No. The horror. "You better be screwing with me. No way are we calling any nephew of mine Herc." Jade couldn't restrain a shudder.

"Okay, maybe we won't. But I can assure you we are definitely not calling him Theodore." The name of the father who'd skipped out on them when Pearl, their youngest sister, was still in diapers.

"We have plenty of time to figure out a name."

"Not really. And what if the sperm donor wants a say?"

"He'd have to man up first."

"What do you think they'll do when they get the card?" Ruby asked, one hand reaching down to rub against her belly.

"If he's got any kind of moral backbone, he'll take responsibility and help you out with the kid." Jade could have yanked back the words as soon as they left her lips.

Ruby's back straightened. "I don't need anyone's help, thank you very much. I can take care of my son myself."

"I never said you couldn't, but that will be a lot easier to do if Mr. Can't Keep It in His Pants coughs up some cash to help out."

"And what if I don't want his money?"

With a narrowed gaze at her sister, Jade said it softly. "You'll take it for the baby's sake so he doesn't have to watch his mother work herself to death like we did." A single mother of four kids—with a deadbeat of a husband—meant Jade's mother had spent more time out of the home earning a few paychecks than giving them hugs and reading bedtime stories.

As the oldest of them all, that task had fallen on Jade, which was why she felt compelled to meddle in her sister's life when she'd arrived on Jade's doorstep, her belly a ripe watermelon. Apparently during their weekly phone calls her sister had neglected to mention that important fact.

"You are so incredibly bossy," her sister grumbled.

"And don't forget I'm right. You know this is the proper thing to do." Jade just hoped the guy had the balls to face the results of his actions. Of course, it would help if she'd sent the possible candidates an address. But Jade wanted the guys to sweat a bit first. To spend a few sleepless nights thinking on their actions.

She felt only a twinge of guilt at the thought that she was stressing out seven men instead of one. How else was she to ferret out the right one? She'd managed to discover, and not easily—she spent a few hundred dollars bribing someone on the catering staff—who the guys wearing the Zeus outfits were at the fateful party. Brothers and cousins all from the same family as it turned out. Problem was the public pro-file pics Jade found didn't ring any bells with Ruby. Her sister didn't recognize any of them, but maybe they'd re-member her.

"What if he wants nothing to do with the baby?"

"Then we'll take him to court and make him face his re-sponsibilities."

"Seems rather harsh for a few minutes of bump and grind." Her sister flopped onto the couch, right on top of Jade's belly, drawing an oomph.

"Cow. You're going to squish me flat."

"Whiner." Ruby grinned, a dimple popping in the left cheek. "Thanks again for letting me crash here. With the baby getting close, I didn't want to be alone."

"You'll never be alone." Because Jade would always be there for Ruby and the baby.

Or so she hoped later that afternoon when she opened the door to find a big menacing dude with craggy features standing there. The dude, who looked straight out of a mobster movie in his pin-striped suit, loomed over her in the doorway.

"Ms. Cadeux?"

"Yes, but you're not the UPS guy," she managed to say. She'd expected her package of shoes. Bought on sale and a decadently beautiful red.

However this guy didn't hold a package. He did, however, hold her gaze, locking his eyes to hers and causing her heart to race. Something fluttered in her.

Fear. Anticipation. Arousal . . .

What the hell? "Who are you?" she whispered.

Oddly enough she could have sworn she heard someone growling, *Mine.*

CHAPTER 3

I'm your mate. You're mine. All mine.

Yes, mine.

Grawr.

The realization hit Ark the moment the door opened. A vanilla-honey scent drifted out to him, the sweet fragrance wrapping around his limbs, stroking his skin. It even managed to ignite his taste buds.

Want the yummy thing.

Bear and man both wanted the same thing. The woman standing before him.

The certainty that she was his mate hit him much like that baseball bat had in third grade. It punched the air out of him with an almost audible whoosh.

Unlike many boys, Ark didn't mock the mating instinct. He knew, when it hit, a man was a goner. He didn't stand a chance.

And to think what took me down isn't even chin high. Then again, he was rather tall for a bear—and he wasn't even a Kodiak. Or so his grandmother claimed. Funny how none of her kids looked like their dad.

Jade eyed him, cute as could be with her hair pulled back in a ponytail, drawing attention to the high cheekbones, rounded cheeks, and full, pouty lips. Dark lashes blinked over darker eyes. The tip of her pink tongue wet her lips. Her skin was a creamy cocoa he wanted to lick.

Good enough to eat.

Reality bitch slapped him, and he realized her lips moved. "Can I help you?"

Well, yes, as a matter of fact she could. She could help him by letting him gather her into his arms, bend her back, and plunder those luscious lips and maybe nibble on that throat, have a little suck at the skin. Perhaps leave a little bite to mark the spot.

Bite.

Now, most men might have shied away from wanting to leave a permanent mark on a strange woman. But this woman was his. Earmarked by fate. Handed to him wrapped in track pants and a T-shirt that read, *Mine*. Okay, so it actually featured a princess making a rude gesture. In his mind though, he could totally picture it.

He might have stared overlong without talking. His brothers weren't there to slap him and tell him to stop freaking out the pretty girl. It caused her brow to knit, adding to her cuteness.

"I said can I help you? On second thought, I don't care why you're here. Whatever it is, I'm not interested." She went to slam the door, and he snapped out of his stupor long enough to insert a hand in the door.

Crunch. Apparently his fleshy doorstopper wouldn't stop her from slamming his fingers. Repeatedly. And when he didn't remove them, she threw herself against the door in an attempt to ram it shut.

Ouch. Not something he uttered aloud. Hello, he was a bear, not a puny man.

"Are you done trying to amputate my fingers?"

"Take. Them. Out. Then," she huffed as she kept pushing at the door.

"Not until we talk." And maybe kiss. He wasn't averse to groping either.

"I don't talk to crazy dudes at my door."

"I'm not crazy; I'm Greek." The statement gave him plenty of leeway to behave. Such as playing the part of arrogant alpha male.

"Go away." She reared back and thumped the door.

She'll hurt herself. He couldn't allow that. He withdrew his fingers and the door slammed shut. A loud click sounded as it was bolted too.

A grin stretched his face. Playing hard to get. He loved a challenge.

Knocking, he waited. And waited. When she didn't reply, he leaned close. "I know you're there. I can hear you breathing."

"You cannot."

Actually, he could, but he could see why a cute little human like herself wouldn't understand his special power.

"I am sorry if I startled you." In his defense, she startled him first.

"Apology accepted. Now go away."

"I can't. I need to talk to you." Talk, touch, taste. Possibly in reverse order.

"I have nothing to say to you."

"I disagree." They had many things to talk about, such as where they'd live after the wedding, how many cubs they'd have. He was thinking a half dozen but was open to more if she insisted.

Another knock only netted him some heavy breathing. Hers not his. She too found this whole courtship exciting.

Since she didn't seem inclined to open the door, he pulled out his lock picks. It might seem like an odd thing to carry around, if you didn't know his family. Usually he'd have even more tools, however the airport frowned on so many things these days; crowbars, machetes, blowtorches. Explaining he had to use them in his quest for new flavors of honey, straight from the hive, failed to sway them.

The basic lock didn't take long to pick and keeping the tips of his tools in the hole meant she couldn't reengage it. A twist of the handle saw the door move only an inch before she slammed against it.

"I'm coming in," he announced.

"Oh no you're not," she snarled.

Did she dare him?

I accept.

Palms against the painted panel, he shoved it open with ease. It wasn't just his bear that was strong. Ark worked out too, and had the muscle to prove it. What he lacked, though, was a certain finesse with women.

The brute strength, while effective in gaining him entrance, had the unfortunate effect of sending the woman—his mate—stumbling. He could hear his mother now. *"Is that how we raised you?"* Followed by a whack with her dish towel. *"To bully women?"* Snap. "The shame." Yes the shame, because he'd just mistreated the woman he would spend his life with.

"I am terribly sorry."

"You will be," she snarled.

So cute. Everything about Jade was cute.

And just who was Ms. Jade Cadeux? He knew the basics; age twenty-seven, born and raised in Montreal, Quebec, but moved to New York City after the death of her mother. The only reason he knew that much was because she'd been arrested for possession of an illegal substance at eighteen while still living in Canada. It was enough to require a fingerprint on file that drew up her record with border services. A fingerprint that matched a partial print on the card he'd received.

One thing was for sure; he'd never met her before. When Stavros had emailed him a picture, Ark had not felt a spark of recognition. He blamed it on an awful DMV mug shot. Yet now, in person, while his bear might be grumbling and mumbling this woman belonged to them, the man did not recall a single thing about her at all, which meant he wasn't her baby daddy . . . if she was even pregnant. He eyed her flat belly with skepticism.

"Get out," she yelled.

"Or else what?" he asked, shutting the door, narrowly missing the first shoe aimed at his face and snatching the second midair. "You have excellent aim." He wondered how she'd do at plate tossing. It was now a yearly event at Aunt Karina's summer barbecue, and it was time someone dethroned his cousin Mabel. "I get the impression you're a tad agitated."

"A tad? I am very agitated, you thug," she huffed. "Get out of my apartment. Right now. Or I'm calling the cops." She whirled and darted for a cell phone lying on a living room table.

"Is this how you want the story of how we met relayed to the children?"

"What children? Stay away from me, you psycho." She brought up the phone, and her fingers scrabbled on the screen to enter a passcode.

It took but a moment to stop her from dialing, his large hands circling her wrists and prying them apart, forcing her to stop her frantic actions. He wasn't quite sure how to calm her. When his mother got mad, his father bought her something. He'd not thought to bring a gift. Perhaps he could use words? That doctor on TV was always going on about talking. "I think we got off on the wrong foot."

She stomped his foot. Since hers was bare, it didn't do much.

"This might seem sudden, but if you hear me out—"

She kneed him but hit his thigh. His poor woman wore herself out trying to fight her probably overwhelming attraction to him. "You are going to hurt yourself. You need to calm yourself, *koukla.*"

"I'll calm myself when you're out of here," she said with a snarl as she wrenched at his grip.

Much as he'd like to hold her forever, he let her go. Best to not overwhelm her with his magnificence too quickly.

"Why would I leave when you dared me to come? I got your card."

"Card?" She froze. Brown eyes peered upward at him. "What's your name?"

"Arkadios Pietro Matis. But my friends call me Ark." *And the women call me* Dios*, god,* but that wasn't something he felt he should share. Especially since his seduction days were now over. He was in the presence of his mate, the only woman he'd ever touch again.

"You know about the baby."

"You mean there really is a baby?" His brows rose. It couldn't be. For one, he was always so careful with his paramours. Not to mention he usually remembered sleeping with them. He didn't recall this lady at all. If she did indeed carry an infant, it wasn't his.

Which obviously put him in a big dilemma, especially

considering the cards she'd sent to the other possible fathers. Most of them were related to him. If one of them were the father of her cub, then . . .

We'll eat him. End of problem.

Seemed simple, but he could just see his mother having a fit over getting rid of one of his many cousins.

He could always send a message to Stavros and advise him to tell the others she and the babe belonged to him. *I will be her baby's daddy.*

Eep.

Who made that sound?

"Yes, there really is a baby. It's why I sent the card," she stated with an eloquent roll of her eyes.

"It was very unexpected."

"Which explains why you're here all pissed off."

He arched a brow. "On the contrary, I am not angry in the least. I am delighted to have found you." It called for a hug.

She danced out of his reach. "Good for you because I'm a little freaked out that you just showed up."

"I'm spontaneous." And he had long arms, which meant he got his bear hug. He lifted her off the floor and she sounded quite breathless when she said, "Put me down."

"But I'm happy to see you."

She pushed at his grip. "Would you let me go?"

No. Even he knew better than to say that out loud. "Yes I will let go, but only if you promise not to call the police." His uncle might be a lawyer, but he charged an exorbitant fee whenever Ark needed help avoiding jail time. Uncle Jorgi didn't believe in a family discount.

He deposited her again.

The fear in her subsided, and she angled her chin as she said, "Behave yourself or I'll have your ass put behind bars."

Such spunky spirit. Such a good match. He could see

them having fun together. "Having me arrested will delay the wedding."

Her mouth rounded. "You're planning to get married because of the baby?"

"There is no other choice." Even without the baby, he would marry her. She belonged to him.

For some reason those words, despite the lack of romance, softened her features. "I knew Ruby was wrong. Contacting you was the right thing to do. But just so you know, you don't have to get married. It will be enough if you're there for the baby. Maybe toss a couple bucks in each month to help out with costs."

"Money is no issue." The family had more than enough. "And I will be a part of the child's life." As if he would do any less. Family was everything, the one motto he and everyone else, except for maybe his crazy cousin Cole, lived by.

"You're not what I expected. Then again, I guess I didn't really know what you'd be like."

"What did you expect?"

Her lips twitched. "I didn't expect you to show up."

"Expectations are a dangerous thing." And anticipation was pure torture. All he wanted was to draw this woman into his arms and plunder those lips.

"So I guess if you called in some favors you know who I am."

Of course he did. *You're my mate.* But he managed to hold those words back, given she regarded him still with suspicion. He'd have to sweeten her up first.

With honey.

Mmmm. Honey. The kind drizzled on her skin needing a good tongue lapping.

The door behind him suddenly opened and he whirled to see a woman with similar features as his mate, her hair loose and straight. Her features a little rounder, hair a little curlier, and sporting a giant pregnant belly.

The earth tilted and he heard himself query as if from far away, "Who is that?"

"Are you fucking kidding me?" gasped the woman he still held, the woman his gut still screamed was his mate. "That's my sister, you asshole. The one you impregnated."

A roaring noise entered his mind at that point as she continued to yell at him. She also resumed stomping his foot with her bare feet and trying to kick his shins.

He managed to ignore that craziness because, in that moment, only one thought kept paw-slapping him over and over. What cruel joke had the universe played? The woman he might have impregnated was the sister of his mate?

Talk about a honey of a clusterfuck.

CHAPTER 4

The big dude, Ark as he called himself, still sat on the couch staring at Ruby's belly. He bore the look of a man struck with a wrecking ball.

"And you think it was me." The third time he'd asked.

"Actually not just you. I never got the name of the guy I was with that night." Ruby folded her hands over her belly. She bore a fierce, unapologetic look. "He hit the party dressed as a hot god and I was a kitty in heat."

"Ruby!" Jade couldn't help but exclaim, her cheeks hot.

"Well I was. I was horny and had a one-night stand. Get over it."

"It's not right," she mumbled, aware of how she sounded but unable to stop herself. Jade had this funny belief in only being with the right man. A man she loved. It was why she'd been with only two guys in her life, and only after a long period of dating.

"You're right. It was bad. *Soooo* bad," her sister purred.

Jade cleared her throat and tried to bring them back to Ark and the fateful party. "So you don't deny you were at that Halloween party, the one out in Beverly Hills?"

His brow furrowed and his shoulders sank. "Yeah. I was there."

Her heart almost sank too. For some reason, despite knowing who this playboy was—*the possible father of my sister's kid*—she couldn't help her initial reaction upon seeing him. Instant molten attraction. Then annoyance as he'd manhandled her—gently manhandled she might add. Not once during his imprisonment of her hands had he ever actually exerted any pressure, and this despite her savage attempts to maim him.

The man oozed virility. She hated to even mentally admit it. Dude was totally not her type, and yet, at the same time, he was. Big, over six feet by a few inches. Like a giant tower—*that I totally want to invade*—with thick arms, a solid trunk, and powerful-looking thighs clearly defined by his khakis.

He possessed a swarthy complexion, with dark hair, thick brows, and stark features, very Mediterranean-looking and hot.

He was also extremely off-limits.

This could be the guy who impregnated Ruby. And the sad thing about it? Neither remembered a thing about the other.

"Did you hook up that night?"

He shrugged. "Yeah. I mean I guess."

"I guess?"

"Most of us were pretty wasted."

"Ditto what he said," Ruby added, raising her hand. "Those gelatin shots were wicked good."

"The tequila was even better," he added with a shared grin.

Jade frowned at them both. "Can we stay on track here?"

"As my *koukla* wishes. I was there at that party, drinking heavily, which is why parts of the evening are a blur. But if I did get frisky, I guarantee I wore a rubber."

"They're not foolproof." Jade couldn't help but play devil's

advocate. "And you were dressed as Zeus." Or as Ruby recalled, big-built dudes wearing togas, white wigs, and giant
bushy white beards.

"Me and my cousins. We do it every year. It's a family joke
on account we're Greek."

"And do all of the men in your family not call a girl the
day after?" Jade arched a brow.

He scratched his head. "Why would they?"

"You're kidding, right?"

"You haven't met my cousins. And I will add that I would
never stoop to writing a number on my hand. I use my cell
phone to store numbers." He waggled it.

She held out her hand. "Let me see it."

"Why?"

"To see if it's in there."

He handed it over. Even typed in the passcode for her. It
took her but a few minutes to eye him. "It's nothing but
guys in there. Are you gay?"

"No." He barked the word, but it didn't change her appraising look. He grumbled. "My turn to ask questions. Such
as, why are you only contacting us now and not earlier in
the pregnancy?"

"I wasn't planning on contacting you or any of the others,"
Ruby admitted with a roll of her shoulders. "But Jade thought
the daddy should know."

"She did, did she, and why is that?" He narrowed his gaze
on Jade, seeming inexplicably annoyed, which she couldn't
figure out.

When he'd first arrived, he seemed all gung ho about
doing the right thing and taking responsibility. Hell, he even
said he would marry her sister. Now he acted as if he wanted
nothing more than to find a way to ensure he wasn't the
daddy.

"That baby needs support."

"So it's about money?"

"No. It's about doing the right thing for that child and giving it a father." Jade crossed her arms. She missed out on having a daddy growing up and she didn't want to see it happen to her nephew.

"Stavros was right. You want a daddy to pay child support." He shook his head. "I'm going to need a paternity test, of course, to determine who the child belongs to before we do anything."

"Are you going to tell the other guys?"

"Of course. They'll probably also want to meet Ruby. Perhaps they will recall a certain night spent with a mocha kitten."

The compliment didn't sit well with Jade. "And if they don't?"

"Once we prove via DNA this isn't a scheme to get money then—"

She sucked in a breath. "Are you accusing us of blackmail?"

"Actually the correct term is 'extortion.'"

"Get out." She sprang from her chair and pointed to the door.

"Don't worry, *koukla*. I am not shocked by your savvy financial sense. Rather pleased. My family doesn't always obey the letter of the law either."

"We are not crooks and we want nothing to do with you or your cousins if you are. Ruby was right. Contacting you was a bad idea. You need to leave."

Instead, he leaned back and folded his big arms over his chest. "I don't think it's up to you to order me out."

"My name on the lease. My rules."

"Possibly my baby." He pointed to Ruby's stomach. "That trumps all your excuses."

The reminder of what he might have done caused something in her to snap. She threw a remote. She didn't even remember grabbing it. But he saw it coming and snatched it in midair.

"Are you going to throw things every time I say something you don't like?"

"Probably." Some people counted. Others screamed. She threw stuff, mostly shoes now since she no longer owned any knickknacks and she kept the knives in a child-proof drawer. It took paying out of pocket to replace three cell phones to teach her to throw shoes instead of smart devices.

"Stop freaking out, sis. I happen to agree we should get the test," Ruby interjected.

That stayed the slipper she'd yanked off her foot. Jade stared at her sister. "Excuse me."

"What if I am wrong? I mean, there were a lot of folks dressed up that night. And like seven or eight Zeuses. Who's to say we even have the right ones?"

Getting tested was the logical thing. So why did it still enrage her? *Why does the thought of Ruby and Ark being together make me so uncomfortable?* The jealousy made no sense.

"If the child is mine"—which his very expression said he doubted—"I will do right by it."

"Him. It's a him," she corrected.

"How can you be sure?"

"The way she's carrying." Jade pointed to her. "It's all in how the belly hangs."

"Don't let her screw with you," Ruby said. "I saw his little thingie on the ultrasound. It's a boy. Now, if you'll both excuse me, Junior needs a snack." She rose from the couch, Ark quick to give a hand and haul Ruby to her feet. With a nod of thanks, her sister waddled to the kitchen.

"Your sister is living with you?"

"For the moment. She didn't want to have the baby alone." So her sister had embarked on a long bus ride across the country.

"Does she have a doctor?"

"Kind of. I had her see the one at the clinic by my work." All they could afford on their medical plan.

"That is not good enough. We shall have her see my family one."

Jade's brow wrinkled. "Is he flying out here? Because she's too pregnant to fly out west."

"Fly? No. She is obviously in no shape to see my uncle Ken. However, my great-uncle Huego still maintains his practice in New York."

"Our insurance won't—"

"I will cover this."

"And what if the baby isn't yours? We won't be able to pay you back."

"This won't cost either of you a thing."

This kind of altruism after his odd reaction didn't sit well for some reason. "Why do you seem so reasonable again? Less than half an hour ago, you were looking like you wanted to pass out, and now you're Mr. Nice again."

"Just a little shocked. But I'm over it."

"Because you don't think the baby is yours." She shook her head.

"I know it's not mine. The gods have other plans for me."

Such an odd thing to say. "And what are your plans for the future?" How did he support himself? Because that suit he wore wasn't cheap. And the watch? More than she made in three months. "What do you do for a living? When I did my search to find out who you all were, the only mention I saw for you is under a company called Kalameli."

"I'm a businessman."

"Of what?"

"Imports. Exports."

Wasn't that what the criminals called their enterprises in the movies? He certainly looked a bit gangster. "Is that a polite way of saying you're a drug dealer?"

His laughter barked out loud and boisterous. "No. Although our product is considered addictive." He smiled. "We deal in honey."

"As in sticky honey?"

"And creamed. We also do lotions and lip balms. We have an entire division devoted to the creation of new honey products. I can have some sent to you, if you'd like."

Jade couldn't help a wrinkle of her nose. "I don't eat honey. It's too sweet."

He looked utterly appalled. "That will have to change. Honey rules the world." Except, given where his gaze dropped, it seemed doubtful he was thinking of honey that came in a jar.

"Eyes up here," she growled. Perhaps it would be a blessing if the guy turned out not to be the father of her sister's baby. He was obviously a bit of a playboy.

"My apologies." He said it and, by his grin, obviously didn't mean it. "And now that I've answered some of your questions, my turn. Are you single?"

"None of your business."

"How do you feel about full moons?"

"Why do you care? Are you going to tell me you turn into a werewolf and run through the woods naked?"

"That's crazy." He smiled, a little too wide and toothily as he said, "Everyone knows werewolves don't exist."

"But bedtimes do." She tapped her watch. "While this has been fascinating, Ruby and I need our sleep." Mostly Jade, though, given she was expected to work in the morning.

"I take it you're not inviting me to spend the night, even though I've flown all this way."

"Our hotel industry would love the business."

"I will call you in the morning."

"Why?" She wrinkled her nose.

"To make arrangements."

"Oh, you mean the doctor."

"And we need to schedule the paternity test."

"That is going to have to wait until the baby is born."

"Born? Isn't there a way we can clear this up now?"

"Not without risking the baby." Amniocentesis could give the kind of results they needed, but she'd heard scary things about it. Besides, given her size, Ruby would probably deliver soon. Or explode. Surely her skin couldn't stretch any further.

"How long until the child comes?"

She shrugged. "The doctor is ballparking it from the Halloween party. It could happen any week now."

"Call me." He pulled a card from his pocket.

"I'll leave that up to Ruby if she wants to talk to you."

"Or you can call me."

Her lips flattened. "Not likely. Or have you forgotten why you're here?"

"I didn't touch her."

For some reason he seemed so determined to convince her. A pity it wouldn't work.

Jade opened the door and held it as he walked past, but he no sooner crossed the threshold than he whirled around.

"Once we clear up the baby issue, I would like to take you to dinner."

"Did you just ask me out?" Jade ogled him in disbelief then slammed the door in his face.

The nerve of him.

She should have been outraged. Pissed that in the midst of such a serious accusation he'd hit on her.

But the womanly part of her, the part that roiled with jealousy, bloomed with warmth.

I'm such a traitor.

CHAPTER 5

The door remained closed and Ark did not kick it down. Nor did he pick the lock again.

Yeah, he was proud of his restraint too.

What an entirely bizarre hour. Welcome to his new hill-billy life, or so his cousin named it when Ark related it to him over a few beers. Stavros, unwilling to miss out on the action, had accompanied Ark on his trip across the country.

"So let me get this straight: Your mate is the sister of a woman you don't remember poking who is carrying your bun in the oven."

"Possible bun. It's more likely someone else's." He refused to believe it without proof. Refused to believe fate would fuck him over like that.

"If it's yours, then maybe they'll want to do some sister-wife thing like you see on those reality shows."

Ark didn't even look to see where his fist landed. He did, however, enjoy the *oomph* Stavros emitted as Ark struck him. His cousin rubbed his jaw. "Someone is a little sensitive."

"I don't want the sister."

"Maybe not, but if that baby is yours, then you are going to run into some issues."

"Do you think?" He stared morosely at his drink. "This kind of shit doesn't happen in the movies."

"You mean it doesn't happen to the good guys. Have you forgotten who we are?" Stavros spun on his stool and snapped his fingers at the fellow passing behind him. "This pasty-faced fellow here knows who we are, don't you?"

"I don't know what you're talking about," stated the skinny guy as he tried to pass them on his way back from the bathroom.

"Are you sure about that?" Stavros asked, not letting the guy by. "Because I know I saw you on the flight over here from L.A. and again this afternoon sitting in a coffee shop, which is coincidentally right across the street from the building my friend was visiting. That seems like a big coincidence, don't you think, Ark?"

Ark fixed the guy with a stare that made him fidget. "Huge coincidence and very unlikely given the size of this city."

The scrawny fellow hunched his shoulders. "Don't know what you're talking about. And since you're the one who kept noticing me, how do I know you're not following me? I was in this bar first."

"I know because I followed your ass to this shitty little dive." Stavros grinned.

"I wouldn't call it shitty. The beer is cheap and the wings are good," Ark noted. He also couldn't help a mournful look at the now empty plate.

As the guy went to move around Ark he put out an arm to block him. "Not so fast. We still haven't discussed why you followed us from the West Coast."

"Fuck off. I ain't following you."

Ark shook his head. "Why did you have to go and lie? I hate liars."

"I don't like his face." Stavros grabbed the guy, who wore entirely too much cologne, and yanked him down, smooshing his cheek against the bar top. "It's why I followed him when I saw him lurking outside the building we were visiting."

"Who are you working for?" Ark asked nicely—and people said he was rash. He only got hotheaded if he had to ask a second time.

"No one hired me to do nothing."

Stavros sighed as he adjusted his grip on the guy, grabbing a fistful of hair instead. "Didn't your mother ever teach you not to lie, boy?"

"I know nothing. Whoever you think I am, you got me mistaken with someone else."

Slam.

Ark leaned forward as Stavros lifted the bruised visage of the street thug from the bar. "Wrong answer. I've seen you twice now, which is two times too many. Why are you following me?"

"I am not—" Slam. "Following you. Fuck. I'm telling you the truth." The skinny twerp glared before shouting, "Is anyone gonna stop these fuckers?"

The bartender didn't even glance their way, simply asked, "Ready for another round?"

"Yes, please." Ark loved a good shot of honey Jack. "And some more of those honey-glazed wings too." The money he slid at the bartender more than covered the request and included a sizable tip.

Stavros yanked the guy who had been following them since they flew out from the coast upright. What a rather embarrassing specimen to send to spy on Ark. *I deserve a better adversary.* Or at least a bigger one.

Ark stared the guy in the eyes. "Since I'm a nice man"—Stavros snorted—"I'm going to give you a warning. Stay away from me, or next time I won't be gentle."

"Like I said, I wasn't following you. I'm here investigating something for my boss."

"Who is your boss?" Ark asked. When the guy hesitated, Ark arched a brow and cracked his knuckles.

The guy swallowed. "Some rich dude. He says his girlfriend took off with something of his."

"You're an investigator?" Stavros eyed him. "Where's your camera?"

"On my phone."

"What did the girl take?"

"How the fuck would I know." The fellow seemed rather agitated. Probably not enough honey in his diet.

"If you don't know then how will you find what your boss lost?"

"How about none of your fucking business. Jesus, would you give it a rest already. I'm not following you or your buddy. We just happened to cross paths. So fucking chill."

"I will chill, little man, but don't let me run into you again or we will have a problem." Because in the cutthroat world of honey, Ark and his family didn't take kindly to interlopers. Was someone thinking of taking him out so they could make another run at bear territory?

Excellent. It had been a while since they'd enjoyed a good brawl, and after the exercise and bloodshed, his aunt Zuna always made ribs. Honey-glazed ribs. *Mmm.*

Stavros shoved the skinny guy away from them. The pathetic specimen fled, and Stavros asked, "Should we follow him?"

"If he's lying, he'll be back. Think of the fun we'll have." Ark grinned. Not to mention he could use the distraction of the little man.

A platter was set in front of them forestalling any further

talk and the rest of the evening passed with wings and beers. Tasty stuff that did nothing to forestall the bear grumbling inside his head.

Worse than the bear bugging him, the man found his curiosity aroused. He couldn't help but think about Jade.

He tried to find it within him to feel guilty about it. After all, there existed a possibility he'd slept with her sister, but in the man guide, it didn't count as cheating. He'd never met Jade at that point. Never knew she would be the one to make his beast want to roll over and demand a belly rub. It wasn't just dogs that liked them.

Curiosity drew him back to the apartment building, back to the woman with the vanilla-honey scent. The woman who'd slammed a door in his face. A woman undaunted by his size. A woman he wanted to lick from head to toe, and especially in between.

Sigh.

She exuded utter perfection. Even in sleep, her face composed, she appeared very angelic, so was it any wonder he took a picture? She didn't have to scream.

CHAPTER 6

The scream barely managed to pass Jade's lips before it was stifled by a hand over her mouth. Her heart fluttered, but stupidly enough not in fear.

Through the dim light coming through her window, she recognized that beaked nose and those dark eyes.

"Hsgdsgjhew," she mumbled against his hand.

"Did I wake you?"

She arched a brow.

"Sorry."

He said it, but she didn't believe it for a second. "Gnng," she growled.

"I agree you should move over and make some room." He shoved at her, one hand still over her mouth.

Enough was enough. She bit him.

Hard.

White teeth gleam as he grinned. "Is that supposed to be foreplay?"

She bit him again in answer.

"So that's a yes?"

Grrrr.

"No? Shame. If you change your mind, let me know."

Change her mind? He was completely unbalanced if

he thought she'd for one second consider getting involved with him.

Look who I'm talking about. He's already insane.

She squirmed against his hand.

"Very well, *koukla*, I'll let go if you promise not to scream. Some neighbors can be so nosy, calling the cops just because a man likes to use a window to get in. Others seem to think screaming is a bad thing. If you ask me, they should be so lucky to have someone who makes them scream in bed." He winked. "The hand is coming off now, but keep in mind, if you insist on making noise, I have other body parts that can gag you."

Try it, she dared with her eyes. She'd bite whatever came her way—and lick it and . . . The very idea was so wrong. So very wrong.

"Tempting." It was if he read her mind.

He pulled his hand away and she exclaimed, "What the hell is wrong with you?"

"Depends on who you ask. Dad says I am an imbecile, probably on account of the concussions I got playing hockey. My brother says I'm an idiot. Personally, I think I'm perfect, and my mother agrees."

"Does she also agree with you breaking into women's bedrooms and attacking them?"

"Attacking? I'm the one with injuries here." He held up his hand that barely had an indent from her teeth.

"I attacked because you thought to subdue me and—"

"I just wanted to snuggle." He drew her against him, his arm a solid anchor around her waist that wouldn't let her escape. And dammit, she should want to escape and not have it feel so good.

"We are not snuggling," she growled through gritted teeth as she tried to pry herself away. The thrashing did nothing but coil his arm tighter. "You're being disrespectful to my sister."

"Not really since it's not my baby."

"We don't know that for sure."

"I do."

"So you're calling her a liar?"

"Nope. She is obviously pregnant, just not by me."

"Even if you're not the daddy, I still wouldn't be with you."

"Why not? I'm in good health. Have all my teeth. I'm employed. Is this because I'm not like you?"

Was he calling her a racist? "It has nothing to do with the color of your skin."

"I meant, is it because I'm Greek? I realize we sometimes get a bad rap. We are loud at times. Very arrogant too. But I see that as a character trait not a flaw. I should also admit my mother is a devout Orthodox follower, but I'm more loose in my beliefs. So church is only every other Sunday, and you'll only need to learn to celebrate a few holidays."

"We won't be celebrating anything because, if you're right and the baby is not yours"—and she couldn't help but hope it wasn't—"you'll be out of our lives."

"Not likely. I rather like it here." He snuggled deeper into her sheets and somehow managed to roll her atop him. He laced his arms around her, trapping her against his body. "That's better."

Better for him since he sported an obvious erection currently pressing against her thighs.

"You are unbelievable."

"So they say," he agreed with a sage nod.

"Let me go."

"Make me."

She braced her hands on his shoulders to push herself

away from him, and yet, she couldn't escape. His strength frustrated her, mostly because the more he held her tight the sexier he got.

That wasn't supposed to happen. She was supposed to hate the aggressive guy who invaded her bed, not want to kiss him!

"Are you always this stalkerish? There is a word for a man who won't listen to the word 'no.'"

"Persistent?"

"More like psycho."

"How else is a man to show his admiration?"

"Maybe by not crawling through windows in the middle of the night."

"Dating is hard. No wonder I've avoided it."

"This is not dating. This is freaking me out."

"And that's bad, right?" Did he somehow fake the authentic-sounding query?

"Very bad."

"Do you really want me to let you loose?"

No. The word almost left her lips. Almost and he knew it. She could see it by the gleam of satisfaction in his eyes. Somehow, he knew of her attraction for him. Knew of the molten heat moistening the crotch of her panties.

But he didn't take into account her fierce devotion to her sister—and her intense jealousy that he might have slept with Ruby first.

What do I mean "might have"? Don't tell me I'm starting to believe his assertion that it wasn't him?

"Let me go. I mean it."

His arms loosened, and she rolled from the bed, standing alongside it in her nightgown, all too aware of him still. She crossed her arms over her chest, lest he notice the hard nubs of her nipples protruding.

He rolled to his stomach and stared at her. "You really should stop fighting it."

"Fighting what? Your obvious insanity?"

"Can I help it if you drive me to crazy acts? Although, I should mention, that climbing through a window is considered rather tame by my family's standards. I have an uncle who once jumped out of a plane, landed on a skyscraper, and rappelled down to my aunt's balcony."

"Does your family have a problem with knocking?"

"That would make for a rather dull story, don't you think."

"It's called respect. Perhaps you should look it up."

"But *koukla*, I do respect you. How could I not when we're destined to end up together."

As in a couple? "Did you forget to take some medication?" And did she need meds of her own because for some crazy, inexplicable reason his words had her heart racing in excitement.

Jade didn't do excitement.

"What ails me is something only you can fix."

"I think you're delusional, and given your obvious mental imbalance I am really hoping my nephew was conceived by another guy—"

"So we can be together."

"No, in case it's hereditary. I don't need craziness in my life."

"I'm not crazy. Just Greek. And I will mention I am not as bad as some of my uncles. You'll meet them soon. We've got the Pentecost coming up. It's an Orthodox holiday. Which means lots of food. Wear stretchy pants."

"There will be no weight gain because you are going to leave. Now. Go. Before I call the cops and report you for breaking and entering."

"As if I would be so clumsy as to break anything. The lock on your window was easy to undo. You really should invest in a better mechanism."

She would. But first to get rid of her intruder.

"Out." She pointed to the door.

"Very well. I will go." His head drooped low. He seemed so put out, but he moved in the direction of the door.

He stopped with his hand on the knob.

"Keep moving. I mean it—"

She never finished her sentence because he whirled and covered her mouth with his hand again.

"Gsfpldgadhfh," she mumbled angrily.

"Shhh. Listen." He whispered the words hotly against her ear.

She went still, aware of his body pressed against her back. Aware of the heat radiating from him to her. The stillness meant she noted the sound of a door opening with a tiny squeal.

The front door.

Her eyes widened.

"Shhh." A soft susurration against her ear before he removed his hand from her mouth.

He crept to the bedroom door and opened it, peering through the slim crack.

"What's wrong?" she whispered.

"You have a visitor."

"What? Impossible. No one has a key."

"Who said a key was being used?"

Mental note to self: Get a better lock. At the very least, she should have shoved a chair under the knob. But she'd not wanted to seem scared or paranoid in front of her sister.

"But I locked the door."

"Your lock isn't very good," Ark advised. "Shh. They are coming inside."

The claim clamped her lips tight. Who came inside?

Apparently, Ark intended to find out because he flung open her bedroom door and stalked out.

She padded on bare feet to the door and peeked out. Ark held a slim fellow by his shirt, dangling him at least a foot off the ground. Holy smokes, that took some strength.

Impressive but not the most important thing to focus on.

Since Ark had the situation in hand, she studied the guy who'd broken in. He sported scraggly blond hair and a scruffy beard, but seemed otherwise clean. He didn't look like a burglar with his khaki pants and button-down shirt with a sports jacket; then again, she didn't know many burglars so she didn't have a basis for comparison.

How he looked didn't matter though because this stranger broke into her apartment.

What does he want? Had he planned to attack Jade and Ruby while they slept?

It made her kind of glad Ark was here to deal with it. So glad that she didn't stop him from shaking the intruder while haranguing him.

"What are you doing here? Did your mother drop you on the head? Do you not understand simple instructions? I told you to stop following me."

Following? Ark knew the intruder?

"What are you doing here? You shouldn't be here," the burglar babbled.

"I'm here because my woman lives here."

His woman. Ark, of course, meant her sister.

Don't be a ninny. Your sister isn't who he tried to cuddle. It meant nothing. Sure, this time he attempted to cuddle Jade, but that would change the moment he ran into another woman he found attractive. The man didn't deny he slept around.

For some reason it made her want to throw something. At him.

Jealousy didn't seem appropriate for the moment because, hello, who the hell was the guy breaking into her place?

"Who is this man?" she asked.

"He is an annoying cockblocker who apparently doesn't understand simple commands," Ark growled. Then to the intruder, "I thought you weren't following me."

"I'm not," said the burglar.

"You say you are not following me and yet you're here." Ark glared.

"I swear I didn't know you were seeing one of them," the man blubbered.

Meanwhile, Jade was completely lost. "What's going on, Ark? I want an answer. Right now."

Ark stopped shaking and stared the fellow in the eye. "You heard my woman. Speak."

The burglar babbled. "I already told you. My boss wanted me to find his girlfriend."

"And his girlfriend is one of these women?" Ark queried.

The plot thickened, but before the fellow could answer more questions, Ruby took that moment to emerge from the second bedroom. "What's going on?"

Distracted, Ark turned his head, as did Ruby. Neither noticed the knife the burglar pulled. Jade caught only a glimpse of silver flashing and turned in time to see the blade slash across Ark's side.

Ruby squealed. Jade grabbed the nearest thing—a DVD case sitting on the television credenza—and threw it. Except the guys shifted position as the case was still mid-flight, and it bonked Ark in the face. That caused him to lose his grip and the guy with the knife hit the floor and bolted.

Being a stupid man, Ark made to follow. Jade grabbed his arm to hold him back. Yeah, that didn't work so good. He kept walking, although he did look down. "I've got this."

"You can't go after him."

"Why not?"

"Because you're hurt."

"It's nothing. Just a tiny flesh wound."

"That's what the dark knight said and he ended up being just a head and a torso."

"A girl who's watched *Monty Python*." He stopped. "That's fucking cool."

"I'm glad you think so. Now get back in the apartment so I can put some pressure on your wound." Because the dampness of his shirt suggested a lot of bleeding.

He peered down the hall at the elevator, which was long gone. "Might as well. I'll catch up to him later." Said with an ominous undercurrent. It was also rather optimistic. As if he could track down a burglar in a city this size.

He followed her back into the apartment. Ruby still stood in the bedroom door, her face ashen.

"Is he all right?"

"A scratch," Jade lied. "You should lie down until the cops get here. They'll probably want a statement from you."

"No police." Ark shook his head. "There's nothing they can do."

"A guy just broke into my place and stabbed you. I am calling them. And if you keep pissing me off, I'll tell them you broke in first and have you arrested too."

"But jail food sucks." His lower lip jutted out.

"Then shut up and behave. Ruby, grab my phone."

"Ruby, don't you dare touch it."

"Don't you order my sister around." Jade glared at him.

"Fine, then I'll order you around, *koukla*."

"Resorting to name-calling along with bullying and stalking?"

"Um, you know what, I'm too tired for this. I'm going back to bed." Her sister turned around and shut the bedroom door, leaving Jade nose to nose with Ark.

"You upset my sister," Jade snapped.

"You are very attractive when you are angry."

The man had no shame.

She whirled away from him and went to grab her phone, only to have him grab her and reel her back against his body. His lips hovered by her ear. "No police."

The fabric of her nightgown got damp, moisture resulting from his blood. "You need medical attention."

"It's nothing."

"I wouldn't call a gash on your body nothing."

He turned her in his grip, and the white of his teeth gleamed as he grinned down at her. "Are you worried about me, *koukla*?"

"Why do you keep calling me that?"

"It means 'darling.'"

"But I'm not your darling." She pushed at his chest, and he let her go, uttering a soft, "Yet."

She made it to the bathroom and flipped on the light. A quick glimpse in the mirror showed her disheveled, her eyes bright, and her cheeks faintly flushed. She also noted the crimson staining her gown. It reminded her of why she'd come in here. She opened the cabinet and pulled out a first-aid kit. She returned to find him sitting on a chair in the kitchen.

Shirtless.

Oh my.

"That's a lot of hair," she remarked, managing to bite her tongue before she said, "And a lot of skin."

The man was built like a mountain, slabs of muscle across the shoulders and chest and with arms as wide as her thigh. She should have been mature enough not to stare.

Should have been. She should have also not been turned on by the sight of him half dressed, especially since his flesh was stained with wet blood. She dropped the kit on the table and went for a wad of clean paper towels that she wetted under the tap. She turned around to find him swiping at his wounded side with his T-shirt.

"Get that away from there. It's dirty," she scolded. The mothering habit she'd grown up with came back naturally. How many scrapes and bruises had she tended with her siblings growing up?

"I've had worse." Indeed he had, and some had left scars.

"Is that a bullet wound?" she asked as she pressed the damp towel to his side.

"The one above my left clavicle was a silver bullet. Damned things burn. The one down by my ribs was from a knife."

As she swiped at the blood, she frowned. "You make it sound as if it's nothing. As if those kinds of things happen all the time. I thought you said you worked in the honey business."

"I do. And some people are buzzkills." He grinned.

She pressed a little harder against the gash. He didn't even wince.

"Is the fact you didn't want me to call the cops because you knew the guy who broke in?" she asked as she exchanged the bloodied paper for a fresh batch.

"I don't know his name, only that I've been seeing him around quite a bit. I thought, initially, he was following me."

"Why would anyone follow you?" she asked.

"Who wouldn't follow me?" He seemed surprised by her question.

"You're right. I'll bet the men in the white coats are always chasing after you."

"Actually, I have to be more careful around hunters. Thankfully most have shitty aim."

Jade shook her head. "Why can't I ever get a straight answer out of you? Is it that hard to tell me why that guy was looking for you?"

A noise at the kitchen door showed Ruby standing there with her hands on her belly. "That guy wasn't here for Ark. He was looking for me."

CHAPTER 7

In a surprising twist, it turned out the scrawny intruder wasn't after Ark after all.

It took a moment to bring Ark up to speed as to why Ruby declared the intruder had come for her. Apparently, Ruby thought it might be an ex-boyfriend who was having a hard time letting go.

It only took a little prodding for Jade to reveal the whole story, which started out romantic enough with Ruby and some dude named Xavier meeting and taking an immediate shine to each other in December. Things were going great until Xavier's fiancée showed up to surprise him at his condo. Once Ruby discovered he was already hooked up with someone else, she put an end to things. But her boyfriend didn't want to let her go.

He sent her flowers.

Called constantly.

Showed up at her door.

So Ruby moved out of her place, subletting it to a friend. She moved cities and got a new job, not hard given she worked mostly from home as a website designer and easily found work under a male pseudonym.

"She moved and changed her name because of a man?" Ark sounded a little incredulous.

"I agree it was a touch drastic," Jade remarked. "I told her she should have gone to the cops instead."

"And said what?" Ruby exclaimed, spreading her hands wide. "That he won't stop professing I'm the woman he wants to spend his life with. That his fiancée means nothing. To give him a chance to fix things. Which maybe I could have handled, but how was I supposed to explain to him I was pregnant with another guy's baby? It was best to break things off."

"But now your ex-boyfriend is after something," Ark noted. "The man who broke into your apartment claimed he was here to find a woman."

"Gee, I wonder who hired him? Not." Jade glared at Ruby.

"I thought things were over. I mean, I haven't heard from him in months," Ruby stated. Her lips turned down. "I figured he'd moved on."

"Yeah, moved on to breaking and entering. And then what? Kidnapping? Murder? Why else send a guy with a knife? I told you to press charges against him or at least get a restraining order."

"Restraining orders don't stop a determined male."

"Neither do locks," Jade remarked with a pointed look at him.

He could sense she admired his tenacious pursuit. She had seen nothing yet. "Have you thought of arranging a more permanent demise for this ex-suitor? It wouldn't be hard to arrange." Ark would even take on the task himself.

"No!" The vehement rejection came from Ruby. "I don't want to see Xavier hurt. I hurt him enough when I left."

"Perhaps I am misunderstanding, but you sound as if you still care for him?" Ark's brow creased.

"I do. I love, I mean *loved* Xavier. Being with him was the most exhilarating thing I've ever experienced. When he talked about our future together, I could picture it. I wanted it." Ruby's lips turned down. "But, I guess it was a lie. I mean, what guy professes forever when he's got a fiancée?"

"And you've not heard from him since you disappeared?"

Ruby shook her head. "I thought he gave up on me." She sounded so sad, which in turn caused Jade to frown.

"It's been months, though. Surely he's given up. And even if he hadn't, why would he be sending someone to break into my place?" Jade asked.

"Maybe I'm wrong." Ruby patted her sister's hand. "We don't really know for sure if it was Xavier who sent that guy to break in."

"Who else would be crazy enough to go looking for his ex-girlfriend?" Jade sat up straighter. "Oh my God, the guy who broke in had a knife. What if your ex knows you're pregnant and has gone into a jealous rage and is trying to kill you?"

"He wouldn't kill me. I think." Ruby gnawed at her lower lip and Ark knew it was time to put a stop to this kind of talk.

"No one is killing anyone while I am around."

"And how will you make sure of that? Once you're gone no one will be here to protect Ruby."

Ark admired how his mate put her sister's well-being above her own. She'd make a fine mother to their cubs. But first, he needed to prove to her what a worthy mate he'd make. "Don't worry about your sister's safety. I just need to make a few phone calls." *And set some things in motion.*

The news the investigator was after Ruby, not Ark, changed things. Before the petty thug had proved a pest. Now, he posed a threat to Ark's mate—who still seemed determined to hate him—and the sister his mate loved, which made her family.

And no one fucked with his family.

So, he said all the right placating things. He behaved while Jade slapped on a bandage and told him to get to a hospital, but he refused to leave until Jade allowed him to put them both in a cab and have them sent to a hotel. His hotel, as a matter of fact, in rooms across the hall from his own. A call to Stavros meant he would be waiting for them in the lobby and shadowing them to their floor. Then keeping guard out of sight in case that puny investigator thought to come back.

In the end it didn't matter what this ex-boyfriend or the investigator wanted with the women. Ark was going to put a stop to it, and that meant paying a call to yet another cousin. Matthias—who really hated the nickname Matty—ran the New York City sleuth, a fancy term for a bear clan, four hundred strong, and scattered throughout. The Big Apple sleuth was the biggest of its kind in the United States and they were snotty about it. Thought that living in the city made them better than their cousins from the country. Ark had to teach little cousin Matty a thing or two about pride when they were younger. Taught that snooty bear not to mock his wilder cousins.

Taught the lesson so well that apparently his cousin Matthias hadn't forgotten about the broken nose Ark had given him as a teen. *I gave him character.* But did Ark get any thanks for it?

None. It also appeared as if Matty might not have forgiven the fact that Ark borrowed his car the night of the prom, which happened to hold his girlfriend, who later that night dumped Matty for Ark.

Matthias never did thank him for showing just how fickle she was. It didn't even last two weeks.

But his cousin's vendetta? Still going strong more than

a decade later. It explained the gun pointed at his forehead when the metal reinforced door to the townhouse swung open.

"Give me a good reason to not pull the trigger."

Ark smiled. "Cousin, so good to see you. We have business to discuss."

"Is that business your imminent demise?" Said with a sneer, and yet Matty stepped aside.

"Are you still bent about the girl in high school? So what if she chose my big *péos* over yours. Get over it."

"You think this is about the girl." Matthias shook his head as he headed past Ark into a living room. He went straight for a decanter full of amber liquid. "It was never about the girl but the fact you ruined my fucking car." A sweet convertible with supple leather seats—before the storm.

"I didn't know it was going to rain. I'm sure it was fine once it dried out."

Matthias leveled him with a glare.

"Okay, I'm sorry about the car. In retrospect, I should have put the cover up."

"Finally, he apologizes." Matthias raised his glass. "About time. Drink?"

"Make it two."

"Double fisted. By my recollection, you only resort to that when really giddy or really pissed."

He should have been giddy about finding his mate, but events kept conspiring. "There's a thug in the city. I think he's on a contract, and he's made a move on my mate."

"A mate? You got mated? When did this happen? The aunts usually keep me well informed."

"The aunts don't know yet." And would probably meddle to ridiculous lengths once they did. "Anyhow, this rather irritating fellow broke into her place tonight."

Matthias arched a brow. "I take it you foiled that plan."

"Yes. But the guy got away."

"Has someone been hitting the burger joint instead of the gym lately?"

"My mate required my attention." Actually, she wanted to doctor him, which he would have enjoyed more if it had involved a bed and the pair of them naked. Instead, they talked. What a shitty way to end his evening.

"She was attacked, and yet here you are with me. Don't tell me you left her unguarded. Are you sure it's wise to leave her alone? Perhaps she should have some company." Matthias smiled, not the jovial smile of a friend.

Ark grinned right back as he said, quite pleasantly, "Lay a single body part on her and I will murder you and scatter the ashes. She. Is. Mine."

"So you licked her."

Did in his head count? "Not quite. There's a bit of a problem. We're waiting to see if I impregnated her sister."

The admission had Matthias laughing and he kept laughing as Ark explained the situation. "That's a fucking mess. Glad I'm not you."

"Which is another reason why I'm here. Weren't you at that Halloween party last year in Beverly Hills?" Ark thought he'd smelled him, but Matty took the art of avoidance to great levels.

"Yeah, I was there. Why?"

"And were you dressed as Zeus?"

"Yes." His cousin frowned. "Where are you going with this?"

"The sister I was telling you about, the pregnant one, she was at that party. Claims she slept with a god."

"Doesn't mean it's me. I counted at least eight other Zeuses that night."

There could have been more, hard to tell through the alcoholic haze. "I don't suppose you hooked up with a cat woman?" There were plenty of them roaming around, meowing and in heat.

His cousin blinked. "I think we need more alcohol."

Copious amounts of it were drunk, which led to Ark weaving back to the hotel and relieving Stavros from his post in the hall so he could keep a watch on his mate's door—with his eyes shut.

It was the giggles that woke him. "Look, Matilda, he's naked."

"And hairy."

He was also in so much trouble according to the look in Jade's eyes when she flung open the door.

CHAPTER 8

"What is wrong with you?" Jade hissed as she ushered him into the hotel room and slammed the door shut to hide the giggles of the other hotel patrons.

"Nothing. I'm perfect." He raised his arms and spun, tossing her a devilish smile.

He was indeed quite perfect in shape and contagious in his madness because, when he crooked a finger at her, she almost went to him.

"What are you doing here, naked?"

"Well, I kind of lost my clothes on the way here."

"How do you accidentally lose your clothes? Did you accidentally put your dick in a woman too?"

The accusation apparently annoyed him. His back straightened, and his dark eyes flashed. "I haven't touched another woman since we met."

"Wow, what's it been? A whole day?" She rolled her eyes. "Feels like forever."

"See, you also feel like we've known each other longer."

"That isn't a good thing in this case." She turned away from him, even if all she wanted to do was stare. He made it so hard to remind herself why he'd come into their lives.

Don't fall for it. He might have slept with Ruby. She clung to that "might have" part because it helped with the guilt. He was the forbidden fruit, and she began to under-stand why Eve caved to temptation in the garden.

"I don't suppose you have some clothing I could borrow."

"Sure because I'm such a slut I keep men's clothes lying around and pack them when I go to hotels in the middle of the night."

Actually she did have men's clothes, mostly their boxers and T-shirts, which she bought, she might add, and didn't steal, because they were freaking comfortable to lounge in.

Thing was her T-shirts and shorts were much smaller in size than Ark. The bottoms didn't make it up his thighs be-fore getting caught on his backside.

As for the shirt, it stretched and threatened to split at the seams. Add in his below-the-waist bareness, and she laughed.

She laughed so hard the door to the second bedroom in the suite flung open and her sister peered in, uttered a gasp, and fled.

"Shit." Jade took off after Ruby while Ark grumbled, "Way to shrivel a man's confidence."

It would take a lot of shriveling to shrink him enough for that. Yes, she'd noticed, how could she not? The man took well endowed to a whole new level.

Jade found Ruby in the bathroom, getting a glass of water.

"It's not what it looks like," she said.

Her sister whirled. "Are you going to tell me you didn't have a naked man in your room?"

"Well, I did, kind of." As her sister's gaze narrowed, she sighed. "Fine. But he didn't spend the night. I found him in the hall. Naked. And he won't say how it happened."

"Oh dear God. This nightmare is getting worse." Her sister placed her head on the counter.

"What nightmare? No one is going to hurt you. Most especially not that two-timing prick harassing you."

Ruby waved her glass of water. "I'm not worried about him hurting me. Xavier would never harm me."

"And yet you ran away from him."

"What else could I do?" Ruby scowled. "Even if he did dump his fiancée, how was I to explain this?" She pointed to her belly. "'Hey, sweetie, I love you but guess what, I hooked up with someone else before we met. Surprise, I'm pregnant with another man's kid.'"

"I should have never let you move out west."

"We are not arguing about this again. What happened, happened. I'm more interested in what you're going to do with the naked guy in the other room."

Do? The problem was she wanted to do so many things.

Jade shrugged. "I don't know what to do about him. He seems determined to keep popping up. And given that other dude who broke into my place last night, I really think we should go someplace for a few days. Maybe go stay with Pearl until the baby is born."

"The three of us in that tiny studio apartment?" Ruby grimaced. "No thanks. I'd rather stay in a hotel."

"Great plan," Ark announced from the doorway, the sheet from her bed tied sarong style around his torso. "But not this hotel. I know just the place we can go."

Which was why an argument, a phone call to her work, and a hastily packed suitcase later, they were at the Jersey Shore, booking into a penthouse suite with two bedrooms. Stavros, the man who'd shown up with clothes for Ark and a car to drive them there, had just left, leaving her with just a warning to not leave the suite unless he or Ark accompanied them. Apparently, he was staying a floor down.

As for Ark, he'd only seen them off, and she had no idea if

he planned to join them and surely she wasn't disappointed about the fact he hadn't yet.

She wandered out to the living room to find Ruby staring out the window. "You look awfully serious," Jade noted.

"Maybe I should talk to him."

"Who? Not your stalking ex?"

Ruby nodded. "He deserves an explanation for why I left."

"Isn't the fact he was engaged enough?"

"It's not like that. He didn't love her. Their families arranged it."

Jade rolled her eyes. "Well then, that makes it okay. I can't believe you ever got involved with a practically married man. At least you had the sense to end it."

"But not because I wanted to." Ruby whirled, her body tense and her eyes flashing. "You seem to keep conveniently forgetting that part of the reason I left was to save Xavier from the pain of watching me raise another man's child."

"And what of your pain of seeing him with another woman?" She couldn't understand her sister's mindless devotion to the guy.

"I already told you he didn't have a choice."

"He could have chosen to not brainwash you into loving him."

"Sometimes you can't fight fate. One day you'll understand."

One day? What about now? She'd been separated from Ark only a few hours and yet already she anticipated his return. Kept expecting him to appear.

Yet, the day passed. They ordered room service.

Got hell from Stavros for letting the room service guy in.

They watched a movie . . .

Got hell again from Stavros for screaming at the scary parts.

And during all that, still no Ark.

Surely she didn't suffer from disappointment. She latched the deadbolt on the door. Then went to bed.

Alone.

Always alone.

Sigh.

Why did she find herself suddenly bothered? This was the way it should be. The way she liked it and yet despite her usual preference for solitude she could have sighed with relief when a voice whispered in her ear, "Did you miss me, *koukla*?"

Yes. I did. But it would be so much easier to handle if she didn't.

CHAPTER 9

Expecting Jade to react, Ark was ready when she tried to shove at him. He grabbed her wrists and pinned them over her head, which made it easy for him to settle his body atop hers.

"What are you doing?"

"Saying hello. Can you not feel my obvious delight?"

"What I feel is you crushing me. Get off me, you giant oaf."

"I wouldn't have to get on you if you'd not hogged the bed."

She stopped struggling and said, in a tone pitched with incredulity, "I will hog it if I want to. This is my bed."

"Ours," he corrected just because he wanted to see how round her mouth could curve.

She made a spectacular O. Perfect for—

"There is no *ours*. You are deluded." She writhed under him. It proved distracting, enough that he found himself bucked off and hitting the floor.

Her playfulness had him bouncing to his feet with a smile. "You never fail to please me."

"Do you have a problem with the word 'no'? I'm not interested in you."

She claimed it and yet her arousal perfumed the air. Her heart beat fast. Her nipples pressed against her thin shirt, the sheet covering her having gotten pushed down during their foreplay.

"Why do you keep denying your attraction to me?"

"Do you really have to ask? Pregnant sister for one."

"Which is not mine." For some reason he felt that certainty, especially since the more he thought back on that night, the more he recalled, and those memories did not include sleeping with a cat woman. Making out with one, yes, but a certain cockblocker interrupted before he sealed the deal. Of course, telling Jade would accomplish nothing. He doubted she'd believe him.

"Claiming it's not your baby doesn't make it the truth. And even if you aren't the daddy, I'm still not interested. You're a little too aggressive for me."

"I can't help it. You drive me wild." He pounced back onto the bed, framing her body with his, drawing close enough he could nuzzle the skin of her cheek with his nose. The intimacy of the gesture made her squirm—which he very much enjoyed.

"You can't force me to feel the same way."

"How have I forced you to do anything?"

"Asks the guy pinning me to the bed."

"Have I hurt you? Done anything you don't want?"

"I don't want to have you on top of me."

"You're right, you'd rather I was in you. Sinking balls deep into your heat." The dirty words slipped from him and she reacted by sucking in a breath.

"I do not want you!" she exclaimed.

"Liar," he chided before he nipped her chin. He heard the hitch of her breath. She was not unaffected, but she was certainly stubborn. "If you really wanted me to leave, I would go."

"I really want you to leave."

He didn't move.

"Now who's the liar?" she chided.

"I said if you really wanted me to I would. But . . ." He leaned down until their foreheads touched. "You don't want me to go." She might not be able to admit it, but he sensed it on a primal level. The same level that claimed she was the one for him.

"I do want you to leave."

"If you insist, then I will go." He rolled off of her, and stood beside the bed.

She seemed surprised by his capitulation. Didn't she yet understand he'd do anything for her?

"You're really leaving."

"Your wish is my command."

"What happened to making me yours?"

A crooked smile pulled his lips. "It will happen. You cannot fight destiny. Even now, your desire rages inside. You want me."

"I . . ."

He could see she wanted to deny him. She fought so hard against fate. But the soft words spilled out of her in spite of it.

"I do, but I shouldn't."

"Don't be afraid," he said as he climbed back onto the bed and cradled her body. She felt so right against him, and this time she did not push him away. He stroked her hair, loving the springy curls of it. He ran his knuckles over her cheek, heard her breath catch.

"We shouldn't be doing this."

"Why?" he asked.

"Surely this is wrong."

"On the contrary, I think you're afraid because you know we are so right."

She closed her eyes before his gaze, but she couldn't hide the tremble in her frame.

He wouldn't let her hide from him. "There is something between us, *koukla*. Something that won't be denied."

"It's just lust. It will go away."

"What if it's something more?" He couldn't help but brush her lips lightly, feeling the tremor that shook her.

"Is this your suave way of convincing me to have sex with you?"

"If I wanted to convince you, I would kiss you."

"You really think you can seduce me with a kiss?" She laughed, a high and breathy sound that held a note of fear, anticipation, and . . . challenge? She dared to meet his eyes, provocation dancing in their depths.

"Are you daring me to try?"

She finally uttered the permission he'd been waiting for. "Yes."

Drawing close, his lips touched hers, more than with just a brushing glance. He took her mouth with a fierce, possessive embrace. He branded her with his kiss, and finally—fucking finally—tasted her sweetness.

Given her complaints, he expected some kind of attempt to freeze him, to pretend she was not affected. To his surprise, it took not even the barest second to push past her weak defenses. Her mouth went immediately pliant under his, her body softened and accommodated his weight.

The parting of her lips allowed him to plunder with his tongue, starting a sinuous dance that made him hum. The sound rumbled against her, and she stopped the slide of her mouth to tug at his lower lip. "What is that noise?"

"It's my happy sound. Which is not as loud as my really happy sound. I can't wait to see what noises you make." He ground himself against her.

"Who says I make any sounds?"

"You will." Said perhaps a little more ominously than the moment merited. "I just need to find the right spot to lick."

"There will be no licking."

"Oh, there will be lots of licking. And touching. And other things involving less clothes."

"No, there won't."

"You really need to stop arguing about it. I've already proved you wrong once."

Her mouth rounded with a gasp. "The fact you're a good kisser doesn't make this right."

"I'm good at a great many things. You'll see. Most definitely feel, and did I mention enjoy?" He winked before rubbing his nose against hers.

"I wish you wouldn't do that," she grumbled.

"Why?"

"Because it's cute, and I don't want you to be cute."

She thought he was cute? His pride swelled, as did his dick. Perhaps the seduction of his mate wouldn't be as difficult as he'd feared.

The scream proved shrill and more chilling than cold water. Jade froze, her body tensing under his, but Ark acted, immediately rolling off Jade and moving to the door.

There was another shriek and a hollered, "Get away from me!" Then a bellow of annoyance, but a bellow more animal than man, which kind of described the sound Ark let loose as he went bolting from the room, stripping as he went, not pausing to answer as Jade yelled, "What are you doing?"

Doing? Why protecting his mate of course.

Upon hitting the main living area between the bedrooms, he scented another bear.

Who dares come so close to me and my mate? The need

to protect drove Ark over the edge. He didn't think. He didn't pause. He shifted into his beast.

Of course, he might have forgotten that, while he was more than ready to take Jade as his mate, he might have neglected to inform her of his ability to change into a bear.

Jade screamed. Screamed. And screamed.

They all screamed for ice cream. Actually, his woman screamed, "Bears! There're fucking bears in here!" as he roared a challenge at the dark brown beast lumbering around the living room.

For anyone else, anyone human, this might seem odd. Not to Ark.

Playtime.

Ahem, he meant *protect* as he charged the intruder, not holding himself back, even as something about the other bear seemed familiar.

He should have knocked. The rudeness of entering his territory unannounced, and, yes, hotel rooms counted. For the record, he didn't give a damn if this wasn't his usual den. *You came in uninvited.*

They met in a hard clash of furry bodies, hundreds of pounds of muscle and flesh pounding and grappling. Since his opponent didn't immediately try to draw blood, Ark held back. It would make the fun last longer.

As they snapped their jaws and clacked teeth at each other, he caught a glimpse of his adversary's eyes. The scent might not have jostled him, but those mismatched orbs did.

Matthias. What was that prick doing here? And here as a bear no less.

What an idiot. A total ilithios. Putting their secret at risk without thought. Ark cuffed him upside the head with a paw before stepping back and shifting. Crack, snap, and holy fucking pop of the joints. No one ever claimed shifting shapes was easy.

It might have enhanced his annoyance just a little. "You fucking moron, what are you doing here in the middle of the fucking night?"

"Did I scare the teddy bear?" Said with such mockery. Rubbing his jaw, Matthias stood, and they made a point of ignoring the naked junk hanging between them. *Just two bros hanging, dicks swinging in the breeze.* His was bigger of course.

"What were you thinking? Do you want to die young?" Ark would accommodate him if necessary.

"Would you believe I wanted a sniff of the girl?"

"And you couldn't ask?"

"It was late. I figured I'd pop in, do a sniff test, and leave. But the girl woke up and saw me. Someone taught her how to have great aim. The alarm clock she whipped at my head hurt."

"I think the tossing thing is a family trait," he confided. Speaking of family, he noted the open door to the penthouse suite. "Ah fuck it." The women had bolted, which meant finding clothes to get them back because naked men running with flopping pricks—not a pretty look for any guy—were somewhat frowned upon in public. So were bears, and all that screaming hurt his poor ears. Which meant . . . "I need my pants."

"Toss me a pair and I'll give you a hand wrangling the women."

It didn't take a genius to recognize the subtle jab by his cousin that Ark couldn't handle the situation on his own. It was only two women. Piece of cake. His mother's cake of course, maybe soaked in a bit of rum.

With whipped cream.

And three cherries.

Not that he was craving it or nothing.

Before he could tell his cousin to fuck off, Stavros marched into the suite, wearing pants and a shirt—which totally gave him an advantage—and he didn't arrive alone. He prodded Ruby in, her belly leading the way, and a scowling Jade followed, feet dragging, arms crossed, and lip jutting mutinously.

Very cute.

Her eyes widened at the sight of him and then widened some more as they also spotted Matthias. Her eyes started at his face and moved down.

Oh hell no. "You will cease looking at him," he growled, jealousy prickling his furry side.

Her gaze flicked back to Ark, but she didn't give him the same once-over. Some guys might have thought she wasn't interested. He knew better.

She's not looking because she doesn't want to publicly lust after my eminent virility. He couldn't blame her. He was very well endowed. And proud of it, which meant he had to put his hands on his hips, throw his shoulders back, and puff his chest a little.

Another grand gesture wasted on his mate of the stoic expression.

Her gaze never once wavered from his. "There you are, in the flesh. Is it me, or weren't you a lot hairier a few minutes ago?"

"He's still pretty hairy if you ask me," Matthias interjected. "Have you seen his back?"

"My back is not hairy." Yet. He'd seen his father's, who claimed the same thing at Ark's age. Nowadays, any attempt to wax would hurt.

A crease marred Jade's perfect brow. "Stop twisting my words instead of answering the question: Were you or were you not a bear a few minutes ago?"

Lying would serve no purpose. As his mate, she'd find out eventually. "Yeah, I was a bear. A real one as opposed to a grumbly one when we run out of honey for my coffee." An office without honey was like peanut butter without the jam. Good thing bread was optional.

"You're a bear." She crossed her arms and cocked her head. "You know that's impossible."

"But you saw it."

"Did I? What I saw was you run out of the bedroom. Then I saw a bear. Not you. A freaking giant ass bear. So I ran from the room and lo and behold, when I return the bear is gone and you're here standing buck ass naked."

"Because I was a bear. He is too." He jabbed his finger at his cousin.

Oops. That caused her gaze to flick to Matthias. Not long. She glanced over at Stavros. "I suppose he's a bear too." A slender finger pointed.

"Yup, but he's not as big as me." Seemed best to get that out there now.

A small tic jumped by her eye, and she said nothing. Ruby, on the other hand, rubbed her belly. "Does this mean there's a possibility I'm carrying Yogi?"

For some reason that drew a half-snort, semi-laugh from Jade. It also drew her ire. She whirled on her sister. "Are you joking about this? Were you not paying attention? These guys turn into fucking bears. Which sounds utterly insane, even if I kind of saw it with my own two eyes."

"You did see it because I saw it. And now having seen it"—Ruby flicked her gaze at Matthias then Ark—"I'm wondering about the baby I'm carrying."

"Dear God, if your mutant sperm kills my sister . . ." Jade jabbed a finger in his direction.

"I didn't touch your sister." But given his cousin's sudden urge to smell Ruby, it looked like Matthias was worried he might have.

"Well, someone did," Jade snapped.

"The baby is fine," Ruby assured. "I've seen him on ultrasounds. Hands and feet, not paws and claws."

"Of course it doesn't have bear parts. It's just a baby. As human as you are," Stavros said. "Our condition isn't hereditary. It comes from the transmission of the ursinethropy virus. It's usually passed on from father to son, although, in some rare cases, outsiders are considered for inclusion to the sleuth."

"'Sleuth' as in detective?"

Ark grinned. "As in a clan. A bear clan."

"And you make your members?" Jade made the sign of the cross. "Don't you even think of changing me or my sister."

A faint smile tugged at Ark's lips. "You don't have to worry. The awesomeness that is animal-thropy is something that affects only those with a Y chromosome. In other words, girls can't catch it. It's rather sexist if you ask me, but that is just how it is."

"I don't believe all this. This can't be happening." Jade shook her head, and her hair bobbed in a wild dance. "I am obviously sleeping and having a dream. I am so totally hallucinating. When I wake up, I'm going to laugh at all this. Shape-shifting men. Insane." She closed her eyes.

And she kept them closed.

"Jade?" He waved a hand before her face "This isn't a dream. I'm still here." He angled his head before asking Ruby, "How long will she stay like that?"

Ruby rolled her shoulders. "I don't know. She's usually the sane one in the family."

"And the sane one doesn't believe in fairy-tale monsters," Jade muttered, eyes still clamped shut.

"I'm only a monster to my enemies." He stepped close to her, close enough that her skin noticed and reacted, heating, and her heart picked up its pace. "There is no point in hiding, *koukla*. I'm not going away."

"You should."

"I can't." She might not understand it yet, but she was stuck with him for life. He just needed a nicer way of explaining that to her, a way that wouldn't have her throwing knives.

She cracked open one lid. "I wish I'd never sent those cards."

"I would have found you anyway." He gave her a gentle chuck of the chin. "It's fate. Before the end of this year, you'll be bearing my name." It slipped out. Okay, maybe he did it on purpose.

She looked so cute when her eyes sparked. He was also prepared to catch the fist she aimed low at his gut. It hit hard rock. She looked down, made a small sound, and then leaned over to grab a cushion from the couch and shove it at him.

"Cover yourself," she snapped. "It's indecent—"

"—ly large," he corrected. "I know. But I promise it will work."

"But obviously has done brain damage in the past. Lack of oxygen and all."

He grinned. "Yes. It is that big." And her recognizing it meant he sneered in triumph at Matthias.

As if his longtime foe would let him win without a fight. "What about me?" Matty asked, holding his hands wide with a grin. "Do you need me to cover up? Or I could cover you?" Wink.

Oh hell no. Ark dove on his cousin. By the time they finished wrestling, which didn't last long given their lack of pants, the women had disappeared again, this time the pair of them into a single bedroom, which left three men in the room, two of them naked.

A grin stretched Stavros's face from ear to ear. "Look at you bloody morons. Swinging your dicks around like clubs. No wonder the ladies left. Probably worried you wouldn't have anything left for them."

"Fuck off," Ark grumbled as he left to find pants, a new pair since he'd kind of ruined the last ones when he'd charged out of the room. When he returned, also sporting a shirt, they were all more or less clothed. Stavros, one side of his face ruddy and puffier than the other, glared at Matthias.

Damn, he'd missed it. Ark flopped in a seat and eyed his cousin. "So care to explain, again, why you came over in the middle of the night?"

Matty shrugged. "I tried calling."

Which he'd never heard because Ark had shut off his phone. He'd hoped to avoid interruption, but cockblocking knew ways around a simple trick like that. "So when I didn't answer, you thought you'd drive in from the big city and break in for a visit?"

"I was planning to be in and out, with no one the wiser."

"As if I wouldn't have smelled you." Any bear worth his weight in honey would know if another crossed his path.

"Only after the fact." Matthias grinned. "Alas, the woman was a light sleeper."

"Don't give him too much shit. I knew he was here," Stavros added to the conversation.

His killer glare moved to his other cousin. "You let him in?"

"The man wanted to see if he recognized the pregnant one. In a sense, you could say I was trying to help you with your mate."

"I don't need help with my mate."

The other two guys snorted.

Since there was no hiding it, and it was best to let them know before he had to murder and dispose of them for looking at her, he admitted, "Okay, so I'm having a few issues. Mainly that she wants nothing to do with me. And then, when I finally get her to melt a little, you go and interrupt."

"I didn't interrupt. I was just going about my business when you came barging out."

"You scared Ruby." Which, in turn, meant the cockblocker had put a stop to his seduction of Jade.

"She wasn't supposed to wake up. Blame her."

"I can't blame her, so I blame you." Ark went back to glaring.

"Go ahead. Be a little cry bear about it. Maybe I'll make it my life's mission to make sure you never get laid again."

"Don't make me start a war when I rip your head from your shoulders."

Stavros stepped in at this point. "Why don't you both settle down and discuss what's important?"

"He's right. We should discuss the pregnant girl."

Given she was practically his sister now, Ark had to growl, "Her name is Ruby."

"Whatever. Am I the only one peeved she called us Yogi?" Matthias grumbled.

"Maybe you shouldn't have sniffed her like a picnic basket," Stavros replied.

"I wasn't sniffing her that hard and she still screamed."

"My mate screamed too when she saw me." His bear was still offended.

"What did you expect?" Stavros asked.

"Admiration. Maybe some thanks for protecting her."

A snort left Stavros. "You are so whipped, and you haven't even bitten her yet. *So* pathetic. I am telling you both right now, I am never letting that happen to me."

"Or me," Matthias chimed in.

"When fate brings the right one your way, you won't have a choice." But that wasn't a bad thing. Left to his own devices, Ark would have probably never gotten around to settling down.

"That sister is awfully violent. She called me a bad bear." Matty pouted.

"Were you nosing around her crotch?"

"No!"

Stavros held out his hands. "Just wondering. For some reason, that freaks the ladies out, and yet dogs get away with it all the time."

"No, I did not sniff her girl bits, and she still yelled at me, and then threw something. Who does that?"

"She's feisty." Almost as feisty as his Jade.

"And she is also in demand," Matthias added. "That's the other reason I came here. I heard through a certain police grapevine that your girlfriend's apartment got hit. It looks like a tornado went through it."

Was it that bloody investigator again? Did it really matter? They'd invaded his woman's place. That meant war. Also known in bear terms as more playtime. *Grawr.*

CHAPTER 10

"You knew about them, didn't you?" Lying alongside her sister in the hotel bed, Jade found herself unable to sleep.

"Knew about what?"

"You knew they were bears." *Bears!* Just saying it aloud made her want to commit herself to an asylum and ask for drugs.

"Not exactly, but I heard things while living in L.A. Saw stuff too. So I wasn't surprised, no."

Implying she'd met other kinds of . . . What had Ark called them, something *thropy* something or other? "Exactly what kind of freaks were you hanging with out west?"

"They aren't freaks. Just people in touch with their animal side."

"In touch is pretending you're a cat. Or dressing in pony costumes and prancing around. They changed into fucking bears."

"Don't swear in front of the baby."

"Sorry."

Ruby snickered. "You do know I'm screwing with you, right?"

"You're right though. I should watch my tongue. Once junior gets here, no more potty mouth."

"No more lots of things," Ruby grumbled. "No more sleeping in. No more taking off to do cool shit when someone calls with an offer. No boyfriend."

Ruby fell silent and Jade reached out to grab her hand. "It will be okay. You won't be alone."

"Yeah, I will be because I'm not into incest."

"I'll buy you plenty of batteries for your vibrator."

"A vibrator can't give me a hug."

Jade didn't have a reply for that.

Ruby tugged her hand free. "I'm tired. I'm going to sleep."

"But what about—"

"It can wait until the morning after breakfast. I need my sleep."

Sleep? Who could sleep when the world had tilted on its axis and tumbled all her long-held beliefs? There were shape-shifting men in her new reality.

Bears. Maybe other weird werewolf-type creatures.

And I was making out with one.

She should probably preface that with she enjoyed making out with one.

Very much so, and the guilt of it made her blurt out in the darkness, "He kissed me."

"Cool."

"What do you mean 'cool'? I said he kissed me. Ark did." Jade braced herself for a verbal lashing, something from her sister.

"Is he any good at it? Or is he sloppy? I hate it when they slobber all over you and think it's sexy."

"I agree slobber is gross, but why are you asking me about his skill level? Shouldn't you be freaking out? Ark kissed me."

"So what?"

"So, we still don't know if he's the daddy of junior."

The covers shifted as her sister shrugged. "I doubt it."

"What do you mean you doubt it? He was at that party."

"And? He's not the right size. He's too big for one. And I mean *big*." Snicker.

Yes, he was and Jade couldn't help the heat in her cheeks. "So you're not mad?"

"Sis, if you like him, then go for it."

"I never said I liked him."

"Whatever. I don't really care, but don't use me or the baby as an excuse to reject him."

But . . . But Jade needed something to keep him at arm's length, the constant reassurance that the baby wasn't his was not enough. Jade had to know for sure if Ark had slept with her sister because she refused to have her sister's sloppy seconds.

It made no sense. They hadn't even known each other when it happened, but it bothered her. "I don't want to date him."

"Who said anything about dating him? You don't have to be boyfriend-girlfriend to have a good time. Although, lube is everyone's best friend."

Jade could practically see the smile from her sister's tone. "I don't even like him. He's a bully."

"He's assertive. I wonder if it's a bear thing. I noticed Stavros is that way too."

"Why does it seem like you want me to hook up with him?" She tried to pierce the darkness but couldn't even make out the hump of her sister's body under the covers.

"Because you need somebody in your life. You aren't getting any younger."

"I am not over the hill." But thirty was approaching kind of faster than Jade liked.

"Why can't you just admit you like him?"

"Because."

Because then she'd have to open herself up to the reality that someone could hurt her. As the oldest, Jade had watched her mother pine after a man who never looked back. She'd listened to her sister mope about the lover she couldn't have.

She didn't want to have her happiness that dependent on someone else. But that resolution would work a heck of a lot better if she could get away from Ark. *I can't think when he's near.*

The next morning, she found herself outvoted—even by her sister—as to their next move.

"I think Ruby and I should go back to my place," she announced having finished her bowl of sugary cereal topped with a glass of chocolate milk, a meal ready and waiting for her when she staggered from the bedroom, showered, dressed, and unable to stop herself from a certain giddy anticipation.

"No." Ark didn't even look up from his laptop. As he put away a breakfast fit for a family of six—stacks of pancakes drizzled in maple syrup, along with bacon, sausage, roasted potatoes, whole wheat toast slathered in honey—he tapped away on his keyboard, only speaking to her once to say, "You should eat more."

"You are not the boss of me." The childish taunt—thrown often at her by the siblings she tried to wrangle—came easily to her lips.

"Yes I am."

There was a hushed "ooh" as the others listened with too much interest.

"I'm leaving."

"No, you're not, because it's not safe." He folded the lid of the laptop down. "Someone is after you or your sister."

"Why? We haven't done anything."

"Perhaps someone who received a card has a jealous girl-friend."

A possibility, given none of the men she'd mailed the announcement to was married. "Assault is a crime."

"If they get caught. That's of little consolation if you're tied to cement blocks and dropped in the river."

"That won't happen."

"You're right it won't, because I'm going to make sure you're protected."

"I don't need your protection."

"Did I say you had a choice?" He arched a brow. Arrogance at its finest. "Now will you come nicely, or make me put my hands all over you?"

"You're just looking for an excuse to maul me."

"I am." He didn't even try to deny it.

"Keep your dirty paws off me," Jade grumbled.

"Listen and I won't have to get physical. At least until our wedding night."

"We. Are. Not. Getting. Married."

"I would prefer to live in sin too." He shrugged. "But my aunts and mother will have something to say about that. You'll meet them soon."

Soon because his plan was to transport them out west to be with his bear gang or sleuth or whatever he called it.

"We can't travel. She's too pregnant to fly." Jade waved her hand at Ruby—who savored a Danish with more relish than it deserved. "It would take days to drive, and she's got to pee like every five minutes."

"I do not," retorted Ruby. "It's usually fifteen. Sometimes a half hour if junior is sleeping."

"I won't have my nephew born on the side of the road."

"I've got weeks still to go," Ruby said before setting out to devour another pastry.

"We are going west, but I understand your concerns. We need to find a comfortable method of transportation with a working washroom. Lucky for you, I know just the thing."

Hours later . . .

"A train?" Jade stood on the platform and balked at boarding the centipede of connected cars.

"It's fast and has all the amenities we need."

Jade might have protested more just for the hell of it, but Ruby waddled to the stairs and climbed them.

Apparently, they were going along with his nutty solution.

They boarded an actual train. The passenger caboose they were in held several sleeper cabins. Producing a key card, Ark ran it over a scanner, and the door unlocked. He'd secured a spot for the four of them, Matthias having opted to remain behind.

As cabins went, it proved pretty damned small. Four bunks, a pair stacked on each wall, a window in between. A small table could be propped between the beds.

"Bathroom?" Ruby asked, dancing from foot to foot.

"Middle of the car." Stavros accompanied her while Jade tried to keep from brushing against Ark. Kind of hard in the tiny space.

"How many days do we have to stay in here?" she asked, already sexually hyperventilating at the fact that they'd be in close quarters for hours on end.

"A lot. Plenty for you to get used to me."

"I won't get used to you."

"No, you won't. As a matter of fact, I expect your craving for me to intensify until you can't handle it."

"You wish."

Undaunted, he smiled. "Soon you won't be able to pretend."

Such determination and she feared he was right. Something about his nearness addled all her wits. He inflamed her senses and set her on fire.

He also had no concept of space. As Ruby returned, her pregnant belly needing room to maneuver, he seated himself hard on the bottom bunk and drew Jade onto his lap.

"Coming through, wide load," Ruby announced, but it was the truck beeping sound she faked that made Stavros snicker.

Laughter was the farthest thing from Jade's mind. All she could think of was how hard Ark felt against her. How right.

So wrong. She sprang from his lap, but there was nowhere to hide, and when Stavros pulled out a deck of cards, the spot beside him was the only place to go.

As the train chugged, and the hours passed, Jade couldn't help but notice Ark found any excuse he could to touch her. He was constantly putting his hands on her. Gently. Never anything truly overt, and yet, she found herself hyper aware of him.

Surely everyone felt the sizzling tension between them, yet no one said anything—and Jade did nothing to stop him.

More hours passed. A whole day. The train made periodic stops. The rattling yet smooth gait lulled her, and after the third picnic basket Stavros and Ark produced, she learned to not question how they got the food. Good food she might add. These men didn't skimp when it came to nourishment, which probably explained why, that evening, the urge to snooze came early to some.

Stavros currently slept in the top bunk while Ruby

snored on the bottom. Several cups of coffee and jangling nerves meant Jade sat wide awake across from them.

I'll never sleep.

The inability to slumber might have had to do with the man who sat beside her. Ark. Ark the bear who liked to touch. Touch her.

She shivered.

"Cold?" He placed an arm around her frame.

She shrugged it off and moved to the side. "I'm fine."

"Are you sure?" He sidled closer and squished her against the wall. She wiggled free and stood. He also got to his feet, and there was no room. Nothing but him. It would be so easy to—

She grappled only a second with the door before sliding it open and entering the narrow hall.

It didn't surprise her that he followed, sliding the cabin door shut behind him before he pinned her against the wall, out the window a fast-moving backdrop of twilight-lit lush fields and the darker glimpse of trees bordering the cultivated areas.

Thick arms bracketed her body, and his lower half pressed against Jade. She placed her palms against his chest to shove him away, as if she could budge a rock. "Give me some space."

"You can't sulk forever."

"I am not sulking."

"You've barely talked to me all day."

"Maybe I have nothing to say."

"Are you still angry at the decision to head back west? You know it's for the best. I'll be better able to protect you on my home turf."

"I didn't need protection until you showed up in my life."

"It's a good thing I arrived when I did. Now you don't have to worry. I'll protect you." His nose rubbed across hers.

"You're being deliberately obtuse."

"Only because I must be to counter your stubbornness."

"Why are you so determined to have me?" She wanted to understand, because she'd never seen someone so ardent over her before. It flattered and frightened.

"Because you're perfect."

"Bullshit." The crass word slipped from her lips.

It only served to make him laugh. "Perhaps I should explain a bit better. In my culture—"

She interrupted. "Are we talking Greek or bear?"

"A little bit of both." His lips quirked. "With my kind, there is something known as the mating instinct. It's a feeling, an absolute certainty that a woman, not just any woman but a specific woman, is meant to be yours. Forever."

Was he talking love at first sight? "And you think that's me?" She couldn't help the incredulous query. "We barely know each other."

"We will have a lifetime to discover each other."

"What if we discover I can't stand you? What if you're the type who leaves his socks on the floor? That drives me absolutely nutty. What if you do it and I get pissed and I stuff them in your mouth one night and suffocate you with them?"

"Or I could just always put them in the hamper."

"I'll bet you're the type who eats healthy." He had the body of a man who probably didn't own any caramel-covered chocolate.

"Nothing wrong with being a good boy who eats his veggies."

"I hate peas." With a passion.

"Then I'll take care of those for you."

"I love Brussels sprouts."

"Then you can eat mine."

"Do you have an answer for everything?"

"Nope."

Another answer and not the one to cure the turmoil within. "What will it take to make you go away?"

He leaned closer. "I'm here to stay, *koukla*."

There was that word for her again; "darling" in Greek. But the way he said it, the soft rumble of the consonants affected her.

But it was the promise that scared the most. He kept swearing he wanted her forever. That he would never leave. But, her daddy left . . .

It was hard to overcome abandonment issues. Hard to believe.

She wouldn't look at him, because she feared she'd melt. "I don't have time for a boyfriend. My sister needs me."

"I need you." He spoke the claim softly.

"You're not human."

"You're right. I'm not. I'm something more. Something special. Which makes you special because you're mine."

Sweet words shouldn't have the ability to seduce her. Soft claims shouldn't make her want to clasp him tight.

He took a finger and dragged just the tip down her cheek and across to her lips. He rubbed across her flesh, and her mouth parted.

"Come with me."

"Where?"

"Somewhere we can be alone."

"But Ruby—"

"Will be fine. Stavros is with her."

He leaned back and held out his hand. The reasons to

abstain weighed heavily on one side, but that didn't stop her fingers from lacing with his.

He tugged her up the length of the train car. He slid a key card from his pocket and slapped it against a door at the far end.

"Hold on a second. You mean all this time you actually had two cabins?"

"Actually, I might have bought all the tickets for this and a few other cars," he admitted with a grin.

Which explained why they never saw anyone. "So why did you cram us in the same one if you had all of these to use?"

"Because I wanted you close to me."

How was a woman supposed to fight those kinds of words?

He stepped into the small cabin and dragged her close to him. He shut the door, and she wondered if he could hear her heart pounding over the clacking of the train.

"You're scared," he stated as he ran a finger down her cheek.

"Yes. No. I don't know. I get so confused around you."

"Because you think too much."

"I have to. All my life I've been the responsible one. The one to keep my siblings out of trouble." And not doing a very good job apparently.

"You're not their mother and they're adults now. It's okay to want something for yourself."

"I do things for myself. I moved to New York."

"Because your baby sister got accepted to a dance academy there."

"How do you know that?"

He drew her close. "I know many things about you, Jade. But the most important thing I learned is you are mine."

"That seems unfair. I hardly know anything about you."

"You know my biggest secret."

As she stared up at him, Jade tried to remind herself Ark was a bear. A wild animal who only looked like a man. As if her body cared. "Tell me something else I don't know."

"How about I show you how badly I've wanted to do this." He drew her on tiptoe and rubbed his mouth over hers. A simple kiss that came fraught with complications, and need.

She pulled back, hesitating, and he let her. Gave her time to absorb the fact he made her feel things. That for all his pushy nature, he would respect her if she walked out the door. She even had her hand on the latch, ready to leave.

He did nothing.

Stay or go, this was her choice.

My choice.

My life.

She whirled around and threw herself at him, and he caught her, lifting her high enough for their lips to mesh.

Their first true embrace proved scorching. It literally stole her breath and any lingering doubts she might have had. With one kiss, he ignited her and continued to set her on fire as he took his time with her, savoring each lick and nibble. Exploring her with a gentleness that brought a gasp to her lips. He left no part of her untouched, his tongue meshing wetly with hers and tracing along the edge of her teeth. For her part, Jade clung to him tightly, her arms cinched around his neck, pressing herself against his thick body. He replied by moving his hands from her waist to her ass, cupping the full cheeks and growling, a grumbly sound. "I can't wait to bite into these."

Dear God. She almost sank into a puddle at his feet. Her knees definitely trembled and her legs wobbled. Sensing her weakness, or perhaps suffering a weakness of his own, he sat down on the bottom bunk, drawing her down with him.

With her seated on his lap, they continued to kiss, but only for a short moment. His lips moved to her neck. Her head arched back to give him better access, and she uttered a soft sigh as he licked and nipped at her skin. When he took a moment to actually suck, surely leaving a mark, she trembled.

"I want to eat you all up," he murmured before capturing her mouth once again.

"I thought that was the wolf" was her dorky reply between kisses.

He drew his head back, his mien completely serious. "Dogs can't compare to a majestic bear."

"I thought lions were king."

"Only of their litter box."

She giggled.

"No laughing. We are about to do some very serious things," he said with a devilish arch of his brow.

"Such as?"

Why tell when he could show? In between one startled breath and the next, he'd leaned her away from him, but only so he could give himself room, room to bend his head and grasp the tip of her breast in his mouth. He didn't seem to care that a bra and her shirt barred his way. He sucked, each tug pulling at the core of her, sending a jolt of pure pleasure straight to her core.

But soon that wasn't enough for him. Jade found her shift pushed up and over her breasts, and instead of pulling off her bra, he simply popped her breasts out of the cups, the tips of them puckering under his intense perusal.

"I love dark berries." And he showed her how much by sucking the tip into his mouth.

And then biting down!

"Ark." She half cried, half sighed his name, and he chuckled, the sound vibrating against the bare skin of her breast.

"Say my name again."

"Make me."

"With pleasure." His head dipped, but instead of taking her breast into his mouth, he swirled his tongue around the throbbing tip. Sucking it into his mouth, he sent a never-ending stream of electric zings down to her already damp cleft. He switched breasts, paying equal torturous attention to the other.

When he stopped, she mewled in loss, but he seemed determined to torture her. He moved down her body slowly, his lips caressing her skin softly, driving her crazy with need. He nuzzled the apex of her thighs, and she parted them, her chest heaving as she fought to capture her breath. She lost it in a whoosh as his tongue jabbed at her damp core. Her fingers found his hair and hung on tight as he ate her, his tongue and mouth alternating between nibbling and flicking her clit then delving into her sex. He inserted two fingers into her channel, pumping her with his digits as his tongue skimmed over her sensitive nub. Her pelvic muscles clenched his fingers tight, her hips rocking in cadence to his thrusts.

When he bit her swollen clit gently with the sharp points of his teeth, she bowed off the bed with a scream. He pushed her back down and anchored her with his hands and did it again, applying even more pressure. Her climax crested and crashed with an intensity that made her lose her mind.

But that was okay, because she'd already lost her heart.

CHAPTER 11

The spasms of her climax gripped his fingers. How tight and hot she felt. He couldn't wait until he could sink another part of him inside her.

He leaned down to kiss her, kiss those lush and swollen lips, only to freeze.

What is that?

His predator side roused and cocked a wary ear.

There it was again. *Thump. Scrape.* Given the train was moving, those sounds were not normal at all.

Ark rolled off Jade and peered at the ceiling overhead.

"What is it?" She pushed up on the bed, her shirt still shoved over her breasts, her bra tucked under them, presenting them so delightfully. They really needed more attention from his tongue.

Imagine sliding my shaft between them and watching her as she sucks the tip. A vivid fantasy he wanted to make reality. It made it ever so hard for him to say, "I need to check something out."

What he'd heard was probably nothing. Just the odd contraction of the metal skin covering the train car or perhaps a low-hanging branch not yet trimmed away from the track.

Maybe it's something else. Something that squeaks. His bear's optimistic thought.

Not likely. Only in the movies did adversaries have the means or balls to attack a moving train. In real life, attacks happened on the ground. But just in case . . .

He exited the room, closing the door, shutting Jade inside. A movement down the hall caught his eyes and he saw Stavros stepping out as well. It appeared as if he wasn't alone in hearing things. They eyed each other, passing a silent communication.

The door out of the car had a window, but it was dark outside, and the dim illumination inside made it so that the interior reflected back.

It's probably nothing.

A probably nothing that had interrupted his time with Jade.

It better be nothing or he might kill something.

He flung open the door with one violent motion. Slam. It bounced off the outside frame and stayed open from the force. He'd taken a step out—*to check out nothing*—when a body landed on top of him.

He stumbled, but the railing linking the cars kept him from tumbling off the moving train into the dark landscape.

The heavy attacker grappled with him, his features obscured behind a mask, his scent stifled by a cloying cologne.

Wham. His fist met the jaw of his attacker.

Slam. He whirled and threw him against a wall. The fellow was clearly outmatched and yet he continued to fight with Ark.

What did the guy want? Did it matter?

Grabbing the attacker by his dark combat vest, Ark leaned him over the railing and shouted, "Who do you work for?"

The reply came in the form of a dirty knee to his balls. Ark managed to divert most of that blow to his thigh, but it still smarted, and the sudden jostle by the train, a big shake, caused him to lose his grip.

Screech. The metal chugging serpent ground to a halt, throwing him forward. Ark gripped the railing and cursed as the big dude shoved away from him, into the car.

Oh no you don't.

Ark followed and noted the guy sprinted past the first door, down to the end of the hallway where Ruby sat on the floor watching with one hand on her belly while Stavros straddled a bloke, punching him.

"Heads fucking up," Ark hollered as he bolted toward his cousin.

Stavros paid him heed, sprang off the prone body, and flipped in time to face the rushing male.

The timing of his fist proved to be pure perfection. The guy hit the floor and didn't get up.

But these two attackers were only the beginning. With the train sitting still, Ark could hear the sound of approaching dirt bikes. Rapid and slick machines that could get in and out of tight places—and scatter if anyone took chase.

Nice. It was something Ark might have done if he had wanted to pull a fucking train heist.

And, yes, he was annoyed. Annoyed he'd not thought of it first. Talk about sounding like fun. Against him it proved a challenge. Ark had two women to protect. Good thing they had two badass bears who were pretty good at that sort of thing.

"First one to the house doesn't have to share your mother's famous cherry pie," Stavros challenged, a grin on his lips and a sparkle in his eyes.

"You're on."

Ark sprinted away from Stavros back to Jade, who peeked out the door.

"What just happened? Are we under attack?" She peeked around him and noted the bodies on the floor. "Are they dead?"

"Sleeping."

"That is not any more reassuring. Why are they attacking us? I thought you said that type of thing didn't happen." Her eyes widened. "Are you like some kind of spy bears? Like Double-O Yogi?"

Okay that was funny, but he didn't chuckle, not with the enemy fast approaching. "We are not spies."

"And yet you just handled this attack like a pro."

"Can we talk about this later?" While naked in a bed, with honey. "We need to get out of here before they converge in numbers."

He grabbed her by the hand and pulled her out the still open door. He didn't know why the train had stopped but he guessed it might have something to do with the crisscrossing beams of the motorbikes.

The first one zipped by.

Chug. Shudder.

The whole chain of cars shivered as the wheels began to turn with a squeal. But it took time and momentum to get something of this size moving. They didn't have the luxury of waiting, not if they were going to provide a diversion for Stavros.

"We have to jump."

"Are you nuts?" she hissed, yanking her hand free.

"Do you want to lead those guys away from your sister?" She nodded.

"Then we need to draw those bastards away from the train."

Her eyes widened. "If they're looking for Ruby, then they're looking for a pregnant lady." Jade darted back into the room and grabbed the thin blanket on the mattress and balled it under her shirt.

The sloppiest pregnant belly ever, but it would do in the dark.

"Smart thinking. Let's go, and head toward the lights."

"Toward? Isn't the recommendation to head away from it?"

"Not this time. Trust me."

"I must be insane, but I do."

Of course she did, because Ark would never let anything happen to her. He swung himself over the railing and slotted his feet through the bars. He offered her a hand. "Hurry up and get over before the train picks up any more speed."

"I hate climbing." A grumbled complaint uttered even as she brought her leg over the rail. She'd no sooner joined him on the other side than he wrapped his arms around her and dove from the side of the train. It was a lot harder to land with grace when a guy had a suddenly terrified woman clinging to him and shrieking.

Loudly he might add. Awesome. That would draw attention.

Worry first about landing, idiot. Luckily for them both, Ark hadn't made it to his ripe age of twenty-nine without a few bumps and bruises. He took the brunt of the dive, ensuring his shoulder hit the ground first, and then tucking as best he could around Jade as they rolled to a stop. Not the worst dismount, he recalled getting bucked off a bull a lot harder as a teen, and look who was on top of him. He peered up at her and couldn't resist a very husky, "How you doing?"

"You're out of your bloody mind."

"Isn't it wonderful? Let's go." He rolled off her and sprang to his feet, his eyes scanning the open field around them.

The railways kept a cleared swath on either side of the track. Moving away from the train, car after car clacking by, he noted, in the distance, the red taillights of the motor-bikes.

Dammit. They'd missed them.

A red light flashed bright but not as bright as the head-light that slashed over them as a dirt bike spun around and spotlighted them.

He waved. "Get ready. We're going to steal some wheels."

Draping his arm around Jade's waist, he set off at a light jog, zigging and zagging to keep them erratically spot-lighted by the head beam. He even angled her once or twice to show the big belly she held, the baby bump blanket threatening to fall.

The whine of the small engine grew loud. He pushed Jade to her knees, mostly to make her a smaller target and not for dirty things, and whirled to face the bike. The driver raised a baton. As if that would save him. Ark sidestepped at the last moment and eased his torso back in a deep limbo before he kicked out, connecting with the body of the bike as it went past. The sharp strike of his boot set the bike off balance, tumbling its driver with it, pinning him under the chassis. Ark nicely yanked it off him, then smashed it down, then pulled it up again. Then down.

When he noticed no movement, he lifted it one last time and straddled the machine. "Get on," he yelled as the small-engine scream of more bikes filled the air.

Eyes wide, Jade stared at him as if she'd seen something amazing. Or really scary. But since he was saving her ass, and her sister's, she was going to stick with amazing.

"Now," he yelled before he gunned the motor.

She scrambled to her feet and slid onto the back. The seat

didn't provide much room, but the motor was strong enough for two.

"Hold on tight."

Her arms wrapped around his waist—*Squeeze me tight!*—and he twisted the throttle. The bike lurched ahead, and she tightened her arms anaconda-style.

Riding a metal beast wasn't new for him, but his mate on the back—in a strange place in the dark—added a certain element. Given escape, and not doing donuts, were his ultimate goals, he drove away from the train tracks, straight across the open strip of field to the woods. Most of the bobbing lights followed him instead of the train.

As they hit the edge of the thin forest, he stopped the bike and got off, holding it steady for Jade.

"What are you doing?"

"Drive this in that direction." He pointed.

"But—"

He planted a hard kiss on her lips. "Go. I'll be along to find you shortly."

"I can't do this."

"You can, and will." He gave her another hard embrace. "Go now."

Because with her out of the way, he could do what needed to be done.

Grawr!

Only later could he have ripped off his own head for letting her go off on her own. She'd wobbled away safe enough, and he'd charged the oncoming bikes, his big bear form lashing out and knocking them off. On the ground, they were easy targets. One even cried.

Ark was a good bear. He didn't kill them, because that would result in some difficulties later, but he did shake them and make them wish they were the load of cum their mother had spat out. He did wish he'd eaten a few, though, especially once he loped off looking for Jade and found the bike and only the bike.

No Jade. Nothing but the lingering smell of pussy. The shifter kind. Get your mind out of the gutter and into the game.

Someone in the feline family had taken his mate. Someone dared to take his honey. And he was going to get her back.

CHAPTER 12

In the movies, a heroine awoke looking rumpled and sexy. She didn't have to pee or worry about a pasty tongue and surely foul breath. She also didn't have to endure the wide ass of some dude in ill-fitting slacks standing in front of her and, judging by the *pfft* sound, killing them all slowly with stealthy noxious gas.

Of more concern than his lack of manners about bodily matters was the fact that she recognized him. The twerp standing over her was the same guy who'd broken into her place.

"You!" She lunged at the guy and hit him in the leg.

"Ouch. You bitch!" The skinny fellow raised his hand but stopped when a velvet voice said, "Hit her and I'll have you tossed from the plane."

A freaky threat, but freakier still was the fact that she appeared, as the speaker claimed, to be on a plane.

Oh shit. She went from slumped and drooling on the armrest of the couch to rigid and straight-backed. The skinny fellow slouched as he moved away to a group of men huddled around a laptop at the back of the plane.

A plane. Eep.

She heard a chuckle and she whipped her head around in time to see a wiry fellow take a seat across from her.

She could guess who it was. The platinum hair, shaved on both sides, the earring dangling from one ear. The tribal tattoo her sister had mentioned when describing him wound around his arm in thick bands.

"You must be Xavier." A name she'd forbidden in her apartment because Ruby still seemed so hung up on the guy.

"She spoke of me." Stated with satisfaction.

"Complained about her creepy ex, yes." The little lie punctured his small pleasure.

His features darkened. "Are you the reason she's refused to talk to me? Won't even see me?"

"Maybe the fact you were practically married and showed yourself to be a two-timing douche nozzle is why she wants nothing to do with you."

"Merina meant nothing to me. It was an alliance of convenience. I broke things off the moment I found Ruby. But Merina refused to listen. Kept acting as if we were still engaged. I tried to explain that to her, but Ruby wouldn't talk to me. She ran and hid!"

"Stalking has that effect."

A low laugh rumbled from him, not the anger she would have expected at her. "Don't kid yourself. She loved my ardent pursuit."

"Loved it so much she hid from you? Yeah, I totally see that now." Jade rolled her eyes.

It had no effect on his conviction. "She succumbed to a fit of jealous rage. She is a female. It happens. But she misses me. I know she does. She wants me back. She just needs some time to get over her tantrum."

"Tantrum? You're delusional." And she might have added more except the plane chose that moment to do a little shaking.

Shaking in the sky.

Way above the ground.

Way, way above.

Gulp.

Her fingers dug into the seat as her phobia shoved past their inane chatter to remind her she was scared of planes. Really scared.

"It's just a little turbulence," Xavier noted.

"Is what I'm sure everyone said before their plane went down."

"You are quite safe."

"You can't be sure of that."

A smile tugged at his lips and only a blind idiot wouldn't see the charm that could illuminate his features. She could see why Ruby might have fallen for him.

"I can be sure," he said, "because for you to die, this plane has to crash, and I am not in the mood to die."

"Who said anything about dying?" A high-pitched giggle seeped out of her. "People fly all the time. In the air. In giant metal cans." With wings. Wings! Who the hell ever thought it was a good idea to put wings on machines?

"Do I need to drug you again?"

Her gaze narrowed. "Don't you dare. You're just as vile as Ruby claims."

"You lie. She wouldn't say that about me." He sprang into an immediate defense.

"She said a lot of things. First and foremost was the fact she never wants to see you again."

"No. I don't believe it." He shook his head.

"In case you hadn't noticed, she ran away from you and cut off all communication."

"Again, a momentary lapse of judgment."

"No, your relationship was the aberration. She wants nothing to do with you."

"If that's true, then I want to hear it from her lips."

In some ways, his odd determination reminded her of Ark.

"If you wanted to talk to her then why send that thug to my apartment with a knife."

"He was only supposed to confirm her presence. No harm would have come to either of you."

"I don't believe you. What about when those guys attacked the train?"

Xavier's gaze darkened. "In their enthusiasm to please me, my men might have gone too far. I told them to locate Ruby, and shadow her movements until my arrival. They were never to harm her."

"How reassuring. Not," Jade snapped. "Was it their own initiative that led to them kidnapping me, or was that your plan to use me as bait to lure her?"

"Nothing has gone as planned. Rest assured kidnapping you wasn't my idea, but now that I have you, then yes, I will turn that to my advantage. If I must dangle you like a carrot to get Ruby to talk to me then I will."

"All you'll do is piss Ruby off."

His lips flattened. "I expect she'll be a tad miffed. So what do you think? Diamond earrings or a bracelet for her forgiveness?"

She gaped at him.

"You're right. Both. At the very least. I will give her anything she wants when she comes back to me."

"Why would she come back to you?"

"Because she's mine." His eyes flashed, hinting of yellow and perhaps a touch of insanity.

Freaky. "You won't get away with this. Let me go."

"I can't and I would add that we wouldn't have to do this if you'd tell me where Ruby is. I need to see her. At once." It should have sounded imperious, but it emerged more as a plea.

She hardened herself against him. "Ruby doesn't want to see you. So why don't you crawl back to your fiancée?"

"I've already told you I am not engaged anymore. I called it off the day Ruby and I met. But it took time, to make it sink in, especially since Merina and her family fought it."

She snorted. "You don't really expect me to believe that?"

His piercing blue eyes pinned her. "I knew Ruby was mine the moment I met her."

"You say something psycho like that and you expect me to tell you where she is?" Jade laughed. "You are out of your freaking mind. And just wait until Ark finds me." *He's going to eat you. Maybe.* She wasn't too sure what shape-shifting bears ate, but she would wager it was some kind of meat.

"Ah yes, Arkadios."

"You know him?"

"Quite well in fact. How entertaining that I managed to steal his paramour right from under his nose. I do hope he pays a visit. It's been a while. Did you know we attended the same college? The good old days. He never could beat me when we played against each other, and now it seems history will repeat and I will get to beat him again."

"Obsess much? Is it me or do you have a hard time letting things go? First Ark, then my sister . . . You need help."

"I just need Ruby." His features tightened. "She shouldn't have left. I was planning to propose. To show her I meant it when I said she was my mate."

There was that word again. *Mate.* Ark used it too. "I'm going to go out on a limb here and say I'll bet you're some kind of shape-shifter."

"Was it the teeth that gave it away?" He smiled widely. Big. White. And . . .

"Are you like a polar bear or something?"

He recoiled. "That's rude, and if you weren't Ruby's sister, I'd probably kill you for the insult. I come from much more majestic stock than that."

"Moose?"

His glare narrowed.

"Rabbit? What," she exclaimed. The man appeared ready to explode. "How am I supposed to know what kind of freakish animal you turn into?"

"I am a white tiger. We are very rare."

"A good thing. I don't think the female population could handle two psychopaths at once."

"You are twisting my actions into something ugly."

"Maybe that wouldn't happen if you backed off."

"Ruby cares for me." Did he say it to convince Jade or himself?

Problem was Jade knew Ruby loved this guy. For a moment, Jade took pity on him. "She did, but she had more than one reason for leaving."

"You know why she left?" He froze her limbs with his laser-like eyes. "Tell me."

"If she wanted you to know, she would have told you."

"She will speak with me if she wants you back." With that threat, Xavier turned away from her and ignored her the rest of the flight. She would have preferred they continued arguing so she could forget how high above the earth she was. High enough to land and splat like a bug.

Gulp.

Her nails definitely left some crescent moon scars in the leather when it began its descent and the plane landed with a bump and whistling scream of the engines.

Her fingers only trembled a little as she undid the seat belt. Now was not the time to turn into a girl freaking out.

She'd survived her first plane ride. She'd survive what came next.

"Let's go." The man with the strange platinum hair pushed her toward the opening in the side of the plane.

"Where are we?"

"A private airstrip outside of Los Angeles. We were rerouted."

She emerged ahead of Xavier onto the top step of a staircase, where she froze upon seeing a sea of eyes. Wild, glinting eyes set in very ursine faces. The many big brown bears let out a very big roar. Jade could handle a lot of things. She truly could. Blood, stitches, overcooked food. But that many carnivores in one place?

She promptly fainted.

CHAPTER 13

His grandfather handled the blah blah part of the threats. Ark had eyes for only one person. Jade. Alive, appearing unharmed, shocked at the greeting he'd arranged.

Overjoyed, she fainted the moment his sleuth said hello.

It took him too long to reach her, and when he did, Ark cradled Jade's limp body and growled at anyone who got too close. Perhaps he'd calm down—doubtful—once he got over his fear from when he realized she'd been taken.

Someone had taken Jade. *My Jade.* His. Did they understand how badly they trespassed?

Sharing was for others. He wanted Jade for himself.

In those first few moments in the woods when he realized she was gone, he'd panicked. It wasn't pretty or manly. It involved the punching of some trees. The drinking of some moonshine—an unexpected surprise found in a shed in the woods.

Once Stavros found him, it was Ruby who gave him his first clue as to who might have her.

"Do you think Xavier did this? The Boudrion family has got the kind of money to send guys after me."

His head almost spun a hundred and eighty degrees.

Which would have hurt. Good thing his body spun with it. "What did you say?"

"Do you think my ex did this?"

"Before that. The name. Did you say Boudrion? As in Xavier Boudrion? The feline scourge of Hollywood. He is the one stalking you?" He couldn't help raising his voice.

She crossed her arms and glared at him, much like Jade would. "Don't you raise your voice to me. I am stressing a little bit right now, which isn't good for the baby. That means you're going to tell me why you're saying Xavier's name like he's some kind of super villain."

"Because he is a villain."

"I thought he was a businessman," Ruby retorted.

"He is, and he's been dipping his toes into the honey business. Trying to steal our clients. Totally unacceptable," Ark roared.

"He's a villain because he's giving you competition?" Ruby snickered.

"The man is also an ass. Arrogant. Cocky."

"You speak like you know him."

"Unfortunately, I went to school with him," Ark grumbled. Back then, Ark had size, but lacked finesse, and so Xavier constantly taunted him. "I can state with confidence that Boudrion is an asshole."

"Says you. He was always rather sweet to me. For a two-timing jerk." Her lips pulled down. "Then again, I'm one to talk about honesty given I was pregnant at the time."

"Will he think it's his?" Ark eyed Ruby's belly.

"I never told him I was pregnant even after I dumped him. I didn't see the point. So I guess if he saw me, he'd probably wonder."

"Are you aware he's like me?"

"As in changes into an animal?" Ruby shrugged. "I knew there was something different about him. He had the same kind of wild energy that the guy I slept with at that Halloween party did."

"Did he ever call you his mate?"

"Xavier said a lot of stuff. Very macho and possessive claims. Which is the reason why, when I found out about his fiancée and then the baby, I thought it best to break things off."

A man like Xavier would snap if it turned out Ruby was his mate and she carried another man's child. He might even harm them, which meant there would be no trade. Ark had a duty—a need—to save Jade, but he also had to keep the sister safe.

Xavier Boudrion, you stupid son of a kitty. You just opened up a huge jar of sticky honey.

Such excitement happening in his life. He made a few phone calls. More than a few people owed him a favor, and those that didn't, he threatened.

In some cases he plied the guilt, ranting and raving how Mother didn't love him until she agreed to make him his favorite dessert. He'd need something sweet to calm his adrenaline after he got Jade back.

Apparently, he did his job well because he met the plane holding his mate—registered to MeoX, Xavier's company—with at least a hundred bears. He got there first because a buddy in the control tower delayed Xavier's landing for a few hours, before diverting the plane to a smaller airport to refuel. Guess who was there to meet them?

Grawr.

When a hundred bears roared, it brought a shiver. Really it did, because it vibrated the very air.

The show of strength was meant to intimidate Xavier.

Instead, Ark's welcoming committee scared Jade, and dammit all, when she fainted, Xavier, that slick jungle cat, kept her from falling. Xavier touched Jade when he caught her and now Ark would have to wash the smell from her because it bothered him.

"Hey, Ark, are you going to need some pants?"

Grrrr. Translated: *Go away.* He hugged her tighter.

"Is he gonna eat her?"

Probably. After he washed the stink of cat from her skin and burned her clothes.

"Auntie sent a text and said they just put some ribs and potatoes on the 'cue for when we're done."

Ribs? Grumble, the tummy kind.

"He's got the girl so I say we're done. There's a store with cold beer on the way home."

Home. Good plan. Take his mate to his home, where she would be safe from dirty cats and they could be fed. She'd probably need food to keep her strong for when he locked her up in his fucking room. To keep her safe. *Because I don't like it when she's not safe.*

Didn't like it at all. *Grawr.*

"I think he's going to rampage."

No, because I have more control than that.

Deep breath. Another. It didn't calm his bear down, which was why he rode in the box of his brother's pickup truck, his furry body wrapped around Jade. At least she didn't scream when she woke.

However, she did growl. "About time you came for me. I'll find you he says. Nice job finding me. You let a psycho kidnap me and put me on a plane. Do you know how high those things fly? And then, as if I'm not already traumatized, you bring the whole Bear-y Bunch to the rescue. Next time warn me so I pack extra underwear." She harangued him, but she snuggled closer. She might vent, but she knew she was safe with him.

The quiet moment didn't last.

The truck pulled to a halt in front of the farmhouse, his grandparents' he should add. His family had owned the place for a few generations now, the original structure long buried as they added on to the main house. The freshly painted white clapboard gleamed, as did the white pickets containing his grandmother's flower garden, protecting it from roaming chickens—and the pounding feet of cubs as they ran through screaming, playing a game of . . . It didn't have a name, and the rules consisted of yell and run and tackle each other until someone screamed for mercy or an ear got yanked by an adult.

Good times.

Lots of great memories were made on this farm and even better food came out of it. Something delicious came wafting his way. Lifting his head, he scented the air, almost able to taste the roasting ribs. Rubbed with a blend of spices and brown sugar that caramelized onto the meat.

His mouth watered. Rumble. That was his belly insisting it needed sustenance. But his grandma wouldn't feed bears.

"Never feed the wildlife," she'd told him when he was but a cub, not even waist high, with a slap of her wooden spoon on his hands. He'd shrugged and mouthed, "Sorry, Grandpa," to the black nose pressed against the kitchen window. Grandma showed no sympathy for his hairy hungry grandpa as she said, "He knows the rules."

If Ark wanted to eat, he'd have to change.

So unfair.

The staggering notes of plucked strings filled the air. The haunting sound went well with the rhythmic clap of hands. The music came from the backyard, but he didn't have time to make his escape. His aunts poured out of the house, his grandmother in the lead, his mother part of the invading posse.

How nice of them to provide a welcoming party. He could have smiled—but his muzzle wasn't built for it. He prepared himself for a few hugs, only to gape when they ignored him.

"There she is. Let's get her inside before these *vlakas* frighten the child again." Yiayia spoke, offering Ark a glare as her minions of darkness in their aprons scurried to obey. The women arrived in a swarm and departed with a dazed Jade in their grips, his grandmother pausing only long enough to pat him on the head and say, "Good boy. About time you settled down. Get changed and find some pants." But it was the "The ribs are ready" that got him moving.

CHAPTER 14

Jade tried a few times to peek over her shoulder and catch a glimpse of Ark. *My big ol' teddy bear.* While a little late, he'd come for her—with an army no less—and taken her from Xavier, only to turn coward and let a bunch of women kidnap her. Worse, they seemed determined to judge her.

"Nice teeth. Do you brush?"

"Yes. And floss," she answered without thinking.

"Can you cook? Ark is a growing boy. He needs his food."

"And meat. Lots of meat. He loves my ribs best." One of them beamed smugly.

"He would ditch your ribs for my pie in an instant." A retort by another woman.

"Unless it's my cake with that buttercream frosting. I don't know how many times I slapped his paw for sticking his fingers in the bowl as a boy." The reminiscing gaze refocused on her with laser intent. "You didn't answer, girl. Do you cook?"

"Yeah, I can cook but—" As if they'd let her finish a sentence.

A rotund woman with her hair cut short and trendy in a dark bob halted in front of her and held out her hands about waist height. "She has good birthing hips. Good thing because she'll need them. I still remember Ark's big head when he was born."

"Not as much as his mom Eudora does," snickered another.

Exactly how many women surrounded her? Hard to tell because they kept changing places as they herded her along to the house.

"Excuse me. Um, can we slow down for a second?" Jade tried to interject, but they simply spoke over her.

"I'm thinking she needs Grandma Alicia's."

A woman tapped her chin and eyed her neck to toe. "Maybe, although I would have said Annalise."

"Can't. It didn't survive Sofie's wedding night."

"Men!" They all hmphed together.

"I think she'd go perfect with Kalienta's."

"Oooh." Nods all around.

She managed to squeeze in a "Who is Kalienta?"

"She was Ark's great-aunt on his father's side. You'll look perfect in her dress."

"What dress?" She blinked as her confusion grew.

"Wedding dress, of course."

"Should we have her IQ tested?" someone whispered. "Seems a little slow to me."

"It's on account she's not Greek" was the sage reply. Again, heads nodded all around.

In that moment, Jade quite felt like Alice. She'd fallen down a hole of some kind, a bear hole with crazy ladies smelling of baked goods at the bottom. "Can someone explain what is going on? And who are you?"

Bright blue eyes, peering from an ancient face, caught her gaze. "I am Ark's grandmother. You may call me Yiayia."

"And I am his mother, Eudora."

More names were tossed at her: Athene, Lydia, Nerine,

Reah, Titaia, and those were just his aunts. Once they started tossing the female cousin names—*Mabel is the one about to get married, about time too, her parents have their eye on a condo for sale by the beaches. Kloe is going for her masters. Smart as her mother that one. Then there's Julia . . .* —Jade was lost. The size of this family boggled the mind. It made her want to hide. It also fascinated her, given the apparent complex relationships floating around.

This was a family that stayed together. A family that celebrated. She'd never had that. Her mother's family lived scattered, and they never spoke, much less saw each other. Jade did her best to keep in touch with her siblings, but their diverging paths meant the only one she saw with any regularity was Pearl.

Thinking of her sisters made her think of Ruby. No one had really said what happened to Ruby. "Where's my sister? Does anyone know where she is and what's happened? I haven't seen her since the train and—" She stopped talking for a second as she reached the door to the house. Less door, more a portal made of wood and at least eight feet in height with a curved top. The door had a medieval feel with its chiseled etchings, a beautiful rendition of Greece, the coliseum peeking from the edges, bears roaming the streets on two and four paws amid the eclectic buildings. She no sooner stepped past the fabulous carvings than she noted Ruby ensconced in a chair, her feet on a stool, a blanket over her belly. A plate of food balanced on the baby bump and she held a glass of lemonade—with an umbrella and straw!

Meanwhile, Jade was pretty sure she looked wretched and smelled even worse. Still, though, she didn't resent her sister because she looked the most content Jade had seen her in weeks. Okay, she maybe resented the lemonade a little, and she coveted the cookies.

"Hey, sis. About time you got here."

"Don't you sass me. I was so worried." A chastisement that promptly turned into tears, which led to a very naked Ark rushing into the house, eyes wide and yelling, "Who hurt her? Who dies?" He paused, legs slightly bent, fists held upraised in a pugilistic ready pose. His cheeks turned a lovely shade of ruddy crimson as many sets of eyes perused him.

"The pregnant one did it," Reah said with a smirk and pointed finger.

"I'm okay, Ark," Jade said to reassure him with a swipe at her eyes. "Just so happy to see my sister."

"So I don't have to hurt anyone?" He sounded so disappointed.

"Oh, someone needs a hurting," said Eudora. Jade winced with Ark when his mother snapped a naked haunch with a dish towel and barked, "Get some clothes on. We have guests. Mind your manners."

"We are not a hippie commune." Said by Aunt Athene.

"Except on full moons," whispered Titaia to titters.

"Are you sure you're okay? You're crying." He looked so adorably confused and her sister so amused. As a matter of fact, everyone was amused.

And she was so . . . overwhelmed. "I'm crying because I'm happy, you idiot. Can't you tell?" she wailed.

"I think I'm going to find some pants."

"Maybe you should!" she yelled. Because trying to keep her gaze averted was hard. The man was built like a Greek god. All muscle and tanned skin.

When Ark turned around, she was treated to a lovely

view of his ass as he walked away. Just as good-looking as the front. Sigh.

"I know. Always a pleasure to watch. He's got my husband's glutes," confided the old lady. "It skips a generation, so don't expect your children to get the Stover ass. But your grandchildren might."

"Um, why are you all assuming I'm going to be getting hitched with Ark?" Bad enough Ark kept alluding to it too.

For some reason, the query brought guffaws of laughter.

"Sweet child, that fate was sealed the moment he set eyes on you."

More of the assertion that they belonged together. It wasn't just Ark now but these women, his closest family relatives, who acted as if it were a foregone conclusion.

Did she not get a choice? Attraction wasn't the only thing to aspire to in a relationship. She had yet to decide if she even liked Ark. He was pushy, arrogant, overbearing . . .

A bear. Cuddly and sweet and protective.

I think I'm screwed. Which led to more sighs as the madness continued. It had been over an hour since she'd arrived. Given her emotional wreckage, a pair of women whisked her away via a few hallways, possibly through a portal, then another hall or two before arriving at a bedroom. They'd shoved her in a bathroom and told her to take a relaxing bath. She'd opted for a shower instead, wishing the soothing hot water would wash away the strange feeling within her.

It took her a while to figure out what bothered her. So much had happened. The world she thought she knew had turned upside down. She got the feeling nothing would ever be the same again, and that scared her. Just like Ark and his family scared her, not because she worried about them hurting her but because of what they represented; belonging. She'd spent her life trying to hold her family together, taking care of them on her own. And here was family that wanted to not just absorb her in their midst but seemed determined to coddle her for once. The very idea was baffling. But it also intrigued.

What would it be like to belong to a family that, at the request of one member, would converge en masse to rescue another? What would it be like to be one of these women who so readily accepted her and assumed she would join them as a happy wife to a crazy Greek bear?

I kind of want to find out. Something she wouldn't accomplish hiding in the shower.

Emerging a while later from the bathroom, she found a plate of food waiting for her, along with the aunt called Nerine, who pulled out a brush and told her to "Sit."

It seemed best to not argue with the matronly woman. While Jade ate, the aunt brushed and then weaved strands of hair. The combination was like a euphoric relaxation pill. It made her say more than she should have. "Do you really believe I'll marry Ark?" Sleep with him? Sure. They'd made it to third base, and she wasn't averse to the idea of a home run, but forever?

"You will marry. And soon. You are fated mates."

"I don't know if I can wrap my mind around this whole fated thing you guys take for granted." The idea that love was instant, and not something built over time, seemed impossible. But then again, perhaps there was an esoteric formula, a magical combination of souls that was just meant to work together.

Could that be true of me and Ark?

"We all have a bit of adjusting to do when we first find out about it. You're not the first one to wonder." Nerine took a seat across from her, the ledge on the window wide enough for a cushion to sit on. "When my Giorgi first found me and told me I was his, I laughed at him. Who was this man to declare I belonged to him? I refused to date him just on principle." A smile of fond remembrance lit her features. "He was so persistent, though. Every day he would come to the dry cleaner I worked at. One day he would bring me a large bouquet of flowers. The next, jars of honey. Chocolates. I finally agreed to go on a date with him if he'd stop. We became inseparable after that night, and I've now been with my Giorgi for eighteen years."

"So it worked for you."

"Not just me. My older sister Athene didn't even try to play hard to get, and she has been with Yohan for thirty-four."

"Surely there are some relationships that fail?" Jade had seen love die firsthand.

"Not if they were fated."

It gave her something to think about. How could she not ponder such faith? The question was, should she give in to this wild feeling she had for Ark? What of her sister? They still didn't know who the daddy was.

But it's not Ark. The certainty wouldn't waver.

It took an eternity of hallways and possibly a trip through some kind of wormhole before they emerged at last into the yard. It took her a moment to take it all in. Large oak trees bordered a yard the size of a hockey rink. Soft white lights, strung in the trees, lit the darkness. There were picnic tables and patio sets and even a few fire pits scattered around. Closer to the house, long tables, laden with platters, mostly empty of food.

Music played, fun and upbeat. Bodies swayed to the rhythm, boisterous stomping and swinging. Plenty of clapping and laughing too.

She couldn't help but note the men; big, burly, and boisterous, their laughter loudly exuberant, their hands often gesturing. Many of them danced, doing their own thing and smiling as they did, their cheeks flushed and eyes bright.

There were an equal number of women it seemed, but unlike the men, they came in a wider variety of shapes and heights. Whereas the men stuck to trousers or jeans and collared shirts, the ladies seemed to have covered every single fashion from sedate knee-covering skirts to a plaid shorts ensemble that just covered some cheeks.

Jade was lucky in that her luggage, last seen getting loaded on the train, actually made it to Ark's home. She was quite comfortable in her well-washed blue jeans and her shell-colored long-sleeve knit jersey. Pausing by the back door of the house, she hesitated to enter the large group celebrating. "Are you sure my sister is out here?"

"Right over there." Nerine pointed to where Ruby held court, a bunch of men hovering, big dudes who all appeared to be talking and smiling.

"Who are they?"

"Possible fathers. We did our best to round them all up to meet your sister."

Jade almost choked. "You know?"

"Of course we know. It's family business."

A family they wanted her to become a part of. "You know what, since she looks fine, maybe I'll go back to my room and lie down. It's been a—"

"Nonsense. You are not tired. Don't be scared. No one will hurt you here. Ark would kill them. So go. Have fun." A shove at her back sent her stumbling a few steps forward. "You should find Ark before he gets growly again. New mates are always so protective."

Find Ark? No, what she should do was grab Ruby and run away from these crazy people. She wasn't ready for this kind of blunt chaos in her life. She whirled to march back into the house, only to hear an exuberant, "There you are, *koukla!*"

"Eep." She uttered a sharp scream as her feet left the ground and she found herself hoisted over a brawny shoulder. Bottom up and head down, the startling reversal in gravity made her screech. "What are you doing?"

Before answering, he dropped her down until her feet touched the ground, but he didn't let go. His arm curled around her waist. Brown eyes glanced down at her. "I'm dancing. With you." Spin.

She clung to him, and only when they stood in one spot swaying again did she manage to sputter, "What if I don't want to dance?"

"Are you tired?" A look of concern creased his brow. "Fear not. I'll dance for both of us." Again, she was hoisted, her feet leaving the ground by more than a few inches, bringing her high enough that they hugged, cheek to cheek.

It was kind of cute. Real cute. Panty-melting cute.

She had to fight his allure. Bad enough his family already planned a wedding. This would just cement their mistaken belief that she and Ark were destined to be together.

Would it be so bad? Not while it lasted. But what if it ended?

I don't want to end up like my mom.

She needed to distract herself from the temptation he represented. "I think I met half the western seaboard. Apparently they are all related to you."

"Not all. But we do have plenty of scattered lines through the United States."

"How do you remember all their names?"

"It's easier than you would think." He spun her and, keeping only a single arm wrapped around her waist, pointed with his other hand. "That's Cyndi. Makes the best chocolate chip cookie dough ever. Then Mallory." Another jab. "She works as a chiropractor and can make your spine crackle from top to bottom. That's my second cousin Fiona. She used to hunt frogs with me until she got boobs."

"You have an insane amount of family."

"It's not crazy it's—"

"Greek. So I keep hearing. You know, your family seems convinced we're going to get married and pop out babies for, them to fatten." She assumed they wanted to feed them because chubby babies were cute and not because they were a delicacy among bears.

"They are rather excited. I am one of the first of my generation to find his mate. They will start behaving once we have our second child."

"Second? That might be a little difficult given I have no plans to have sex with you." Obviously taking things any further was not feasible. She wasn't ready for the type of commitment they seemed determined to demand.

"You are going to have sex with me. A lot of sex. You have needs. I will take care of them." Stated with such cocky confidence.

"Or I could take care of myself."

"Can I watch?" He twirled them so fast on the dance floor exhilaration hiccupped her breath, and when she caught it back, she couldn't help but laugh.

"Making me dizzy won't make me change my mind. I think things are moving too fast. So many marriages end in divorce."

"Because it wasn't the right person. The right bear." He smiled as he set her on her feet. He tilted her chin. "We are meant for each other. You'll see." His lips dipped close. "You'll feel."

A shiver went through her at the hot words breathed upon her lips.

Kiss me. She thought it. Wanted it, and yet, before they could press together in an embrace, someone grabbed her arm and spun her with a mirth-filled "My turn, cousin."

"But she's mine," exclaimed Ark as she was pulled away.

"Not until the wedding she's not." The teasing cousin kept spinning Jade until she thought she would fall.

It wasn't Jade that fell but rather her partner as Ark took him out with a left hook. The other fellow hit the ground with a groan. Ark glowered over his cousin. "Mine. Don't touch. Come." He didn't ask, but grabbed her hand and pulled her off the dance floor. He seemed a tad angry. Volatile, like a volcano about to erupt.

Or a bear about to rampage.

A man on the edge and dangerous yet she didn't hesitate to follow him. A part of her wondered at her trust in him.

He's big. Violent. Unpredictable. But also gentle, and fiercely protective, and sensual. So sensual with her, such as when he reached a wide-trunked tree and pressed her back against it. He framed her with his arms and his body.

"I see we're not done with the cave bear act yet."

"I won't apologize. Where you're concerned, I lack control. I can't stand to see another man's hands on you. I want to claim you. Take you and mark you as mine."

"You can't own me."

"You think I would own you?" He laughed. "Don't you see? You are the one who has me. I am yours to command. I need you, *koukla*."

Need. What a funny word. When Jade was young, her mother needed her to do the laundry and make the kids' lunch in the summer. Sometimes even breakfast and dinner. Her siblings needed her to do homework and give them rides when she got her license. She'd been needed her whole life.

But Ark's need was different. This need was about heat and desire. A desire for her as a woman, a sensual being who deserved the touch and affection of a man. Not just any man.

Ark.

He held an insane ability to make her feel breathless. Only he could moisten her panties with just a smoldering look or touch. He made her need too. She didn't just need the way he made her feel; she wanted it.

"I want you." The words were said aloud, and the regret she'd fear in admitting her weakness didn't hit. Not yet.

His lips quirked. "I know."

"That's all you have to say?" She glared at him. "Why do I even like you? You are insufferably arrogant."

"You like it." He drew her closer. "Admit it. You think I'm like hot honey on toast."

"I hate toast."

"How can you hate toast?" His brows rose. "Put some creamed honey on it and it's like the best thing ever."

"I'm more of a cheese spread on crackers kind of girl."

"You will learn to love honey." Solemnly stated.

"How can you be sure?"

"Because I know."

"Incoming!" The shout had Ark turning his head, but it was Jade who slipped from his grasp to catch the Frisbee.

"Nice catch."

She grinned and waggled the disc.

Someone shouted, "Wanna play?"

As a matter of fact, she did. Especially since it was six

cousins against her and Ark. Oh and Ruby, but she was more of an honorary player, given she didn't move from the table and only caught one Frisbee that came her way.

It was a rollicking fun time full of dodging, running, laughing, and the occasional grab by Ark, who held her in the air to catch the higher tosses.

It was the sexiest thing she'd ever done with a guy—and there was nothing they could do to celebrate it. One thing was made very clear to her and that was Ark's grandmother didn't condone any hanky-panky under her roof by unwed young'uns. She and Ark would have separate bedrooms.

"A pity."

"What's a pity?" Ark asked, handing her a glass of punch.

"Do you realize this will be the first night we haven't slept partially together since we met?"

"Says who?" he asked.

"Your aunts. Your grandma. Everyone."

"Have a little faith. My brothers and cousins might be excellent cockblockers, but they also make great wing men."

He'd no sooner spoken than he tossed a nod toward Stavros. The Frisbee hit a beer in an older fellow's hands.

"Hey." The disc was sent back and managed to smack the noggin of a guy by the food table. He fell against it, and rose, face smeared with jelly, holding cookies. He fired them like Frisbees.

It took only a jaw-dropping moment to turn the yard into the world's biggest food fight, and in that chaos, Ark dragged her off into the shadows, but he headed for the house, not away from it.

"Where are we going?" she whispered.

"Your room."

"But I don't see a door," she remarked as they stopped by a wall with lots of windows surrounded by ivy.

"We can't go through the house; we'd be caught. Hold on to me. I'll show you the best way to sneak in."

Perhaps the punch held a little more *punch* than she knew. Whatever the reason, she clung to Ark piggyback style as he maneuvered the awfully strong trellis bolted to the house. At any moment she expected them to get caught, but then again, judging by the yells coming from around the rear of the home, the food fight was still in full swing.

The window was partially ajar. He shoved the screen to the side and widened the space before manhandling her inside.

He hoisted his forearms on the windowsill and vaulted in. The room assigned to her might have seemed spacious before, but now with him taking up an awful lot of space, it became cozy.

"Come here."

The reality of what was about to happen struck her. "Won't we get in trouble?"

"Only if we're caught. And the worst that will happen is my grandmother might beat me. She has wooden spoons made of acacia. The toughest wood around."

"I don't want you to be beaten."

His big shoulders lifted and dropped. "I can handle it since it's for a worthy cause."

"We could wait." The words emerged breathless.

"I can't wait anymore."

Neither could she.

She moved first, lifting herself on tiptoe, bracing her hands on his chest, tilting her lips for a kiss. He drew her close, bending enough that his lips might brush hers.

As usual, when he touched, she melted. A soft sigh of pleasure left her as his lips plundered hers, stroking them apart, tugging at their fullness. His tongue mingled into her mouth, twisting and twining. A sensual dance that tugged at the core of her, making a spot between her thighs pulse.

It wasn't the only thing showing a pulse. The hardness of his shaft pressed against her lower belly, a caged beast in need of taming.

Giggle.

"What's funny?"

"You. Me. This." She laughed again. "I'm a grown woman, who is worried about getting caught and spanked."

His lips curled into a devilish grin. "Anytime you need a spanking, just ask."

Again, she giggled, the moment fraught with sexual tension and yet, at the same time, so enjoyable.

I'm happy. The feeling was unmistakable and shocking. It made her realize something; it was too late. If something were to happen to separate her and Ark, she'd hurt.

Oh hell no. She backed away from him and he turned a puzzled glance her way. "What's wrong?"

"I care for you."

"Is that your happy face? Because you look kind of horrified."

"Because I *am* horrified. I care for you, which means you could hurt me."

"I won't hurt you."

"You could."

His brows drew together. "I wouldn't. Unless I accidentally stepped on your foot on account when I mix tequila and beer I get a little clumsy."

"Don't you see what's going to happen? You're going to knock me up a few times and then leave."

"Why would I leave?"

"Because who wants to be a family man? It's a lot of responsibility."

"Yes. It is. And? I am waiting for the negative." He spread his hands and took a step toward her. "I think the idea of having a family is the best thing. Even better than my great-aunt Frieda's crusted seasoned side of beef au jus."

"Did your stomach just rumble?"

"It's the best meal ever. Makes me hungry each time I think of it, and yet, do you know what makes me even hungrier?" He stepped close enough that she could reach out and touch him. "You are a temptation I can't resist."

"Until you get bored."

"Is that a challenge?" His lips curled. "I accept."

"This isn't a joke, Ark."

"I wasn't laughing. I will make you happy, *koukla*, and I won't ever leave."

"Do you really think it could last?" Could she hope for the kind of happy she saw within his family sleuth? Was it possible to have a happily ever after?

"I know it will last. I dare you to try." He dared her to trust.

And she had to wonder, should she let fear decide her life? Her mother had lost love and then chose to mourn that instead of finding herself a new partner in life. Her mother wasn't lonely because her dad left. She'd spent her life lonely because she feared trying again.

I don't want that to happen to me. Being brave and taking control of her life started now by taking a risk. By jumping in eyes wide open and with two hands grabbing him by the shirt, and kind of tossing him.

Okay, maybe not so much toss as heave to the side, and being a smart bear, he grinned as he hit the mattress. He brought Jade down with him. She landed atop with a squeak.

"Ark!"

"Shhhh." His lips pressed against hers. Pure heat. She melted but, at the same time, was resolved to even the score. Last time it had all been about her pleasure. Poor Ark never got a turn. And the man had saved her. Surely that deserved a thank-you.

How about the real reason she wanted to pleasure him? *Because I want to.*

From the first moment she'd met him, she wanted to maul him. To—she reared back and held herself upward with one arm extended. The tip of a finger on her free hand traced down his body, bumping over the ridges of muscle. She stopped at his waistline.

"Think we could get caught?"

"Possibly. Are you going to let that stop you?"

Snap. She tugged at his jeans and popped the first button. "Nope. But try to be quiet, would you?" She said it low and teasing, and she inched down his body, putting herself on hands and knees, ass up, facedown, her chin dragging down his torso, her lips nipping at the fabric of his shirt, clipping the flesh underneath.

She reached his partially unbuttoned pants. She nuzzled the exposed skin but was foiled by the edge of his briefs. Tight black briefs.

She wanted to see them and rose on her haunches. Her fingers nimbly took care of the remaining fastening to his pants. She worked the fabric open and then tugged it down. He helped her by hoisting his hips. His hands were laced under his head. He regarded her with hooded eyes.

A big man. Straddling him only made that fact glaringly obvious. For the time being, he still wore his shirt, but it couldn't hide the breadth of him, the corded strength. That was a definite quiver down below in her girly parts.

"Take off the shirt."

He didn't argue, just stripped it before lacing his fingers again under his head. It pulled the muscles of his upper body into sharp definition. Her fingers lightly pressed against his flesh, dragged down, the nail tip a pressure on his skin.

A tremor went through him and she smiled. Then smiled wider as he said, "You are so beautiful."

And she was still fully clothed. He didn't look at her body, but at her. That deserved a reward. She removed her shirt, leaving her in only her bra and jeans.

A low growl rolled out of him. The deep vibration caused another quiver.

"Are you all right?"

"I'm getting close, *koukla.*"

"Close to what? Unleashing the beast?" She grinned as she leaned down, lips close enough to blow hot air against the thin cotton that hid him from her. "I'm ready."

Her fingers gripped his underpants and tugged, stretching the tight fabric further to release him. There was so much of him to release.

A cock like his deserved a moment of admiration. He wasn't circumcised, which gave him excellent size. He was long, so beautifully long, and thick. His shaft projected straight with only a slight curve at the end.

She couldn't wait to feel it. Quiver.

The mushroomed head beckoned, fully blushed. She leaned forward and dragged her tongue over the head.

Grawr.

Another rumble went through him. And her next lick tasted sweet.

Like honey.

She sucked at the head, hard strong pulls, and he groaned. His fingers found her head and cradled gently. So gently he was taut with the strain. He wanted to take control. This was a form of torture for him.

Good.

She licked down the length of his very long dick, and she circled his sack as she reached the base and squeezed.

His hips bucked, and she made a humming sound of pleasure. Squeezing his sack, she licked back to the ridged head. She sucked the tip before taking him into her mouth, pulling that long, hard cock of his as deep as she could. It wasn't deep enough. He was much too long. She let go of his balls and wrapped her hand around him. She needed two hands. And still her fingers couldn't touch. So much man.

She started squeezing and releasing, a rhythmic caress to go with the sucking. That caused him to lose his cool. His fingers threaded almost painfully, but she welcomed the sharp tugs as he helped her to rhythmically bounce her lips up and down. The force of her suction grew harder, and her hands fisted him tighter.

Down she slid, her teeth grazing the length. Back up, the flat edges of her teeth dragging over the edge of the head. Down she bobbed again, and his whole body rumbled, shivered, tensed.

She watched him, her gaze fascinated by the play of sensations on his face, his mouth open, his breath panting, his whole expression showing him on the edge of ecstasy. Contorted features as he held on to that edge, not losing himself yet in the bliss.

She wanted him to stop holding back. Eyes locked to his face, she devoured him, pushing herself far, farther than before, and then sucking harder, and harder on the way back up. Her cheeks hollowed as she suctioned, and his body shuddered and shook.

He was still holding back.

And she was so incredibly horny now. As in pussy wet and throbbing, in need of him inside her.

Her hands went to the waistband of her jeans. "Help me get these off."

Rip.

She blinked, and her pants were gone. "Did you just seriously ruin my favorite pair of jeans?"

"But you said to remove them."

"In one piece."

"I'll be careful with the last layer." His fingers tugged at the elastic on her panties.

Her lips curved wickedly. "Those you can rip." And they were gone before she'd popped the "p" on "rip."

She was also flipped onto her stomach, facedown in the pillow and her ass yanked into the air. He nuzzled her, the tip of his tongue swiping her already swollen lips.

"There's my favorite honey," he grumbled against her flesh.

To her disappointment, she was only treated to one lick. Apparently he had other plans for her. Harder plans.

The head of him nudged her sex, teasing her. A short tease as he simply dipped his head a few times before pushing into her, stretching her with his thickness, delighting her with his length. He kept sinking and sinking inside her, and she couldn't help but moan into her pillow as her fingers curled into the blankets, looking for purchase. He stopped. She could have cried.

She trembled all around him, her channel having mini spasms of delight. Deeper. She needed him deep deeper. She rocked back against him, drawing him farther into herself.

Yes. Oh yes.

She let out a whimper as he pulled out, slowly leaving her, only to then slide back in, faster, deep, bumping against that sweet spot inside. Out. Then in again. A pumping rhythm that drove him deep. His fingers dug into her ass cheeks, spreading and holding her so that he might slap his body in and out.

The orgasm coiled in her, each thrust, each grind, tightening her pleasure. Until it was too much. She crested, her lips parted in a scream with no sound. A wave went through her, a clenching and releasing of her muscles. Especially in her sex. Her body squeezed him so tight. Over and over. And he let out a sound as liquid heat bathed her channel.

He shuddered against her and in her. He drew her up against him, their bodies intimately joined. He pulled her bared flesh against his and pressed his lips against the curve of her neck and shoulder. Soft kisses, a rumbled, "You're mine." Then he bit her.

CHAPTER 15

"What do you mean because that's how it's done?" Jade held her shoulder and glared at him. She looked glorious.

And naked.

All naked. *Mine.*

"I marked you." Said with some smugness.

"No kidding. Am I going to need a rabies shot now? Tetanus?"

"I'm not diseased."

"Says you. You're not the one with a giant hole in your body."

The skin had to be broken to make a proper claim. "It doesn't hurt that much."

"How would you know? You weren't the one bitten."

"Yet. I am ready for my turn." He canted his head to the side, exposing his neck. "Make it nice and high so everyone sees it."

"I am not biting you."

"You're not?" He might have pouted. He didn't jut his lower lip for long though, as a pounding came at the door.

"Cousin, is your mate in there with you?"

"Is he serious? Who else would be in here?" she hissed as she dove for her open suitcase and some clothes. "And how did he know you were here?"

"Where else would I go when they caused that diversion?"

"They had a food fight so you could have sex?"

He grinned. "They did. You'll have to thank them."

Bang. Bang. Bang. "I can hear you in there. We have a problem. It looks like the pregnant one is gone."

Jade froze, leg in the air over her pants. Horror turned her features ashen. He, on the other hand, found himself dealing with disbelief. Surely no one was brazen enough to attack Ruby here.

He hopped out of the bed and went to the door, opening it to see his cousin Antoine. "Where is Ruby?"

"Gone. Apparently she wandered away and made it outside the ranch gates at the end of the driveway. She caught a ride with a guy driving a Lincoln Navigator."

A rich vehicle like that, Jade could think of only one person Ruby might agree to meet. "Xavier took her. He took my sister. You said she was safe." The accusation in her tone stung.

"She should have been." He glared at Antoine. "How the hell could that have happened? I thought you and the boys were watching her."

Antoine held up his hands. "I was. Swear on Nana's tombstone. She said she had to pee. Next thing I know she's gone and all I've got is surveillance footage."

"She can't be gone. You don't understand. He's obsessed with her. Once he finds out she's pregnant and it's not his, he might hurt her or the baby. You need to find her." Jade turned a pleading gaze on him. "Please, Ark. Help me."

Of course he would. That went without saying, but that didn't mean he wouldn't twist this to his advantage. And yes, he knew doing this while she was vulnerable was wrong. So fucking wrong, but . . . he never claimed he was a good bear.

"I'll find her if you promise to bite me when I bring her back."

"Are you fucking kidding me?" She pushed away from him and planted her hands on her hips. "My sister is in danger and you're going to blackmail me into scarring you for life?"

"Yup."

A shoe came winging his way and he swerved to the left. Antoine got it in the chest.

"If you won't help me, then I'll call the cops. It's what I should have done in the first place. I don't know what possessed me to come here. I should have stayed home." She spun to march off, to where he didn't know.

He grabbed her before she realized she couldn't leave. "You came here with me because you know we belong together. Because you know you can trust me." He pulled her close. "I will help you find your sister." His head lowered until his words practically stroked across her lips. "But first a little kiss."

As if anything between them thus far could be called little. And she might have muttered a brusque "Fine," but her lips were soft and pliant as they pressed against his. Her touch explosive. The scent of her divine and the taste even better.

He might have groaned a bit. Possibly growled. He definitely grabbed her in a bear hug. He lifted her off the ground, and she wound her arms around his neck while her legs wrapped around his waist. Her mouth devoured his with as much insistence as he showed. Her breath panted hotly into his mouth. His hands palmed the fullness of her cheeks, and he ached to throw her down on the bed and sink into her glorious depths, pumping and—

"Ahem, if you two are done practically fornicating in front of me, shouldn't we find Ruby?"

It was at this point, given Jade's pink cheeks and averted gaze, that he realized he was still kind of naked. He took care of that while asking a few questions of his cousin. "You're sure it was Xavier who took her?"

"The gate cameras are pretty high tech. They capture a lot of detail. You know a lot of dudes who sport a completely white Mohawk with a giant tribal tattoo of slashing claws wrapping up his neck?"

That certainly sounded like Xavier. Ballsy, given they'd confiscated his plane from him already and sent him home to his pride—on a bus.

"Is he trying to start a war?" Antoine asked.

"If she's his mate, he'll do anything." Ark knew it was what he'd do.

"We have to get her back."

So, for the second time in less than a day, the bears mobilized and converged on a place downtown. A motel to be exact, where they found a very naked couple. One of whom was very pregnant.

Only one person was truly shocked.

Jade planted her hands on her hips and uttered a very indignant, "Ruby, how could you? He was engaged to another woman."

"I love him."

"He stalked you."

"Only because he loves me too." Ruby bestowed a sappy smile on him.

Ark could have gagged.

"What about the fact you're pregnant with another man's baby."

"No, she's not." Xavier leaned back completely at ease, and laced his hands behind his head.

Jade's gaze narrowed. "Someone better explain."

"So here's the funny thing, turns out he was at that party too, and you'll never guess what he was dressed as." Ruby couldn't help but grin as she tossed the biggest irony of all at them.

"You mean he . . . But . . ." Jade couldn't seem to form a coherent sentence.

Ruby beamed. "The man I slept with was Xavier."

"But he never called you?"

"Because he lost my number. The lipstick smeared and since we were in disguise and never exchanged names, he didn't know who I was."

Xavier took over the narrative. "But I looked for her. It took me a while but I found her." Xavier laced his fingers through hers.

"Then why didn't you tell her it was you at the party?"

He shrugged. "I didn't see the need. Not to mention I didn't want Ruby to think I was the type of man who casually indulged in sex. From the moment I scented her, I knew she was mine. So when I found her again, I didn't say anything lest she think I was crazy for hunting her down."

"I would have thought it romantic," Ruby said.

This time Jade gagged.

"We were together and happy. Until my ex-fiancée got involved." Xavier scowled.

"He really did dump her, but she's crazy Jade. You should see the texts she keeps sending."

But Jade didn't appear ready to accept things. "Why did he wait so long to find you?"

Xavier replied. "Car accident. A bad one. Totally my fault too. I was so upset at Ruby's leaving that I had too much to drink and got behind the wheel. I paid the price. I shattered a good number of bones in my body when my car hit the tree. The doctors put me in an induced coma for a while. But as soon as I was released, I went looking for Ruby. And found her."

More sappy smiles and nose rubs only served to turn Jade's lips farther down.

"So that's it? You guys are together."

"And we're getting married. Hopefully before the baby is born." Ruby flashed a diamond so big, it was a wonder she could lift her hand.

Ark made a mental note to get a bigger one.

For some reason their happiness snapped something in Jade. A good thing the motel kept everything bolted down because Jade did her best to find something to throw.

Ark let her rant and rave as he carried her out and sent his family home to resume celebrating.

"I can't believe she didn't call and let me know she was okay," she yelled.

"They were busy." Busy doing things he should be doing with Jade.

"He's an arrogant ass."

"Who loves her. Just like I love you."

"What?"

Apparently all it took was a few words to calm his raging mate. As for teaching Jade the joy of honey—it only took one lick at a time from her lovely cocoa flesh. And it was totally worth the beating by his grandmother and the lecture by

his mother about ruining perfectly fine sheets with his de-
bauchery.

To ensure no more defiling would occur, the wedding
happened late the next day, with Jade wearing a wedding
dress she chose off a rack—to his mother's and aunts'
horror—but it was probably a good thing given the dress
didn't survive the wedding night.

Grawr!

EPILOGUE

Liana Zelda Boudrion was born a few weeks later without a *thingie* and a shocking amount of platinum-blond hair.

Ark frowned down at her as they watched the angel sleep in the hospital bassinet while Ruby took a well-earned shower, Xavier keeping a close eye on her.

Funny how things worked out. All this time, Ruby ran from Xavier out of fear he couldn't accept another man's child, and yet it turned out he was the daddy all along.

As for Xavier's ex-fiancée, even though he dumped her after that fateful Halloween party, the deluded girl remained convinced they were together. Ruby and Xavier's big wedding did nothing to sway her either, and when the priest asked, she stood up and objected—loudly and with much f-bombing—which the videographer edited out of the final film. After that incident, the crazy ex-fiancée was taken by her parents on an extended trip to Europe.

As for Jade, she cried. She cried at her wedding. She cried at her sister's wedding. She also cried at the birth. What she didn't do was lament the fact Liana was born without a certain body part.

"I can't believe it's a girl. I was going to teach my nephew so many things." Ark pouted.

"So you'll teach them to her instead. I mean, think of it, she's your niece, and one day she'll grow up and boys will notice her."

His expression brightened. "She'll have to know how to defend herself."

"Indeed she will, and you'll need the practice so you're an expert when it comes to teaching our child." She placed his hand on her stomach.

It took a second. First his eyes widened. Then his lips parted. His fingers pressed into her, and he gasped. "You're pregnant. For real?"

About five or six weeks, but already the life growing within her made its presence known. "I saw the doctor to be sure." She leaned close and whispered, "And the doctor heard two heartbeats."

He fainted, six feet five inches of flesh hitting the floor like a sack of potatoes.

"Unbelievable." Jade shook her head and was still shaking it when his mother entered the room and held out her hand, palm raised.

"I thought for sure he could handle it," Jade grumbled as she handed over the twenty she pulled from her bra.

"He will handle it. Once he gets over the shock."

"Are you sure?" She looked down at Ark somewhat dubiously.

He stirred and opened an eye and growled, "Sure about what? Who hit me?"

"I'm pregnant with twins."

His eyes rolled back, and he slumped again. But it lasted less than a second before he leaped to his feet. Grabbing her around the waist, he lifted her and swung. He set her down just as quickly. "I'm sorry. I probably shouldn't do that. Or should I?" He spun a panicked look at his mother. "Shouldn't she be in bed? With her feet up?"

It was his mother who slapped him. "Did you ever see me with my feet up?"

He gave her a wicked smile and winked. "All the time. Laziest mother ever."

"Ungrateful cub," his mother grumbled.

"Love you, Mama." Heartfelt and sincere. That was what Jade loved about this family. There was so much freaking affection. And she got to bask in that affection as Ark turned to Jade and drew her into his arms. He gazed down at her, affection so clear in his eyes. "I love you."

Which is why she threw her arms around his neck, hugged him tight, and bit him, really hard. "Awk." He might have coughed up a hairball. He certainly made a sound.

"You bit me. You finally bit me." He couldn't contain his exuberance. "You see it, right?" Ark pointed at his neck, and his mother rolled her eyes.

"Yes, I see it. You do know you've been married several weeks now."

"But she bit me." He pointed again.

"If you think that's cool, then guess what else." She pulled forth the legal confirmation that she'd changed her last name. "Look. I now bear his name. Get it?" She snickered. "Bearing his name."

Her attempt at humor might have been met with groans, but she knew this act of trust meant the world to Ark. Heck, it meant the world to Jade since she'd finally decided to stop hiding from life and take a bite out of love.

The coppery undertone of blood hit him as soon as he exited the bar. The heavy metal door clanged behind him, and

Stavros pulled his gun. Off duty didn't mean he went around unarmed.

His nose twitched, but his bear didn't rumble and growl, which he took to mean no danger. Using the blood scent as his guide, he used his nose to lead him, his shifter side stronger than most even in his human shape. It was what made him such a good detective—until he'd gotten suspended.

Who knew they'd care about the baggie of weed he'd taken to make brownies. The stuff was legal in just about every other state. He didn't regret it. The brownies were that good. And the suspension wouldn't last forever. He hoped. Or else the boredom might just kill him.

Out in the alley, the bass beat of the music still exuded a muted thump. The witching hour had passed and the street out front had only minimal passing traffic. The alley itself was a dead end with a roll-down garage door that was bolted more often than not. A pair of trash bins, tall suckers on wheels, were lined like sentinels along the brick wall. They might have been emptied that morning, but the smell clung, a miasma that did finally make his inner beast grunt in annoyance.

Smells.

Yes it did and, above it all, the sharper scent of blood.

Stavros found her wedged between two trash bins, her head turned away from the alley as if by not seeing she could prevent being seen.

He crouched down and noted she stopped breathing, her body going still.

An anticipatory hush fell, and he studied her, studied her hunched frame, the tattered clothes, the scratches on her arms, the fading and fresh bruises.

Trouble.

So much trouble. Despite finding her battered and broken, a part of him knew he should walk away, knew if he didn't run that his life would change.

He didn't budge. How could he leave when she turned bright green eyes his way and said, in the softest whisper, "Help me."

OWNED BY THE LION

Milly Taiden

CHAPTER 1

Ally collapsed onto her buttery soft leather couch and sighed in weary relief. The apartment was unpacked and things were starting to come together in at least one aspect of her life. Now if she could only get the rest to follow suit, life would be perfect. Her cell phone let out a loud cacophony of sounds so suddenly that Ally jumped and nearly fell off the couch in surprise. "Son of a . . . who messed with the volume level?" She grumbled as she fumbled for the phone and quickly pressed talk without looking at the caller ID.

"Hello?"

"Open your door, woman. We're not going to stand out here all night knocking."

Ally frowned in confusion as she suddenly became aware of the persistent knocking on her apartment door. She quickly raced to the door, opened it, and stared slack-jawed at the two women standing there with pizza, wine, and big smiles.

"Don't just stand there, let us in," Josie said as she gently hip-checked Ally out of the doorway and sauntered past.

"Did you forget about us?" Shawna asked curiously as she set the pizza down on the small table in front of the couch.

Ally shrugged sheepishly. "It's been a hectic couple of days."

"Is this a bad time? Should we do it another night?" Josie asked gently before winking at Shawna. "We can wait for any juicy details later if you're too tired."

"You can stay, but only if you promise not to bring that overgrown manwhore's name up." Ally growled low in her throat and flopped back down on her couch. "Pour the wine, I need it more than you can imagine. That man is going to drive me either to become an alcoholic or a nun. And at this point I'm not sure which is better."

"So you admit you have the hots for He Who Shall Not Be Named?" Shawna asked with a wink. "I have to admit, the sexual tension at dinner the other night was off the wall."

"Sexual tension, are you kidding me?" Ally gaped at the two women, who nodded their heads vigorously in agreement. "That was not sexual, that was mutual disgust and horror at having to be stuck with each other thanks to Julia's misguided offer of help."

"Did he end up helping you move in and get settled?" Josie questioned tentatively.

Ally rolled her eyes. "Yes. Honestly, I'm surprised we got anything done with the way he was constantly answering his phone. At one point he left it on the counter, and I sneaked a peek. He'd turned it to silent mode, and he had fifteen missed calls and twenty text messages. All from women."

"Wait, how do you know it was all from women?" Shawna asked in confusion. "I mean, did you actually see their names or messages?"

"No, I'm not that much of a snoop." Ally bit her lip as she tried not to laugh, "Okay, I am, but he came back before I could look. The calls he did take were women though, I heard him use words like 'honey,' 'babe,' and 'sweetheart.'"

Josie laughed, "I can guarantee he wasn't talking to Xander then, I'd have heard about it. Though I would've loved to have seen his face if Keir did talk to him that way."

"Enough about him, it's pizza and wine time. I need it desperately," Ally cried in frustration.

"Thanks for inviting us, even if you did forget," Josie joked.

"I need girlfriends in this town. I love your mate, but it's not the same as having women friends, you know?"

Shawna cleared her throat as she searched the cabinets for wineglasses. "I don't mean to pry, and I know you said to let it go, but can I ask one more question? Then I'll stop, I promise."

Ally huffed good-naturedly, "Guess this is what I get for wanting girlfriends, isn't it? Sure, hit me."

"You bet it is. But seriously, are you annoyed that he was on the phone with these girls instead of helping you move—even though you already said he did help—or because he didn't flirt with you?"

"Are you kidding me?" Ally gaped in astonishment. "When he wasn't on the phone, all we did was argue. He's such a pig."

Josie frowned. "You know, I don't quite get that impression of him. I know he dates a lot of women, and has a different woman on his arm every time I see him, but he's never come across as anything other than a guy enjoying the company of women. Xander even said he's up front with them, saying it's not going to be long term."

"Please, no more, let's just have some girl time. I have to see him in a few days to begin setting up the new campaign and that will be soon enough. I have enough on my plate without adding him to it," Ally complained with a pout. She didn't want to think about Keir and what he made her feel. Her body lit up like a damn Christmas tree every time his smile or those gorgeous eyes came into her mind. Stupid hormones.

"What's up? Talk to us. That's what we're here for after all," Shawna asked in concern. "Is there anything we can do to help?"

"Only if you have a way to get some quick, easy cash. I'm getting desperate and time is running out."

Josie and Shawna grinned at each other. "Do you know how Josie met Xander?" Shawna asked with a mischievous twinkle.

"No . . . but with that look I'm definitely curious. And it better not have been illegal. Oh, who am I kidding? If it was fun and you met the awesomeness that is my friend then maybe it was worth it."

Shawna grinned. "You ever hear of Naughty Goddess, the lingerie company?"

"Who hasn't? They make the best lingerie for curvy girls. I love their stuff, hell, I think I shop in their stores at least once a month," Ally gushed in admiration. "But what does that have to do with anything? I work for an ad agency, I can't model or anything like that." Not that she was scared to. She knew she was curvy but she had a body men drooled over.

"I work for them. The owner, Hawke Kingston, started a side business, and my boss handed it over to me to run. It's called mateforhire.com. It's almost like a matchmaking service, but for shifters," Shawna explained. "Shifters mate for life, but sometimes it can be hard for them to find their mates. So mateforhire.com matches them with a woman to fill the role for various functions, events, and things like that." Shawna cleared her throat. "Like a fake mate. Or in human terms, a fake girlfriend. Just to have someone they can take to events and nobody will know."

"It's how I met Xander. Shawna entered my name and I got matched with Xander. It turns out I really was his mate. I balked at first when she told me she signed me up, then I saw the pay and I was in complete and total agreement. It was enough to do everything I needed and wanted to do and have a bit left over."

"I don't think even a fake mate could pay what I need to cover," Ally said with a sigh. "My mom's been selected for a new regimen of chemo. It's got a high success rate, but insurance doesn't pay for it. It's part of the reason I'm here, the company offered me a raise and a bonus for opening the branch here."

"I'm not sure how much you need, but let me put you in the system and see what happens. These shifters pay seriously well, and if it's not enough to cover the whole thing, maybe it can at least put a dent in it."

"Shawna's right, it can't hurt. Plus, who knows, maybe you'll meet someone that will make Keir jealous."

Ally gasped. "I don't want to make that manwhore jealous, he can go fuck a goat for all I care."

Josie burst into laughter. "Something tells me you might be protesting just a little too much for me to believe you."

CHAPTER 2

"Dad, calm down. You're not old enough to be thinking of retiring. I don't care about your sense of smell. You've been running the bank for close to forty years, no one can pull one over on you. The employees have all been there for years, nothing has changed. There's no way anyone can lie to you; besides, no one knows about your loss of smell. Everyone knows your reputation in the banking world, no one is going to take a chance anymore. You spent years proving no one could lie to you; that's not going to change."

Keir had to rein in the growl that wanted to rise up his throat and the urge to slam his fist on his desk. Instead, he listened halfheartedly as his father continued his tirade, begging and pleading for him to come take over the bank. Keir loved his job at XJ Financial and didn't want to leave yet. Eventually he'd take his dad's place, but right now there was no need to.

"Dad, I love you, but I have to go. I have a meeting I can't miss."

Keir hung up and leaned back in his leather desk chair. He wasn't sure which was going to kill him first: his father and his demands or Julia and her demands for him to settle down. Which, luckily for him, suddenly didn't seem such a bad prospect. He'd spent most of his life playing the field, dating women, and then moving on to the next. Each one he treated with respect and courtesy, but they all knew the end game. Nothing past a couple of dates max. No forever; there were too many amazing women out there for him to settle down with just one.

Then he'd met her. The only female who'd driven him to distraction. The only smile that made him want to fall to his knees and cherish her. The only body he wanted to explore and kiss and do some things he would probably get arrested for. Her. Ally.

His reputation as a womanizer wasn't exactly exaggerated; it was true he was with a different woman almost every night. What could he say? He loved women, their smell, their taste, their curves, everything about them enthralled him. Now all he could think of was if her skin was as soft as silk, and if her pussy as sweet as he imagined. Then there was the nightly dreams of licking his way down her body, taking her in every way possible and coming inside her, immediately branding her as his mate.

He couldn't fight his body. The desire to rush up to her, rip her clothes off, and give her so many orgasms she wouldn't be able to use her legs for a week. He wanted to listen to her moan and scream as she came. Every. Single. Night. Of. His. Life.

Ally Fosey, one of his closest friend's little sister. It boggled the mind and made his lion purr with the need to mate.

"Seriously?" Xander exclaimed as he walked in and slammed his hand down on the desk, startling Keir.

"What?" he snapped.

"Meeting, remember? We've been in the conference room waiting on you for ten minutes. Ally is getting pissed and I don't blame her."

"Fuck!" The word came out a loud growl. Xander raised

a brow but shook his head. "I'm sorry. I was on the phone with my father and got sidetracked. He's driving me nuts."

Xander frowned in sympathy. "Still pushing you to come work for him?"

"It's getting worse, he swears he's going to be swindled since he can't smell their lies anymore. I'm holding out, but I don't know how much longer I can do it." Keir sighed. "I just can't work under him again, he still treats me like a little kid and second-guesses everything I do. It's so aggravating."

"Normally I'd say you're a damn hard worker and I'd hate to lose you, but I understand you'll have to go sooner or later though. For now, you better get in there and fix things with Ally before we lose her. You know what she can do for us, it would be a great push for the company." Xander turned and started out of the office before stopping and glancing back over his shoulder. "And I don't know who you were just thinking about, but damn, you've got it bad."

Keir snarled and grabbed a pen to toss at Xander, but he was already through the door laughing. "Bastard," he grumbled as he gathered his supplies and headed to the conference room. But first a quick stop by his secretary to hopefully tame the scary hellion he kept waiting.

"Mr. Harper," Keir's secretary stopped him as he came out of his office. "I forgot to tell you, I called Mr. Kingston's office and got you added into the database for possible matches."

Keir froze in place as he registered her words, he'd completely forgotten he'd asked her to do that for him. Another thing to lay at his father's doorstep. The man was determined to see him settled and his persistent meddling was becoming a major pain.

"Bess, I don't know what I'd do without you, but in this

instance, I wish you weren't so damn good at your job. Any chance you can call his office back and get that canceled?"

"Sure, I can do that," she agreed in puzzlement. "Mr. Kingston gave me the direct number for the manager of the project, a Mr. Clark Benoit. I'll call right away and have your name removed."

"I don't know what I'd do without you, Bess. You're a life-saver."

"You'd work yourself to death, alone and sad. But good thing I don't plan on leaving anytime soon. It's too much work to train you young guys properly and I'm too old to start over."

Keir laughed. "You're not old, and I'd never leave you. When I do have to go, I plan on stealing you away from here," he said with a wink as he started toward the conference room again. "Oh, and can you do me a huge favor?"

CHAPTER 3

The insufferable ass was keeping her waiting for a meeting that he'd set up. Xander said he'd find him, but it was just plain rude. It was probably one of his women who he just couldn't tear himself away from long enough to be on time. The longer she sat, the worse her temper became. By the time he showed his face, she was going to show him what a pissed-off Latina looked like and it wasn't going to be pretty.

"Ally, I'm—" Keir began as he sauntered into the conference room.

"Don't. Unless you are about to talk about the business we're here to discuss, don't say a word. I don't want to hear it," Ally interrupted with a scowl.

How dare he breeze in here like he hadn't kept her waiting for half an hour and try to explain why he was late. She was not in the mood for his lame attempts at apologies. She wanted this meeting over with, she had a date with a bottle of wine, her tub, and a bit later, her trusty vibrator.

"I can explain, if you'll just let me," Keir tried again.

"No, let's just get this meeting over with," Ally said as she pulled out some papers and slammed them down on the desk in front of Keir. "Here's my proposal. I need you and Xander to look it over and highlight any changes you want made. As soon as you approve it, I can get the campaign unveiled and start bringing in more business to XJ Financial."

She watched as Keir cocked one eyebrow as he scanned the papers. Why did the manwhore have to be so damn gorgeous? She could feel her breathing quicken as he bit his lip in concentration, reading her ideas. Ally frowned as she realized where her thoughts were going; no way could she be attracted to the playboy, even if he did make her want to strip down and scream *"Take me now."*

"This is . . ."

Keir trailed off as he focused on Ally. She fought back a blush as she saw his nostrils flare as he scented the air.

"Ally?" he growled deep in the back of his throat.

Ally jumped to her feet. "I've got to go, let me know when we can get started," she stammered in her haste to run away from the tempting man staring at her with naked hunger burning in his eyes.

She could feel his eyes on her as she raced down the hallway. This wasn't going to work. Her traitorous body was going to give her away; no way could she ever let that man know how he turned her on. Just the sound of his voice was enough to make her squirm in need. If he'd growled in that sexy-as-fuck voice for another moment, her clothes would have disappeared as if by magic.

Ally closed her eyes and took a deep breath as she pushed the elevator button repeatedly. "Come on, you slow bastard," she mumbled. "Finally." She breathed a sigh of relief as the doors slid open and she raced inside and pressed the close button. Just as the doors slid almost shut, a hand shot out and caused them to reopen.

Keir stepped in, followed by another employee. She glanced up into his smoldering eyes and quickly looked away. Lust burned bright in those beautiful emerald eyes. The floors ticked by as she felt his eyes on her, burning a hole. Five floors to go, she wasn't going to make it. She was going to crack under the pressure or come just from his powerful intoxicating stare.

"Excuse me, this is my floor," the employee said as he edged around Keir and stepped off the elevator.

She looked up in panic, saw she was alone with Keir, and jumped forward in an attempt to follow the man.

"Oh no, you don't," Keir said in a silky smooth voice as he grabbed her around the waist and pulled her back. "I need to talk to you."

Ally fumed as she saw that he'd hit the button for the tenth floor, also known as the floor she'd just run from. "Let me go," she demanded. "I have another meeting and you have no right to manhandle me."

"I'm not, but you know you can't lie to a shifter anyway. I can smell how much you like my hands on you. What would you do if I pushed the emergency button and stopped the elevator?"

No way in hell was she going to allow that to happen; the two of them in a small cramped place was enough to make her whimper in need. She had to get away, and it had to be sooner rather than later.

The ringing of her phone saved her from responding to his question. She pulled it out with a vow to kiss whoever it was calling, saving her from making a fool of herself with the manslut standing inches away.

"Xander, hi," Ally said breathlessly.

"Where are you? I came back to the conference room and you both had disappeared. I wanted to look over your pro-posal."

"I'm on the elevator on my way back up to you, actually,"

Ally said as she turned her back on Keir and his sinful good looks. "Want me to bring them to your office?"

"No, that's okay. I'll meet you at Keir's. I have to talk to him anyway. See you in a minute."

Ally hung up and glanced over her shoulder at Keir. "Did you hear it all?"

Keir nodded slowly. "This isn't over, baby."

Right then the elevator dinged and she flew off without replying. She had a new goal in life: never be alone with him again. She wasn't sure she could trust herself around him after today.

"Mr. Harper," Bess called as she stood up and held out a stack of messages. "Can you please tell those women to stop calling here over and over again? It's getting ridiculous. I can't get any work done with the way they've been calling the last few days. This Jasmine alone has called fifteen times in the last two days."

Ally stopped dead in her tracks and gaped at Keir. He had his secretary taking messages from his women now? This was getting to be too much. Whatever lust she had been feeling quickly evaporated under the disgust she felt for the scoundrel in front of her.

Keir sighed and glanced sheepishly at Ally before turning back to Bess. "I swear, I'll talk to her again. I'm sorry, Bess."

"Maybe she needs something stronger than a talking to, I explained to her that you were off—"

Keir quickly interrupted Bess with a wide-eyed panicked glance at Ally. "I understand, Bess." He stressed, "I'll take care of it, as soon as I'm done with this meeting."

Ally frowned. What was she missing? It felt like they were trying to hide something from her, but for the life of her she couldn't figure it out.

"Hey, you guys coming?" Xander called from Keir's doorway.

"Ally, go ahead. I'll be right behind you," Keir said as Ally brushed past him. Whatever was going on wasn't her business, she decided. Bess was probably just pissed that this woman had the audacity to call her to keep tabs on him.

"Hey, stranger," Xander said with a wink. "I promised Josie I'd invite you to dinner. She wants to do a welcome party and introduce you to some of our friends."

"You've got one hell of a mate there. She's already made me feel so welcome, but I'd love to. If nothing else just to spend more time with two of my favorite people."

"You've agreed, so you can't back out now. Shawna will be there, as will Keir, and my friend Hawke and possibly a few others."

Ally groaned. "You bastard. You did that on purpose."

Xander laughed. "Hell yeah, I did. I know all about the tempers you women have. You may be shorter than me, but you scare the shit out of me too."

Ally brushed her long brown hair over her shoulder and smiled. "My work here is done."

"Now, down to business. Where's that proposal?"

"I've got it," Keir said as he walked in carrying the papers. "I ran down and grabbed them from the conference room. It's brilliant, in my opinion."

CHAPTER 4

A date. He needed a date to Xander's dinner party, but how did he do this and show Ally he only had her in his sights? For the last three days he'd agonized over this, coming no closer to an answer. No matter what he came up with, it was bound to fail. If he went stag, it would look weird since he was never alone. He could play it off, but she wasn't ready to hear the truth yet.

"Mr. Harper, I'm leaving for the night. Anything you need before I go?" Bess asked from the doorway.

"Bess, can I ask your advice?" Keir called desperately.

Bess cocked an eyebrow, but entered the room and sat across from Keir at his desk. "What's on your mind, son?"

"Ally's my mate."

Bess smiled. "I know. You've been kind of obvious about it."

Keir frowned. "What are you talking about? How have I been obvious?"

"Well, maybe you weren't, but word has spread. All those women calling asking if it's true, begging me to tell them you're pulling a prank on them. Word's spreading you're off the market. Ally needs to be careful, some of those women are jealous as hell."

Keir didn't say anything as he processed her words. He'd thought he was doing the right thing by letting them down gently like that. Had he caused a potential problem for Ally instead?

"I wouldn't be too worried, honey. Ally is feisty and has a wild cat buried down inside. So tell me, what do you need advice on anyway?"

"Xander and Josie are having a dinner party, they told me to bring a date."

Bess bit her lip and tried to hide her smile. "I guess asking Ally to be your date is a no?"

Keir groaned. "She wouldn't agree. Ally being my mate is driving my lion crazy."

"It's simple, you need to bring someone she won't see as competition then. Someone nonthreatening," Bess concluded with a soft smile. "You'll win her over, I know you will."

Keir smiled with more frustration than happiness. Oh, he knew he'd win his mate over. That hardheaded curvy goddess wasn't going to be without his mark for much longer, but it was going to take a lot of fucking patience. Something he didn't seem to have lately when it came to Ally. She drove his basic desires and all he wanted was to strip her, fuck her, and mate her. Not necessarily in that order. "Thanks. You're the best. Why don't you take the rest of the day off?"

"You're a scoundrel, you know that, boy? It's a good thing I love you," Bess said as she made her way out of the office.

An idea suddenly went through his mind. A damn great idea.

"Bess, wait. That's it," Keir cried in triumph.

"What did I miss?" Bess asked as she turned around.

"You're going to be my date, beautiful."

"No, I'm not. I may not be competition, but it won't work. How about you take my granddaughter? She recently broke up with her girlfriend and could use some cheering up. You two get along and there is no sexual tension between the two of you. It's perfect. Ally can see how you treat a woman you genuinely like and respect, instead of those fill-ins you usually go around with."

"How is bringing a beautiful woman with me going to help?" Keir asked in exasperation.

Bess mock-glared at Keir. "I'm going to let that insult go, because I know what you meant to say."

Keir blushed. "Sorry."

"Anyway, my point is that before the night is over, and I'd hazard a guess within an hour of you showing up with her, Ally will know the truth. But don't you dare let that change anything. You treat my granddaughter like a princess, laugh, have fun, and for heaven's sake, don't ignore Ally."

Bess was a woman. He should trust her. Still, his lion didn't see how it was going to be that easy. Ally was too feisty and would see him bringing any date as a sign of his womanizing ways not being over. "I trust you, but I will say this plan sounds insane."

Bess didn't reply, just smiled and left, leaving Keir confused and reluctantly agreeing to her plan. What did he have to lose at this point anyway? He didn't have a better plan and time was running out.

Keir jumped as the ringing of his cell phone startled him out of his preoccupied mind. He glanced at the phone and groaned.

"Hey, Dad. I'm still at the office so I don't have much time to talk."

"Make time, boy. This is important," Kenneth Harper growled.

"If this is about me coming to the bank to take over, you can hang up now. I can't deal with that while in the middle of this project I'm working on."

"It's not, but I still contend it's the smart move. I was calling because I finally hired a contractor to do some work on the house. Redo the kitchen, add on to the back porch, and a few other things."

"Good, you've been wanting to do that for a long time," Keir said through clenched teeth as he waited for his father to get to the point of the call.

"I can hear that tone in your voice, I have a point, you pain in the ass. When you moved out, I converted your room into a home office. All your stuff you left behind is in the shed out back, which is why I'm calling. I need you to come get it."

Keir frowned in confusion. "Did I leave a lot of things? And why now anyway?"

"Just a few boxes of stuff you had packed in a hall closet, old trophies and memorabilia from school and your friends. And now because I'm having the shed redone into a workshop and greenhouse so that when you do take over at the bank, I can concentrate on my love of gardening."

"I knew you'd get in something about me taking over," Keir growled in frustration. "But fine, I'll get over there as soon as I can. I've got to get back to work before I end up sleeping here tonight."

"One last thing. The annual bank party."

"I know, it's on my calendar. I'll be there."

"Son, don't bring one of your girls. It's time you settled down and started making a family and future."

"So you've told me every time we've talked."

"Fine, love you, son."

"Love you too, Dad."

Keir sighed as he hung up the phone. If his mother were still alive, he knew she'd keep his dad from pushing the bank job on him. It's not that he didn't want to take it over, he just didn't want to do it under these circumstances. XJ Financial had given him the confidence he'd needed to be the successful man he was. He could bring that to the bank easily, but was it wrong he wanted to do it on his own terms though?

"Hey, bro, you going home anytime soon?" Xander called from Keir's doorway.

"You're still here," Keir pointed out.

"Josie is meeting me here so we can head to dinner."

"Is this an invitation and are you paying if it is?" he joked.

Xander laughed. "No and hell no, you cheap bastard."

Keir shrugged. "Can't blame me for trying."

"What's wrong, anyway? You looked upset when I first came by."

"Just hung up with my father." Keir scrubbed a hand over his face. Man, he was tired all of a sudden. "For once he didn't badger me about taking over, it was subtle."

Xander nodded but didn't say anything; there wasn't much he could say at this point. Keir knew it all and understood his friend would support whatever decision he made.

"Dinner is Saturday, you still good to come?" Xander asked in an obvious attempt to change the subject.

"Yes, and I'll be bringing a friend."

Xander cocked an eyebrow. "Your funeral, but I've got to admit, I'm looking forward to the fireworks. Anyway, Josie should be here any minute, don't stay too much longer. Go home and relax, this will be here tomorrow."

Keir nodded and wished his friend a good night before going back to the paperwork in front of him. His dating life and his father could wait till later, right now he needed to make sure this deal was the best he could make it for XJ Financial.

CHAPTER 5

"Good news, you're all signed up and as soon as you're matched, I'll send you his information," Shawna's excited voice said on Ally's voice mail. "By this time next week, you'll be earning enough money to get your mom that treatment."

Ally sighed in relief, finally something was going right. Now if she could just find some place to get dinner. She was starving and the thought of going back to her empty apartment and cooking was enough to make her cry.

"Ricardo's," Ally said as she read the sign outside the small restaurant. This was perfect; she'd loved the food when she'd come with Xander and Josie that one time. And on a Wednesday night, they probably wouldn't be too busy, so it wouldn't look weird to eat alone, she attempted to convince herself.

"Fancy meeting you here," Keir said as he came to a stop beside Ally at the entrance door. "Going in?"

"Hey, Keir. Have a hot date?" Ally grumbled out at the same time. "Yes, I am. Thank you," she replied sheepishly as he pulled the door open and waved her through.

"No, by the way, I don't have a date. I'm starving and I don't like to cook for just one. I made a reservation earlier."

Ally frowned. *Reservation?* That did not bode well at all. She approached the smiling hostess and opened her mouth to ask for a table when the blond bombshell saw Keir standing behind her.

"Hey, sexy. Where have you been?" the hostess cooed, completely ignoring Ally.

"Hi, Stephanie. How are you?" Keir asked politely as Ally fumed and stared holes into the blonde's head.

"I'm good. How are you? It's been forever, we should do dinner some time. I've missed you," the hostess continued, still ignoring Ally.

"My friend here was hoping to get a table, think you can help her out?" Keir said with a smile as he winked at Ally.

Oh sure, now the bastard remembered she was there. She watched as the hostess's smile fell slightly and she turned back to Ally.

"I'm sorry, ma'am, but unless you have a reservation we're booked solid tonight."

"Ally, if you don't mind sharing a table, you can join me," Keir offered tentatively.

She stared at Keir with mixed feelings: on the one hand she was starving, but on the other, could she stand to sit there and watch women fawn over him as he lapped up their admiration?

"I promise I'll be on my best behavior." Keir leaned forward to whisper so only she would hear, "Unless you ask me otherwise, of course."

"Fine, yes, I'll join you. Thank you," she replied grudgingly as she tried to drown the lust that filled her at his words and the images they conjured. This man didn't have to do anything but whisper and she was ready to jump him right there on the hostess stand.

"Right this way," Stephanie said with a sneer as she led them to a table.

Ally nodded her thanks and sank gratefully into a chair.

Keir had moved forward to pull her chair back, she saw with surprise, but was stopped by the hostess's hand on his chest as she leaned forward and whispered in his ear. Ally couldn't hear what was said, but by the blush on his face, she didn't want to know. She quickly picked up the menu and did her best to ignore the two of them.

"Thank you, Stephanie, but I have to refuse." Keir's words startled Ally and she quickly glanced up to see what was happening.

"So it's true then?" the hostess asked in disbelief. "You really are . . ."

Keir glanced to Ally and nodded before the woman could finish. "Yes, I am."

"Wow, good luck then. I'm happy for you," Stephanie said as she walked away in dejection.

"What was that all about there at the end?" Ally asked in confusion.

"Nothing important. She asked me . . . out, and I turned her down. That was it."

"Out? Something tells me that wasn't what she was asking, but I was referring to the part after that. You cut her off before she could finish what she was saying."

Keir shrugged as if it wasn't a big deal. "She isn't known for her tact, after all."

Ally knew he was lying but she had no idea why. Within moments the waiter arrived at the table and the woman's words were forgotten over her haste and excitement for some good food.

An hour later, she was contemplating the dessert menu when a shrill voice broke through her rapt attention of the delicious options.

"She said it, but I didn't believe her. I had to come see for myself."

"Eliza, how are you?" Keir said with a smile as he stood and embraced the beautiful bombshell standing next to their table.

"I don't even want to know what she said," Keir said with a fake laugh. Now that Ally had been watching him so closely, she'd come to know when he was genuine about his smiles. This was not one of those moments. "But it's always a pleasure to see you."

"Liar." Eliza laughed. "Are you going to introduce me or what?"

Keir turned to face Ally. "Ally, I want you to meet a close friend of mine. She also happens to be the sister of the hostess you met earlier. Eliza meet . . . Ally."

Ally cocked one eyebrow at his stumbled explanation of who she was, but decided not to make a scene. She'd known when she'd agreed to eat with him that peace wouldn't last long.

Eliza smiled. "It's a pleasure to meet you."

"Likewise," Ally said in confusion. "If you'll excuse me, I've got to run to the ladies' room. I'll give you a moment to catch up."

Ally fled the table and her conflicting emotions. For a few moments during dinner she'd forgotten Keir's much deserved reputation. They'd conversed, laughed, flirted, and had a great time. Then another one of his bimbos showed up and it was all lost. Not that she was complaining exactly. She needed to keep focused on who he really was after all.

"Listen, lady," a nasty woman sneered at Ally from her place in the bathroom doorway. "I don't know who you think you are, but don't worry, you won't be around for long. He'll never settle down with you."

Ally frowned. "Excuse me? I think you have me confused with someone else, and if you don't then go fuck yourself."

The woman narrowed her eyes and stepped closer. "Keir is mine."

Sarcastic laughter bubbled out of Ally before she could control it. "Yours you say, then why is he here with me? You and your bleached and badly dyed hair, if I do say so myself, can get out of my face, or let me try out the new moves I learned in kickboxing class."

"I'm warning you, he's mine," the woman said as she slowly backed away and moved out the door.

"No," Ally growled with more aggression than she'd felt in her entire life. "He's not. He's *mine* and if you lay one fucking hand on him, I'll kick your nonexistent ass all over the street. Got it?"

The woman's eyes opened wide in horror. "You're a hood rat."

"Yeah? Why don't you come closer so we can examine how ghetto you think I am."

The woman rushed out the door with a gasp.

Ally slumped against the bathroom wall and shook her head in dismay. How was it that no matter where she went, one of Keir's women was always there? This was the first time she'd been threatened, but still. They were everywhere and it was kind of sad and disturbing. The number of them was mind boggling.

"Are you okay?"

Ally jumped in startled surprise and turned to see Eliza standing beside her with concern in her eyes. "Yes. I'm fine."

"What did she look like?" Eliza sighed. "Let me guess, I bet it was the tall brunette with the rather overabundant breasts and the really bad hair dye."

"How did you . . ." Ally trailed off and moved to the sink to splash some cold water on her face.

"Don't worry about that one, she's pretty harmless. Keir

met her at one of our friend's parties, she's been slightly obsessed ever since."

"No offense, but that seems the norm."

Eliza laughed. "Yeah, I know what you mean. They can be a bit pushy, even with me, if you can believe it."

Ally frowned. "I don't understand."

"Long story, but the gist of it is Keir helped me out of a rough patch with my family. My mother didn't accept me and my lifestyle choice. So when she came to visit, he pretended to be my partner for the night." Eliza winked. "My father is a client of XJ and a wonderful man who raised me. My mother is a socialite wannabe more interested in money than her family."

"I'm sorry, but what does this have to do with me? Why are you explaining? I don't know you and you certainly don't know me after all."

"No, but I'd like to. Nena and I spend a bit of time with Keir, and we don't want things to be awkward. And from what I've heard and seen, I think you are a perfect fit for him."

"For him? And who is Nena?" Ally asked in exasperation.

"Him is Keir and Nena is my wife." Eliza chuckled. "I'm saying I approve of you and Keir. I think you fit well together is all. Now hurry up and get back out there before those vultures descend on your man."

Ally groaned. "He's not mine. I only came here for dinner and happened to run into him."

"That's not what you just told the chick who tried to intimidate you but ran out of here scared shitless."

"He's not mine though," she sighed. As much as she'd assured the other woman he was.

"Just keep telling yourself that, honey."

Ally didn't reply, she turned on her heel and headed back to her table to say good night. She'd had enough excitement for one night. It was time to head home and curl up with a good book and forget the sex god known as Keir.

"Hey," Keir called as Ally approached the table. "You look upset, what happened?"

"Nothing, I'm fine. I just want the check so I can go home."

Keir whistled softly. "Those happen to be two of the scariest words in the dictionary when said by a woman."

"What are you talking about?" Ally snapped in frustration. "What two words?"

"'I'm fine,'" Keir replied. "My dad taught me that whenever a woman uses those words, my first reaction should be to apologize and buy chocolate, because somehow I've screwed up."

Ally couldn't help the small laugh that escaped at his serious tone. "It wasn't you. One of your ever-increasing number of let-down women cornered me in the bathroom. It pissed me off is all."

Keir flinched at her words. "I'm so sorry. I swear, I—"

"Stop, there isn't anything you can say. You didn't send her in there and it's not your fault they're like rabid dogs with a bone. I just want to go home now." Ally sighed in weary exhaustion.

"I paid for dinner. Thank you for joining me, it saved me a lot of turmoil and aggravation from unwanted female attention. Can I walk you to your car?"

"No, I'm good. Thank you for dinner. I had a mostly wonderful time. I'll see you later."

Ally rushed out of the restaurant without another word, her emotions all over the place. Stress, worry, and lust were starting to take a toll on her sanity. She laughed out loud and glanced around sheepishly as she realized what she'd just done. Yes, lust was definitely at the top of that list, which in turn caused her stress to escalate too. Keir was too tempting for her peace of mind.

Fifteen minutes later, she threw off her shoes and sprawled out lengthwise on her couch with a groan. How had her life spiraled so far out of control so quickly, she wondered as she glanced at the clock and sighed. It wasn't too late to call her mom; she needed to hear her voice and remember where her priorities were right now, and they didn't include a playboy, no matter how wet he made her.

"Hey, Mom," Ally said softly with a gentle smile.

"Sweetheart, I was just thinking about you. How are things going, settling in okay?"

"Yes, and I'll tell you all about it, but first, you. How are you? Have you heard anything from the doctors yet?"

Arlene sighed in resignation. "Ally, stop worrying about me. You're going to put yourself in an early grave with all the stress you put on yourself."

"Mom." Ally growled in frustration. She hated when her mother stalled and tried to change the conversation.

"Fine. I'm doing the same. Doctors say they're doing everything they can. There's still room in the trial, but they can't hold it for much longer. That man is as stubborn as you are, he refuses to listen and let someone else have the spot," Arlene grumbled.

"Actually, I have some good news on that front," Ally said as tears fell down her face. "I've got the money, or I will in a few days."

"Ally Jane Fosey, what have you done?" Arlene scolded.

"Mom, calm down. Nothing illegal or immoral, I promise. You remember Josie, Xander's mate I was telling you about? Well, she met him through matesforhire.com, which her friend runs. These men need a fake mate for one reason or another and they pay out the ass for the woman's time. I signed up and just found out tonight I've been matched. We have enough for the treatment and some left over to hire a helper for you during the treatments."

"Ally—" Arlene started to say before she broke off into a bout of coughing that left her breathless.

"Mom, don't argue. Let me help. This might be your best shot and I will do absolutely anything to make sure you get to take it."

"Your sister and brother could still come up with the money in time. You don't have to do this."

"Mom, we both know it's not going to happen. Sara has her own family to support and she's struggling. Maxton is MIA right now and we don't know when he'll be reachable again. I've left messages with his commanding officer and anyone else that would listen, but it's the military and they run on their own time."

"I know, honey, I just don't like the idea of you taking chances like this. What if the guy's a serial killer, or rapist, or even a self-absorbed, insecure ass that only wants tooth-picks? Not all men can handle our curves. We're big, beautiful, and luscious and that's a lot for some men."

Ally burst into laughter at her mom's words. "I'm so lucky to have you for a mom. Not many mothers would have taught me to love my body like you did."

"Size isn't what matters in the world, I've told you that. It's all about being healthy, smart, and proud of who you are. Men will see that and fall head over ass for you. At least the ones worth having will."

"I love you, Mom."

"I know, baby. I love you too."

CHAPTER 6

"Any word from Kingston yet?" Keir called as he sorted through the mail Bess handed him.

"Nothing. I'll call again this morning," she replied with a shrug.

"No, I'll handle it."

If he could only go back a few days and redo things, he would in a heartbeat. After all, what were the chances he'd sign up for his friend's matchmaking site and then meet his mate the next day?

"Pick up, you overgrown housecat," Keir grumbled in frustration as he listened to the phone ringing in his ear. Times like this he missed having a landline phone he could slam down. Jabbing the end button just didn't cut it. Finally, Hawke's clipped tones came on the phone, urging the caller to leave a message. Keir growled, "Answer the phone, this is my fourth call. I am desperate here and you are probably sitting on your cushioned couch in that luxurious office laughing at me and my pathetic pleading." He paused and took a deep breath. He was losing his mind, that's all there was to it. "Look, just please get my name off matesforhire .com."

"Bro, what's gotten into you? I could hear you growling from down the hall."

Keir glanced up and frowned as his best friend and boss walked in the door. "Hawke isn't answering and I've left four messages over the last few days."

"What's got your dander up?"

Keir rolled his eyes. "That's the best you got? After all these years, that's the first time you've thought of that one? Really?"

Xander laughed. "No, but just never felt like the right time to use it before now."

"It's still not, if you were wondering. What did you want anyway?"

"I wanted to see if you were set for dinner. Josie is excited and if it helps, Hawke's supposed to be there too. You can get him to pull your name then. In the meantime, I'm dying to know, who are you bringing as your date? Did you actually get Ally to agree to go with you?"

"I haven't even brought it up to her yet. I ran into her at Ricardo's last night, and let's just say I seem to take one step forward and fifteen backward every time I'm in her company."

Xander flinched in sympathy. "How bad was it?"

"Two that I know of approached or made comments. I saw another three eyeing us from the bar area, but I don't know if she noticed or not. Eliza stopped by as well."

"Wow, yeah, I can see the problem. Well, I guess this isn't going to help your mood any, but Josie and Shawna have decided to hook her up with a friend of theirs. I tried to convince them it was a bad idea, but they don't believe me that you're her mate."

"Dammit to hell," Keir growled out. "This is my punishment, isn't it? All those years of meaningless sex with any woman I wanted and now the one I want, I can't even get to give me the time of day."

"She had dinner with you, that's something. And just think of all those nights as practice so that you could blow your mate's mind when she finally got in your bed."

Keir grinned. "That's a given."

"Anyway, back to business. I've got that meeting this afternoon with the new investor. Have you had time to look over Ally's proposal and if you did, what were your thoughts on it? We need to share it with Julia, but I wanted your input first."

"I think it's solid and a great plan, and by the way, I'm not telling Julia anything or going to lunch with her. That woman is scary as hell, she knows everything even before we do."

Xander laughed but quickly sobered as he heard Julia's voice from behind him.

"Should I be flattered or insulted?"

Keir winced. *Damn.* She'd caught them talking about her. They'd never hear the end of it now. "Fuck!"

"Bess, I do believe we surprised them," Julia said with a cackle of amusement. "Xander, come give me a kiss. Keir, sit your pretty ass down, we need to talk."

"Julia, I didn't know you were coming today. What's the occasion?" Xander asked as he moved to his grandmother's side.

"I have to keep you on your toes, and besides, I've heard some things that I needed to see for myself." Julia smiled and moved farther into the room. "Xander, if you and Josie are free, let's have dinner tonight. But for now, I'm stealing Keir here for a little talk."

Keir cursed under his breath. "Can we do this another time? I've got a packed day and nowhere on my schedule do I have any time for you to tell me how to live my life."

Julia rolled her eyes and sat down, "Stop fussing, boy.

This will only hurt for a few minutes. Now tell me how things are going with your mate."

Keir raised a brow. "Really, Julia. If I didn't know better, I'd say you have cameras following me around."

"I have spies everywhere. Ally is your mate, but your past is making things difficult for you. It's understandable, and part of me wants to laugh and say I told you so. My question instead is what are you going to do about it?"

He wasn't sure what he was supposed to say to that. Julia always knew everything that went on, how she did it they'd never been able to figure out. Now she expected him to give her answers when he had no idea himself how he was going to do it. The soft ticktock of the clock filled the silence of the room as the two of them continued to stare at each other.

Julia finally gave in, much to Keir's surprise. "I don't have all day to sit here and stare at your handsome face. So let me tell you what I think. First off, this ridiculous idea of bringing a date to my grandson's dinner party is absurd. You go alone. Don't think I haven't heard how your past women are reacting to the news. Second, you need to show her that she's special to you and not just a hookup."

He already knew that. He wanted to roar at her but she was an elder so he had to shut the fuck up and let her talk all she wanted. This was going to be a long day if this was any indication. He let his mind wander as he half listened to Julia's meddling. He knew she meant well, but she didn't understand shifters. Things were different for them than for regular humans. His cat was climbing the walls, pushing for him to claim his mate, to be near her. The more he fought to calm the animal, the harder it pushed back.

His mate was perfect for him, feisty and stubborn, beautiful and curvaceous. She made him and his lion want to roar in triumph and lust every time she came close. Ally wanted him too, he could smell the lust that wafted off her, and it made him drool and dream of the things he wanted to do to her.

"You're not listening to me, are you? Your head is stuck in the clouds. Useless men, always thinking with their third leg, and now look at where it's gotten you," Julia said reproachfully.

"Yes, ma'am," Keir responded automatically before shifting slightly in his chair in the hopes of releasing some of the pressure in his groin.

"So tell me what your plan is. Aren't lions supposed to be king of the jungle? From what I've been hearing, you're not doing well winning her over yet. So tell me, king, how are you going to get your woman and keep her?"

Julia's words made Keir and his lion growl in protest, they had not grown soft or compliant. Sure, sex had been easy and very enjoyable, but it hadn't weakened them. If there was one thing he and his lion knew how to do, it was plan an attack and execute it with precision. With a little help from his friends and family, she'd be his in no time.

"That's the smile I've been waiting for," Julia quipped with satisfaction. "When you're ready, give me a call and I'll do my part in whatever plan you come up with."

Keir stood and moved to sit beside Julia, "In case I haven't told you recently, thank you."

"You're welcome, my boy. I love you like a grandson and just want to see you happy. Now, before I go, tell me how much longer are you going to be able to stay here at XJ? Rumor has it your father is pushing harder and harder for you to take over after all."

CHAPTER 7

"I know you mean well, guys, but I'm taking someone to the party. I have too much on my plate right now to worry about meeting some blind date," Ally stressed into the phone she had propped between her shoulder and ear.

"Fine, I get it. I won't push. I was just trying to help," Shawna replied as Josie finally relented and agreed.

"Since you're both on the phone, help me out here. What do I wear? I don't want to be over- or underdressed."

"Something with easy access would make a certain someone's night a lot sweeter," Josie interjected quickly. "Xander swears Keir wants you desperately, Ally."

"You know that old saying, don't you? 'Want in one hand and shit in the other and see which one fills up faster,'" Ally quipped back with laughter tingeing her words. "He can want all he wants, but I've seen the women he's been with. Trust me, they bombarded us at dinner last night."

"Wait, shut the door," Shawna screeched. "You had a date with Keir and you didn't tell us?"

Ally groaned at her stupid mistake and tried to quickly fix the rapidly escalating cries of disbelief. "No, it wasn't a date. It was a chance meeting is all. Stop and I'll explain."

"You bet your ass you will," Josie exclaimed. "We want details, woman."

"I went for dinner and he happened to be there. There weren't any available tables so he invited me to join him. I was starving and didn't feel like going anywhere else so I agreed."

"And?" Shawna growled in frustration. "Details, remember?"

"We had a great time. He was entertaining, charming, and on his best behavior. That's after the hostess sat us and blatantly ignored me to flirt with him. She was one of his flavors of the night, then I went to the restroom where another of his floozies threatened me."

Ally had to pull the phone from her ear as she listened to her two friends threaten to castrate Keir and shave the heads of the women who had dared to accost her. She smiled and waited for them to calm down. These ladies were priceless.

"It wasn't directly Keir's fault, guys. Yes, it was because of him, but he did his best to include me and introduce me. He was attentive and I can't believe I'm saying this, but he was a perfect gentleman and a sweetheart."

Josie giggled. "So where there's smoke, there's usually fire."

Ally groaned, she shouldn't have said anything. "Stop right there. I'll admit he's beyond hot and he might star in a fantasy or two of mine, but that's all it is. I don't have time for the kind of drama he'd bring with him, if he was even seriously interested, which he isn't."

"Denial is not just a river in Egypt," Josie said at the same time Shawna piped in with, "Even I've seen the looks he gives you."

"Shut up and help me figure out what to wear tonight," Ally grumbled as the two women laughed.

"It's casual, most of the guys will be in jeans and polo shirts, if that helps. Personally I have no idea yet what I'm wearing either. I'm too busy making sure things are going as planned here. The caterer is giving me fits about the menu. The cleaning lady is running late and Xander is busy trying to distract me with looks of lust and it's driving me freaking insane."

Shawna and Ally burst into laughter as she growled the last words, with a whispered "stop" to presumably Xander who was interrupting her phone call.

"I'll see you tonight. Josie, go relax and let your man take care of you," Ally replied with a smile.

"Ally, why don't you meet me for lunch? We can get a mani-pedi and relax, I'll even help you pick out an outfit if you want."

"That's perfect. Where?" Ally cried with enthusiasm.

They quickly made plans and hung up. Ally slumped down on her bed and smiled. In some ways her life was going to drive her insane, but at least she had awesome friends to help her through them.

For the next couple hours Ally puttered around her apartment, putting things in their places and straightening up from the last few hectic weeks. Overall, she was happy she'd moved here, now if she could just get her mind off Keir and what he could do to her body, she'd be perfect.

Ally stopped in her bedroom doorway and stared at her bedside table, she'd done her best to avoid thoughts of the sexy lion shifter. It was a losing battle though, he heated her blood and made her yearn for things she couldn't even describe. He brought out a side of her she hadn't even known existed. Yes, sex had always been good and she enjoyed it, but never had she ached for a man like she did Keir.

"Fuck it," she growled as she pulled the drawer open and pulled out her nubby finger vibrator. "Perfect," she said as she made her way to the bathroom and turned on the shower. She knew it wouldn't take long, she'd been on the edge since dinner last night.

Ally couldn't wait; she jumped in and yelped when the freezing water pelted her overheated skin. She quickly adjusted the temperature and sighed as the heated water cascaded down her body.

Now the big decision, play then wash her hair or maybe play, wash, and then play again. Who was she kidding, she needed that release and she needed it now. She gathered her loofah and body wash and gently stroked it across her sensitive nipples and gasped. *Definitely not going to last long,* she thought as she soaped her body and moaned at the sensations.

The loofah fell to the tub and her soapy hands cupped her full breasts. Ally moaned as she pulled and pinched her taut nipples, delighting in the painful tugs. Her breaths were coming in short gasps as she trailed one hand down her rounded belly and stopped at the apex of her thighs.

Her legs trembled in need as she slowly and with deliberate care pulled her lips apart and stroked her exposed clit. She circled the small nub and gasped at the tingles that spread through her lower belly. "Oh hell," she whispered as she imagined Keir's hands touching her, rubbing her. That it was his tongue trailing the wet path down her body and not the shower water.

Ally glanced around for the vibrator and sighed as she pulled it on her finger. With a gentle flick, the small machine hummed to life with the promise of ecstasy. She bit her lip as she moved the vibrator to her extended nipple.

The rough nubs combined with the vibration sent her need into heightened levels, she whimpered as she moved it back and forth between her nipples.

Her other hand continued its torture of circling her clit,

but not quite touching it. She was driving herself insane as she imagined Keir whispering into her ear.

"Are you wet for me? Do you need me to give you the pleasure your body craves? Can you imagine what it would feel like if I pushed you against the wall and took you into my mouth? What it would feel like as I licked, nipped, and sucked your clit. Would you ride my tongue?"

Ally gasped as her imaginary Keir pushed her closer to the edge of an orgasm. With trembling fingers, she brushed the vibrator against her sensitive nub. She slumped against the wall as her legs wobbled and she cried out from the intense pleasure.

"Keir," she whispered as she felt herself moving closer and closer to the cliff. Her body was throbbing, pulsing as she rotated the nubby finger vibrator around her.clit.

"Oh God, Keir." She panted as she felt her body tensing as her orgasm crashed through, leaving her spent, shaking, and beyond content for the first time in days.

Forget playing again, she was exhausted now. Ally quickly washed her hair and climbed out of the bath, feeling drained and relaxed. She grabbed her robe, pulled it on her still wet body and made her way back to her bedroom. She faceplanted on the bed and smiled, her body still humming slightly.

"Ally?"

A soft knock sounded on her bedroom door, startling her from her dozing state. She jerked up and spun around in confusion.

"I'm opening the door, if you're not decent you'd better cover up."

Ally's eyes opened wide as she finally registered whose voice that was. "Keir?" she whispered softly, not quite understanding what was happening.

"There you are, is everything okay?" Keir asked cautiously as he stepped into the room and glanced around.

"I'm fine. How did you get in and why are you here?" she demanded as she glanced around in a panic, fear making her voice tight. Had she left the vibrator in the bathroom or had she brought it out with her?

"You missed lunch with Shawna, she's been trying to call you. Josie called as well. They asked me to run over and check on you. I still have a key from when it was Xander's place. I knocked for five minutes, but when you didn't answer I got worried."

Ally frowned and grabbed her phone from the nightstand. Dead. "Shit, I must have forgotten to charge it. What time is it?"

"Two . . . ," Keir said as he trailed off and stared at the ground in front of Ally's feet.

She watched as he licked his lips. She glanced down to see her finger vibe lying there where she must have dropped it in her mind-numbing euphoria. "I . . ." she stuttered as she felt her face flame in embarrassment.

"So many questions, so many things I want to say," Keir said as he took a step closer to Ally and locked eyes.

"I fell asleep," she whispered softly as she licked her lips.

"Did you tire yourself out using your toy? I can smell your need from here. Would it be wrong of me to say I'm going to dream of you and that toy tonight? Of you screaming my name as I worship every inch of your body."

Ally couldn't reply, her breath was trapped in her chest as she gazed dazedly at the man who only a short time ago had made her come, even if it was only in her head. To have him in her bedroom after all the fantasies she'd been having was surreal.

"Oh yes, that's it. Fuel my fantasy with those soft whimpers, baby," Keir said quietly as lust burned bright in his eyes. "I bet you taste as amazing as you smell."

Ally gulped as she saw Keir's lion close to the surface, saw his need plainly evident in his eyes, in the way he sniffed the air and licked his lips.

"Tell me to go away, Ally."

"What if I want to know what one night with you would be like? What if I want to feel how your women felt after being with you?"

Ally wasn't sure what she was saying, all she knew was the primal need in her body was taking over and lust was clouding everything.

"One night wouldn't be enough," he growled as he stalked closer with his feline grace. "I'm already addicted to you, baby."

Before Ally could protest, Keir leaned down and kissed her for all she was worth. His tongue glided in and took possession, robbing her of all rational thought. She moaned and clutched at him as he devoured her mouth.

"I'm leaving. What I want to do will take hours, and we have someplace to be tonight. When we make love, and I assure it will be making love, we need all night, baby," Keir whispered before he planted a soft kiss on her swollen lips. "You are fucking gorgeous, I'll be here at six to pick you up."

Ally watched as Keir turned and left as quickly as he'd arrived. Fifteen minutes later, she roused herself enough to get up and plug her dead phone in, only then did she recall his parting words. He was picking her up at six tonight.

CHAPTER 8

Keir stumbled out of the apartment and slumped against the wall in the hallway. Never had his control been tested so completely before. He closed his eyes and concentrated on calming his raging need down, it wouldn't do him any good to call the girls and Xander back sounding pained. They'd never let him live it down.

"Shit," he cursed as his phone rang and he glanced at it to see his best friend's phone number. "She's fine. She'd fallen asleep and her phone's dead. I just left her."

"Thank you, the girls are beside themselves with worry."

"No problem. Look, I've got to go. I'll see you tonight."

Keir hung up without waiting for a reply and turned to head out to his car and his own shower. Mary Palm and her five sisters were calling to him desperately. His lion was roaring for its mate, if he didn't get out of here quick, he was worried he'd go back in and take her.

Within minutes he was back in his house, pacing the floor like a caged lion in a zoo. His blood was boiling, not just in lust but in anger. He'd lost control of the situation. He hadn't meant to come on that strong, what if he lost whatever chance he had with her because of this? No, he couldn't believe that. He'd felt her response, smelled her need. She was desperate for him, just as he was for her. He could work with this, he just needed to tone it down a bit and show her there was more than just sex with him to look forward to.

Now the hard part: coming up with ways for her to spend time with him. It was time to call in the reinforcements, cunning plans of attack were a lion's specialty after all.

An hour later and things were set in motion. Xander, Julia, Josie, and even Shawna agreed to help. Operation Mate was in play; before Ally knew it she would be his in every way for all eternity.

Now the waiting began, it was only a little after four and he still had almost two hours before he could pick her up. He felt like an adolescent going on his first date as he scanned his closet for the perfect outfit. Never in his life had he felt this way, but she was worth it. He knew that with every fiber of his soul.

Within minutes, the piles of rejected jeans and shirts were getting to alarming heights. No matter what he tried on, nothing screamed out to him that it was the outfit to woo his mate. He slumped on the bed, discouraged and a tad frightened at the mess he'd made so quickly.

"You know I'd laugh, but I can't help but feel sorry for you," Xander said quietly from the doorway, startling Keir, who jumped and spun around with a growl.

"What the hell, man?"

"I knocked, you didn't answer. The door was unlocked so I came in. After our conversation earlier I knew something was up and I wanted to check on you."

"Great, just what I need, everyone to know I'm whipped before I've even gotten her to agree to be mine."

Xander laughed wickedly. "If you'll remember not that long ago, I warned you. I said when you meet your mate, I'm going to laugh my ass off at you as you flounder and try to change years of womanizing ways. Now look at you, my pre-diction came true quicker than I expected, but it's here and I'm enjoying every damn moment of it."

"If you're not here to help me, then get the hell out," Keir grumbled. "I'm already making an ass out of myself, I don't need an audience to make it worse."

"What if I told you I came bearing gifts, or well, advice from the girls, which is basically the same thing?"

Keir paused and cocked one eyebrow at his friend. "Great, are you telling me they know I'm freaking out too?"

"I doubt it, they just hoped. I believe Josie's words were something to the effect that after years and years of not car-ing what women thought, you've finally got one that matters. You've never worried about making a good impression on them, they literally fall at your feet and worship you. Ally isn't doing that and it's probably making you ape-shit crazy."

Keir couldn't help the laugh that bubbled up. "She's got that right. I love women, all women, don't get me wrong, but I've never once had to convince one to give me a chance until now."

"She says to wear your most comfortable, but nice, jeans. No holes or rips, and your blue button-down shirt. She says, and I'm quoting here so don't say one freaking word or I'll hurt you, that 'the blue brings out your eyes and makes them shine' or something stupid like that," Xander grum-bled.

"Thanks, man, I know that probably wasn't easy for you." Keir struggled not to laugh at the disgruntled expression on his friend's face.

"The shit we do for our mates, I swear," Xander grum-bled as he waved and left the room. "See you tonight," he called, knowing Keir with his sensitive shifter hearing would hear him no problem.

He really did have the best people in his life, he couldn't ask for better or more supportive people. Keir glanced at his watch and smiled, time to get cleaned up and dressed. He had a stop to make before he could see Ally and he didn't want to waste any time getting back to his mate.

CHAPTER 9

Ally turned from side to side, viewing herself in the mirror from every possible angle as she weighed the decision. This was her favorite of all the outfits she'd picked out, but she wasn't sure if it was the right choice. The dress was a casual one she'd picked up one day, but she'd quickly discovered it to be one of her favorites.

The black capped sleeves contrasted perfectly with the tight red-and-black-swirled bodice. A belt of silver loops draped around her middle leaving the rest of the black bottom to flair out, giving a small peak to her legs from the slit that ran up the right side.

She stepped into her black ballet shoes and sighed happily. A silver heart pendant necklace her mother had given her and the outfit was perfect. She was as ready as she was going to get.

The doorbell rang and Ally took a deep breath, it was time to face Keir after the soul-searing kiss he'd given her earlier. She was so not ready for this; she had one goal. To get him out of her apartment and away from temptation as quickly as possible. The couch, beds, and well, any flat surface was too close for her comfort. Her willpower was shot for the day.

Ally stopped in front of the door and took a deep breath, hoping it would fortify her resolve. The resolve that went up in smoke the minute she opened the door and saw Keir standing there with a dozen red roses and a stuffed lion holding a heart. She bit her lip and smiled at the gorgeous man standing in front of her with a soft smile and lust flashing in his eyes.

"You smell amazing," she whispered as she stepped back to let him into her apartment.

"Thank you. You look mouthwatering."

Ally blushed and squeezed her thighs together as she felt herself grow moist at the need that infused every word he spoke.

"Are those for me?"

Keir nodded and handed them to her. "You smell as delicious as you look."

"Let me go put these in water," Ally stammered as she turned and raced from the doorway. She needed a minute to get herself under control. He was insanely gorgeous, smelled like the outdoors, pine, and man, and good enough to eat. Ally stopped beside the sink and took a deep breath. "Get yourself under control, girl, you can do this," she said quietly in the hopes of giving herself a pep talk.

"I've been saying the same thing to myself since the moment I met you. Control seems to be the one thing I lack lately," Keir whispered from behind her.

Ally stiffened but didn't turn around. Her need was too great to face him at the moment. "We need to get out of here. I don't want to be late for my own dinner party," she responded weakly.

"I know. I'm going downstairs; just meet me when you're ready. I don't think I can stand in here alone with you and resist temptation. Not when I can smell how much you want me, and see how fast your heart is beating whenever I get close to you."

Ally didn't respond, her words were locked in her throat as she tried to swallow around her suddenly dry mouth. She was tempted beyond belief to make a side trip into the bathroom and insert her ben wa balls. If she didn't get some kind of stimulation soon, she'd go insane.

She turned and glanced down the hallway, to the right was her front door and Keir, to the left her toys. She'd never thought she'd be debating this while getting ready to head out to meet her friends.

That thought did it. Her friends and their heightened senses, no way in hell did she need to be anymore aroused all night with them all around than she was already going to be with Keir so close by.

Before she could change her mind, she grabbed her purse and raced out of the apartment. Temptation was everywhere and it was trying to trap her; the most tempting part was leaning against his car smiling at her with a grin promising wicked delights in his arms.

"You ready, beautiful?"

Ally smiled and stepped closer. She watched as Keir closed his eyes and fisted his hands.

"This is going to be a long car ride, baby."

"Then I hate to ask this, but can we make a quick stop? I don't want to arrive empty-handed."

Keir smiled. "For you, anything. Besides, I didn't say I was going to enjoy the ride, just that it was going to be long."

Ally smiled and waited as he opened the car door and helped her slide in. The smooth interior was as sexy as its owner. Sleek, polished, and gorgeous. Keir climbed in and winked. "Buckle up."

She almost came as the car started up, a sexy purr that

sent vibrations coursing through her body. Yup, just like its owner.

"Where do you want to stop?" Keir asked softly as he gripped the steering wheel with white-knuckled hands.

"Anywhere is fine. I'm not sure what to bring, honestly. Do you have any suggestions?"

"There's always the customary wine, but what about something a little different? I'm sure a lot of people will bring that. I know they are having this catered and they have a cleaning lady, but what about something for breakfast? If I know Xander and Josie at all, they will stay up late picking up and setting the house to rights. What if we stop by the store, grab a basket, and then hit the bakery? We can load it up with scones, donuts, croissants, and things like that."

"Wow, I'm impressed. That's a fantastic idea and something different. I know I'd appreciate that in their place. Especially after being up late the night before, to wake up and have a ready-made breakfast."

Keir smiled. "I'm not just a pretty face, you know, I have some good qualities."

"Pretty, my ass," Ally grumbled under her breath, forgetting about his superior hearing for a moment until he burst into laughter and winked at her.

"Your ass is gorgeous, baby. Want me to tell you the things I've dreamed of doing to it?"

Ally swallowed audibly. "No, please don't."

She was so stupid to think she could be in the closed confines of his car and not want to rub all over him until she came, screaming. His smell was intensified in the small space, she couldn't help but shift and try to give herself some relief from the throbbing that was taking over her body.

"So, Ally, distract me, please," Keir said as he breathed

heavily through his flared nostrils. "I'm fighting to stay in control and whatever it is you're thinking about is killing me here."

"Oh, sorry. Um, okay," she stammered as she tried to think of something to say as her mind emptied. "Well, how come I never met you before moving here? Xander I knew and I've heard of you from my brother and sister and even Xander, but why haven't I met you? You were at the house all the time growing up, after all."

"I asked the same thing actually. I didn't know you existed until just before Xander met Josie. I knew Sara, but I didn't know there was another sister. I'm still wondering if it was a conspiracy."

Ally laughed in delighted humor. "Not so much. I'm the youngest, by the time I came around my parents had learned quickly how wild my siblings were. They were working all the time trying to make the business a success and it was better for me to go to boarding school. I loved the idea of it and, actually, I asked to go. I learned so much, traveled the world with my friends and their families and I saw my family all the time. I really couldn't have asked for a better childhood."

"How did you meet Xander?"

"I came home one summer and he was there pretty much all the time. They told me stories of you and the adventures you all went on, but you were away that summer with your father. It was just after your mother got sick, I believe. After that I wasn't home as much as I was spending more and more time in school and you were with your family making the most of the time you had left with her."

"I understand that, but how come they didn't ever tell me about you? It's like they kept you a secret from me."

"Maybe it was just nothing more than you were preoccupied with everything going on in your life. I bet they did, you just don't remember since we'd never met. I was just an abstract mention in a teenage mind filled with grief and all the other things boys your age were obsessed with."

"I guess so. I know you have a degree in marketing, but what else can you tell me about yourself? I want to know everything I can."

"You'd be bored within minutes. I don't do much but work, take care of my mom as much as I can, read, and hang out with my friends."

"Take care of your mom?"

"She's dying of a rare form of cancer. There's a trial coming up that I'm desperately trying to get her in, but it's a waiting game at this point. Insurance doesn't cover it, and they can only do so much."

"I'm sorry," Keir whispered softly. "I know how it is to lose a parent and be helpless like that."

Ally smiled sadly. "How's your dad doing anyway?"

"He's good. Grumpy as ever, he's pushing me to take over at the bank. He lost his sense of smell a few years back and he's afraid someone will take advantage."

"You don't want to?"

"I do, I've always known that's where I'd end up. I just don't like to be pushed into doing something that he's still capable of. He wants me to settle down, start a family. He doesn't care if it's my mate or not. He settled and was content with my mother. I don't want to settle."

Ally didn't respond, she wasn't sure what to say. She understood what he was saying and she could see his point, but going out with a different woman and having sex every night was not the answer.

"You want to go to the bakery there and I'll run next store and get the basket?" Keir asked with a questioning smile as Ally stared out the window, lost in thought.

"Sure, that's perfect. I'll see you in a minute," she said as she climbed out of the car, still thinking about his last comment.

The bakery smelled wonderful even this early in the evening, the smell of fresh bread and pastries making her stomach growl.

"Hi and welcome. What can I get for you?" an older woman behind the counter called out as Ally walked in.

"Hello. Everything looks and smells amazing."

"Tastes good too, if I do say so myself. It's why I have a few extra curves after all. I can't resist my own cooking."

Ally laughed and surveyed the options. So many choices to choose from.

"Anything particular you're interested in?"

"My friend and I are going to a dinner party. We thought we'd buy some baked goods for them to have for breakfast. Figured the last thing they'd want to do tomorrow is cook after hosting everyone."

The lady beamed. "I know exactly what you mean. I think it's a terrific idea. You know, I have some breakfast goodies in the back. Let me go gather some for you. We'll make that basket full of goodies. You'll be their favorite guests hands down, I promise you that."

"Thank you, that would be wonderful," Ally said with genuine warmth and laughter ringing in her words.

"Why don't you have a piece of my newest cake while I gather them up? You can give me feedback; this is my first day serving it after all."

Ally accepted the chocolate cake with delight and moved to a table. She'd taken one bite when the ding of the door rang and she glanced up, expecting Keir to walk in. Instead, a brown-haired vixen glided in and headed straight for her.

"So you're the one I've been hearing so much about."

Ally frowned in confusion. "Excuse me?"

"Keir's newest . . . friend."

"I assume you're one of his numerous conquests."

The lady laughed heartily. "You could say that. We had fun, but we both knew it was only for the night."

"Why are you here then?" Ally asked curiously as she took a bite and moaned at the delicious flavors that exploded in her mouth.

"I wanted to meet you for myself. It takes a special person to capture his attention. I was curious."

Ally didn't say anything, just continued eating and staring at the woman until Keir walked in a few moments later.

"Carissa," he cried in delight. "It's been forever. How are you?"

"Fantastic. I just stopped in to see my aunt and saw your . . . friend step in here. I wanted to say hello."

Keir smiled at Carissa and turned to Ally. "I got the basket . . . are you eating cake?" he asked, flabbergasted.

Ally smiled. "She offered and it smelled so amazing. Who was I to say no to that? Try a bite, I promise you won't be disappointed." Ally held up a forkful, devilish delight dancing in her eyes.

Keir narrowed his eyes playfully but gave in and leaned forward, taking the bite from her hands. "Holy hell, that is fantastic."

"Told you." Ally smirked before turning her attention back to Carissa and smiling.

"So it is true after all. I'm glad," Carissa murmured as she winked at Ally. "Keir, I like her. I've got to run. Take care and I'll see you around."

Ally waited until the door had shut before glancing up to Keir. "Another of your women? This is getting old quick."

Keir frowned but knew he couldn't say much. It was true, no matter where they went they were accosted by one of them. So far they'd been lucky and things had been civil, but he knew there were a few out there that weren't going to be like that.

"Son, give me the basket and I'll get you all loaded up," the shopkeeper announced as she came back into the room. "I think your friends are going to be very happy with the selection I've put together."

"After the taste of that cake I just had, I have no doubt of that at all," Keir called back as he moved to the counter and pulled out his wallet.

"I've got this, you bought the basket," Ally cried as she raced to the counter to stop him from paying.

"Nonsense. A gentleman never lets a lady pay in his presence." Keir gently nudged Ally before turning his attention back to the baker.

"You two are so sweet together, what a wonderful match you are."

Ally started to protest, but Keir cut her off and thanked the lady for her kind words. He paid for their baked goods, left a generous tip, and headed out. "Come on, we don't want to be too late to your own party."

"Can I ask you a question?" Ally asked softly a few minutes later as they were driving toward Xander and Josie's house.

"Sure, ask me anything."

"You said you didn't want to settle like your father."

"Yes," Keir responded hesitantly, not sure where she was going with this.

"Is that why all the different women?"

CHAPTER 10

He'd figured this would come up at some point. He just hadn't expected it so soon. This was the first time she'd gone out with him, even if it hadn't been proposed as a date, it was damn close to it.

"I love women, the way they smell, the way they look, every shape and size. I like sex; okay, I love sex. I've always been upfront with the woman I'm with. It's a no-strings, one-night affair. A way to mutually satisfy our needs, and before you ask, no, I haven't slept with every one of the women I was with. I love their company, so I chose to spend my free time with as many of them as I could. Sometimes we'd go out to dinner, sometimes we'd just hang out and talk. Some of them I slept with."

Keir sighed and tried to come up with the words to explain. "My father settled and married a woman that wasn't his mate. I didn't agree, but I understood it. Not everyone finds their mate. I don't want to settle for less than my full match, the one person made for me. At the same time, I didn't want to give up spending time and, yes, sleeping with women until I found her. I made sure that no matter what, they knew they weren't going to keep me, that it was temporary."

Ally sighed. "I think I get it, Keir. It's okay. I just wish they would stop attacking. I've done nothing wrong and for them to confront me and warn me off you is ridiculous. I don't own you, I didn't make you turn them down."

Keir cursed and gripped the steering wheel tighter. "I know, I'm sorry, I didn't want that to happen either."

"It's fine, just a bit annoying. I'm not a threat to them. They need to understand that," Ally continued as if he hadn't said anything.

Keir gritted his teeth to keep himself from blurting out the truth. She was his mate, his one and only. The one he never thought he'd find, but secretly hoped he would. "We're here. You ready for this?" Keir said instead.

He climbed out of the car and raced to her side. He took a deep breath and pulled open the door, offered his hand, and smiled as she stepped out to stand beside him.

"Thank you, kind sir," she said with twinkling eyes.

"My pleasure, my lady. Your pleasure will always be of the utmost concern for me." He winked as he reached in the backseat and pulled out the basket of pastries. "You ready?"

Keir smiled when she nodded, he placed his hand on the small of her back and began the trek to the front door. He felt her shiver as he brushed his hand up and down her back in an encouraging gesture. The feeling was mutual, a simple touch and he was shaking like a leaf.

The front door opened as they approached and Keir smiled to see Josie standing there waiting for them.

"About time you guys got here."

"Stop, we're barely late," Keir replied with a laugh.

"Besides, we brought you a present, and trust me, it's worth it," Ally finished as Keir handed the basket over.

"Wow, this smells great. Xander is going to be so excited. We've already fought over who was cooking breakfast tomorrow."

"It was Keir's idea," Ally offered. "I know, it impressed me too."

"Hey now, ladies. I do have good ideas occasionally."

"Come in, everyone's scattered about. Keir, will you introduce Ally around to those she doesn't know while I go tease Xander about breakfast? You should know everyone."

"Sure thing," Keir said with a smile as he gently prodded Ally inside. "Come on, beautiful. Shawna is dying to see you, I'm sure."

Keir glanced around and frowned at the large number of single men he recognized in the room. In fact, other than Xander, every male was a highly sought after bachelor. Who cared that they were also close friends of his and Xander's— that was beside the point.

"What's with the frown?" Ally asked suspiciously.

"Nothing, just surprised at the turnout. Something tells me I'm going to lose you now. Shawna is making a beeline for you and she looks determined."

Keir smiled as Shawna approached. "She's all yours. You can stop scowling at me now."

"You're dismissed," Shawna said with a wink. "We've got some talking to do," she said as she pulled Ally to the other side of the room.

That was fine with Keir; he needed to have a word with his best friend too. They knew Ally was his mate, so why had they purposefully invited all these guys?

"Keir, just the man I was looking for," Xander called out from his spot by the fireplace. "How did it go?"

"Great, she came with me, didn't she?"

Xander cocked one eyebrow and smirked. "Touchy tonight, aren't we?"

"Want to explain the guest list?"

"Nope." Xander smiled and walked off, leaving Keir to

stew in his misery as he watched the other guys being introduced to his mate.

"You're growling, bro," Kingston Hawke said between chuckles. "What's gotten into you?"

"Where the hell you been? I've left you so many messages. Bess has left messages at your office too. Not a word from you."

"Sorry, I've been out of town. Haven't even checked in at the office yet. What did you need?"

"Take me off that damn website. I don't need to hire a mate anymore."

"Oh, well, then I guess you don't want this," Kingston said as he held out a folded piece of paper. "You've been matched."

Keir groaned. "No, I found my mate."

"So I heard, but you might want to read that paper, I promise you it's worth it."

"Fine," Keir grumbled as he snatched the paper and unfolded it. "Are you serious?" he asked in astonishment. "Ally was matched with me?"

Kingston burst into laughter. "Sure was. What can I say, my program is amazing."

"You won't hear any complaints from me and this actually solves so many problems. You are my new favorite person, behind my mate and a couple others, of course."

"Thanks, I think," Kingston said with a chuckle. "Now who is that talking to your mate?"

Keir honed in on his mate and glanced at Kingston. "You don't know? Really?"

"No, should I?"

Keir laughed. "This is awesome. Hold on. Xander!" Keir hollered, calling their host over to join them. "Kingston would like to know who's talking to Ally."

Xander glanced to Ally and bit his lip trying to contain his laughter. "Dude, how big is your company?"

"Why, what does that have to do with anything?"

"She works for you. She's the one who set Josie and me up from your matching program."

Kingston frowned. "That doesn't make any sense. I have one of my managers running that site. He's the only one who has access."

"You might want to check into that, because I can guarantee you that Shawna runs that website. Josie told us that she is always complaining about the work and maintenance the website and software takes," Xander said with a shrug.

"Want us to introduce you?"

"Yes, please," Kingston said with a confused frown.

"My pleasure," Keir said with a gleam. "I don't like that asshat she's talking to right now. He's a womanizer and not good enough for her."

"Wow, did I just hear you say that?" Kingston gaped at him in astonishment.

"What? I'm reformed and that's my mate, after all. Come on, I'll introduce you and claim her while I'm at it."

"Just don't let her know that's what you're doing," Xander advised softly. "I guarantee you that won't fly at all."

CHAPTER 11

This guy was going to drive her insane. He just wouldn't take no for an answer. They'd both told him, in fact, but he insisted on keeping them company. He was being courteous and polite, but they just wanted to talk and do it without this man lurking close by.

"Ally, Shawna," Keir called as he stopped beside them. "Let me introduce you to my close friend, Kingston Hawke. Kingston, this is Ally and our friend, Shawna."

"Ladies, it's a pleasure to make your acquaintance. I've heard wonderful things about both of you."

Shawna scoffed and turned her back to Kingston and faced Keir. "You, mister, were supposed to call me, instead I had to hear it from Xander."

Kingston frowned and glanced around in astonishment. No woman had ever shunned him like that before.

"In my defense, I knew you were here with Josie, so by calling her I filled you all in at once. I'm sorry," Keir attempted to defend himself as Ally snickered beside him.

"Whatever, you can make it up to me by staying here and rescuing us from the letch over there. He won't leave us alone and I desperately need to talk to Ally, since she ditched me for lunch today."

Ally couldn't contain her laughter as Keir was left

standing there gaping in shock as Shawna pulled her down a hallway.

"Come on, I know they'll come looking for us in a second," Shawna said as she pulled out a slip of paper and waved it around. "You've been matched and you so won't believe it."

"What does that mean?" Ally asked, puzzled as she grabbed the paper and scanned it.

"See what I mean."

"I'm matched with Keir? There has to be some mistake. And why would he sign up when he's got a different woman on his arm every night?"

"According to his sign-up information, he needs a date for some functions at his family's bank. As to why he isn't bringing one of his ladies, who cares. Look at your salary for the two weeks."

"Holy hell," Ally said, mouth gaping, "that's more than enough to get my mom in the trial and have enough to make sure she's taken care of for a few months. I told my mom as much, but I was lying and hoping to give her hope."

"I know, I was so excited when I saw his name come up and read what he needed. This is exactly what you need. And did you read the part where it says he'll pay half up front?"

Ally broke down into tears. "I know you told me it would be enough, but to actually see it. I'm . . . I can't wait to tell my mother."

"Go call her, dinner will be ready in a few minutes and I'll make an excuse for you."

Ally didn't have to be told twice, she turned and opened the first door she came to, a spare bedroom. *Perfect,* she thought as she sat on the bed and stared at the paper in her shaking hands. Her mom was never going to believe it. She quickly dialed her mom; this was news she couldn't wait to tell her.

"Mom," Ally cried as soon as Arlene picked up the phone, "I've got the money for the trial."

"Already?" Arlene asked in shock.

"Monday. I'll have it deposited into your account. Make sure you call the doctor right away and get in the trial. Don't wait."

"I won't. I . . ." Arlene trailed off and burst into tears.

"Mom, are you okay?" Ally cried in alarm.

"Yes, love, I'm here. Just a bit overwhelmed. I hoped and prayed, but I really didn't think we'd find the money."

"I'm at a party at Josie's house so I only have a minute. I was just so excited I had to call and tell you."

"Don't let me keep you. Thank you, Ally, I can't even begin to thank you."

"Mom, stop, that's what family does. Support each other, no questions asked, in any way we can. I love you."

"I love you too, baby. Go have fun and I'll talk to you tomorrow."

Ally hung up and sat there for a few minutes composing herself. So many emotions fought for dominance, but happiness and gratitude were winning hands down.

"Ally?" Keir called from the other side of the door. "Are you okay? Dinner's being served."

Ally jumped to her feet and pulled the door open. "I'm fantastic now." *Thanks to you,* she thought silently. They quickly made their way to the dining room and found their seats. Keir was across and down one from Ally and Shawna was next to her on the right.

The food was plentiful and good and the conversations flowed around the room with easy banter.

"Is everything okay?" Shawna leaned over and whispered almost inaudibly into her ear.

"Yes, why do you ask?"

Shawna sat back and tilted her head slightly toward Keir. "He can't stop watching you. Every couple of seconds he turns back to check on you. It's kinda sweet."

"Did you notice the guy staring at you intently with a frown? I can't quite tell if he's trying to figure you out or if he's scared."

"Who?" Shawna questioned in confusion. "I haven't noticed anything like that."

"The guy Keir brought over before you dragged me away. I can't remember his name. I didn't get to say hi or anything after all."

"Oh, you're talking about Kingston Hawke. I work for him, remember? Well, he's my boss's boss or something like that. I've never met him in person before tonight."

"Why did you ignore him then?" Ally asked in confusion.

Shawna shrugged but blushed as she glanced away.

"All right, I'll let it go for now, but tell me one thing."

"Maybe, but I won't guarantee anything."

"What would you do if I dared you to speak to him?"

"I'd have to return the favor, but in this case I'd dare you to kiss Keir, now."

Ally glared at Shawna. "Seems a little unfair, don't you think? And why would you want me to kiss him?"

"Because we're not blind, we see the attraction between you two and we want you to act on it," Josie whispered from behind as she snuck up on the two women.

"Can you be a bit more circumspect? Damn shifters in here will hear every word you say," Ally whispered in embarrassment.

"Oh, honey. Too late for that," Xander called out from his spot at the head of the table, causing Ally to blush and sputter.

"Xander, stop teasing our guest of honor," Josie scolded playfully.

Luckily the rest of dinner went off smoothly and no more embarrassing comments were made. Ally did begin to notice how often she sought out Keir's presence. As she mingled and talked, she found her eyes always searching him out. More often than not he was watching her as well.

"Are you having fun?" Keir whispered as he stopped behind her.

Ally spun around and laughed. "You surprised me. Yes, I'm having fun, and you?"

"I'd be better if some of these guys weren't so persistent, but for the most part yes, I'm having fun."

"Persistent? Are you being harassed by men now too?"

Keir laughed. "Not what I meant and you know it. Any chance you want to step out back with me and get a breath of fresh air?"

"I'd love that. But don't think I'll give you any leeway: best behavior tonight," she scolded playfully.

"I won't touch you unless you ask me to, and something tells me you'll be asking sooner than you think, beautiful."

Ally sighed, he was right. She wanted nothing more than to strip him down and ride him all night long. The more she watched him with his friends, the hotter she became. He really was a great guy, well liked and respected by everyone here. And damn that ass was delectable.

"Stop," Keir growled as his steps faltered and he glanced back at her over his shoulder. "Whatever you're thinking better stop or I promise you, we will be giving everyone here a show as I make you whimper and cry out in torment, begging for me to make you come."

Ally gulped, licked her lips, and quickened her steps. She wasn't exactly sure if she was hurrying to let him fulfill his promise or trying to get out of ear and smell range.

"I'm not sure how to bring this up, so I'm just going to come out and say it. You're my mate."

Ally stumbled in shock. "Excuse me?"

"Mateforhire.com says you're my mate. They matched us together."

Holy hell, she'd thought he meant for real. A mixture of disappointment and happiness passed through her. She wasn't sure if she was more relieved or upset by that revelation and that stunned her even more.

"Yes, Shawna informed me tonight." Ally paused and bit her lip, before adding, "Is this going to be a problem for your other women and why did you need to hire a mate anyway?"

Keir laughed somewhat bitterly. "Not a problem at all. I haven't been dating anyone in the last few weeks actually, and I originally signed up to help Kingston as a favor. He was trying to get the program set up and running and needed test applicants. I'd been trying to get him to take me out of the system for the last week, but it worked out perfectly in the end. I do need you to be my mate."

"Shawna said it was for your company's parties and things. Your family company, I mean."

"Yes, my father runs the company for now."

"He's a shifter too, right? So, how does this work? I mean, won't he know I'm not really your mate?"

Keir laughed sardonically. "He lost his sense of smell in an accident a few years back. As long as you act like you like me, we'll be fine."

Ally snorted out a laugh. "What if I don't like you?"

"Baby, you like me. You'd like me to bend you over this porch railing and fuck you senseless too. You can lie to yourself, but not to me."

She licked her lips hungrily at his words, he was right and she knew it, but that didn't mean she wanted to admit it. "So how does this work, being your mate I mean?" she asked between shaky breaths.

"Nothing too strenuous, we go to the different events, be seen around town together, things like that."

"When's the first event and what is it? I need to know what to expect and anything important about the people there. Things a mate should know to pull this off."

"Monday, dinner with the board of directors and their wives, I'll pick you up at six again. Then Tuesday, dinner and a movie in the park with me. Wednesday you're free, Thursday I'm taking you out again. Friday is game night, we take all the employees and their families to a baseball game. The weekend is free, but I was hoping you'd agree to hang out with me," Keir said with a bashful smile. "The following week, Monday I have a meeting with XJ executives, so you're free. Tuesday is potluck lunch at the bank, Wednesday and Thursday are date nights with me again, Friday is the big fancy party, and Saturday is the picnic and family game day."

Ally didn't reply, just stood there staring at Keir like he'd lost his mind. She'd known the contract had said two weeks, but she hadn't realized it would be just about every night. And what were these date nights with him?

"Date nights with you? How does that help?"

Keir blushed. "We need to be seen together out socially, not just during bank functions. Would it be so bad being in my company?"

"Depends, honestly," she mumbled under her breath.

"There you two are. Dessert's being served, it's informal, so people are mingling while eating, but they are curious where you two disappeared to," Josie scolded from the back door. "Now get in here before they send out a search party to try to catch you doing something scandalous."

CHAPTER 12

Fate was his new best friend. How else could he explain how well things had played out? Ally was his mate *and* his fake mate. He couldn't have asked for things to turn out any more perfect than that. Now to show her how much she meant to him, and to get his father off his back. Two birds with one stone.

"Hey, Dad," Keir said as Kenneth opened the door. "You busy? I came to collect my stuff and visit."

Kenneth smiled and pulled Keir into a hug, "I wasn't expecting you, but this is great timing. Come in, see the renovations. The contractor is here explaining an issue that arose. So if you don't mind hearing him out with me, I'll show you the changes."

"Sure, let's go," Keir said happily. His father looked good, healthy, and content. Something he hadn't seen in a while.

"Chuck, this is my son, Keir. Son, this is Chuck."

Keir nodded a greeting, sat down across from the man at the kitchen table, and frowned at the empty kitchen area. If they'd been doing construction for a week, wouldn't there be something to show for it by now?

"Hello, as I was just telling your father, there's been a slight complication. The piping from the sink is old and rusted. It's got a small leak that has begun to rot the wood and drywall. We'll have to replace the pipes, wood, and walls. This, of course, puts us a bit behind schedule and will also add to the final cost of the work."

Keir frowned and glanced at his father sadly; he'd been right all along. The loss of his sense of smell did put him at risk. He'd spent all his life relying on it and now this was happening. "Chuck, can you show me the area you're talking about, please?"

"Sure," the man said as he stood and moved from behind the table into the open area. Before the man could utter a word, Keir grasped the other guy's shirt with both hands and threw him up against the wall. The guy groaned as he hit the wall.

"What game are you playing? You're lying to us," Keir growled deep in his throat as he lifted the man on his tiptoes. "You can't lie to shifters, you asshole."

"Keir, what's gotten into you, son?" Kenneth cried out in alarm and panic.

"He's lying, Dad. He's trying to steal money from you. There's nothing wrong with the pipes or the walls, is there, Chuck?"

The man gulped audibly as he slowly shook his head no. "Have you been stalling to jack up the price? And remember, I'll know if you're lying."

The man nodded slowly as his face paled to a ghostly white.

"Here's what you're going to do. You'll finish the renovations as promised to my father's specifications without delay and without any more false or real complications, and you'll do it at the original stated price."

"But . . ." Chuck began to stammer as he shook in Keir's arms.

"No buts, you tried to steal from us. I don't take that kindly. Finish the job and then leave the area. You will never work around here again. If I find out you are, trust me, you won't see me coming. Is that understood?"

"Yes, sir," Chuck said weakly.

"Be finished by next weekend. Now get out of my father's house, you piece of shit."

Keir watched as the man grabbed his pile of papers and ran out of the house like the hounds of hell were nipping at his heels. He turned to his father. "I owe you an apology."

"No. You don't," Kenneth replied sadly as he sank into a chair. "He came with good recommendations. I thought for sure he was a good guy. I always thought it would be at the bank I'd get screwed, not here in my home."

Keir sighed and sat beside him. "I'll talk to Xander and Julia and get things settled and moved around. I'll come to the bank on the condition you stay working there too. You love that place and I don't want to push you out. I'll help you run it, deal?"

"It's a deal. It'll be good to see you every day again . . ." Kenneth trailed off and glanced at his gutted kitchen. "It's a good thing you surprised me today. He would have earned a couple thousand dollars extra for work that he wasn't going to do."

"Did he get anything completed yet? For the amount of time he's been here, I figured it would be done by now."

"He did actually. Your old room is completed and the backyard is done. The kitchen was the only thing left. You want to see them? He did a good job on those even if he is a cheating, lying, sack of rotted skunk ass."

Keir burst into laughter at his dad's words. "That's descriptive and slightly alarming."

"So tell me about this woman I've been hearing about. She's really your mate and not another one of your . . . what do I even call them?"

"How about 'friends'? They are my friends, Dad." Keir sighed, annoyed at his father. "But yes, Ally is my mate. She just doesn't know it yet. She's human, so claiming her right away doesn't work as much as I wish it did."

"But she is coming to the bank festivities, right?"

Keir grinned. "She is and as my mate." Keir spent the next few minutes explaining to his father about the Mate for Hire site and how it matched them up. "So you see, it's kinda perfect. When we go out, she'll pretend to be my mate, and I can show her what it means. I have two weeks to show her she loves me, and then I'll explain she's more than just my hired mate."

"Well, damn. You know I loved your mother and I don't regret a thing. I got you. But if this had been around when I was young, maybe I'd have tried it too. Your friend is a smart man."

"Dad, you know the site isn't really designed to match up mates, it's just to give men a mate to help them out for different events and things. It just kind of worked out that Xander and I got matched with our mates . . . okay, now that I've said that out loud, you've got me wondering too."

A few hours later, Keir was lying on his couch and contemplating the conversation with his father. Could Kingston really have designed the website as a matchmaking site, and played it off as a mate for hire? He's that devious and he's always been a self-professed hopeless romantic. It wouldn't be that out of place for him to do that. Hell, he'd even sworn he'd wait for his mate or die alone. He refused to settle, so it would make sense he'd create something that would ensure people found their other half.

Keir fell asleep thinking about the website and Ally and woke in the morning with memories of the decadent dreams and thoughts of seeing his mate in just a few hours. In the meantime, he needed to talk to Xander and get things figured out there. A lot of changes were coming.

CHAPTER 13

Sunday had flown by for Ally as she relaxed in her small apartment and obsessed over her reaction to Keir's announcement that she was his mate. Her heart had done a flip-flop and joy had filled her, before she understood what he'd been saying. His hired mate, not real mate. For some reason she couldn't quite figure out, it bothered her more than she cared to admit.

She didn't know why. How could she wish to be his mate; she knew how he was with women. But then again, he'd been so different with her. She even understood what he was saying about why he spent so much time with all those different women, and truthfully, other than the one in the bathroom, all the women had been so friendly and welcoming. It was a bit disturbing actually.

"Knock knock, you busy?" Josie called as she entered Ally's small office and startled her out of her thoughts. "What's got you so preoccupied?"

Ally laughed. "Just thinking about the weekend. Thanks again for the party. I had fun and got to meet a lot of pretty awesome people."

"Good, I'm glad. Listen, I stopped by for a couple reasons. First to tell you that Xander and Julia loved your proposals and they want to get started right away."

"Fantastic. That's a great way to start this Monday off properly."

"Second, I heard you were matched with Keir . . ." Josie trailed off.

"Yeah, about that. Can I ask you some questions? But I'm swearing you to secrecy on this."

"Of course, what's on your mind?"

"Mates. What can you tell me about that whole thing? How does it work? I mean, how do they find their mates or know it when they meet them, I guess is what I'm asking."

Josie smiled and sat down. "Can I ask why you want to know?"

Ally blushed and rolled her eyes. "Answer first and I'll explain after. Please, I promise I will," she added at Josie's skeptical look.

"Fine, I was matched with Xander, but like you I didn't know we were real mates until that dinner you were at with us. Apparently, everyone but me knew it though. Shifters aren't like humans in this area. We take our time, get to know one another and fall in love. Shifters know instantly if they are near their mate. It's some kind of scent I think. I'm not sure, honestly. I just know that they know within seconds of meeting that they've found their mate."

"Okay, but that doesn't tell me much."

"Hold on, I'm getting there." Jose laughed. "Impatient much?"

Ally blushed. "Sorry."

"Shifters mate for life. Once they find their other half, that's it for them. They'll never look at another woman again. Cheating doesn't exist either, at least on the shifter side. Humans can, but it's almost unheard of. Shifters will spend the rest of their lives making their mates happy, they will do everything and anything to make them happy, feel

loved, and protect them. It's the ultimate bond in my opinion, you can't find a more secure match in all the world.
Mates are two halves of one whole; they fit together like a
puzzle piece. Like . . ."

"Suddenly everything in your world is right," Ally sup-
plied quietly.

Josie nodded. "Exactly."

Ally didn't say anything, just sat in silence and contemplated her words for a minute. "How do you know if you're
their mate? I mean, how does a human know they are mates
with a shifter?"

All Josie could do was shrug sadly. "We don't. I mean, we
feel a connection to our mate. Sexual attraction is out of
this world too, but we don't feel it like they do. I know I just
thought it was lust and chemistry until I was informed otherwise." Josie squinted her eyes at Ally, bit her lip in contem-
plation and finally blurted out, "Why are you asking this?"

"Keir, of course. He told me I was his mate. My heart did
a flip and then he clarified that I was matched with him as
his mate." Ally sighed. "He said he hasn't been dating anyone in a few weeks, which happens to correspond to the
time I've been in town. When I met him at XJ for our meeting, Bess started to make a comment about word getting
out, and he cut her off. The few times we've been out in public, different women have said things along the lines of 'So
she's the one.'"

Josie tried to hide her smile, but knew she was failing
miserably. "I get it now."

Ally groaned. "What do you get?"

"You want to know if you're his real mate, and he's hiding it from you."

"He's hiding something from me, that's for sure." Ally
groaned again as she flopped back in her chair.

"Do you want to be his mate?" Josie asked quietly.

"It would explain things and make things simpler at the same time."

"Like what?"

"Every time he walks in a room, I know it before I see him. I hear his voice and I need to . . . change . . . you know. It's getting embarrassing. I won't even begin to tell you the dreams I've been having involving him either." Ally laughed self-deprecatingly. "It's like he controls a switch and turns my body on with just a glance, but it's more than that. He makes me laugh, we talked for hours over dinner the other night. We have so much in common, it's almost unreal. He's sweet, kind, romantic, loving, and so damn sexy it makes me want to strip down naked and beg him to take me."

"Would this be a bad time to tell you he's here with me and probably heard most of what you just said?"

Ally jumped up in alarm and stared at her in shock. "You're just now telling me this? What kind of friend are you?"

"If it helps he just got here, and only heard that last bit. He texted me, that's the only reason I know."

"What did he say?" she asked with a small groan of embarrassment.

"That it was lunchtime and I needed to leave now."

Ally frowned. "But it's only ten o'clock . . ." She trailed off as Josie gave her a pointed look. "Oh. Oh . . . um . . ."

Josie laughed, stood, and moved to stand beside her at the desk. She grabbed a pen and jotted something down on a piece of paper before winking. "I'll talk to you later."

Ally stared at the paper and the words written there. "He is, but don't tell him you know. Let him do that when he's ready."

"I know it's true," Keir said in a soft growl. "I turn you on by stepping into a room. I bet you're already soaked and ready to take me into your hot tight pussy. It's okay, beautiful, you don't have to agree. The proof is the sexy scent I get coming straight from between your luscious legs."

Ally quickly grabbed the paper and crumpled it. "What are you . . . doing here?" she asked breathlessly.

"I wanted to see you, so I made up some pretense to come by. I couldn't wait."

She watched as he stepped farther into the room, his smoldering lust-filled eyes never wavering from her. He closed the door, turned the lock, and smiled wickedly. "Your assistant, where is she?"

"Vacation this week. I didn't get a replacement because we're not busy enough to need one yet," Ally rambled as she watched him stride closer to her.

"You know, I've got this fantasy and I think it's a perfect time to try it out. Your desk looks sturdy enough. You might want to clear it off, before I throw everything to the floor."

"What . . . are you . . . why?" she stammered as she found herself clearing it off almost unconsciously.

"Do you know how hot dresses are? They provide such easy access." Keir moved in, leaning on the edge of her desk as if testing its strength. "Sturdy. Good."

His eyes walked the full length of her body and back again. With a low growl, he cleared what was left on top before grabbing Ally and spinning her around so her belly pressed against her desk's beveled edge.

"In this room you usually call the shots, but I'm here now." Even as his breath fanned against the back of her ear, his words were a Taser to her pussy.

Her lower belly jumped at the thought of him, his body, his mastery.

Keir grinned against the soft flesh on the side of her

neck, letting his fingers tug the hem of her dress higher on her thighs.

"The door, Keir . . . lock the door."

"Already done. Now, I'm going to do you."

Ally closed her eyes, suddenly thankful she decided to wear a thong under her snug dress. She gasped as his hand palmed one ass cheek, his thumb running under the edge of the lacy split along her crack.

"Sexy. Even easier access. It's like you knew I was going to come"—he licked the side of her throat and slipped his hands lower—"here"—his fingers played with her damp folds—"and deep in here."

Keir shredded the thin fabric and pulled it from her hips. "So, boss lady. How do you want to get fucked?"

Ally slid her legs apart and leaned over her desk, raising her ass higher. "Any way you want."

He chuckled, letting his hands slide over the outside of her thighs as he slipped to one knee. Spreading her cheeks, his tongue licked her from clit to ass and delved into her wet entrance.

"Mmmmm, juicy and sweet." His mouth took her as his fingers worked her clit and her tight hole.

She gasped, her fingers clutching the far edge of her narrow desk as his mouth pushed her toward climax.

"You're so luscious and sexy, Ally. So wet. Come for me, baby."

Keir slid his thumb into her slick entrance and circled her pleasure center. Ally's body tensed as her climax crashed. He kissed the full-fleshed curve of her ass and slipped his thumb from her, straightening behind her.

She turned and watched him lick her wetness from his hand. He was so damned hot, the sight made her pussy spasm.

He leaned in and took her mouth. "Kiss me, baby. Suck my tongue deep and taste yourself."

A small cry left her mouth as he took her lips, his hands slipping under her dress to cup her breasts. "I want every part of you, Ally," he whispered into her kiss. "Your mouth, your cunt, your ass."

Letting one hand drop, he freed his cock and then grabbed her hips, driving his member deep. Ally broke their kiss, the feel of his thick mass making her knees weak.

Keir pulled back, filling her again. "You like that, Ally, don'tcha? A rock-hard length deep in your pussy. I can smell your juice on me, so wet it's dripping down my balls."

His other hand dropped to her hips and he pulled her back, driving his member hard before pulling out.

"Keir!"

He fisted his shaft. "Turn around, baby. I want to watch your eyes as I fuck you. Watch you as my hard length slips in and out of your tight slit."

Ally turned and as she did, he lifted her to the end of the desk, spreading her knees wide. "Stroke me, Ally. Feel my thick head."

She slid her hand down his corded length, her own juice making his skin like silk in her hand.

"That's it, work me, babe. Work my cock."

Her eyes met his, and gritting her teeth she let go of his sex and grabbed his hips. "Keir! Please!"

With a smirk, he jerked her ass to the end of the desk and drove his cock deep. She locked her legs around his hips and he lifted her with a low growl, turning with her until her back pressed against the floor-to-ceiling office glass.

With her ass pressed against the glass, the office windows rattled in their frames behind as he rode her, banging her into the thick panes.

She cried out, her body in spasms as her head pressed back against the cold glass. Her inner walls convulsed as she came and she dug her fingers into his shoulders.

"Look at me, Ally," he ordered and her eyes found his, dark and feral with need.

He snarled, letting his lion raise to just below the surface and her body quivered at the raw animal sensuality. Keir's body tensed and he threw his head back with a roar, emptying himself deep. He held her tight to his hips, letting every drop pump from his sex until he exhaled, his head falling forward onto her shoulder.

The two slipped to the polished floor still entwined, his arms still wrapped tight around her waist. "So, boss lady, how's that for an office introduction?"

She sucked in a breath. "I don't care if you weren't looking for a job, you're hired."

CHAPTER 14

"You got a minute?" Keir looked up to see Xander standing in his doorway.

"Sure, I actually needed to speak to you too. What's up?"

Xander shut the door and moved to sit in the chair beside him. "I just talked to Josie, she wanted to make sure that you were still going to pay Ally to be your hired mate. She's worried that if you tell her too soon, she won't accept the money. Ally has to have that money."

Keir frowned in confusion. "Why? What am I missing?"

"Ally's mom is dying. She signed up for the website to get the money to enroll her mom in a trial of a new chemo that they are hoping will give her a chance."

"Shit, of course I'll pay her. Is it enough to cover their expenses? Does she need more do you know?"

"No, Ally told them it was enough with a bit extra for some help around the house." Xander sighed. "Sara apparently is trying to gather money, but with her kids it's tight. Maxton is MIA with the military and unaware of how serious things have gotten."

"How is she holding up with all this on her shoulders? I can't even fathom it."

"It's why she moved here and opened the branch of her

company. It came with a bonus and a raise. The worst part is now her mom is alone, an hour away."

"I love Arlene, she was always so sweet to us growing up. Is there anything we can do?"

Xander shrugged. "Ally hasn't even confided in you or me about this yet. Our hands are tied until she does."

"This sucks. She filled the hole in my life after my mother died. Even to this day I get Christmas and birthday cards from her. She's never once said a word about being sick."

"I know, not to me either. Julia talks to her at least once a month."

The two men lapsed into silence as they reminisced about Arlene and all the ways she'd been there for them through the years. Come hell or high water, Keir knew they'd figure out a way to help somehow.

"What did you want to talk to me about anyway?" Xander asked a few minutes later.

"My time at XJ is ending. My father was right."

"Shit, what happened?" Xander asked furiously. "I can't imagine anyone cheating him. Everyone he works with at the bank has been there for years."

"Not at the bank. He hired a contractor to redo the house. It was chance I stopped by when the guy was there. It was a Sunday, who would have thought, you know? Anyway, he was spinning some tale about needing more money to replace leaking pipes and rotted floors."

"Lies? Is he still alive or do we need to bury the body?"

Keir laughed. "It's been twenty-four hours. If he was dead, don't you think I'd have called you already? Can't leave him sitting around after all."

"Good point." Xander laughed. "So what did you do?"

"Threatened him, made him promise to finish the work

this week. Oh, and if he attempted to do business with any-one else in this town, I would kill him."

Xander nodded. "Sounds perfect to me. If it's not fin-ished properly, let me know. I'll help you hunt the bastard down."

"I've got a few things to finish up here business-wise, I've already gone through and delegated what I could. I can finish up what can't be given away over the next couple weeks. If you don't mind splitting me for that time?"

"You know I don't and you'll always have a place here if you want it." Xander paused and nodded his head to the area where his assistant, Bess, sat outside his office. "Have you told her yet?"

"Hell no. I'm scared to."

Xander laughed. "I'd hate to see her go, but if she wants to follow you, it's fine with me. She'd be an asset to you."

"Thanks, brother, that means a lot."

"So now one last question. Does your mate know how insane these bank functions can get?"

"Get out of my office, you overgrown carpet, and ask Bess to come in. It's time I told her before she hears it through her spy network."

"I already know, boss," Bess said as she opened the door and passed by Xander as he made his way out.

Keir jumped and spun around to face her. "How in the hell do you do that? You know everything practically before we do. Are you psychic or something?"

Bess laughed. "Gossip, it's the fastest thing I've ever seen. So the only question is when are you leaving?"

"I'm going to go back and forth for the next couple of weeks while I finish up a few things, but for the most part I'll be there. I've handed off a majority of the things I was handling. The only question is . . ."

"That's not a question; I've been with you since you joined the company all those years ago. I'm too old to break someone else in. If you'll have use of me, of course."

Keir smiled. "It wouldn't be the same without you. I kind of hoped you'd want to follow me over. My dad already knew it was a possibility and he was very happy to make it work as well."

"Good, now on to more important things. How's that mate of yours? I hear you've been spotted out together a couple times."

"You really are scary, woman. But to answer your question, she is fine. She'll be attending the bank functions as my mate. Which, by the way, you are invited to attend as well."

"Sounds like fun, I think it might be beneficial for me to attend. Get to know everyone in a relaxed environment."

"Oh, and since you know everything or can find out anything as the case may be, I need your skills put to work if you don't mind."

"For you, anything."

"Arlene Fosey, Ally's mom."

"The nice lady who always sends you the cards and calls to check up on you. Yes, I know who she is."

"That's her. She's got cancer and is dying. Can you find out anything you can, please? Xander and I want to help, but we're not sure what we can do. She's signing up for a trial as well. Can you dig up any information on it you can? Let's try to make sure things are legit, if possible."

"I'll get right on it, boss, but in the meantime it's four and if I'm not mistaken, there is a dinner tonight for the board of directors that you're taking Ally to. Might I suggest you leave a bit early and go get ready?"

Keir laughed. "Yes, ma'am. I'm on my way out the door now."

It was true; he'd been useless since he'd gotten back to the office after seeing Ally. His every thought was of her and when he could see her again. This pussycat had been pussy whipped and he was loving every single moment of it. Hell, he'd actually caught a couple people staring at him with frightened eyes as he'd walked down the hall whistling.

He couldn't wait for his father to meet Ally, they'd get along famously. His little firecracker kept things lively and entertaining and that's just what this bunch at the bank needed, and if things got too boring, he had a special present he'd picked up for Ally that promised fun.

CHAPTER 15

"Mom, stop laughing at me, this is serious. They're bank executives, that almost automatically qualifies them as pretentious assholes."

"Darling, stop worrying. Just be yourself, everyone loves you. Now stop fussing, put on the black dress you sent me the picture of first and relax. Your man will be there shortly and you need to make sure you are dressed and not keeping him waiting."

"I swear, I don't know what I'd do without you."

"Well, if I have my way you won't have to find out. By the way, I called the doctor and told him the money was in. He's set me up for the first round of treatments at the end of the week."

"I'll come up Friday night, I don't want you alone. We don't know what the side effects will be, and I don't want to be so far away."

"Stop right there, young lady. I have the nurse already on standby. You are not to do any such thing. Enjoy this time with Keir. I'll be fine, I promise."

"Mom," Ally protested as tears poured down her face. "I—"

"Ally, stop. I can hear the tears in your voice. You have a date to get ready for, stop crying, go wash your face, and show him how happy he makes you."

"How do you know he does?"

Arlene laughed. "Baby, I can hear it in your voice. Every time we talk love rings through your voice when you mention him. You're constantly texting me little things about him, or things you've done together. You're in love, and it would seem to me he loves you. I've known that man for many years. He's a keeper, you can count on that."

"I love you."

"I love you too, now make sure you call me tomorrow and let me know how many of those bankers fell in love with you and your vivacious personality tonight."

Ally laughed and hung up. Her mom was one in a million. They hadn't been close when Ally was growing up—being away at boarding school had that effect—but they'd more than made up for it as adults. Her mom was her best friend, confidante, and biggest supporter. There wasn't a day that went by that she didn't talk to her mom in some form or another. Cancer was trying to steal that from her and it was unacceptable. They had to find a way to beat it, she couldn't lose her, not after losing her father already.

The doorbell chimed and Ally threw a panicked look at the wall clock. It was only five thirty, what was he doing here so early?

She pulled the door open, ready to yell at him when she was stunned speechless. "Keir?" she asked quietly in surprise.

"I didn't want to bring you flowers again, so I thought this would be fun," he said as he held up a small tan kitten. "It's a mini lion," he joked bashfully. "So even if I'm not here, you won't be alone completely."

"It's adorable. What's its name? Boy or girl? I love it," Ally cried as she pulled the small body into her arms and cuddled it.

"I've got all the supplies in the car, but first, it has no name yet and it's a boy." Keir stepped forward. "I missed you, baby," he whispered as he placed a soft kiss to her lips and turned to head back to the car.

She didn't know what to say, she was overwhelmed. She stumbled to the couch and sat down. "Aren't you the most handsome little man," she cooed as the kitten meowed in reply.

"We have to leave by six fifteen to make it on time. I'll get everything set up for the little guy while you finish getting ready," Keir called as he passed by her and placed his packages down.

"I don't want to leave him now," Ally cried as she hugged the small creature and nuzzled his head.

"Hhhmmm, I might not have thought this one through. I'm getting jealous of the damn thing," Keir growled as he stalked forward. "He's got a play area for tonight. He'll be fine while we're gone."

"He's so little, what if he gets scared?"

Keir laughed. "What if I asked Josie or Shawna to come over and cat sit for the night? Would that make you go get ready?"

Ally laughed. "Yes, it would."

Keir laughed but agreed. Ally smiled and raced back to her room to repair the damage to her face from the earlier crying fit and to remove the tiny cat hairs that were now littering her black dress.

"Beautiful, I've got one other thing for you," Keir said as he followed her into her bedroom.

"It better not involve removing any clothes. We'll never get out of here if it does," Ally joked as Keir handed her a small black bag.

"Well, that would depend on what you're already wearing."

Ally gasped as she pulled out a skimpy pair of panties with an attached vibrator. "I'm so not wearing these tonight."

Keir laughed and held up the remote control. "Come on, if this gets boring just think of the fun we can have."

"No. I want to make a good impression on your father and the board, not come across as some harlot. There's no way, as you found out this morning, that I can be quiet with you that close to me."

"Fine, but you have to promise to wear them another time for me to make up for this." Keir pouted good-naturedly.

"Go away, you perv." Ally laughed as she pushed him out the door. When she emerged from her room twenty minutes later, it was to find Shawna curled up on the couch snuggling with the little kitten. Keir gawked at her as she walked in.

"What?" she asked in alarm as she spun around to face the mirror and see what he was staring at.

"You look like a goddess," Keir said in awe. "I've never seen anyone more beautiful than you. We need to leave before I peel that dress off right here on the living room floor."

Ally blushed and shrugged in apology to Shawna.

"It's sexy. Don't apologize for him wanting you. That's the way it should be. Now, go have fun and rest assured me and the little lion here are all set for a night in. Don't hurry home or hell, don't come home. It's fine either way," she said with a waggle of her eyebrows.

The drive to the restaurant was short. They pulled up to the valet and Ally smiled as the attendant whistled as she climbed out of the car. The poor guy was scared shitless when Keir walked up and growled. "Stop frightening the boy," Ally chided good-naturedly.

"He shouldn't ogle you like that, it's rude."

Ally didn't reply, his caveman tendencies were out in force tonight, but for some reason she found it sexy. To her and all the other women they passed he was courteous, to the men he stared them down if he felt they were watching her a little too intently.

"I think you gave that last patron a heart attack. You really need to stop growling at the old men. Their hearts can't take it."

"I know what they are thinking and it's wrong. They have their own dates they need to be paying attention to, not mine."

Ally couldn't refute that comment, it was true. One or two of them had actually turned around to stare at them as they passed, leaving their partners in the lurch. It was rude and ungentlemanly. She was glad when the maître d' escorted them to the private and reserved room away from the crowds and lingering stares.

"Father, I'd like you to meet my mate, Ally. Babe, this is my father, Kenneth Harper."

"It's a pleasure to meet you, Mr. Harper. I've heard wonderful things about you. Keir speaks very highly of you."

Kenneth laughed. "Is that so. I shudder to think of the things he probably told you in truth, but you're a born diplomat I think. I can say with perfect honesty that he has spoken of you often and with great affection. He failed to do your beauty justice, though."

Ally smiled. "I see where Keir got his glib tongue from. You Harper men are sweet talkers."

Keir laughed and leaned over to whisper in her ear, but Ally knew as soon as the words had left her mouth what he was going to say. "Don't you dare, Keir. I know what you're thinking and you shush."

It was Kenneth's turn to laugh now. "Oh yes, I like this one a lot. She's feisty. You need that, son. Ally, if you'd do me the honors, I'd love to introduce you around while my son fetches us a drink."

"I'd be delighted," Ally said with a slight curtsy, which made both men chuckle.

The hours dragged on as Ally sat through one boring conversation after another. Occasionally she'd catch a glimpse of Keir as she was pulled from one person to the next, everyone eager to welcome her to the bank family.

The first chance she got she was going to apologize for not wearing the damn toy. Keir was right; this party was going to be the death of her.

"Would you mind if I stole my mate for a moment?" Keir interjected when one long-winded executive took a breath of air. "I really need to speak to her, I apologize for interrupting you."

They quickly walked to the back of the room and to a darkened corner. "I think my ears are bleeding. How much longer?" Ally pleaded.

"They're serving dinner now. After that we can escape and no one will think twice. Can you hold up for a bit longer? I promise this is the worst of the events," Keir replied with a soft kiss to her forehead.

"I'll try, but please tell me I get to sit next to you. I can't handle much more of these old men slobbering over me."

Keir laughed. "Yes, between my father and myself. You should have some buffer now. If it helps, everyone loves you. I've been congratulated by most of them on landing a woman as special as you. I have to admit, I agree with them. You are a jewel. Thank you for putting up with this for me."

"If it wasn't for you, I doubt I'd have stuck around this long. Money or not, I'd have walked two hours ago."

Keir had been right, Ally thought later that week. The dinner had been the worst of the events. Not that she could compare Tuesday's date to anything she'd ever done. Keir had outdone himself. A lovely dinner at Ricardo's followed by a leisurely stroll to the park where they'd watched an old black-and-white film on a blanket he'd set out and had held ready for him till they'd arrived.

Wednesday she'd planned on staying home and relaxing, but Keir had shown up with takeout and a movie. Not that she had any idea what movie he'd brought with him. They'd never it made that far. Thursday had been another date, this time he'd picked her up and brought her back to his house where he'd cooked for her. Who would have guessed he was a gourmet cook? The food had been orgasmic, as had the rest of the night, she thought with a blush.

Friday had been her favorite event with the bank. The employees and their families were fun, loud, and everything the board wasn't. The baseball game had been a blast despite the home team losing. They'd shared hot dogs, cotton candy, and popcorn until they got in a fight with it. Kenneth had taken it away with a roll of his eyes, grumbling about kids these days.

It was Saturday and Ally was lying in bed recounting the week's adventures to her mom on the phone, as Arlene listened quietly. She'd had her first chemo treatment of the new trial drug one day before and it was wreaking havoc on her body. Ally had never heard her mother sound so weak and frail.

"I told you . . . he was a . . . keeper," Arlene rasped a

few moments after Ally finished talking. "Sounds like . . .
love to . . . me."

Ally didn't reply, she had a lump in her throat that made it
impossible to speak around. She couldn't help but wonder if
the treatment was worse than the disease at times like this.

"Stop . . . I'll be . . . fine," Arlene tried to stress. "Tell
me . . . what's next . . . for you two."

"Let's see," Ally said as she attempted to clear her throat.
"There's a potluck lunch at the bank on Tuesday, Friday is
the big fancy party for all the employees and their signifi-
cant others. Saturday is a picnic and game day."

"How were . . . the women?"

Ally laughed. "Surprising, actually. No matter where we
went, someone was there he'd dated or been with. They were,
for the most part, nice. He knew every one of their names,
and asked about their lives. It's the weirdest thing. He wasn't
lying, these women really are his friends."

"Told you he's . . . a good man."

"Yes, Mom. You did. I shouldn't have doubted you for a
second."

"What are . . . you going to . . . make for . . . the potluck?"

"Leave it to you, Mom, go right for the food," Ally said,
laughing. "I'm not sure, to be honest. Do you have any suggestions that they might like?"

"No . . . you plan this . . . one out," Arlene said with a
small laugh that caused her to cough uncontrollably.

"Ma'am." The nurse came on the phone. "She needs to
go. I'll have her call you back later. Don't worry, though,
she's fine."

Ally hung up and collapsed into tears. It was so hard to
hear her mother so sick and know there wasn't anything

she could do to help. She wasn't sure how long she lay there and dozed, the last thing she remembered was crying as she hung up with her mother's nurse.

"Babe, what's wrong? I've been calling you for hours," Keir said as he crawled into bed next to Ally and pulled her into his side. "Are you sick? What do you need?"

"I'm fine. It's my mom. She had her first treatment Friday and it's bad, so bad. I can't lose my mom, Keir," she whispered in between broken sobs.

"Why didn't you tell me she was going? I would have taken you up there to be with her."

"She has a nurse, she told me to stay here." Ally sniffled.

"Josie told Xander. We love Arlene, she was a staple in both of our lives. You don't have to go through this alone."

"I was talking to her this morning, and the nurse took the phone and hung up. Said she was too sick then to talk anymore. Keir, I've never heard her like that. I'm scared."

Keir sighed and pulled her closer. "I know, baby, but the one thing I know about your mom is that she has a core of strength. She won't give up without a fight."

"I feel so helpless."

"Why? You did everything you could so she could get into this trial. You, love, are amazing, wonderful, and loving. Do you want to drive up and see your mom?"

"No, she begged me not to. She's going for another treatment on Monday, and it's going to be worse she said." Ally laughed bitterly. "Worse, can you imagine?"

"It's supposed to help, right? It's got a good chance of curing her cancer, right?" Keir asked hopefully.

Ally shrugged. "They don't know. This treatment does have a good success rate, but she's the first for her type of cancer. It's a really rare form and there aren't many treatments that are effective for it yet."

"Then we'll just keep our fingers crossed, send out positive thoughts, and hope it works. In the meantime, let's get you cleaned up and get some food in you."

CHAPTER 16

He was exhausted, worn out, and heart sore. He'd spent all weekend with Ally. They'd played with the still unnamed kitten, watched movies, cooked dinner together, and fell asleep in each other's arms. They'd spoken to Arlene late Sunday night, but only for a minute. The treatment was brutal, and the poor woman couldn't stay lucid for more than a few minutes at a time.

"Keir?" Bess called as he walked by her in his zombie state.

"Yes?" he grumbled.

"Let me get coffee, I'll be right in," she said with a worried frown as she took off toward the staff break room.

Keir nodded, walked to his desk, and flopped down into his chair. Arlene was on the way for her second treatment. All he could think of was how was she going to handle it, when she was still so sick from the last round?

"Here. Drink this," Bess said softly as she placed the cup in front of him.

"Thanks."

"It's Arlene, isn't it?" Bess whispered fearfully. "That's what I've got to talk to you about."

"What?"

"I'm here," Xander called as he came running into the room and stopped short in surprise at the sight of Keir.

"Good, you'll both want to hear this. Arlene's prognosis is not good, as you both know. She's currently maxed out all her credit cards and her house is in foreclosure. I don't think the kids know that part either. The trial she's enrolled in has good success for some types of cancer. Hers is questionable. The side effects, as you saw this weekend, are horrendous. More than a few participants ended up in the hospital due to complications."

"How do you know that?" Xander asked quietly. "If it's a trial, the information is kept confidential. From what I know everyone is given a control number so names aren't even used."

Bess smiled ruefully. "You'd be right, but I have my sources everywhere."

"What else do you know?" Keir asked hoarsely.

"She's going to be kicked out of her house within the next two weeks at the most. Every spare cent the family had was used to pay for treatments and doctors' visits. Arlene needs help, she doesn't need to be worrying where she'll live if she is going to beat this."

"What do we do?" Xander asked quietly.

"I've already talked to the oldest daughter, Sara, discreetly of course. She is strapped financially and roomwise can't handle another body. Arlene is very close to Ally, and I personally think it's the best option. But the woman has a ferocious stubborn streak, as you both probably know already."

Keir and Xander laughed in acknowledgment. "Like mother, like daughter," Keir said with a sad smile.

"I've taken it upon myself to talk to Julia. We have a plan. Julia is going to handle Arlene. Your grandmother is the only person I know who could get her way with Arlene. Keir, you're going to have to tell your mate the truth and get her to move in with you. Xander, with your permission, Julia has offered XJ Financial to pay the rent for your old apartment, for Arlene to live in."

"That won't be necessary, actually," Xander said sheepishly. "I didn't think I'd be moving out of the apartment anytime in the future, so when the building came up for sale a few years ago, I bought it. Figured it was a good investment. She can live there rent-free, for as long as she wants."

"Bess, I love you, you know that. So when I say this, know I mean it with affection. You scare the shit out of me," Keir said straight-faced.

Xander burst into laughter. "I second that. Damn, woman, you are amazing."

Bess blushed and smiled. "Shush, you two."

"So what do we need to do?" Keir asked with the first genuine smile he'd felt in a few days.

"Simple, for now nothing. Julia is already on her way to Arlene's. She has the hard part of convincing her to leave. When that's done, we'll call in the cavalry and move everyone around. Until then, life goes on as normal. But Keir, you better step up your game and get your woman warmed to the truth, come hell or high water she's moving in with you."

"I think she was a general in her past life," Xander whispered as they watched Bess make her way back to her desk with her usual quiet efficiency. "You look awful, what happened?"

"Ally fell apart this weekend. It's killing her to be so far away from her mom. She was on the phone with Arlene Saturday when the nurse apologized and hung up, and said her mother was too sick to talk then."

"Damn," Xander said softly.

"Yeah, I can't even imagine how that felt. From what I've gathered those two have become as thick as thieves. I remember when my mother died, but I was still so young. I don't think I understood it well, you know. It's not like it is for Ally."

"Why don't you take the day off? You're going to be done soon anyway, let me handle the meeting tonight. If you're there, you'll try to take on a new project or something and you don't need that right now. Go get Ally, and go do something fun. Take her mind off what's happening with her mom for a couple of hours."

"You won't mind?"

"Not at all. She needs you, I understand. Keep me updated, though, if anything changes."

Keir nodded, grabbed his things, and raced out of the office. He was sure he broke at least a half dozen traffic laws in his rush to get to Ally. He'd called and spoken to her assistant and explained the situation. All of Ally's meetings were moved and she would be ready when he arrived, she'd reassured Keir.

Within minutes of leaving his office, he pulled to a stop outside her building and smiled as Ally opened the door to his car and stared at him in confusion. "What's going on?"

"Come on, I want to take you someplace and we need to talk."

"It's a workday, Keir. This couldn't have happened on the weekend or at night? You've got too much going on with switching jobs to be taking time off right now," she scolded gently.

"Beautiful, trust me. We both need this."

Ally didn't reply, just rolled her eyes, turned to stare out the window, and got lost in her thoughts. Every once in a while, Keir could see a tear fall down her cheek in the reflection of the side window.

"Baby, we're here," Keir said softly as he gently shook Ally awake. She'd fallen asleep after a few minutes. He hated to wake her so he'd driven around for a while. Finally, his bladder had made the decision for him. They needed to stop.

"Where are we?" she asked groggily.

"The zoo."

Ally blinked her bleary eyes and stared at him in confusion. "Did you say 'zoo'?"

Keir laughed at her disgruntled tone. "Yes, come on. I want to show you something."

"But the zoo? Really?"

"I know it's an odd place for a shifter to go, but come on. My mom used to take me when I was a kid. She loved the big cat exhibits the most. Guess it fit since she ended up with my father."

"You're a lion shifter, why would she take you to a place they keep lions penned up?"

Keir laughed. "Yeah, when you look at it that way. But I didn't see that when I came here." Keir paid their admission and ushered her through the turnstile. "Look around, see how the kids and parents are laughing, smiling, and talking? See how excited they are to see the animals?"

"Yes, it's kind of disturbing considering I'm sleeping with someone who shifts into one of those very animals."

"Come on," he laughed. They stopped in front of the lions and Keir moved to stand behind her. "What do you see?"

"Lions and lionesses in captivity."

"Yes, but you know what I see?" he asked softly as he leaned down so his mouth was next to her ear.

"I see a pride. A family of lions."

"I still don't understand this," she grumbled softly.

"My father wasn't very good at communicating with me

when I was little. Everything I learned about being a lion and what noble creatures they are was from coming here. My mom urged my father to talk to me, but he didn't know how. She did the next best thing she could think of. It's a bit unconventional, but then so am I. I used to sit here for hours and watch them. I studied their behaviors, the way they interacted, and one day I realized that I felt in touch with that half of who I was. For the first time, I felt peace deep within myself."

"That's kind of sad," Ally whispered as she leaned closer to the glass enclosure.

"It is, but it's not too. I was spiraling down a path after my mother passed away. Arlene was the one who brought me back to the zoo. She sat down beside me and we watched the lions for hours. Finally, she took my hand and told me that she'd promised my mom to watch out for me. She held me as I cried and mourned the loss of her. When I thought I couldn't cry for another second, I looked up and there was one of the lionesses standing right at the glass a few feet from me, staring at me. I slid off the bench and moved until we were face-to-face. In that moment, I knew my mom was still there with me. She'd sent that lioness to remind me of who I was."

Ally smiled and brushed away a tear. "I never knew that. I had no idea you were so close to my mom."

"Not *were*, baby. Am." Keir chuckled softly. "Your mother called me the day after our first dinner date at Ricardo's. The one where we accidentally met and shared a meal together."

"She did?" Ally asked in shock. "Why?"

"Because, believe it or not, she calls me once a week or so to check in. She does the same with Xander as well. She still treats us as her kids."

"What did she say when you told her we'd had dinner?"

"She laughed, said she always knew I'd end up part of the family."

Ally sputtered and turned to look at him. "What does . . . I mean . . ."

"I mean that I told her you were my mate, the one I'd spent my entire life searching for. The one person my soul yearned for above all others."

"My mom knows?" Ally said in shock. "She never said a word to me. I was trying to figure out how to tell her, but she already knows."

It was Keir's turn to gape in shock. "How to tell her? You mean you already knew?"

"I guessed and Josie confirmed it for me. Too many odd things weren't making sense, I figured it out. As much as I wanted to fight it, I fell in love with you the moment I met you."

"I can't tell you how happy that makes me and my lion to hear you say that. I'm never letting you go. I hope you know that."

"I don't want you to. I'd be miserable without you."

"There's something else. Come sit down with me," Keir said as he pulled her to a nearby bench. "Your mom is losing the house, it's in foreclosure. I just found out today, but not from her."

"What?" Ally cried in alarm. "She'd tell me if things were that bad. I know she would."

"It's okay. Julia is on her way there now to convince your mom to move to your apartment. She's independent and won't tolerate you hovering, so I was hoping you'd move in with me. I'd ask you to marry me, but I didn't know if that was too soon."

"*Carajo*, you tell me you love me, propose kind of, and tell me that my dying mother is homeless all in the span of a minute. What's wrong with you?"

"Ah . . . I'm not sure how to answer that safely," Keir admitted sheepishly.

Ally laughed. "You are going to keep things interesting, aren't you? Yes, I'll move in with you. We practically live together now anyway. Thank you for doing this, I don't know if I could have handled this without you by my side."

"I love you, beautiful."

Ally frowned. "Wait, did you bring me to a public place on purpose so I wouldn't make a scene if I'd handled this differently?"

"I might have. You can have a bit of a temper, or so I've been informed. I was hedging my bets. But I also thought that maybe if you knew that story about your mom, it would help you see why we want to help so much."

"You are so on the couch tonight."

"You haven't even moved in and I'm already regulated to the couch?"

"It's okay. I'll join you there," Ally said with a wink.

CHAPTER 17

Ally couldn't help but smile as they walked back to the car hand in hand. Never in her wildest dreams could she have imagined the last few weeks of her life. Keir had become so much more than just the irritating manwhore she'd first assumed he was. He was the man of her dreams in more than one way. He'd moved mountains to make things right in her world.

"Beautiful, do you mind if I call Bess and tell her you said yes?"

"No, why would I mind that?" she asked in confusion.

"Because she's a tornado and by this time tomorrow I'll bet you're moved into my house and settled already. Give it another two days, and the apartment will be cleaned and your mom's stuff being moved in."

"She can't have that much power . . . can she?"

Keir laughed and dialed the phone. "Bess—" he began before he was interrupted. "Hold on, let me put you on speaker."

"Ally, I'm so happy you said yes. I've already got a mover at your apartment boxing everything up. Your furniture is going to storage unless you tell me otherwise. A cleaning service is scheduled for tomorrow morning, and your mother will be here by Thursday at the latest."

"Bess?"

"Yes, Ally?"

"How did you know I'd say yes, and how did you arrange all this so quickly?"

"Because it was obvious you were meant to be with Keir, as for the rest . . . I have my ways. You'll be happy to know your mother is home and resting. Julia and the nurse are there and they've informed me she is comfortable. She tolerated the treatment much better this time so far. The doctors are optimistic she won't get as sick."

Keir smiled at Ally. "Don't fight it, beautiful, just accept Bess for the force of nature she is. I do and my life has been so much smoother."

"Keir, you need to go by your father's place and check on the work. The contractor should have been finished yesterday. He's canceled all future work and has put his house up for sale as well."

"Wait, I didn't even tell you about that one," Keir said with a frown.

Ally laughed. "You are something, Bess. I'm glad you work for Keir."

"Thank you, honey. Now, you better figure out a name for that kitten before I name it for you. Have a good day."

Ally and Keir exchanged looks before they both burst into laughter. "Does she have our houses, cars, and offices bugged?" Ally asked, exasperated.

"I'm afraid to ask. Between her and Julia, they know everything that goes on, everywhere."

"Would you mind if I went with you to your dad's? I'm not ready to be away from you yet."

"I'd love it, and something tells me he will too."

The next few days were a whirlwind of emotions as they consolidated their two homes into one and prepared for

Arlene's arrival. Bess had been right, the treatment had been easier and Arlene was already out of bed and overseeing the packing of her house. She'd put up a bit of a fight, but quickly gave in under the combined forces of Julia and Bess.

Ally rolled over in bed and grabbed her phone off the nightstand. "Hey, Mom, how are you?"

"Fantastic. Okay, that might be a stretch, but I'm feeling pretty good, all things considered. I wanted to ask you a favor."

"Sure, anything, you know that."

"When I was in the waiting room the other day, one of the other patients told me about a new drug trial. They're having phenomenal results, or so this patient said. I was hoping you'd come with me to the informational meeting I set up."

"Of course, when is it?"

"Friday night. I know you have the party at the bank, and I hate to ask . . ."

Ally glanced over her shoulder at Keir and raised a brow, knowing he'd have heard every word her mother had said.

"Sure, we can take her, no problem. My father will understand."

"You bet, Mom, Keir and I will be there. Can you text me the details?"

"Sure thing, now I've got to run. We're packing up the last of the house and I'll be there bright and early tomorrow."

"I hope you don't mind a bit of a welcoming party. Last I heard everyone is so excited to see you that we might bombard you."

"In that case, how about we let the movers do their thing and I have Julia bring me to your new home. I'd love to see it anyway."

"That's perfect. See you tomorrow.

Ally rolled over and laid her head on her mate's chest. "You mind if we get bombarded?"

"No, they're family, they can never be a bother. But right now I've got much more important things on my mind."

She raised her brows, curious as to what was on his mind. "Oh, and what's that?"

He licked her shoulder. "I want to make you mine."

"When?" she gulped, loving the wild look in his eyes.

"Now."

Ally went up on one elbow. "Now? But I thought—"

He shook his head. "Thought what? That living together would be it?" Keir chuckled, running a finger down her soft cheek. "When have I ever settled for just 'it'?"

Warmth started in both her cheeks and her lower belly. Keir never settled. Not in life and certainly not in the bedroom, although why he wanted her still boggled her mind.

As if he could read the doubt in her eyes, he cupped her cheek. "It's you, Ally. Only you, and if you don't know that by now then I haven't done my job."

"Job?" She held her breath.

"Working your luscious body until it craves mine every second of every day, the way mine craves yours. You're mine, Ally. My mate, and it's about time I showed you just how much I want you."

He kicked the covers from them both and then pulled her close, his lips taking her mouth. He ran a raspy tongue along the bottom seam and she opened for him. Hungry and determined, he kissed her deep, and she met the challenge.

As their breath mingled and tongues tangled, Ally dug her fingers into Keir's hair as he rolled her beneath him. His mouth moved from her lips to her throat, trailing along the deep cleft between her full breasts. He took one nipple and flicked the hardening peak, grazing his teeth along the puckering bud.

Ally moaned and arched higher and he smiled against her soft flesh, reaching for her other breast. "Fuck, baby. Your skin is like silk." He thumbed her nipple while his mouth sucked and teased the other.

Wetness pooled between her legs and he chuckled. "Mmmm. I love the scent of your wet sex." He slid lower, pushing himself between her legs and knelt with his face inches from her slick pink folds. "But I love the taste of you more."

With his thumb, he circled her clit before dipping his mouth to the hard nub. He slipped the sensitive bud between his lips and pulled, letting it pop from his mouth before spreading her wide to lick her wet entrance.

"Open for me, Ally. Take your hands and let me see you spread yourself."

Ally let her knees drop wide and slid a hand down her belly until she slipped her fingers into her folds. One finger, then another dipped inside as he watched her work herself.

"That's it, baby. Curl your fingers deep. Work those hips."

She arched her back, her hand tense, and, as though he knew she was close, he pulled her fingers from her cleft, lifting the slick coated digits to his mouth.

"Good to the last drop." He grinned, licking his fingers clean.

"Keir! Stop playing!" Ally's eyes flashed, insistent and angry.

His eyes met hers and his fingers trailed the inside flesh of her thighs, just brushing her swollen pink sex. "What is it you want, then?"

"You! Your cock! Your . . . . your . . . ."

He flicked her clit with his thumb again and she cried out, near begging. "My?"

"Your mark! All right? I want it all! Everything. Your hardness. Deep. Coming inside me. I want your babies."

He growled and his lion was there beneath the surface, ready to claim her, take her, own her, have her as his alone.

Slipping his hands under her ass, he flipped her onto all fours and without missing a beat, pulled her hips back, driving his cock into her waiting sex. He buried his cock shaft deep, holding her tight while his head swelled inside.

"You feel that, baby?" He lifted her against his chest, one arm tight around her waist while the other worked her clit. "That's my head ready to blow. Not like before." He kissed her throat, letting the hand on her waist slip over sweat-sheened skin to her breast, pinching her nipple.

"I'm so deep inside you, you're going to feel me for days."

She turned her head and he took her mouth, driving his cock up and in, lifting her with each thrust. "You're mine, inside and out. Always."

He let her climax build until tears pricked her eyes, her body ready to explode.

"Come for me, baby. Milk every drop from my cock." He let go of her waist and Ally fell forward, arching her back so her ass rose high.

Keir grabbed her hips and pulled back, driving his member hard and Ally's body shuddered as she came, her walls spasming against his thickness as he slammed into her over and over.

He held her hips tight, his head back as he roared, his shaft forcing his release deep inside. He held his lion back, allowing only his canines to descend, his fangs piercing her skin as she came again.

Ally cried out, her body trembling as he took her nape

and her pussy, until his tongue swiped the tender spot at the base of her neck. She slumped forward, taking him with her, and the two collapsed on the bed, his arms around her tight.

"You are mine now, Ally. In all ways."

She inhaled their salty, sex sweat scent, her body still trembling with aftershocks. "I always was, Keir."

He growled against her hair. "That kind of talk might get a lady fucked again."

Their bodies still entwined, she ground her ass back and his member thickened inside. "I'm yours for the taking."

CHAPTER 18

She'd done it. Ally had lost her mind and gave into his insistence to go out to do something fun. What his idea of fun meant was a local carnival that had gone up not long ago at a high school near them.

After walking around all over the place, eating all kinds of delicious, fattening—but who cared about fat, right?—carnival food, she was now being coerced into going on a roller coaster. She didn't do roller coasters. She was not the kind of person who found them to be much fun. If he got her to enjoy it, it would be a first.

"No."

"What do you mean 'no'? It's fun, Ally. C'mon. You'll love it."

She gave him a short laugh. "Yeah, right, like I'd like having my head shoved in a lion's mouth."

Keir pulled her close and licked the leftover cotton candy sugar from the corner of her mouth. "No, but you love other parts of you shoved in a lion's mouth."

Heat flamed in Ally's cheeks. "Say it a little louder, why don'tcha? I don't think the people on Thunder Mountain heard you." She pouted and he nibbled the side of her lips.

"It's an amusement park, Ally. Fun, remember? Rides, carnival food?"

She gave him a playful shove and then swiped the bag

of cotton candy from his hand, digging in for another handful. "Carnival food, yes." She plopped a finger full of the spun sugar into her mouth, letting it crystalize. "Speeding down a ninety-degree angle at breakneck speed is not my idea of a fun time."

Keir tugged her arm. "C'mon. You have to try it before you can say that. I'll be there to keep you safe. You have nothing to worry about."

She exhaled reluctantly. "More like you'll be there for them to scrape from under my body when we crash to the ground."

He laughed. "We haven't tried that yet."

"What? Dying?"

"No. You on top."

She groaned. "Sex on the brain, Keir. Sex on the brain."

He kissed the side of her hair and handed the ride engineer their tickets. "Only when I'm with you, baby."

They walked through the turnstile and waited to climb into the next car as it pulled into the end track.

"The front? You're seriously making me sit in the front car?"

"C'mon. It's safe as kittens."

She rolled her eyes, climbing in beside him. "Says the lion."

He laughed as ride personnel checked their safety bars. "Hold on to my arm if you need."

Ally's fingers gripped the pull bar. "You are so going to owe me after this."

The ride ticked to the top of the hill and then paused. She squeezed her eyes shut.

"Here we go!"

She screamed as the car plummeted down the track, her hair blowing back as inertia made her stomach fall. "I so hate you right now, you giant fur ball!"

"No you don't. You love the rush same as me, I can smell it on you."

Ally gritted her teeth. "What you smell is my urge to kill you!" She screamed again as the ride dipped and then stopped. "Oh my GOD! We're stuck. I knew it! Arrgh! Keir!"

He slipped his arm around her shoulder and shook his head. "Trust me. We're not stuck."

"Then why did we stop?"

A slow grin spread across his lips as the car lurched back a foot.

"Oh no!" Her eyes flew to his. "It's not . . ."

He nodded. "Oh, yes it is. Hold on, babe! We're doing it all again. Backwards!"

Ally clutched the grab bar, squeezing her eyes shut. "I hate you so bad right now."

He kissed her hair and then let go of her, his arms going up in the air. "No you don't. You love me."

Her eyes snapped open and she blinked before finding his laughing gaze. Did she? Was that in her scent too?

Keir winked and before she could think, the ride was over. The track click-clacked in slow motion as they pulled into the ride's end, and she watched his face. Did he know when she wasn't sure herself?

He climbed out of the ride and held out his hand for hers. "So, what do you think? Am I right?"

She licked her lips, not sure what question he meant her to answer. The ride or that she loved him. Sliding her eyes to his, she slipped her hand into his waiting palm and let him help her out of the car.

"Well?"

Shrugging, she tightened her hand in his, going up on tiptoe to peck his lips. "I'll let you know."

The rest of the day went by in a blur, but she couldn't

deny how much fun they'd had. Especially when they got home and he'd agreed to help get the carnival grime off her by going in the shower together. That had been a great ending to a surprisingly fun day.

Keir felt antsy as he walked beside Ally and Arlene. There was a weird smell in the air and he couldn't place his finger on what it was. The building was nice enough for a medical facility, stark and white. Everyone seemed competent and pleasant, but there was just something off and it was driving his lion crazy.

"What's wrong with you?" Ally hissed out of the side of her mouth. "You're like a two-year-old who can't sit still."

"I don't know, something's off about this place. Are you sure it's legitimate?"

"No, Mom didn't tell me much about it. That's why we're here, to get information."

"Mrs. Fosey?" a nasally voice called out before the woman stepped forward and caught their eye.

"Alison?" Keir said in astonishment.

"Keir. What are you doing here?"

Ally glared at the tall brunette that had accosted her in the bathroom, warning her away from Keir all those weeks ago.

"I told you I was a nurse, did you forget?"

"No, it was just a surprise is all."

Alison's smile faltered as she noticed him holding Ally's hand for the first time. "Oh, you are with her still, I see."

"Yes, she's my mate. I'll always be with her, Alison."

"Excuse me, but you said Mrs. Fosey, right? That's me."

"Yes, right, I'm sorry. Follow me if you will," Alison said with a tight-lipped smile.

"My daughter and son-in-law can join me, right?"

Alison gritted her teeth and nodded. "Of course they can."

Ally bit her lip and squeezed Keir's hand. "That's the woman who accosted me in the bathroom," she whispered quietly so only he'd hear her words.

"I should have known. I ended our date quickly. Something was never right about her. Figures she'd be here when I have the same feeling about this place."

They followed behind Alison and listened as she praised the doctors and the miracle cures they were accomplishing. Ally frowned, that didn't seem right to her either. She might not be a shifter, but even she knew logically that miracle cures didn't happen very often.

"If you'll all have a seat, the doctor will be in shortly. Keir, it was lovely to see you again, I hope we can meet up sometime."

"Not likely. What part of 'he's mine' do you not get?" Ally growled as she stepped forward before she could stop herself. "Go away and stay far away from us."

Alison retreated with a squeak and slammed the door shut behind her.

"Damn, babe, that was sexy," Keir said as he released his hold on Ally and moved to sit beside Arlene. "Did you ever think you'd see that?"

"Oh, yes. My girl has a temper, and she won't allow anyone to mess with what belongs to her. We don't share well, if you haven't figured that out yet."

"It's okay, I think it's hot," Keir whispered.

"You think everything I do is hot," Ally snapped back with a scowl.

"Are you mad at me?" Keir asked in shock. "What did I do?"

"Nothing, that's the problem."

Ally wasn't sure why she was so upset, but she was. It had to be this place; she'd been on edge ever since she'd walked in the front door. Finding out that that tramp worked here was icing on the cake.

"Hello, everyone, my name's Dr. Brunson. You must be Arlene Fosey, and who did you bring with you?"

"Hi, yes, it's a pleasure to meet you. This is my daughter, Ally, and my son-in-law, Keir."

"It's a pleasure to meet you all. Let's get down to business. As you know, you have a very rare form of cancer. The good news is that my treatment has a very high success rate; the bad news is that insurance doesn't cover it and the cost can be quite prohibitive for some people."

Ally started to reply but before she could, Keir was across the table and had the doctor by the throat.

"Keir, what are you doing?" Arlene cried in a panic.

"He's lying, Arlene."

"What? How?" She stumbled as she paled and looked to Ally for answers.

"He can smell lies, Mom. Remember, I told you about that ability. This piece of garbage is lying about the treatment success."

"Let me go before I call the police," the doctor demanded furiously.

"Ally, call Bess, have her get someone on this place *now*," Keir growled as he stepped closer to the man. "You lying bastard, how many people have you swindled, taken their life savings and promised them a cure?"

"I don't know what you're talking about." The man gasped as his face reddened from lack of oxygen.

"That's what I smell: lies, death, and despair."

"Keir, let him breathe, please," Ally called calmly from her seat by the door.

As soon as he loosened his hold, the doctor yelled for help. Moments later, the office door swung open and two well-muscled men walked in the room scowling.

"Throw these people out, this man accosted me!" the doctor yelled belligerently.

"Touch them and you will die," Keir snarled. "Ally, get your mom out of here."

"Be careful, baby," Ally whispered as she pulled her mom to her feet and out the door.

"Is he going to fight them?" Arlene asked frantically.

"Not if he can help it, but I'm not sure he's going to have much of a choice. He's not letting that doctor get away with the things he's done here. Bess already has someone on their way, she'd been researching the place after Keir gave her their information. She'd suspected something already. Now if Keir can hold the doctor and not allow him to escape, he'll go to prison."

Arlene gasped and glanced back to the closed office door. "That was a rather large thump, wasn't it?"

Ally shrugged. "The bigger they are, the harder they fall."

"Aren't you worried?"

"No, Keir can handle them without a problem."

Minutes later they heard screams from the front room as armed policemen stormed the small office. "Freeze!" they yelled at any workers they came across as they traveled down the hallway opening doors.

"Ally Fosey?" a voice called out above the racket.

"That's me, I'm here," she called as she waved her arm to get the man's attention.

"Ma'am, Bess sent me to help. Where's your mate?"

"In there with the doctor and a few of his goons. The bangs stopped a moment ago, so it's probably safe to go in now."

"I hope they're able to talk," the man grumbled as he motioned one of the policemen to follow him.

"Keir, it's Jeff. I'm coming in," the man said as he slowly opened the door.

"Hey, Jeff, let me guess, your grandmother sent you? This scum cowering in the corner is the so-called doctor. Those two are his goons that attacked me. It was all self-defense, I swear."

Ally could hear the laughter in the two men's voices as they talked in the office. What was it with them? A little violence and they were as happy as a two-year-old on Christmas.

"I don't know what I feel. I'm glad we stopped him from hurting other people, but part of me wants to know if there was some chance the treatment would have worked."

"Oh, Mom. Don't think like that. We're not done fighting. We will win this. I'm not giving up and neither can you."

Keir walked up in time to hear Arlene's words. He silently pulled both women into his arms and hugged them. "Come on, ladies, let's get out of here. They know how to find us when they need our statements. In the meantime, I'll have Bess research more treatment options, we won't give up."

They took Arlene back to their house and settled her in the spare room until her apartment was ready. As the days passed she fell a little deeper into depression as her hope slowly died. Ally, Keir, Xander, Josie, Bess, and even Shawna did their best to cheer her up, but nothing seemed to work. She'd lost faith.

A week after the office had been raided, Arlene's new doctor called to give them the results of the treatments.

"I have good news and bad news," he said flatly over the phone to the assembled group.

"What's the bad news?" Ally asked, fear making each word shake.

"Arlene's tumor is still there."

"And the good news?" Arlene asked with tears pouring down her face.

"It shrunk. For the first time, the tumor's shrunk. We might be on to something with this treatment, but only time and more treatments will tell for sure."

"You want her to do another round of chemo then?" Keir asked in confusion.

"Yes, but this time I want to make it six cycles and spread them out a tad bit. I think we can do some major damage and bring them into controllable perimeters if we do."

"I can't afford that," Arlene whispered brokenly.

"Oh yes, you can," Xander said at the same time Keir said, "She'll do it."

"What are you boys doing? I don't have that kind of money," Arlene protested.

"If you were in our shoes, would you pay for us to have it done if you could?" Xander asked quietly.

"Arlene, you were there for me when I needed someone. Let us help you," Keir added softly.

"Mom, they love you as much as I do. Please do this, fight for us."

Arlene glanced from face to face and smiled. "How can I say no to you all? Okay, Doctor, I'll do it."

"Good, because you need to be here to give your daughter away at her wedding after all."

"Wedding?" Ally asked curiously. "We're mated, do we need a wedding?"

"Damn straight we do. I want the world to know you're mine legally. Besides, just think of the wedding night."

EPILOGUE

Ally smoothed down her wedding dress and smiled at her mother's reflection in the mirror. She was in remission. Just thinking of it made Ally want to cry.

"Oh no you don't!" her mom said. "No crying. Well, not yet."

"I can't help it," she said and turned to hug her mother one more time. Every time she gave her mother a hug or a kiss, it was one more she got to do. One that wasn't promised. She kissed her mom's cheek and held her hands in her own. "Mom, I love you."

Her mom nodded, her eyes filling with moisture. "I know, sweetheart."

"Good. I will never stop loving you. Now let's go find my little mankitty and get me married."

Josie snorted a giggle from the entrance. "Mankitty? That's a good one. Wait until I tell Xander."

Ally laughed, imagining Keir's growl at the name. A sudden need to be with her mate filled her. She picked up the skirt to her dress and started off, everyone rushing behind her. It was Ally's turn to get married. When she got to the outside where Keir stood not far down a path, she turned to her mom, grabbed her hand, and watched as her brides-maids went down the aisle.

"You ready, Mom?"

Her mom smiled sweetly at her. "Are you?"

"I've been ready my whole life."

Who would've known the one man she thought was a womanizer would end up being the most loyal, honest, and committed man she'd ever met. Time to go meet Keir for their happily-ever-after.

NO NEED FUR LOVE

Kate Baxter

ACKNOWLEDGMENTS

Thanks go out to Kevin Courtney, for helping me in my research of all things Lowman, Idaho! Also, huge thanks to my amazing agent, Natanya Wheeler, and everyone at NYLA, my kick-ass editor, Monique Patterson, and Alexandra Sehulster, and the amazing cover artists, copyeditors, and marketing team at St. Martin's Press. You guys rock!

CHAPTER 1

"Can I get a Chunder Chocolate Oatmeal Stout?"

Owen Courtney bellied up to the bar at Bridge Street Bar and Grill. It was the only place in Stanley, Idaho—or anywhere for at least sixty miles—that sold Salmon River Brewery's finest and he wasn't about to drink any watered-down piss tonight. He needed a break from pack life like he needed his next breath of air. And he planned on getting good and drunk before the night was over.

"Here you go." The bartender set a glass filled with the dark brew in front of him. "Want something to eat tonight? I can grab you a menu."

"Nah." Food would take up valuable real estate space in his stomach that was strictly reserved for beer. "Just keep my glass full."

The winter season was in full swing, bringing with it a fair amount of tourist traffic. Snowmobilers ready to hit the backcountry and skiers on their way to Sun Valley to hit the slopes. For a place with a population of not more than a couple hundred full-time residents, the town was pretty damn busy tonight. But since everyone was more or less on their way to somewhere else, Owen was pretty sure the town would be as empty tomorrow as it ever was. Which suited him just fine. The full moon was three nights from now, and the more isolated he was, the better.

Owen needed to run more than usual. He was antsy as fuck and desperate to stretch his legs. Anything was better than sitting around the compound all day as the pack's alpha, Liam, and his mate, Devon, settled into their mated bliss.

It wasn't that he begrudged Liam a little love and happiness. On the contrary, after so many centuries alone, it was pretty damned great to see the male happy. But it was also a sore reminder of everything Owen didn't have. It wasn't like he was looking for a female to tie himself to for eternity right this second. He sure as hell wouldn't say no to tying himself to one for the night, however.

"How are things going out at your place?" Owen looked up at the bartender who'd swung back around with a fresh stout. "Tim Johnson said he heard some wolves howling out your way the other night. You hear anything?"

Liam had moved the pack to Stanley, Idaho, in the hopes of expanding the pack's territory in the sparsely populated area. Nestled at the base of the Sawtooth mountain range, the area was the perfect place for a pack of werewolves to hang out. Unfortunately, it was also an area where the human population harbored a lot of animosity toward wolves. Owen let out a chuff of laughter as he finished off his first glass and moved on to the second. "No." There was no use in bringing any undue attention their way. "Liam said there was some distant howling a few nights back, but any wolves he might have heard had to have been at least twenty miles away."

"Huh." The bartender—gods, Owen wished he could remember the guy's name—cleared his empty glass away. "That's good to know. But if the elk move down into the valley, the wolves won't be far behind."

True. But what the locals didn't know was that whether there was a herd of elk in the area or not, no timber wolf would dare to tangle with a werewolf. They weren't even on the same evolutionary ladder. The chances of any ordinary wolves taking up residence in the area were slim to none. That didn't mean there wasn't a possibility that Owen would be dodging a few bullets come the night of the full moon.

It wouldn't do any good to disagree. "I'll tell Liam to keep an eye out just in case."

"Good idea."

Their conversation was cut short as a party of eight walked through the front door. Owen let out a slow breath of relief as he hunkered over his glass and went back to staring at the pale foam as it began to dissipate from the top of the stout in his glass. He knew the move to Idaho would be better for their pack in the long run, but the isolation was really starting to get to him. It was blind fucking luck that Liam had managed to find his mate in the even tinier town of Lowman, fifty miles down the road. The chance that any other member of the pack would have that sort of luck was slim to none.

At least, that's what Owen had convinced himself of.

Mia Oliver walked into the little bar and grill behind a group of skiers on their way back to the city. She hung back toward the entrance and scanned the entire fifteen hundred or so square feet of space for a viable candidate. She didn't need anything special, just a warm body for the night. Someone to buy her a little time and keep her within the confines of her father's ridiculous ultimatum.

Produce an heir or allow him to find her a suitable mate. Otherwise, she'd be forced to relinquish her birthright.

Seriously, what a jerk. You'd think they were still living in the dark ages or something. It's not like there were viable males around every corner in their little isolated slice of Idaho. And besides that, why in the hell did she need to produce offspring to obtain any kind of leadership status? It's not like procreating would make her any more her father's daughter than she already was. Wood nymphs were notoriously stubborn, and Mia was no exception. What her father wanted was to see her good and mated. What Mia wanted was for him to get the hell off her back and let her live her life on her own terms.

Easier said than done.

"Just one for dinner tonight?"

Mia wanted to laugh at the hostess's sympathetic tone. As though eating by herself were some great tragedy. "Yup." Mia did nothing to hide her sarcastic tone. "Just little old me, all by my lonesome. I think I'll eat at the bar if that's okay."

The hostess replied with a bright smile. "Oh sure! No problem at all. Just go ahead and have a seat."

Mia gave her a bright smile in return as she headed for the bar. Wasn't this the pond that most single girls fished from? At any rate, the night was bound to be marginally entertaining. It should be easy enough to snag an eligible male. Besides, she didn't need anyone stellar. Just . . . passable.

Gods. Were her standards so low that she was willing to settle for any poor slob as long as he could seal the deal? At this point, yes. Because there was no way she was going to enter into a hasty relationship with a male she didn't know in order to make her father happy. If he had it his way, he'd pair her off with someone of his choosing. No way, no how. Arranged pairings might have been the norm six or seven hundred years ago, but it was time for their band of nymphs to jump into the twenty-first century. Feminism for the win!

Well, hel-loooo there!

Mia caught sight of a nicely muscled back at the far end of the bar. Guy looked like he spent a fair amount of time in the gym or outside lifting *very* heavy things. His short-clipped, sandy-blond hair brushed the collar of his T-shirt. Just long enough to appear unkempt in a very orchestrated way. His wide back tapered into a finely formed torso and narrow waist. His ass was planted on the bar stool, but Mia imagined it was just as spectacular as the rest of him. His powerful arms rested on the bar. She couldn't see his face but Mia wasn't interested in whether or not the front of him was as attractive as the back. He was a well-made, warm body. The perfect prospect to help her take care of a little business.

From the looks of it, he was all alone, his head bent over his beer as though he might have had a bad night. Nursing a broken heart, perhaps? Maybe he needed a rebound girl. In which case, Mia was more than willing to help a guy out.

"Is this seat taken?" Mia infused her voice with power as she settled in beside her prey. A nymph with even half her power could easily entrance a human with a single word. The magical properties of her voice certainly came in handy. And even though they were required to follow a strict code of conduct in regard to the use of those powers, Mia decided it would be okay to break the rules tonight.

A girl's gotta do what a girl's gotta do.

The guy waited a beat before he acknowledged her. *Weird.* He should have been champing at the bit from the first sound of her voice. He turned slowly on the bar stool to face her and Mia's breath caught in her chest. He was way better-looking than she'd anticipated. And he definitely *wasn't* human.

Wow.

It had been forever since another supernatural faction had lived in the area. Her band came across the occasional shifter, but for the most part, they were pretty scattered throughout the remote rural areas. His gaze roamed over her and a golden spark lit in the depths of his blue eyes. Werewolf. And a damned impressive one at that. Mia took in his finely chiseled features. The straight line of his nose, his square jaw, and sharp cheekbones. One tawny brow arched over a bright blue eye and the corner of his mouth twitched with amusement. Arrogant. So typical. Werewolves had insufferably large egos. But they were also virile—especially in the days before the full moon. No doubt he was antsy and looking for a little action. Mia couldn't have asked for a better setup.

His lips spread into a sardonic grin and Mia's stomach did a pleasant backflip before settling back into place. "It's all yours." Hell, yeah it was. The deep rumble of his voice vibrated through her and Mia suppressed a moan. "I'm Owen."

He held out his hand. If he knew what she was, he didn't give any outward indication. Pretty civilized for a werewolf. Sort of disappointing. Then again, what did she expect? For him to just lay her out on the bar and go to town? Nymphs weren't exactly modest creatures, but in a town as small as Stanley, Mia didn't need to do anything that might draw attention to her or her band. The fact that Owen was a werewolf made hooking up with him a little more difficult as well. Dual-natured creatures like werewolves and shifters weren't susceptible to her powers of persuasion. Which meant, if she wanted to bag this big game, she'd have to do it the old-fashioned way.

Good thing Mia wasn't opposed to rolling up her sleeves for a little hard work.

"Mia." It had been a while since she'd actually had to charm a male. Hopefully, she wasn't too rusty. She hopped up onto the stool beside him and rested an elbow on the bar as she turned her body intimately toward his. "So, what brings you out tonight, Owen?"

A human would be more fitting for her purposes. But there was something about the werewolf she couldn't resist. Mia just hoped her curiosity over the male wouldn't wind up getting her into more trouble than he was worth.

Then again, there was only one way to find out.

CHAPTER 2

Mine.

The word resounded in Owen's mind with such clarity that it drowned out all other sound. This close to the full moon, his wolf was nearer to the surface of his psyche, but that wasn't what triggered the visceral reaction that took him by surprise. *Holy shit.* His wolf had claimed her as their mate.

"So, what brings you out tonight, Owen?"

His brain had a hard time latching on to her words. He was too preoccupied with the sudden shock of lamenting his lack of a bond only to find himself claiming a mate in the very next moment. A rush of electric heat shot through him and Owen found himself wishing he was outside in the cold winter air. His brain was entirely too full of her delicious scent for him to focus on anything else.

"Probably the same thing that brought you out tonight." *Eloquent? Nope.* But it was all he could muster until his brain decided to get its ass in gear.

A slow, sensual smile spread across her full lips and Owen damn near swallowed his tongue. "I doubt that."

Her voice was a purr that struck low in his gut, awakening his lust. Good gods, she was beautiful. An outdoor enthusiast's wet dream, she looked as though she'd walked right out of the woods and into the bar. Fresh. Natural. Her face as dewy as a spring morning. Her pale cheeks, colored with a blush of summer, despite it being the middle of winter, only enhanced her otherworldly appearance. Her forest-green eyes ran with veins of gold that held him rapt. Long, wild locks of golden wheat–colored hair framed her face and cascaded over her shoulders and back. What was she? Owen could identify most supernatural creatures by their scent, but he'd never smelled anything like her before. Not floral or sweet. Not musky like a shifter. She smelled like the river on an early summer day. Clean. Crisp. Amazing. She wasn't human, that much was certain. A mystery. It excited him even more.

Mia reached up and lightly traced her bottom lip with her fingertips. Owen's cock hardened behind his fly and his stomach gathered into a tight knot as his gaze locked on her luscious mouth. *Jesus.* He blew out an emphatic breath. The female was one hundred percent concentrated sex appeal.

"Can I buy you a drink?" Owen almost laughed at the question. Here he was, acting as though this was nothing more than a casual conversation at the bar when he'd liter-ally just met the female who would be his mate until the day he died. Did she know? Did she recognize the connection? Gods, he hoped so. Otherwise, their conversation was bound to get more awkward as the night went on.

"Sure." She flashed another seductive smile. Gods, she was so hot she made him sweat. "What're you having?"

"SRB, Chocolate Oatmeal Stout."

"Sounds great. I'll have one of those."

And she drank good beer? Could Owen have gotten any luckier?

Owen got the bartender's attention and ordered her a

beer. A few seconds later, he returned with a tall glass of the dark, delicious stout. Mia took a sip, and her lids drooped almost imperceptibly. "Mmmm."

Holy fuck. Owen swore he felt the soft hum at the base of his sac. His wolf gave an appreciative growl in the recess of his mind. *Down boy.* He was a disgusting, horny son of a bitch for lusting after her like this. For shit's sake, they didn't even know each other! His wolf didn't have a fuck to give about that, however. She was theirs. Period. That's all the wolf needed to know.

"So . . ." Owen figured he might as well do whatever he could to keep the conversation rolling along. Anything to distract his dick from taking over his brain. "Why did you come out tonight?"

Mia took a long sip from her glass. She fixed Owen with her entrancing stare and licked her lips. "Right now, I'm looking to get laid. How 'bout you?"

Whoa.

So she *did* recognize the connection between them. Owen felt the urge to pump his fist in the air and give a celebratory "whoop!" He thought about Liam and the difficulties his alpha had faced when he'd found himself mated to a human. The trials they'd faced at Devon's reluctance as she'd been thrown into a world she'd known nothing about and forced to decide whether or not she wanted to say good-bye to her humanity to become a part of it. Owen would never have to surmount those difficulties. For the first time in months, he felt as though his luck might finally be changing for the better.

Would it be in bad taste to pound down the rest of his beer so they could get the hell out of here? His wolf was more than ready to go, yipping in the back of his mind like an excited pup about to go out on his first hunt. She might have claimed to be every bit as ready to go as he was, but Owen needed to play it closer to the hip. Besides her name, he didn't know a damned thing about her. It might be a good idea to make a little small talk before he took her up on her offer and got right to it. He brought his glass to his lips to keep from saying something he'd regret.

Mia leaned in closer and her clean, spring water scent washed over him. "Owen, do you want to get out of here?"

Owen inhaled at the same moment he swallowed, choking on the beer that became lodged between his gut and his sternum. His gaze went upward and he gave a silent thanks to the heavens. No nonsense. No pretense. *Perfect.*

Mia's lips curled in a pleasant smile as Owen recovered his composure. He gulped down what was left in his glass and looked pointedly at hers. "Did you want to finish that first?"

He hated that he couldn't help but sound like an eager frat boy, but already she had him so wound up he could barely think straight.

Her smile brightened. "Honestly? It's not what I need to quench my thirst."

Hot. Damn. Owen hopped down from the bar stool like it was on fire. Finally, things were looking up.

Who needed powers of persuasion when there was a randy werewolf around? Mia had worried that it would be tough to seal the deal with such a strong-willed supernatural, but she'd barely thrown out her line before Owen jumped on the hook. Either the werewolf was hard up or Mia was much more powerful than she'd given herself credit for. Did it matter? She was one step closer to securing her place at the top of her band's hierarchy. With the sort of clout that providing an heir would bring, Mia would finally make sure she and the other females of the band had a voice. When it came to having a say in how things were run, Mia wouldn't have any power until she took a mate or provided their bloodline with an heir. And since she wasn't interested in tying herself to any male, her only option at this point was to get knocked up. She only hoped the werewolf would be able to seal the deal.

Because this wasn't going to be anything other than a one-night stand.

"Oh yeah?" Owen gave her a lopsided grin that caused Mia's heart to pick up its pace in her chest. Tonight's hookup certainly wasn't going to be a hardship. "What do you need?"

Any other night, she would have enjoyed the innuendo and playful banter. Who didn't like to flirt a little? Mia didn't have time for games, though. Her fertility cycle was coming to its end and it would be another six months before it would swing back around.

"I think you know what I need." It was time to get down to business. She only hoped they wouldn't have to get down to it in a bathroom stall. She might have been desperate, but Mia had standards. She asked again, "Do you want to get out of here?"

A bright gold light shone behind Owen's eyes, revealing the animal part of his dual nature. The wild glint was a total turn-on and a glow of pleasant heat gathered low in Mia's stomach and fanned outward through her limbs. Nope, tonight wouldn't be a hardship at all.

Owen leaned in close. Mia took a deep breath and held his delicious, masculine scent in her lungs. She tilted her head toward him and his mouth brushed her ear as the one heated word left his lips on a breath. "Absolutely."

"Do you have a place nearby?" *Gods, please don't let him suggest the ladies room.*

"About fifteen minutes from here."

Mia said a silent prayer of thanks. She could wait another fifteen minutes to put her plan into action. "Perfect."

Owen pulled away and gave her a wide, mischievous grin that turned her insides to mush. She hadn't come across such a spectacular male in years. "Let's go."

Mia hopped down from the bar stool. Owen followed but before she could turn to leave, he reached out and took her hand. His brow furrowed as his gaze delved into hers. The wonderment in his expression nearly stole her breath. The depth of emotion was unexpected and it caused her stomach to curl into a tight knot.

"I almost reconsidered going out tonight." The deep rumble of his voice resonated through her in a pleasant vibration that coaxed goose bumps to the surface of her skin. "You have no idea how glad I am that I didn't."

There was way too much sincerity behind his words for Mia's peace of mind. It could have been that he was laying it on thick in order to make sure she wouldn't change her mind about leaving with him. A twinge of guilt tugged at Mia's chest. Was it wrong to take advantage of him when she clearly had the upper hand? She'd come here tonight fully prepared to use whatever powers she had at her disposal to seduce a bedmate. Now wasn't the time to let her conscience get the better of her.

"I'm glad too." She let her voice go low and breathy as she infused the words with her inborn seductive power. A little insurance to make sure she kept the werewolf's engine nice and revved.

His fingers twined with hers as he led the way out of the

bar. The contact was too intimate, as though they were more than two strangers looking for a distraction for the night. Mia fought the urge to pull away, to sever the connection between them. There was something about Owen that threw her off her game. Unnerved her. She couldn't put her finger on it and that bothered her more than anything. She'd been so certain she was in complete control of the situation, but with every step she took, she became less confident that anything was in her control.

Gods, she hoped she wasn't about to make the worst decision of her life.

Owen led her through the parking lot to a Toyota pickup parked at the far end. The midsized truck seemed to suit him: not ostentatious and ready to go anywhere at a moment's notice. Mia wondered at how firmly the thought had planted in her mind. As though she knew Owen much better than she should for having only just met him. Strange.

"Where's your place?" Nymphs were notoriously sexual creatures. It was simply part of their biology. There was no shame in taking someone to bed without having vetted them first. Supernaturals didn't need to worry about things like diseases, and humans were so comparatively weak that they were more often prey than predators. Owen wasn't human, though. Far from. On the supernatural food chain, werewolves were pretty high up. Strong both of mind and body. Resilient to damage except when exposed to silver. Mia didn't feel threatened by Owen. In fact, something told her that she was safer with him than with anyone. But that didn't mean she wasn't going to exercise a fair amount of caution. She was desperate, not stupid.

"About fifteen miles outside of town, near the Bench Lakes trailhead. It's a bit of a drive and sort of out in the middle of nowhere." Owen paused and his gaze searched hers. His brow furrowed once again, this time with concern. "Is that all right?"

His consideration for her comfort level caused a warm bloom of emotion in Mia's chest. Despite the fact his dick was taking the lead tonight, Mia knew that deep down, Owen was a good guy. He wasn't the only one having second thoughts, dammit. She was about to use him in the worst way possible. But her time had run out and Mia was out of options. It was either take him to bed or be forced to pair off with a male of her father's choosing. She refused to lose the battle of wills her father had pushed her into. Owen would simply be a casualty of war.

"I know the area," Mia replied. In fact, her band didn't live too far from there. "And I'm totally fine with it. We're both adults. We both know what's about to happen. I'm not going to change my mind, Owen."

His bright smile nearly buckled her knees. "Good. But I want you to know that if you're not totally sure . . ." He reached back to rub the back of his neck as though to banish the sudden tension that had formed there. "I'm okay with that. I can go slow. Whatever you need."

Dammit, he was killing her! The Mr. Nice Guy ploy could have been a routine, but Mia didn't sense any duplicity in his words. Why the sudden tenderness? Maybe taking him back into the bar and going to town in a bathroom stall was a better idea. Already, she'd formed an intimacy with this stranger that left her shaken.

No. Mia couldn't afford to have second thoughts. She'd made her decision. Whatever happened tonight, she was prepared for the fallout. Her future depended on it.

"I don't want to go slow." She'd give Owen all the reassurance he needed and then some. "I'm a big girl and I know what I want." She stepped up close to his chest and let out a slow breath that ended on a sigh. Even with the added layer of his puffy winter coat, she knew Owen might as well have been chiseled from marble. She looked up at him from beneath her lashes and gave him a slow, seductive smile. "I want you."

Owen reached up and cupped her cheek in his palm. Mia had heard that werewolves' body temperatures ran a little hot and that wasn't an understatement. Seriously, why was he even wearing a coat? The delicious heat that flooded her turned her bones to Jell-O. She couldn't wait to feel the heat of his naked body against hers.

"Good. Because I want you too."

His head dipped and Owen's mouth met hers. *Holy shit.* Her knees did give out this time and Owen's arm went around her to crush her against him. Tonight was going to be one hell of a ride.

CHAPTER 3

He should have waited until they were back at his cabin, but Owen couldn't help himself. Instinct took over and his animal nature drove him to claim some part of his mate as soon as possible. He didn't even know her, but already he craved the intimate contact. Her clean, freshwater scent drove him wild. He knew he wouldn't be satisfied until he tasted her.

Owen wasn't disappointed.

The dewy sweetness of her mouth had no equal. Her petal-soft lips brushed his, tentative at first, and then moved with purpose as he deepened the kiss. She responded as though she was just as starved for him as he was for her. As though they'd been reunited after centuries spent apart. Such was the mating bond, though. It formed an immediate attraction that drowned out all reason in its intensity.

Nature's way of solidifying their bond.

Owen tightened his grip as he held Mia against his body. His mouth slanted over hers, hungry, desperate. He couldn't get close enough, couldn't taste her deeply enough to satisfy his need. There were too many layers of clothes between them. Too much separating the skin-to-skin contact that he craved. His pickup was too cramped for what he wanted to do with her and his mate deserved so much better than a quick fuck in the front seat.

He needed to get a grip on his damned lust and treat her with the respect she deserved. A nearly impossible feat when his senses were awash with her scent, taste, the feel of her body against his. Gods, she was heaven.

"Mia." He whispered her name against her lips. He loved the way it sounded, the familiarity of it, as though he'd spoken it a thousand times over a hundred years. For weeks he'd sulked around the compound, jealous of Liam's mate bond with Devon and bitter that his alpha had moved their pack into a sparsely populated territory where the other members of their pack would have little to no chance of finding their mates. Perhaps there was more to life than random chance. Fate had brought them to Idaho. Fate had brought Owen to her.

"Owen." Her playful tone caused his gut to knot up tight. His cock throbbed hot and hard behind his fly as a renewed rush of lust coursed through his veins. "Unless you plan on getting down to business right here in the parking lot, you'd better take me back to your place."

Her words coaxed a cleansing breeze of common sense to blow through his lust-addled brain. The animal part of him wanted her right here, right now. The wolf didn't give a single shit about who might see them. All the wolf wanted was to claim what was his. Owen couldn't let that part of his instinct take over. He might have been dual-natured, but he wasn't completely wild. He let his forehead rest against Mia's as he took several cleansing breaths.

"You're right. We need to go."

Her warm laughter was better than a long soak in the nearby hot springs. It relaxed him from head to toe and quieted the sound of his wolf in the recess of his psyche. Amazing. He took her hand and by a sheer act of will put a little much needed space between them. The winter air helped to further clear the haze from his mind and he let out a slow breath that fogged between them.

A clear sky full of twinkling stars stretched out above them. It was going to be another cold night. Thankfully, Owen wouldn't have to pass the hours alone, huddled under the blankets as he questioned every single one of his alpha's recent decisions. His life had finally taken a turn for the better, and tonight, he'd have a warm body beside him in bed. It was like he'd been reborn. And he had this extraordinary female that he knew nothing about to thank for it.

He led her the thirty or so feet to where the pickup was parked. He might have had the good sense to put a little space between them, but that didn't mean Owen was ready to sever all physical contact. The reassurance of her touch was a balm to his troubled soul. It calmed his wolf and kept him level. The mate bond was truly extraordinary.

He unlocked the passenger door and opened it for her. She gave him a reassuring smile that sent his heart racing in his chest before she gave his hand a light squeeze and released her hold. She settled into the seat and he closed the door, taking off at a jog as he rounded the front end of his pickup to unlock his own door and climb behind the wheel. *Damn.* He was so anxious to get her home that he could barely get the key in the ignition.

Owen laughed as he turned the key and the engine rumbled to life. He reached over and turned up the heat as Mia buckled her seat belt and turned to face him. "What?"

"Just wondering how fast I can safely drive to get us home," he replied. "It's about twenty minutes when the roads are plowed. I'm thinking I might be able to shave that down to fifteen."

Mia laughed. She reached out and ran her palm up the length of his thigh. "Let's get back to your place in one piece. Five extra minutes isn't going to kill us."

Oh no? Owen was worried he wouldn't last fifteen seconds let alone fifteen whole minutes. She was right, though. He wasn't about to risk her safety. His mate was irreplaceable. Priceless.

Her forest-green eyes sparkled as her fingertips grazed the outline of his erection through his jeans. "I promise I'm worth the wait."

Fuckin' A.

Owen's hips gave an involuntary thrust as he put the pickup into gear and pulled out of the parking lot. If he didn't get them home soon, he was pretty sure he'd spontaneously combust.

Mia reached for the dash and turned on the radio. She fiddled with the buttons until she found a station that played something mellow, but Owen's brain was too full of her to make sense of what he heard. The drive passed in relative silence as she gazed out the window at the scenery illuminated by the nearly full moon. Her hand never left his thigh and her occasional, purposeful caresses over the length of his cock nearly prompted him to pull over to the side of the road.

Seven minutes down. Another seven or so to go. . . .

Time passed in a blur. Before he knew it, Owen turned onto the long, winding driveway that led to the pack's compound. He'd never been more grateful for his own space as he pulled into the narrow parking area outside of his tiny cabin. It might not have been a palace, but at least he wouldn't have to worry about any nosy pack members bothering them tonight.

"This is me." *Ugh.* Of course this was his place, where else would they be? He resisted the urge to bang his head on the steering wheel as he parked the truck. His muscles had grown taut during the drive, his excitement cresting with each mile they covered.

"I like it." Her response was genuine and Owen's chest swelled with pride. "It's the perfect house. Doesn't leave much of a footprint."

At just under seven hundred square feet, that was the truth. His mate smelled of the forest and it shone in her eyes and complexion. She seemed to be a force of nature herself. Again, Owen wondered what type of creature had he claimed? Sprite? Nymph? Sylph? They were all creatures who lived close to nature. Even the fae had a kinship with the earth that surpassed his own. What he didn't know about her didn't matter right now, however. All Owen knew for sure was that she was his. For tonight, that was enough.

Mia didn't mind small talk, but she had other things on her mind that had nothing to do with Owen's quaint cabin. Not that she didn't like it—in fact, it was absolutely perfect—but they were wasting precious minutes that they should have been spending getting each other's clothes off. Owen killed the engine and she took it as a sign to get out of the pickup. She didn't look back as she headed down the path that had been recently cleared of snow and made her way to the front steps of the tiny porch. A smile curved her lips at the sound of Owen's door opening and closing and the rapid crunch of his footsteps as he hurried to catch up to her. She wanted him ready. Eager. Which was why she'd made a point of remaining silent as she stroked him through his jeans during the drive here. Empty words were a total mood killer. Mia would rather talk with her hands.

She stopped at the front door and waited. Owen had no choice but to press his chest to her back as he reached around her body to unlock the door and let them inside. His heat permeated the layers of clothes that separated them, and once again, Mia couldn't help but marvel at the warmth he threw off. She had a feeling he could easily survive a blizzard wearing nothing more than a smile.

The door swung wide and Mia stepped inside the modest cabin. Her preternatural vision didn't need light to take in her surroundings. The place was exactly how she'd expected Owen's house to look, though she wasn't sure how she'd known such a thing. Masculine. Understated. Not a bachelor pad by any means but it wasn't a pristine showplace either. Homey. Comfortable. The sort of place Mia would be at home in as well.

Stop it! She wasn't here to assess the place for a move-in. She had one job to do and only one. It wouldn't matter if the place was a palace or a shack. Besides, Mia didn't plan to be here much longer than the night. Her stomach tied into a knot at the thought of walking away from Owen. She hated the connection she felt so easily and so quickly with him. All the more reason to leave as soon as possible. Mia couldn't afford attachments of any kind. She'd fought too long and too hard for her freedom to be tied to anyone or anything right now. Hit it and quit it. It was the only way.

Mia turned to face Owen. More than ready to get the show on the road before she had another attack of conscience and lost her nerve. She grabbed him by the lapel of his coat and pulled him to her as she worked down the zipper in a mad rush to get his clothes off.

"Not here." His voice rasped with restraint as he reached out to stay her hands. "Let's go to my bedroom."

NO NEED FUR LOVE   289

Mia didn't need a slow, practiced seduction. She'd already told Owen she was a sure thing. She couldn't allow him to do anything that would endear him to her more. He was already starting to worm his way past her all-business, crusty exterior. Still, she didn't want to turn him off with her impatience. Her gaze wandered to a set of stairs to her left that led to a loft. "Up there?"

Owen nodded. "Yeah. I need to get you upstairs. Now. I'm dying to fuck you."

Now we're talking. Mia could spare a few extra seconds to climb the stairs to the loft. A rush of excitement coursed through her veins. Not only at the prospect of achieving her goal, but at the thought of having such a fine specimen of a male between her thighs. Mia knew any number of females in her band who would have considered Owen a prize. And at least for tonight, he belonged to her.

Rather than turn, Mia kept her gaze locked with Owen's as she stepped backward toward the staircase. He mirrored her movement, one step forward for every one of hers back. His hands moved to her waist and a feral light shone in his eyes as his thumbs brushed upward, beneath the hem of her shirt to brush against her bare skin.

Mia shuddered as the back of her calves met the first step. Owen's grip on her tightened. He lifted her as though she were nothing more than a feather, and Mia could either dangle there or wrap her legs around his waist. Honestly, it wasn't a tough decision to make. Her arms went around his neck as her hips gave a gentle thrust. The hard length of his erection brushed against her core and Mia sucked in a sharp breath as the contact fired against sensitive nerve endings.

Power surged within her, a magic unique to nymphs as they became swept up in passion. The residual effects would last for days afterward and Mia would be riding quite a high. All thanks to the magnificent werewolf currently carting her up the stairs. She'd owe him more than he'd ever know.

Owen continued up the stairs as he lowered his mouth to hers for a ravenous kiss. His tongue thrust past her lips, demanding that she answer with equal fervor. *No problem there!* Mia kissed him as though she were starved for him, her mouth slanting over his as one of her hands moved from the back of his neck to dive into the locks of his hair. Her fingers curled into a fist around the strands and Owen gave an approving grunt. His progress stalled and he turned to press her back against the wall as he ground his hips against hers. Who needed a bed? Mia wouldn't say no to being fucked on his staircase up against the wall . . .

"Gods, you drive me crazy." His mouth moved to her throat and he nuzzled her there as he inhaled a deep breath. "Your scent. Your taste. Your skin . . ." He let out another indulgent moan as he continued to thrust against her. "I'm out of my mind with fucking want."

That made two of them. Mia didn't know how much more over the clothes action she could take before her head exploded off her shoulders. Need built within her, a storm that refused to calm. Her brain buzzed as a dizzying wave of euphoria swept over her. Tremors rocked her from head to toe, the intensity of sensation was unlike anything she'd ever felt.

"We can take care of that want right here and now, Owen." Gods, she wished he would. "It only takes a second to get our pants off."

A low growl gathered in his chest. The scent of his arousal bloomed around her and Mia was positively drunk on it.

"In good time." The heated promise made Mia's stomach do a pleasant backflip. "I'm going to take my time with you, Mia. The sun will be high before I'm done with you."

Any other time, Mia would have gladly surrendered to the werewolf's pace and let him spend hours seducing her. Unfortunately, she didn't have that kind of time. "Get me to your bedroom, Owen." Mia needed to do whatever it took to speed things along. "I need you inside me. Now."

He turned and took the last three stairs in the space of a second. Maybe her powers of persuasion weren't as rusty as she'd thought.

CHAPTER 4

Owen didn't need to be told twice. Instinct overrode common sense—or any sense of decorum—as he took the last three stairs in a single leap. Mia wasn't interested in a slow seduction or a long courtship, and as far as Owen's wolf was concerned, that was A-okay. The animal's only priority was laying claim to what was theirs. The quicker, the better.

He put his boot to the bedroom door to kick it ajar.

The mate bond eliminated the need for seduction and courtship. It was immediate. Intense. A call that demanded to be answered. Owen wished he knew whether or not Mia recognized their bond in the same way. She had to have, though. He refused to believe otherwise. She wouldn't be here with him now, begging for him to take her if she hadn't.

"What are you?" He had to know that much. He had all the time in the world to learn more about her. But his curiosity on this one issue needed to be sated. What was this beautiful female his wolf had claimed?

Owen's shins met the bedframe and he stilled. He kept his mouth near her ear and breathed in the intoxicating aroma of her natural perfume. Mia's fingertips teased his hair where it met the nape of his neck and a pleasant shiver traveled the length of his body.

"Does it matter?" Her guarded tone caused his gut to knot up.

"No." That was the truth. The mate bond was absolute. It wouldn't matter who or what she was. Still, he craved to know some small thing about her. Anything. "You know what I am, though. Don't you?"

"I know." Her voice was a husky murmur that banished his earlier worry. "Werewolf."

Most supernatural creatures possessed physical traits that identified them to one another easily. Their scent, mannerisms, the way their eyes changed . . . Mia was a mystery to him, though, and it bothered him more than it should have. His inability to recognize her by scent, or sight, or by the spark of magic that might have clung to her, was an affront to his usually keen senses.

"Tell me."

"We're surrounded by miles and miles of forest." Mia's mouth brushed his cheek as she spoke close to his ear. "What do you think I am?"

"You're not fae." Owen knew that much. He was certain he would have sensed it. "Not sylph." They could become one with a passing breeze and there was nothing gossamer about his mate. "I'd know if you were a shifter." He nuzzled her neck and took a deep breath. "You smell like the forest."

"Uh-huh."

The smile in her tone encouraged him. He'd heard stories about small bands of wood nymphs that still populated remote wilderness areas. For the most part, they were thought to be reclusive. Forest sirens who lured hikers and hunters to their deaths in much the same way mermaids were thought to tempt sailors to their ends. Could it be that Mia was one of those elusive creatures? Owen marveled at the possibility.

"Wood nymph?" He was only partly kidding as the words left his lips.

Mia's answering silence sent a shiver over his skin. "Bingo." She pulled away to study him and her brow furrowed. "Does that bother you?"

She could have been a damned yeti and his wolf wouldn't have given a single shit. "No." All that mattered was that Mia was his. "Why should it?"

Her expression changed to one of relief. "Good. Now, that's enough talk, don't you think?"

Hell yeah it was.

Owen deposited Mia on the bed. His brain fought with his body as a million thoughts assaulted him. Would she be okay with living here with him? Would she adapt to pack life? Did wood nymphs have an opinion one way or another in regard to werewolves? What did the details of their mate bond entail? Was there a ceremony? A ritual? Some act that was needed to solidify the bond? His body—hell, his wolf— didn't care about any of those nonessential details. His sex drive didn't care if they'd be required to stand under a full moon and drink from a cup that had collected the dew of the first fall morning or any other crazy shit.

None of that mattered. Not now, anyway.

Mia's gaze met his and Owen's breath caught as she discarded her jacket and peeled her sweater off. She tossed both garments to the floor and reached around her back to unfasten her bra. She didn't waste any time as she freed the clasp and pushed the straps down her shoulders to reveal the perfect roundness of her pert breasts. She fell back onto the bed and kicked off her boots before she planted her feet on the mattress. Owen stared, transfixed, as she thrust her hips up to unbutton her jeans. She slid them down her thighs, along with her underwear, leaving her completely naked except for her socks.

A grin tugged at his lips as he admired her. "You planning on leaving your socks on?"

Her soft laughter rippled over him. "I thought I'd leave you something to take off of me."

She lifted her legs, toes pointed toward his chest, to drive her point home. The sweet scent of her arousal drove Owen so mad with desire, he wasn't sure he had the presence of mind to perform the simple act. His gaze was drawn instead to the glistening flesh of her pussy and Owen let out an almost tortured groan. She wanted him to reach for her socks, but his hands went to his jeans as his fingers fumbled for the button and then the zipper.

"I'll make it fair and leave my socks on too," he said with a sheepish shrug as he kicked off his boots and yanked his jeans down over his thighs. He shrugged off his coat and reached behind his neck for his T-shirt as he pulled it over his head and discarded it on the floor with the rest of his clothes. "I don't want to waste another second."

Passion sparked in the depths of her forest-green eyes. "Perfect. I don't think I can wait another second either."

There was no reason to wait. Owen was more than anxious to claim his mate.

A riot of butterflies swirled in Mia's stomach. You would have thought she was some untouched virgin, experiencing passion for the first time. Seduction was her freaking wheelhouse. Inborn. A part of her very nature. Owen made her feel as though she knew nothing about raw sexuality. This was uncharted territory, and her own sudden insecurity rattled her. She had no control over the situation or even her own damned emotions. She swallowed down the lump in her throat as she took in the magnificence of Owen's naked body. For the first time in her existence, a male had managed to leave her speechless.

He let out a nervous chuff of laughter and the sound vibrated in a pleasant ripple over Mia's skin. A rush of wet warmth spread between her thighs as Owen reached out and let his palms caress a path from the tops of her thighs, down the length of her still extended legs. Her lids drooped at the sheer pleasure of his touch and she extended her arms high above her head as she stretched out on the mattress. "What's so funny?"

"Just a little blown away by my good luck." Owen's low response ended on a deep growl that caused Mia's stomach to clench with lust. "You're fucking perfect."

As a wood nymph, sensuality sort of came with the territory. Mia wasn't vain, but she also knew her very biology made her alluring. Somehow, though, it meant something to hear Owen speak those words. They weren't empty flattery, or a statement of fact. She was perfect to *him*. As though he saw her differently than anyone else ever had or ever would.

Warm emotion blossomed in Mia's chest. Tonight wasn't about that, though. She couldn't afford to lose herself to Owen or anyone else. She compartmentalized that shit and focused on the task at hand. "You're the one who's perfect." It wasn't a lie. She couldn't have asked for a more perfect male to spend the night with. "I want you so bad, Owen. I can't wait anymore."

He needed to know it was okay to answer to his desires. Mia was more than ready to answer to hers.

Thank the gods, her words were all the encouragement

he needed to move forward. Mia came up on her elbows as Owen lowered himself to her. She scooted up on the bed to give him room to work and he prowled up the length of her body, looking every bit the predator that he was. A thrill raced through her veins as his mouth captured hers once again in a ravenous kiss that left her breathless and shaking. Her knees fell open as he settled between her legs and she drew in a sharp breath as the hot, swollen head of his cock probed at her opening.

"Gods yes, Owen. Now. I need you."

His hips pressed forward in a single, desperate thrust. Mia drew in a sharp gasp that ended on an indulgent moan as her nerve endings fired with pleasure. He stretched her, filled her. His body fit so perfectly with hers that a shudder racked her body from head to toe. Owen's panting breaths teased the hair at her temple as he stilled, as though just as shaken as she was by the intensity of sensation.

"Perfect."

The word was almost indiscernible. He brought his head up to look at her and his eyes glowed in the darkness with a feral golden light that made him look every bit an animal. His lip pulled back as his jaw clenched and Owen pulled out, only to thrust home once again, this time with more purpose. A tremor shook him and his brow furrowed as though in pain. Mia knew exactly how he felt. She'd never known such all-consuming want. A sense of desperation overtook her and she thrust her hips up to meet his.

"Don't stop." Her lips could barely form the words, she was so gone with desire. "I need you hard and deep." She needed him to banish the sensation of gnawing want that threatened to swallow her whole.

Owen let out a low groan that echoed perfectly how Mia felt. He pulled out and thrust again, just as she'd asked, nearly jarring her with the force. She responded with a moan that was more relief than anything as her back arched off the mattress.

"Is this how you want it?" He repeated the motion, coaxing another, louder moan from her lips. "Do you like that, Mia?"

"Gods, yes." She couldn't say more than the two simple words. Her arms went wide and she gripped the coverlet in her fists as though to anchor her to the earth. Her chest heaved with breath as her legs hooked around the backs of Owen's thighs in an effort to encourage his vigorous thrusts. It seemed she couldn't get enough, would never be satisfied, and it only made her that much more desperate to find release.

Owen braced one arm beside her as the other went around her. His muscles grew taut and every hard inch of him brushed her body as he continued to thrust. Unintelligible words left his lips, mingling with each groan of pleasure. His breath came in ragged pants that brushed her skin like wind carried from a wildfire. Sweat beaded her skin from the intense heat of his body and her own moans became desperate whimpers as she released her hold on the coverlet to grip his shoulders.

Gods, if she didn't come soon, Mia worried she might die from want.

Her clit throbbed in time with every wild beat of her heart, the blood rushed through her veins to drown out the sound of her own moans, and her muscles tightened with every vigorous thrust of Owen's hips. Her nails dug into his skin and she gave an approving moan that only seemed to spur him on. He liked a little pain with his pleasure and it only served to heighten her own enjoyment.

Power flooded her in a dizzying rush. She'd never known

anything so visceral. So immediate and intense. Her back came off the mattress and she put her open mouth to Owen's shoulder. Without thinking, she bit down and he let out an approving groan as her teeth sank into his skin.

His reaction was all the encouragement she needed to push her over the edge. The orgasm hit her in an instant, sweeping her up in a violent storm that refused to release its hold. Wave after wave of sensation stole over her, to the point that Mia wondered if it would ever cease. Violent tremors shook her as her muscles went rigid. Her teeth bit down harder and Owen let out a shout as he moved to pull away.

"No!" Her fertility cycle was at its crest; this was Mia's only opportunity to free herself from an arranged pairing. Owen might have wanted to exercise a little caution, but Mia wasn't interested in playing it safe. "I want you inside of me when you come."

He thrust hard and deep, burying himself to the hilt inside of her. A rush of warmth flooded her as Owen's thrusts became wild and disjointed. His grip on her tightened and he grew still as he collapsed on top of her. "Gods, Mia." Concern sharpened his tone. "Are you sure?"

Anxiety replaced the warm glow of pleasure. In her experience, most males didn't need an excuse to play it fast and loose. She'd heard werewolves were particularly virile close to the full moon, and Mia was banking on it being true. Unwelcome guilt tugged at her chest. She didn't want to feel an ounce of regret over her actions, selfish as they might be. It wasn't like she was trying to trap Owen, or corner him into a situation where he'd be forced to take care of her and any potential offspring. Just the opposite. Mia wanted nothing more than to live her life on her own terms, and to claim the birthright that should've been hers whether she had a mate, a baby, or neither.

"Thank you, Owen." Her breathing had yet to slow and her heart still raced in her chest. He'd never know what he'd done for her tonight. "You're amazing."

His low chuckle coaxed a renewed flush of heat to her skin. "You're the one who's amazing. I should be thanking you. I couldn't ask for more from my mate."

Mate?

A cold lump of dread formed in Mia's gut. Her situation had just gone from bad to catastrophic.

CHAPTER 5

Owen didn't think it was possible for his situation to get any better. For the hundredth time tonight, he said a silent prayer of thanks for his good fortune. His mate was beautiful, unique, fiery, and passionate. And though he'd wanted to exercise a little bit of caution, she'd thrown it to the wind. Pregnancy was a definite likelihood. She hadn't shied away from the possibility. Instead, she'd welcomed it. So far, their mate bond had gotten off to an amazing start. Owen didn't see how it could possibly get any better.

Mia stilled beneath him and Owen cleared the haze from his lust-addled brain. No doubt he was crushing her beneath his bulk and he shifted away, though it pained him to put even an inch of space between their bodies. He lowered his head and kissed her, a simple glance of his lips to hers. Tonight was the first of many nights together and Owen couldn't wait to start a life with her.

Mia rolled over to her side, putting her back to his chest. His wolf worried in the depths of his mind, sensing her change in posture as some sort of warning. Had he been too rough? Too eager? Too . . . *what*? His arms went around her and he held her close. Too intimate, maybe? Owen recognized her as his mate. That was all that mattered. He shouldn't have presumed that she would recognize it in the same way.

"I'm not sure how this works." It was best to start an open dialogue now. He listened to the quiet rhythm of her heartbeat as he whispered against her ear. "I mean, I know how it is for werewolves. I knew you right away. I was shocked that you recognized the bond as quickly." He laughed. "I don't know where to go from here."

A space of silence passed and it only helped to ratchet his anxiety tighter. Owen didn't want to press her. Now that the euphoria of their passion had passed, she might have needed a few minutes to wrap her head around what had happened. Just because the bond was immediate didn't mean it was simple to accept. It might have been the norm in their world, but they were still creatures with emotions. Owen needed to be mindful of Mia's. He might have been anxious to be mated, but it could've been a shock for her. He could give her what she needed. Anything for his mate.

"Honestly?" Mia let out a slow breath. "I don't know either."

Not exactly a confidence booster, but Owen reminded himself that this was a marathon and not a sprint. They had centuries to navigate the intricacies of their bond. They didn't need to have it all figured out tonight.

"Has this ever happened before?" Owen hoped to keep her engaged in conversation to distract her from whatever worried her. "I mean, werewolves often find their mates outside of the various packs. I wasn't sure if it was the same for nymphs."

Her expression would have told him so much more than her words. It bothered him that he couldn't see her face, giving Owen no choice but to gauge her reactions by scent.

Deception was nearly impossible for supernatural creatures. Lies were easy to detect through heartbeat, scent, the dilation of pupils, the twitch of a muscle, or other physical tells that a human might not notice.

Silence once again stretched out between them and Owen tensed. His wolf grew restless in his psyche and he did his best to calm that very impatient animal part of him. Mia tucked her elbow under her head and the slight shift put another inch of distance between their bodies. It might as well have been a mile, but Owen refused to pay any heed to the worry that knotted his gut.

"I didn't know how the mate bond worked for werewolves . . ."

Not an answer. She was deflecting, but why? Owen wanted to believe her guarded responses had more to do with her own uncertainties than anything else. Why would she know anything about werewolf mate bonds? The bond was the only commonality between them.

"It's immediate." Owen decided the best way to break the ice was with complete and open honesty. He had nothing to hide from her. There was no such thing as secrets between mates. "My wolf recognized you in an instant and I knew you were mine."

"Yours?" She hid the sarcasm in her voice well, but not enough to mask her disdain. "Now I belong to you, is that it?"

"Not at all." Apparently their mate bonds weren't as similar as he'd hoped. Owen let out a sigh as he searched for the right words to explain it to her. "It's not about ownership. I'm yours too, Mia. The wolf knows its mate and the bond is everlasting. The only thing that can sever it is death. I don't want to own you. But you're mine. No other male can claim you. Ever. On that point there can be no argument."

If the rumors were to be believed, the seductive powers of nymphs were the stuff of legend. Their allure was unquestionable. Their sex drives, impressive. Owen could satisfy all of her needs and then some. He wouldn't share her. Wouldn't tolerate another male so much as looking at her with lust in his eyes. He'd put a swift end to any creature that sought to come between them. It was true that he didn't want to own her like some chunk of property. That didn't mean he could do anything about the possessiveness he already felt toward her. Nothing would ever curb that.

"Our mate bonds aren't the same." She didn't elaborate and it was what she didn't say that worried Owen. "But I will admit that I knew there was something between us."

It was a start. Something they could build from. Owen knew that trust wasn't something that happened with the same immediacy as their bond. And he also knew that sex wasn't synonymous with trust—or even love.

"What can I do to help you understand all of this?" Anything that might help make it easier on her.

"Owen . . ." His muscles grew tighter with every awkward pause. Something wasn't right and it agitated the hell out of his wolf. "Being with you . . . it drained me. I can barely keep my eyes open let alone talk." Her scent spiked with a sour tang from the lie she'd spoken. "Can we sleep for a while and talk later?"

More deflection. Panic welled hot and thick in Owen's throat. His wolf reared up with an urgent need to hold her to them and never let her go. He forced himself—and the wolf—to remain calm. He reminded himself that he didn't know anything about her. It was too soon to come to any conclusions one way or the other about her reaction. It could be that all she needed was some sleep.

Too bad his wolf couldn't get on the same page with the lie he'd told himself.

Mia took a deep breath and tried to quell the fight-or-flight urge that rose up within her. It wasn't that she didn't like Owen. On the contrary, she liked him a little too much. And she certainly wasn't afraid of him. In fact, she hadn't been able to shake the feeling all night that she was safer with him than with anyone else in the world. That didn't mean she wasn't ready to bolt, though.

Seriously. A mate bond? How in the hell could this have happened?

"You should rest." Owen's arms tightened around her and he put his lips to her temple for a quick kiss. "I'm sorry if I came on too strong."

He was apologizing? Mia swallowed down a snort as a fresh wave of guilt washed over her. Owen had only obeyed his own instincts and she'd let him believe—though totally unintentionally—that the feeling was mutual. She'd been in for the night while he was in for gods-damned eternity. Mia's heart pounded in her chest and she forced herself to calm. She didn't want to hurt Owen, but eternity simply wasn't in the cards. Mate bond or not.

"You absolutely didn't come on too strong." She shouldn't encourage him, but Mia couldn't bear to hear the disappointment in his deep, rumbling voice. She gave a short laugh. "I think we both know who did that."

"Not at all." Owen nuzzled against her. "Gods, you turn me on."

The feeling was one hundred percent mutual. Another complication. Mia might have told Owen that he'd worn her out, but in truth it was the complete opposite. She'd never felt so energized, so flooded with raw, unchecked power. Her brain buzzed, her skin tingled, and her heart pounded in her chest. The lazy quality to her words wasn't from exhaustion. Mia was absolutely drunk from a few minutes of passion with Owen.

"Mmmm." Her eyes drifted shut as she replayed their moments together in her mind. Pleasant chills danced over her skin. "Believe me, I know exactly how you feel."

"Are you cold?" Owen laid his cheek to hers. "Let's get under the blankets."

Mia couldn't help but laugh. "Owen, I'm not sure if you realize this or not, but your body might as well be a space heater. I'm anything but cold."

"Werewolves," Owen said with a chuckle. "We run hot."

Boy, wasn't that the truth?

"Your skin is a lot cooler. It feels so good."

She wanted to tell him that her body temperature changed with the seasons. Cooler in the winter, warmer in the summer, and so on. She opened her mouth and just as quickly clamped her jaw shut. Anything deeper than small talk would foster an intimacy between them. She couldn't let that happen. Already Mia felt as though she were in too deep.

"I don't need blankets." It might be harder to sneak away if they were entwined in the sheets. Then again, it might be impossible now with the way her body was tucked close to Owen's. "Just . . ." Again, Mia fought the urge to blurt out something too emotional, too intimate for having just met him.

"What?" The warmth in his voice caused her chest to ache.

You. Gods, she couldn't believe she'd almost said the

word out loud. "Just rest." Mia pushed the lie past her lips and prayed he wouldn't pick up on it. "A little cat nap and I'll be fine."

Owen settled his head on the pillow beside her. "We could both probably use a nap."

That's what she was counting on. Mia didn't respond, she simply let her body relax against Owen's. She might not have had any intention of falling asleep, but that didn't mean she couldn't lie here and enjoy the peaceful moment.

Hours passed—or at least, it felt like hours—before Owen's breathing became deep and even. She hadn't planned to sneak out. Hell, if she'd managed to snag a random hookup, she would've been out of here by the time he'd gone to the bathroom to clean himself up. But her situation had changed drastically and now Mia was in escape mode. Owen couldn't have been more attached to her if they'd been sewn together in the middle of the night. He wouldn't simply let her walk out the door without a few more hours of dialogue and careful planning. From what she'd heard, werewolves were notoriously covetous of their mates. She didn't think he'd go so far as to keep her prisoner, but he'd expect some sort of relationship. That wasn't going to happen. Mia had gotten what she needed from him and that was the end of it. She only hoped that her leaving wouldn't be too hard on him.

How did a werewolf react when his mate ran out on him? Mia refused to consider the possibilities. Already the guilt of what she'd done gnawed at her, leaving open wounds that she worried might not heal.

The only sound in the room was that of Owen's even breaths. He lay close to her, one arm slung over her waist. Inch by torturous inch, Mia scooted away, careful not to jostle Owen even a little bit. She let out a relieved breath as she managed to get out from under him. Without a sound, she slipped out of the bed and gathered her clothes from the floor.

Wood nymphs were particularly light-footed. Quiet. Able to move about the forest without stirring so much as a leaf. Her ability to move nearly undetected was enhanced by the power that flooded her. Owen didn't even realize that he'd enabled her escape to be even stealthier.

Mia didn't even chance a backward glance as she ghosted out of the room. Why bother? She'd gotten what she wanted. She had no feelings toward Owen one way or the other.

So why was there a cold lump of regret knotting her stomach?

CHAPTER 6

"Calm down and try not to jump to any conclusions."

Owen stared agape at his alpha. If Devon had run out on Liam in the middle of the night, he would have torn the entirety of Boise County apart in his quest to find her. So many unanswered questions clogged Owen's brain that it was hard to form a logical thought.

Why?

They'd been on the same page last night. Hadn't they? Owen scrubbed a hand over his face as he slumped down on the bar stool in the center of Liam's large, custom kitchen. His elbows came down on the granite countertop of the island bar as he let out a long sigh that ended on a growl. The full moon was only two days away and his wolf was agitated as fuck. The sense of despair that welled in his chest choked the air from his lungs.

"Don't jump to conclusions?" Owen did nothing to hide the incredulity in his tone. "My mate walked out on me in the middle of the night without so much as a word. You don't think that's something I should worry about?"

Liam's brow furrowed, echoing Owen's own worry. They both knew what happened to a werewolf when it lost its mate. Already Owen felt unstable. As though the two parts of his nature warred with one another and threatened to split. It wouldn't be long before the worry deteriorated the part of his psyche ruled by the wolf. Owen would succumb to madness and Liam would have no choice but to kill him.

"Maybe she had a good reason?" The doubt in Liam's voice only helped to solidify Owen's worry. "I don't know anything about wood nymphs. Do you?"

No, and that was part of the problem. Owen assumed bands of wood nymphs lived in remote wilderness areas. Probably why no one ever saw them. The Sawtooth wilderness was vast. He could search for weeks—months—and possibly never find her.

No. His wolf refused to accept that. They'd track her to the ends of the earth if that's what it took.

"Whatever her reasons, she should have told me." Owen still couldn't understand what would have prompted her to walk out on him without a word.

"You've got to admit," Liam said. "Mated males can be a little intense."

That was an understatement. He'd known something wasn't right last night. She reeked of deception and he'd pushed his own concerns to the back of his mind, so gods-damned blinded by his own happiness to accept anything less. She'd recognized their mate bond, hadn't she? Owen thought back to her guarded answers. She'd alluded to it, but she'd never actually admitted to feeling the connection.

Why lie about it, though?

"I might have been a little eager, but I managed to dial down the intensity."

Liam gave him a look that said, *"Yeah. Sure."*

"I'm not going to find her sitting here." What good would it do to stay cooped up in Liam's kitchen when Owen needed to be out *there*, looking for Mia. Hell, she hadn't even had a car to get her back to town. She'd had to have walked the fifteen plus miles back to Stanley. Owen knew that for a supernatural creature, fifteen miles might as well have been fifteen feet. But still . . . She'd chosen to walk out on him— *her mate*—rather than explain her situation or give him a reason why she needed to leave.

His wolf gave a desperate whimper in the back of his mind. He'd been so happy last night. He'd thought a mate bond would solve all of his problems. Instead, it had only managed to create more.

"You're not going to find her if you run out of here half cocked either."

Damn Liam and his levelheadedness.

Owen let out a forceful breath as he tried to ease the tension that pulled his muscles taut. It didn't help that it was so close to the full moon. Owen could let that part of his nature out any time he wanted, but when the moon cycle reached its apex, it was impossible to deny the animal's supremacy. It took over both his body and his mind without Owen's permission. If he didn't find Mia before the night of the full moon, the wolf would run them to death in his search for her.

"Feel like telling me how to form a plan of attack, then?" It wasn't like Owen could ask around and see if anyone in town knew anything about bands of wood nymphs in the area. "Because I'm at a loss."

Owen might have been at a loss, but his wolf knew exactly what to do. *Find her scent. Run the forest and track her. Bring her back here and never let her leave again.* He gave a violent shake of his head as though to dislodge the wolf from his thoughts. Mia was his mate, not his prisoner. He should have articulated the parameters of the mate bond to her better last night. It was obvious that all he'd managed to do was scare her off and he despaired he'd be able to repair the damage he'd done.

He needed to find her before the full moon. Otherwise, the wolf would have his way and there wouldn't be a damn thing Owen could do about it.

"Devon's lived in the area for about a year. Maybe she knows of some reclusive commune?"

Liam was grasping at straws and they both knew it. Devon had lived in Lowman, a town even smaller than Stanley that was about fifty miles north of them. She wouldn't know of any reclusive groups of humans, let alone nymphs, in the area.

"We're surrounded by thousands of square miles of wilderness. If we don't know about nymphs living in the forest, there's no way Devon knows."

Liam shrugged. "It's worth a shot."

"Hell, what if her band doesn't live anywhere near here?" A knot of anxiety twisted Owen's stomach. "What if she'd been passing through on her way to somewhere else?" His wolf could easily track her across a three- or four-hundred-mile radius, but not even the wolf could hold on to her scent if she'd hopped in her car and driven that far. Fate was indeed a cruel motherfucker to allow him to find his mate only to rip her from him.

"If I don't find her . . ." Gods, Owen could barely say the words. "I don't want you to hesitate."

Liam's brow furrowed as he braced his arms on the countertop. He knew exactly what Owen was talking about. There was no need for Owen to elaborate. If he couldn't find Mia, he didn't want to live anyway. A wolf without his mate was volatile. Dangerous. His death would protect more than the pack. It would protect anyone and anything Owen might happen to come into contact with.

"That's not going to happen." Liam's optimism was laughable. "You're going to find her."

Owen hoped so. But in the meantime, he knew it would be foolish not to prepare for the worst.

It would be at least a few days or so before Mia knew for sure whether or not Owen had managed to get her pregnant. She let out a derisive snort. Didn't most females pray for the opposite outcome after a one-night stand? Instead, she was crossing her fingers that his superior werewolf sperm had managed to get the job done. Walking out of that bedroom last night had been one of the hardest things she'd ever done. Mia needed to do something—anything—to get Owen out of her head as soon as possible.

Easier said than done.

Mia climbed the rough-hewn wood steps to the door of her father's yurt. Their band, like all wood nymphs, lived simply. They made their homes in remote wilderness areas; created small, self-sustaining communities; and remained isolated from the world at large. For centuries, they'd been believed to be the vengeful stewards of nature. In truth, they lived in tandem with nature but they were in no way protectors. Just like anyone, all they wanted was to be left alone to live their lives. At least, that's what she'd always believed.

"Come in, Mia."

Leave it to her father to invite her in before she even had a chance to knock. Mia rolled her eyes as she pushed open the door. She was already annoyed and they hadn't even said two words to each other.

She stepped into the yurt and paused. "You wanted to see me?"

If this was going to be another lecture about pairing her off with some shifter or vampire, he could save his breath. Wood nymphs were unique in that they were the only supernatural creatures who couldn't procreate with one of their own kind. And even more unique was the fact that no matter the coupling, their offspring were always wood nymphs. There were no hybrids, no chance of their children being born with attributes of their other parent. Their powers of seduction came in handy for the purpose of producing offspring. Especially if they weren't interested in any entanglements. For centuries, Mia had rejected the notion of motherhood. She'd never wanted to be tied down in any way, shape, or form. A child would have stifled her freedom as much as a mate would have. But thanks to her father's ultimatum, Mia had been forced to choose the lesser of two evils.

"Did you know that a werewolf pack has moved into the valley?"

As of last night she did, but she wasn't about to let him in on that. James Russell Oliver painted quite the portrait as he regarded her from his makeshift throne at the far end of the circular tent. He fit the description of the egomaniacal commune overlord well with his flowing linen clothes, long dark hair, and wild beard. He could have passed for someone in his mid-thirties, but the truth of his age rested in the depths of his dark green eyes. He'd guided their band through the centuries, adhering to ancient doctrine and antiquated ways. Mia wanted more than to live suspended in time. She wanted to join the rest of the modern world. She wanted to move forward instead of remain inert. And the first step to achieving her goals was to produce an heir to their bloodline.

"I hadn't heard." No way was she going to show her hand. "Why do you care if a pack is in the area or not? Werewolves have never been a problem before." Honestly, why would he even bother with a small pack of werewolves who didn't want anything but to be left alone? Wasn't that exactly what he wanted? "Live and let live."

"You think it's that easy?" His disdainful gaze made Mia want to scream. She'd endured his haughty, entitled attitude most of her life. Their kind wasn't any more superior to any other creature that walked the earth. "We've occupied this territory for decades. We have a right to defend it from usurpers."

Usurpers? He had to be joking. "We're surrounded by thousands of square miles of wilderness," Mia replied. "Are you seriously saying you're not willing to share?"

"This is *our* territory."

That wasn't an answer. "Says who?" Mia was pretty sure the human governments—and a few private landowners—would have something to say about that. "We live here because we can get away with it without being detected. Do you think the U.S. Forest Service would be very happy to find our little community in the middle of one of their national forests?"

"They won't find us and you know that, Mia."

True. Wood nymphs—in groups—naturally deterred humans. Unlike the fae who could easily cast a glamour on their community to make it appear as though they weren't even there, wood nymphs had the ability to produce a deterrent that made humans want to keep their distance from their encampments. Werewolves and other supernatural creatures, on the other hand, didn't experience the sensation that they should turn away and run in the other direction. Owen's pack could easily stumble on their community. But why did it matter?

"It's not like nymphs and wolves are natural born foes. The only territoriality a werewolf would take issue with would be another pack in the area. I know for a fact there aren't any other packs for at least a couple hundred miles. I'm not sure I understand why you care."

Her father let out a soft chuff of laughter that grated on Mia's ears. Gods, did he have to be so smug? "Werewolves are thugs. They're base creatures who rely on their animal instincts to guide them. It won't be long before they find us. And when they do, they'll demand that we pack up and leave."

That sounded a hell of a lot like paranoia to her. "And you know this how . . . ?" Seriously, how in the hell had her father come to such a ridiculous conclusion?

"I don't have to explain myself to you or to anyone else. This band is my responsibility. Our people look to me to keep them protected."

Again . . . from what? Nymphs had no natural enemies because even the bulk of the supernatural community believed them to be creatures of myth. With hundreds—hell, thousands—of square miles of wilderness in Boise County alone, there was no chance of a territory dispute. Mia didn't know much about Owen, but if the rest of his pack was anything like him, they were about as dangerous to their band as the actual wolf packs that roamed the area.

"What is this really about?" Mia knew her father. He didn't do anything without good reason, and though he was usually an ambitious, power-hungry, selfish pain in her ass, she had to admit his calculating mind didn't miss a beat. He had ulterior motives for wanting Owen's pack gone. She just wished she knew what they were.

"Until you produce an heir, or you find an acceptable mate?" Her father cocked a brow as he studied her. "None of your business."

Mia gave him look for look. With any luck, last night with Owen would prove fruitful and she'd finally be out from under her father's thumb. What's more, she might be in the know sooner than he thought.

CHAPTER 7

The best and worst thing about occupying the Stanley territory was the fact that it was a sparsely populated area. It's not like Owen could ask around, see if he got a lead on any bands of wood nymphs hanging out in the forest. A werewolf's greatest asset was his sense of smell, and in Owen's case, a mated werewolf had the advantage in that his mate's scent would carry to him over miles and stand out among all other scents. He couldn't be sure if he'd be able to track Mia or not. She could have lived fifty or sixty miles away or five or six hundred miles away. It wouldn't be difficult for any supernatural creature to cover that distance on foot in the space of a day. Mia could have driven to Stanley for all he knew. In which case, she could have been in another state by now.

Gods-dammit. He never should have let Liam talk him out of searching for her. Another day wasted. Another day for Mia to put too much distance between them.

Owen's wolf let out an agitated growl in the recess of his psyche. The animal was tired of sitting around inert. Tired of waiting for their mate to return to them, because he knew better. She'd flown and wasn't planning on coming back. What had her reason been for leaving? The whys plagued

Owen more than anything. He wanted Mia back. Now. He wasn't about to waste another second in his search for her.

It was either that or succumb to madness.

Owen brought his Toyota to a stop at the Bench Lakes trailhead. He had no idea why he'd chosen this location to begin his search, but the wilderness area surrounding Redfish Lake seemed to fit Mia's personality. He could totally picture her living in the densely wooded area with easy access to the many high mountain lakes in the area. Maybe she bathed in the lakes in the summer, the early-morning sun reflecting off her sun-kissed skin . . .

Okay, so maybe that was a bit of a romantic notion, but Owen didn't know enough about wood nymphs to do anything other than make assumptions. Maybe she lived in a mansion with all the amenities somewhere far from here. His wolf disagreed, though. Owen's own animal instinct had guided him here and you could damn well bet he was going to heed it.

He got out of the pickup and grabbed his daypack from the backseat before locking the doors. He'd hike all day and all night too if that's what it took to pick up on even a hint of her scent. Bench Lakes was a moderate hike and a good starting-off point. The least amount of time he had to spend battling the snow and brush, the better.

Mount Heyburn loomed in the distance and Owen took a sip from his water bottle before reaching back to stuff it in his pack. He stretched his neck from side to side as another wave of anxious energy danced over his skin. The wolf wanted supremacy. This was in his wheelhouse and that part of his nature obviously didn't trust Owen in the driver's seat. He could shift. Let the wolf take the lead and control of his body. The transition would be painful and in the long run it would weaken him. He couldn't afford to risk being anything less than one hundred percent. His anxiety over finding Mia wasn't the only thing tickling at the back of his mind.

Danger.

The wolf sensed it even when Owen didn't. Even when neither of them knew exactly what to make of it. He wasn't armed. Didn't have so much as a pocketknife. That didn't mean he couldn't be deadly. If he ran into anything hostile, Owen could protect himself. He might have looked like an unassuming hiker, but he was every bit the animal.

Fresh snow covered the ground, masking the footprints of anyone who might have been in the area. His breath fogged the thirty-degree air and Owen pulled his beanie farther down on his head even though he didn't need its warmth. He might have been decked out in full winter gear, but his preternatural metabolism made it nearly impossible for him to feel the harsh bite of the winter chill. He'd much rather be searching for his mate in the dead of summer. The snow made it harder to track scents, but Owen could work around that. Mia was his mate. He'd find her no matter the distance.

He had to.

Cold air filled Owen's lungs as he took a deep breath through his nose and held it. Clean, crisp, the scent of snow and pine, but not his mate. That didn't deter his wolf, how-ever. Owen headed up the trail and though he wanted to go right, instinct urged him to go left. He changed course, head-ing higher up instead of down. His feet sank into the snow as he walked—the only disadvantage to being a werewolf was an above-normal body density—and he wished he'd had the good sense to pack a pair of snowshoes. The climb would be a workout, that was for sure.

The crunch of his feet busting through the crust of snow

filled Owen's ears as he hiked. His breath fogged the air and he paused as the breeze changed. Faint. So faint that he almost didn't pick up on it at first. All of Owen's senses fired at once as the wolf fought for supremacy in his psyche. He walked another ten feet, twenty, fifty . . . before he stopped and took in another deep breath through his nose.

Mia.

Unmistakable. A scent he would recognize anywhere at any time. Owen supposed it would stand to reason her band might choose to live higher rather than lower. Discoverability was no doubt a concern and the wood nymphs probably chose as difficult a location to find as possible to make their homes. Good thing werewolves weren't easily deterred.

The wolf would have a better chance of tracking Mia from this point. The animal was more agile in the snow, his senses were keener. Owen knew that allowing a shift was the more logical choice. He didn't have time to waste and the wolf was more than eager to be released from the confinement of their human form.

Fuck it. Owen was too damned desperate to find her at this point to play it safe.

He shucked his pack and tucked it into the bowl of a large pine tree. His coat was next, followed by his boots and the rest of his clothes. Cold air kissed his heated skin but Owen didn't so much as shiver. The cold didn't bother him. What was coming would cause him a hell of lot more discomfort that a little snow.

Owen's jaw clamped down tight and he let out a low, painful groan as he went to his knees in the snow. Icy granules bit into his skin but he barely noticed as the transition took hold and his bones began to break and re-form. His mind clouded, his thought process shifted along with his body as the wolf pushed to the forefront of his mind. Owen let out a roar of anguish that transformed into a mournful howl that echoed off the surrounding mountains. The chill of winter disappeared completely thanks to the thick coat of fur that covered his body. He shifted as his paws settled into the snow, his weight displacement better under the weight of all four legs, rather than two.

Mia's scent intensified, banishing the remnants of pain that clung to him. Owen gave a shake as he settled into his animal form completely and he let out a chuff of breath to clear his nostrils. She was closer than he'd initially thought. Twenty, maybe thirty miles.

His body ached, his muscles twitched from the severity of the shift. Full moon transitions were virtually trauma free in comparison and Owen had considerably weakened himself by shifting outside of the moon cycle. He took off at a lope, bounding through the snow rather than trudging through it. The sense of danger intensified, sending a shiver over his body. Whatever the omen was, he hoped it kept its distance until after they found Mia. Otherwise, he might regret his decision to shift.

Mia stoked the fire in the small potbellied stove that occupied one end of her tiny yurt and added a small log before closing the heavy cast-iron door. A chill settled over the circular space, not enough for her to be uncomfortable, but she still grabbed a fluffy fleece blanket from her bed and wrapped it around her shoulders. Now that she was alone, she had too much time to think. Her thoughts inevitably led her to Owen. Dammit. What was supposed to have been a one-and-done had become a hell of a lot more complicated.

She needed to get him out of her head, ASAP. Especially after her father's ominous warning. No doubt he was about to stir up a hornets' nest of trouble with the werewolves. She couldn't help but wonder how he'd react when he found out she'd taken one to bed and had managed to get pregnant by one of the very creatures he wanted to drive out of the area.

At least, she hoped she was pregnant. Mia wasn't about to give up on her quest to circumvent her father's ridiculous ultimatum.

The fire in the tiny woodstove began to burn in earnest and, in no time at all, managed to heat the confines of her yurt. The canvas structure might not have seemed like it would be enough to shelter anyone through a harsh winter, but the four-seasons yurt had been constructed for just that purpose. The green and tan canvas and heavy-duty rubberized roof blended in perfectly with their forest surroundings and the domed skylight at the peaked roof's apex provided a gorgeous view of the moon when the weather permitted.

Mia didn't own a cell phone. She didn't have a TV nor did she spend hours searching for entertainment on social media. In fact, outside of their band, she had very little social interaction. Her night in Stanley had been the most exciting thing she'd done in months. Life within the structure of their band was very routine. Simple. She didn't mind simplicity. She loved being surrounded by nature and she never felt any regret over her lack of technology or technological knowledge. But the world was slowly passing them by and soon they'd be as lost to the modern world as they were forgotten out in this forest. There were probably remote tribes in the middle of the rainforests of South America with less exposure to the modern world than Mia got. She should have considered herself lucky rather than feeling like she was missing out.

So why did regret well up so hot and thick in her chest?

It wasn't because she'd walked out on Owen.

Mia had done what she'd had to do. He'd never have to know what had come of their night together. He'd find another mate—Mia settled down on the tiny love seat across the room from her bed—wouldn't he? She wasn't exactly sure what a werewolf mate bond entailed. It's not like she'd given Owen the opportunity to explain it to her. The wood crackled and popped in the stove and Mia started. Gods, she hoped that in her selfish quest to claim what should have been rightfully hers, she hadn't caused any hurt to someone who didn't deserve it.

She'd never forgive herself otherwise.

Mia tucked her legs underneath her as she huddled under the blanket. A storm was coming, both literally and figuratively. Her skin tightened and tingled with the shift in barometric pressure. Mia felt it throughout her entire being just as every blade of grass, every tree, and every bush felt the change in the weather and seasons. That union with nature made her unique from every other supernatural creature save the fae, and even they didn't feel that sense of kinship in quite the same way.

Mia's hand wandered almost absently to her belly. She'd been so sure the path she'd chosen had been the right choice. Simple. Victimless. No strings attached. Never once had she considered the consequences of her actions. She'd never considered the possibility of forming a bond within seconds of meeting someone. She'd never imagined she'd feel a spark of interest that went beyond her own selfish wants.

Maybe she wasn't so different from her father after all.

In a matter of hours, Owen had managed to shatter the carefully planned outline of her future that she'd constructed for herself. And in the same amount of time, her own father had planted a seed of fear for Owen's safety that rocked her to her foundation. Should she warn him? Give him the opportunity to urge his pack to leave before her father made them go? Would he hear her out or would he berate her for walking out on him in the middle of the night as though she'd been ashamed of what she'd done?

In the long run, she supposed it didn't matter. Mia knew she was too gods-damned chicken shit to face Owen again. Her only hope of diffusing a potentially volatile situation was to try to dissuade her father from continuing on his path. Mia snorted. She probably had a better chance of convincing a horse it was really a dog than she would convincing her father the werewolves weren't a threat to them.

She needed a buffer. Seven or so days before she knew for sure whether or not she was pregnant. The prospect of an heir would shift her father's focus from the werewolves. At least, temporarily. Maybe then she could buy Owen's pack some time. But for what, Mia had no idea.

Her ears perked at the sound of footsteps whispering through the snow outside of her yurt. It wasn't anyone from their band. A four-legged creature circled and Mia listened intently to the rhythm of its steps. A predator stalking prey.

What in the hell?

Predators rarely came this close to their community. Wolves generally stayed closer to the valleys in the winter, following the elk herds. Coyotes and foxes also tended to live in the valley. It couldn't be a bear. They were all hibernating. Maybe a cougar or a bobcat. They were the most likely candidates, anyway.

Mia held the blanket in place around her shoulders as she got up from the couch and crossed to the vinyl window on the north end of the yurt. It might not have given her the clearest view outside, but she didn't need a pane of glass to see the abnormally large wolf perched on a granite boulder

a few yards away. The animal stared at her with such un-
yielding intensity that it caused Mia's breath to stall in her
chest. It wasn't a timber wolf that watched her with disturbing intelligence.

"Shit." The word left Mia's lips on a breath and the wolf
canted his head as though he'd heard her. Wily pain in the
ass. "Gods-dammit, Owen. You shouldn't have come looking for me."

A cloud of steam rose from the wolf's massive snout as it
let out a chuff of breath, letting her know exactly how he felt
about that. So much for deterring or distracting her father. If
he caught Owen anywhere near here, it would only reinforce
his belief that the werewolves wanted to encroach on their
territory and drive them out of the forest.

"Get the hell out of here, Owen!" He hunkered down on
the boulder as though to show her he had no intention of
leaving. "Go! I'm not kidding. You can't be here!" Any argument, any plea, would fall on deaf ears. Stubborn werewolf.
"It's not safe for you, dammit!"

He settled down on the rock and made himself comfortable. Mia got the message loud and clear. The wolf didn't
need words to tell her that he'd stay all night if he had to.
Owen wasn't going anywhere. Period.

Mia crossed to the door in a huff and swung it wide. She
let out an exasperated sigh as she swung her arm in reluc-
tant invitation. "Well? Are you going to sit out there in the
snow all night, or are you going to get your ass in here?"

She didn't think an animal could look smug, but it was
obvious in the wolf's expression as he hopped down from
the rock and leaped through the snow and bounded up the
steps to her front door. She was in way over her head with
Owen. So much for making a plan. Mia had a feeling she'd
be flying blind from here on out.

CHAPTER 8

Owen capitalized on his heightened senses as he entered Mia's yurt. Her scent covered every inch of the space and he let out a relieved breath that he detected no other presence to indicate she lived here with anyone else. Which meant she hadn't walked out on him because she was obligated to another male. Then again, the absence of any other scent might not mean anything. He let out a territorial growl and Mia stilled as she fixed him with an appraising stare.

"You need to get out of here, Owen. Now."

A sentiment he'd heard already from her and one that didn't make a damn bit of difference. He wasn't going anywhere.

"I'm not kidding."

The alarm in her voice was real and his hackles rose. Something—or someone—had her spooked and as soon as he discovered the source of her discomfort, Owen would put a swift end to it. His animal form had been more than useful in tracking her, but now that he'd found her, Owen wanted to be able to communicate with her. Another shift right now would be difficult as well as incredibly painful. It wasn't going to happen. Not immediately anyway. That didn't mean he was any more or less inclined to do as she asked. He could wait a few hours to shift so they could have an actual conversation. Until then, Owen was more than happy to let Mia complain and order him around to her heart's content.

"Do you have any idea how much trouble you're going to stir up?"

What in the hell was she talking about? What sort of trouble? Owen had never been so frustrated over his inability to communicate. Mia paced back and forth, covering the diameter of the circular living space several times over as she muttered unintelligibly under her breath. Her agitation soured her usually clean, outdoorsy scent and Owen's snout wrinkled as he blew out a forceful breath to clear his nostrils of the offending odor.

"You know." Mia stopped dead in her tracks and turned to face him. Her caustic expression amused him more than anything. His mate had fire. He liked that. "It's real convenient that you show up here completely unable to talk to me. And about that . . . How in the hell are you like that anyway? The full moon is still a day and a half away."

Owen supposed it was a common misconception that werewolves could only assume their animal forms during a full moon. It's not like the packs advertised what they could or couldn't do—that was no one's business—and someone who lived as secluded as Mia would adopt those same misconceptions. There would be time enough to discuss their various differences once things settled down. Owen canted his head to one side and he snorted. She could interrogate him all she wanted right now. As soon as he regained his human form, he'd be turning the tables on her.

"Gods, how did you find me?"

He sensed the question was rhetorical. She'd learn soon enough that as his mate, he'd be able to find her virtually anywhere. It rankled to think that she'd hoped he wouldn't find her. She'd run from him, fully intending never to see him again. Owen let out a low growl as he stalked toward her. If Mia had been a wolf, he would have given her a nip to the nose to convey his displeasure. She wouldn't understand the gesture though, and he might only serve to frighten her. Owen took in her infuriated countenance and reevaluated that opinion. Not frighten. He'd only manage to piss her off.

"You can't stay here. You have to *go*."

He'd thought he'd gotten his point across well enough outside. Guess not. Owen settled down on the rug that covered the wooden floor and made himself at home. He folded his front paws in front of him and rested his snout on them. His contented groan caused Mia's eyes to widen with disbelief. He let his tongue loll out of his mouth to convey his amusement at her indignation. Owen could play this game all night.

"Ugh!" Mia threw up her hands and Owen's body shook with humor. "I'm serious, Owen. You have to leave!"

Not gonna happen. He rolled over and showed his belly, turning toward the heat of the potbellied stove a few feet away. He'd spend the night on her floor like a house pet if he had to. Owen wasn't about to back down.

"Has anyone ever told you that you're a raging pain in the ass?"

Liam told him almost on a daily basis. So did several other members of the pack. Owen prided himself on his ability to push the occasional button and he was especially proud of himself for accomplishing the feat with his mate.

"I can make you leave."

Yeah. Right. Owen let out a chuff of breath.

"Owen, *leave*."

Power radiated from the one word, settling like a mantle over Owen's fur. He rolled back over, no longer playful, but both curious and concerned over the sensation of magic that washed over him and clung to his mate's voice. He sat at attention, ears laid back. A warning growl gathered in his chest and rumbled there. She tried to exercise some power over him. Power that he didn't understand. How could he circumvent it if he couldn't identify it? Owen stilled. Some part of him sensed her intent to influence his will. But his wolf sloughed off the magic like beads of water on its coat. She could compel others with her voice? Vampires could perform a similar trick, though he couldn't comprehend just how they accomplished it. Mia tried to do the same thing to him now.

Owen withstood her influence, though. His will was stronger.

Mia's lips thinned. Frustration boiled under the surface of her expression and Owen suppressed the urge to howl his satisfaction at having thwarted her. It would be a few hours before he'd be able to regain his human form and until then he planned to stay right where he was. Maybe if he managed to work her up enough, she'd come clean on what had her so riled without him having to interrogate her for the details. Silence could be a hell of a motivator under the right circumstances, and in his animal form, passive aggression was as good a tool as any.

"Quit looking at me like that!"

Yup. He had her right where he wanted her.

"Owen, please." The appeal in her tone fell on deaf ears. Owen knew the game she played and he wasn't about to let her get away with it. "If you leave now, I promise I'll come by your place tonight so we can talk."

No way, no how. Owen wasn't about to fall for it. If he left, she'd take off again, maybe deeper into the woods this time, and he'd lose all of the ground he'd gained. He let his eyes drift shut as he let out a slow and steady breath. What he needed was a little rest. Time for his body to recuperate what it had lost in the transition. The only way he'd make the next transition easier was to let his body do its thing and replenish what he'd depleted.

"You're going to sleep?" Her incredulous tone pleased him and he settled down on the rug for a nap. "All right, then. Fine. I'm sleeping too."

He was totally okay with that. But this time, he wouldn't allow himself to get too relaxed. He wouldn't allow her to run out on him a second time.

He cracked one lid and watched as Mia crossed the room. She threw back the covers on her bed, flounced down onto the mattress, and covered herself up with a huff of breath, turning her back to him without uttering another word.

Owen let his head rest on the thick rug as he continued to watch her. He supposed he could consider this their first fight.

Delicious warmth enveloped her. Safe. Secure. The comfort had no equal and suffused Mia with a sense of contentment so intense, it filled her chest to the point she thought it might burst. Strong arms encircled her and Mia snuggled into the reassuring embrace that welcomed her body as though it was almost meant to be there. A soft contented sigh slipped from between her lips. She could lie like this all night.

Conscious thought rooted deeper in Mia's mind as she came more fully awake. She wasn't happy or content. She was annoyed and angry as hell, or at least she had been when she'd fallen asleep.

Owen.

The underhanded sneak had waited until she'd fallen asleep to shift back into his human form. And he hadn't wasted any time crawling into bed with her. Mia stiffened beside him and reached down to circle his wrist with her fingers. She lifted to move his arm from around her and met with resistance. *Shit.* She turned to face him and found Owen's hungry gaze trained on her face.

"Good morning."

A sardonic grin curved his full lips and it was all Mia could do not to slap the smug expression from his face. She'd slept all afternoon and through the night. *Wow.* She couldn't remember the last time she'd been so exhausted. Most nights she slept three, maybe four hours at a time, always too restless for anything else. Now, even after almost twelve straight hours of rest, Mia felt as though she could sleep six or seven more. Seriously, what was going on with her?

"Funny, I don't remember inviting you into my bed."

Owen's smile grew. "You looked cold. As your mate, it's my responsibility to make sure you're taken care of."

A riot of butterflies took off in Mia's stomach and she forced the pleasant sensation away. She knew if she gave Owen an inch, he would take five or six miles. "If you're really interested in taking care of me . . ." Mia averted her gaze. "You'll switch back to your four-legged form and get the hell out of here."

Owen's expression fell. Mia didn't want to hurt him. He really was a nice guy. Infuriatingly stubborn, but that was another issue altogether. He couldn't be here, though. Not with her father ready to do whatever it took to force the werewolves out of their territory.

"I already told you." Owen's jaw took on a stubborn set and Mia suspected they were about to go another round. "I'm not going anywhere."

Gods, why did he have to be so pigheaded? It was hard enough to argue with him and being cuddled up next to him in bed wasn't helping the situation. Mia braced one hand on the mattress as she moved to push herself up to sit. Owen wasn't having it, however, and reached out to haul her body against his.

"I don't have time to play games with you." Mia's lids drooped at the sheer pleasure of being held in his strong embrace. His heated skin was a brand against hers, permeating the thin fabric of her T-shirt. "You need to get the hell out of here before someone sees you."

Owen's brow furrowed. Dark clouds gathered in his gaze and Mia shivered. "Who are you trying to hide me from?" A low growl gathered in his chest. "Another male? Whoever he is, he needs to know that you already have a mate. *Me.*"

Oh, it was another male all right. But not what Owen thought. The possessive edge to his tone caused her indignation to flare. She wanted to tell him that she wasn't some bauble he could put in his pocket, and that she'd give herself to anyone she pleased. But it certainly wouldn't get Owen out of there any faster. If anything, he'd more than likely tear their encampment apart in search of whoever she thought she was hiding from him. Her only option at this point was to tell the truth.

"Owen, if my father finds you here, you're as good as dead. So please quit acting like a stubborn ass and go home."

Owen chuckled. Mia didn't think she'd ever met such an arrogant male. No doubt the big, bad werewolf thought himself more formidable, tougher, stronger than any potential opponent. Her father might not have been as bulky as Owen, but Mia knew her father would have no problem taking a single werewolf down.

"Is that all? I thought there was actually a serious problem." So damned confident. "I'm sure once we explain the situation to your father—"

"Absolutely not." Mia felt completely foolish having this conversation with Owen while he held her in his arms. It was much too intimate. Too comfortable. And it put her on edge. "We won't be explaining anything to him. Ever."

Gold lit behind Owen's gaze. A warning. "Why not?"

The question hung in the air. Mia knew honesty was the best policy. That didn't mean she was anxious to get everything out in the open. "None of this is as easy as you think it is, Owen."

"It's as easy or as hard as you want to make it."

Whatever. He could think that now, but he'd change his mind soon enough. "He wants your entire pack out of the Sawtooth territory. And if you don't leave voluntarily, he's prepared to use force to make it happen. That easy enough for you?"

Owen answered her with silence. Good. It was about time he took something seriously. Owen's nostrils flared as he inhaled a deep breath. Mia expected him to loosen his hold on her but instead, he held her tighter.

"What do you mean he wants us gone?"

"Just what I said. I don't know the particulars, and he's not going to share any details with me until—" Mia bit off her words before she said too much. The only way she'd be allowed the privilege of knowing the inner workings of her father's mind was to produce an heir. Mia definitely didn't want Owen to know that.

"Until *what?*"

Mia clamped her jaw down tight. She could be just as stubborn as Owen and then some. His gaze bore into hers as though he could somehow compel her to answer him. *Sorry buddy, not gonna happen.* Owen let out a heavy sigh. He stared at her for another silent moment before his expression turned to one of resignation.

"All right. Fine. Where is your father? I'll ask him myself."

Well, shit. That plan sure as hell backfired.

CHAPTER 9

Owen wasn't about to sit back and let Mia dictate to him. And he sure as hell wasn't going to simply accept that her father wanted him gone and leave. She was going to come clean with him or he was going straight to the source. If she thought it would go down any other way, she had another think coming.

Mia's expression transformed from indignant anger to shock. She obviously thought he was a male of weak convictions and that bothered Owen more than anything. Her gaze slid to the left and she worried her bottom lip between her teeth. The tang of her anxiety soured the air and Owen blew out a breath. She was afraid for him to confront her father? Why? Did she not think him strong enough?

"You are *not* going to speak to my father."

"The hell I'm not." Owen would be damned if he slunk away like a fucking coward. Mia was his mate. Nothing and no one could change that fact. "I don't need an escort. I'll go by myself."

Owen pushed himself up from the mattress and Mia reached out to grab him by the arm. "No!" The urgency in her tone set his wolf on edge and a low growl gathered in Owen's chest. She was afraid of her father. Why? "Owen, please. You need to leave this alone. Confronting my father will only make it worse."

"So you want me to play the coward, is that it?" Anger surged through Owen, constricting his chest. His pride demanded that he prove to his mate he was anything but a coward.

Mia let out a frustrated breath. Owen wanted to laugh. "I don't want you to play the coward. But I do want you to exercise a little gods-damned caution."

"Really?" Owen didn't bother to mask his disdain. "Because it sounds a hell of a lot like you want me to run."

"I want you to play it safe." Mia's voice rose with each word. "I want you to not stir up trouble. I want you to let me deal with this because this is my father, my band, and my responsibility."

"I see." Owen was becoming more agitated with every word out of Mia's mouth. It was clear that she thought him incompetent. "So even though it is *my pack* your father is trying to run out of the area, this is none of my business?"

She flinched as though stung. *Good.* She needed to know Owen didn't appreciate being treated as though he couldn't handle the situation. "That's not what I meant and you know it."

Owen cocked a challenging brow. "Oh no?"

"Argh!" Mia's frustrated growl only egged Owen on. "You don't know my father. I do. I need a few days to figure out what is going on. What if our situations were reversed? Would you be okay with me rushing to interrogate your pack?"

She had a point, but Owen wasn't about to let her know it. "It would be a nonissue because pack rules are different."

Mia's expression turned skeptical. Apparently she wasn't buying his bullshit. "Different from what? Don't sit there and pretend like you know anything about the infrastructure of our band."

"You're right. I don't know anything about you because you ran out on me."

Mia sat up straight on the bed. She pushed herself away from Owen and practically vaulted from the mattress. Her forest-green eyes lit with an angry spark and the air thickened with her agitation. She opened her mouth to speak. Closed it. Her eyes narrowed and her jaw squared, and still she said nothing.

"You had no intention of staying, did you?" The reminder that he'd meant nothing to her punched Owen in the chest, knocking the breath right out of him. "I was nothing more than a one-night stand. You made me think that you felt our bond." He gave a derisive snort. "That's not true. I let you *make me* think that you felt our bond. Because I didn't want to believe otherwise."

Mia's brow furrowed. "You're right." The words left her lips with reluctance, as though the admission were hard to make. "I don't feel the mate bond like you feel it. There's something different about you, I know that much. And you're right that I never intended to stay the night. I'm sorry, Owen. But I wish you'd try and understand that staying away from me is the best thing you can do."

Mia knew as little about werewolves as he did about wood nymphs. Owen sat up on the bed. He brought up one knee and slung his arm to rest on it. Gods, what a mess. He'd hoped everything would fall into place once he found his mate. Instead his life had grown increasingly complicated.

"That's not going to happen. It can't happen. Do you know what happens to a werewolf who's lost his mate, Mia?"

She studied him for a quiet moment. "No. What happens?"

"A werewolf who's lost his mate eventually succumbs to

madness. The bond is so strong that without it, it becomes nearly impossible to function. The synchronicity of our dual nature deteriorates under the stress and the animal part of our psyches splits from our minds. The longer I'm forced to live without you, the harder it will be for me to keep it together. I'll become wild. Rabid. And my alpha will have no choice but to put me down."

"Gods, Owen." Mia let out a slow breath. "I had no idea."

Mia's scent sharpened once again to betray her anxiety. Was their bond so unsavory that it filled her with such intense worry? Bound to a female who didn't want him. Owen couldn't think of a worse fate.

"I . . ." Mia dragged her fingers through the length of her hair. "I don't know what to do. What to say. I don't even know how to move forward from this."

That made two of them. Owen hated to admit that he had no idea where to go from here. But one thing he knew for certain, and that was that he wasn't going to walk away. Mia was his mate. Period. Their bond was absolute.

"I need something to take back to my alpha." Owen could agree not to seek out Mia's father, but he refused to keep this a secret from Liam. "Any little bit of information you have."

Mia's eyes widened a fraction of an inch. "If you tell anyone in your pack what's going on, all it will manage to do is agitate an already volatile situation."

Hardly. The situation would be volatile no matter what. Liam was settled. Mated and happy. The Stanley area had quickly become their home and there wasn't a force on this earth that could drive them out. A tiny knot of worry gathered in the pit of Owen's stomach. Liam wouldn't hesitate to go to war with a band of nymphs to protect what was his. Owen just prayed that he and Mia wouldn't be caught in the crossfire.

"Liam needs to know. If anything, so we can be prepared. You can't possibly want me to keep this a secret? What if your father decides to ambush us? Would you condemn my pack in the interest of buying yourself a little extra time?"

"Of course not!" Mia seemed appalled at the notion and for that Owen could be thankful. "I'm not trying to put you in danger. I'm trying to buy the time I need to convince my father that he has no need to feel threatened."

What could her father possibly be hiding to feel threatened? Owen's wolf gave a nervous whimper in the recess of his mind. Things were bound to get a hell of a lot worse before they got any better.

Mia didn't want to fight with Owen. In truth, she didn't even want him to leave. The simplest touch sparked something within her that filled Mia with euphoric power. She might not have felt the bond that connected her to Owen, but she felt *something*. And it wasn't anything she was ready to discount.

"Liam is a reasonable male." Owen's deep voice vibrated in his chest and Mia swore she could feel it over every inch of her skin. She was a little surprised to learn that Owen wasn't the alpha of his pack. His personality fit the title to a T. If he wasn't in charge, he was definitely a prominent figure in their hierarchy. She found herself growing more curious by the second, and that was a very dangerous thing. "He's not going to go off half cocked and march up here to pick a fight."

"You say that," Mia began. "But can you be sure?"

"Without a doubt. I've known Liam for centuries. Besides, he's not interested in picking fights with any of the local supernatural population. When we moved into this area there were no other wolf packs for miles. All he wants is to live here in peace. I'm sure your father wants the same."

Did he? Mia was beginning to wonder. Something fueled his desire to run the wolf pack out of the Sawtooth territory. Mia just couldn't figure out what it was. She planned to get to the bottom of it though, and soon.

"How did you find me?" The question came out of nowhere, but Mia had been curious since yesterday. "The snow would've covered my scent. Even an expert tracker would've lost the trail."

Owen flashed an arrogant smile that turned her insides to mush. "You're my mate. I could find your scent anywhere, even diluted to the point that there was barely a trace."

Interesting. Just one more fun fact Mia didn't know about werewolves. A familiar ripple of anxiety spread from her stomach outward. What Owen had so simply told her was that it didn't matter if she ran or tried to hide. He could find her *anywhere*.

"Good to know." She gave a nervous laugh that she hoped masked her worry. "If that's the case though, I think it's safe to say you can trust me when I say I'll come to your place tonight if you leave right now."

Owen studied her. She saw a hint of the animal in his gaze. Mistrustful. Wary. On edge. If Owen was stubborn, the wolf was one hundred times more so. Getting rid of him would be a lot tougher than she'd thought.

"What does my leaving accomplish?" His smile dimmed to almost a scowl. "Besides getting me out of your hair?"

Mia cringed. She'd done very little to build any trust between them so it wasn't like she could blame him for exercising a little caution. Still, he'd said himself that he could track her no matter where she went. What would be the point in running? She needed him to meet her at least halfway on something.

"My father is ready to do whatever it takes to push your pack out of our territory. What do you think he'd do if he found out one of those werewolves had claimed his daughter as a mate?"

Honestly, if a pairing with a werewolf would've been somehow advantageous to her father, he would've welcomed Owen with open arms. But Mia had a feeling Owen wouldn't pull up camp and leave his pack in order to live here with her. Likewise, Mia had gone through too much to walk away from her birthright. She wasn't about to give up all of her ambitions for a male, no matter how amazing he might be.

Amazing? She barely knew Owen. It was a little early for adjectives like that, wasn't it?

Owen bristled. "He'd hurt you?"

Her father was a lot of things. Self-serving, arrogant, at times ignorant. Stubborn, vindictive, and a little hotheaded. But he'd never raised a hand to her. He'd make her life miserable in other ways, but she didn't think he'd physically harm her.

"He won't hurt me. But he's not going to be happy with me either."

Owen scrubbed a hand over his face as he shifted on the bed. Mia's gaze wandered to where the sheet gaped away from his torso and for the first time since she'd woken in his arms, she was painfully aware of his nakedness. Gods, he was a magnificent specimen. "I want to trust you, Mia. But . . ."

Okay, so maybe she hadn't done much to invite his trust. They barely knew each other, though. What did he expect? "But what?"

"But . . . it's too close to the full moon and the wolf wants supremacy in my mind. Making rational decisions is a little more difficult."

"Owen." Tender emotion swelled in Mia's chest and she tried to swallow it down. She couldn't afford to feel anything for him. There wasn't room in her life for a mate. For a relationship. For . . . *him*. "I promise I'll come by your place tonight. Give me some time to figure out what's got my father so riled and we'll decide how to deal with the situation. Together."

That last word seemed to be the tipping point for Owen. He studied Mia for a quiet moment and she squirmed under the intense scrutiny. "Together?"

"Yes." No matter how she felt about a future with Owen, Mia knew she couldn't dissuade her father from his course of action on her own. Especially since she wasn't yet sure if she'd managed to buy her place in their hierarchy by producing an heir. "I need to know his reasoning before we can form a plan of attack moving forward."

"And what if he explains himself to you and you find that you agree with him?"

Mia suppressed the urge to laugh out loud. She'd agree with her father when hell froze over. "Believe me, Owen. That isn't *ever* going to happen."

"All right then." Finally, he'd come to his senses. "But if you're not at my place by nightfall, I'm going out to find you."

"Fair enough." It would likely take all day to drag even one little piece of information out of her father. She'd managed to buy herself some time and whether or not she had anything to offer Owen, she'd be sure to keep her word and show up at his house by sundown. "I'll be there."

At least, she hoped she would.

CHAPTER 10

Liam fixed Owen with an incredulous stare. "What do you mean he wants us gone?"

Owen hadn't wasted any time in retrieving his clothes and daypack from the bowl of the tree where he'd left them the day before and hightailing it home. The sooner they got this mess straightened out, the better. Any strife between their two groups would ultimately affect his and Mia's bond and Owen wasn't about to do anything to disrupt the small amount of progress he'd made with her.

He'd enjoyed Mia's surprise when he strode from her yurt completely naked and ready to trot through the snow back to his pickup. He couldn't initiate another transition so close to yesterday's without it weakening him considerably. With the threat of Mia's father's supposed machinations looming, Owen couldn't risk being anything less than one hundred percent.

He needed to hope for the best and expect the worst. And he needed to be prepared for anything.

With any luck, Mia would open up to him even more tonight. He'd never known a more guarded female. She coveted her secrets, masked her emotions, and hid her intentions well. Owen realized she didn't feel their bond in the same way he felt it, but she'd confessed to feeling *something*. He held on to the glimmer of hope that accompanied the word. Something was better than nothing. He could work with something. Mia could feign disinterest all she wanted but Owen had noticed the way she'd looked at him when he'd crawled out from under her sheets and left the comfort of her bed. His blood raced through his veins at the memory of her heated gaze as it settled between his thighs.

"I literally know as much as you do right now." As the pack's beta and Liam's second-in-command, Owen prided himself on being on top of everything. His lack of knowledge in regard to the current situation was a serious thorn in Owen's side. He just had to hope his mate would come through on her end. "Mia has no idea what her father's problem with us being here is or why he wants us gone."

"I thought moving us here would help to eliminate our problems," Liam said. "Instead, it seems to only be creating more."

Liam's regrets were misplaced. Moving the pack had proved to be the best thing that ever happened to Owen. And he was sure it was the best thing that ever happened to Liam. A guiding force had brought them to Idaho. They were meant to be here. Owen wouldn't discount that certainty, and he wouldn't let some power-hungry wood nymph push him out of his home.

"It's not going to be a problem because I'm not going to let it become one," Owen replied.

"This isn't your issue to sort out." Liam blew out a forceful breath. "You didn't create the problem. In fact, your mate bond might have given us the upper hand."

Maybe he hadn't created the problem, but it sure as hell felt that way.

"Are you sure Mia will come tonight?"

As sure as he could be. Owen hadn't sensed any deception in her words. Owen wanted to trust her because he had no other choice. The alternative would only take him down the road to ruin. "She'll come," he said without an ounce of doubt. "She doesn't want conflict any more than I do."

"Fair enough. We'll wait until she shows up tonight and go from there. It's a waste of time to form a plan until we know for sure what's going on."

Owen nodded in agreement. There was no point in jumping to conclusions yet. He only hoped he could get through the day without worrying himself to death. Mia would keep her word. He repeated the mantra to himself over and over again. His mate wouldn't let him down.

"I think this might be the most time we've spent together in decades."

Mia was less than thrilled with her father's smug tone, but he had a point. She usually went out of her way to avoid him. Too bad that was no longer a possibility. Mia was going to have to step up and be assertive, especially if she wanted to assume any sort of leadership role within their band. An heir would secure her birthright, but proving she was a competent leader would earn the respect of her people.

"I'm pregnant." Okay, so it was a little early to make that sort of declaration. Mia wasn't entirely sure she was, but the bluff was necessary to gain her father's confidence.

Her father's eyes narrowed as he studied her. His gaze raked her from head to toe as though he could tell whether or not she was lying. He sat back in his chair looking every bit the king he thought himself to be. Mia was so tired of their antiquated pseudo-monarchy and part of the reason she fought so vehemently for her freedom and birthright was the opportunity to initiate change within their band.

"How and when did this happen?"

His suspicious tone did nothing for Mia's already frazzled nerves. She threw back her shoulders and bucked her chin up a notch. She refused to let him intimidate her.

"I suspect you know how it happened." Mia did nothing to hide her flippant tone. "As to when, I went into town a couple of weeks ago and found a suitable male." More like a couple of days ago, but Mia needed her story to be convincing.

"Who?"

For someone who generally didn't give a shit about her, her father had grown pretty damned interested in her personal life. "Who isn't important. What matters is that I've secured my birthright and a place in this band's leadership."

His answering laughter caused Mia's hackles to rise. "You think it's that simple? Do you actually think you can come to me, claim a pregnancy, and simply usurp my position?"

In a perfect world, that's exactly how it would happen. But Mia knew better. "No. But I do expect you to honor our agreement and allow me my rightful place within the leadership."

"That's not going to happen. At least not now."

Of course. Mia should have known the bargain they'd struck was nothing more than a ploy to get her out of his hair. He would never share power. He'd use any excuse to fight change and Mia suspected that his beef with the werewolves was just one more sleight of hand to keep their people preoccupied and their focus shifted from the real issues that affected them.

"Because of the werewolves." Mia was through playing nice, done with mincing words. If her father thought her intentions were to usurp his position, maybe she'd do just that.

"They pose a serious threat and I won't suffer their presence here for another day."

Her father had seriously gone off the deep end. What was he even talking about? He knew nothing about Owen's pack aside from the fact that they'd moved into the valley. As far as she knew, her father rarely left their encampment. He was no better than a mountain hermit and his only source of information came from the members of their band who occasionally ventured into town.

"They pose about as much of a threat as the squirrels who chatter at us from the trees." There was no way he'd be forthcoming with information. The only way Mia would get anything out of him would be to goad him into a fight. "You should get out a little more, venture out of the camp and see what's going on around you. You've gotten paranoid over the past several decades and your people will suffer because of it."

He responded with a bark of laughter. "My daughter has suddenly grown wise it seems." He gave a sad shake of his head that only served to infuriate Mia. "Just because you are drawn to civilization doesn't mean you know anything about how the world works."

Insulting her intelligence was a low blow but not surprising. His only defense for his actions was to lash out at her, discredit her, and beat her into submission with his words. Mia was stronger than he gave her credit for. His tactics wouldn't work.

"But you do, is that it?" Her father had hidden himself away for so long that he knew ridiculously little about the surrounding communities of humans and supernaturals alike.

"I know what's best for this band," he replied. "And as a member of that band, you will accept my word as law."

He pushed himself up from his chair and Mia fought the urge to take a cautious step backward. She kept her feet planted firmly to the floor and gave her father look for angry look. He crossed the space between them in three purposeful strides and came to a stop mere inches from where she stood. A deep crease marred his brow and his green eyes sparked with indignant fire.

"Don't think for a second that I believe the claims you've made today. I intend to find you a suitable partner. One who will keep your rebellious attitude in check. After tonight, the werewolves will no longer be a problem. You will see what it takes to be a true leader. I will protect our band and our territory from anyone who thinks to encroach on it."

A cold lump of dread settled in Mia's stomach. "What are you going to do?"

"That, daughter," he said, "is none of your business."

So much for taking control and bringing a little common sense into the mix. It looked like Mia would be paying Owen a visit sooner than she'd thought.

CHAPTER 11

The minutes seemed to crawl by on broken legs. Owen was antsy as hell and couldn't settle down long enough to sit. He paced the confines of his cabin, ready to venture out and go to Mia even though he'd promised not to until after nightfall. It was barely three in the afternoon. It would be another two hours before the winter sun set. He still had a couple of torturous hours left before he could expect to see Mia.

"Owen! Can I come in?"

Mia's urgent voice preceded a round of knocks at his door. Owen crossed the space of his cabin in a couple of steps and threw the door wide to let her in. Panic joined the sense of relief that flooded his system and Owen's limbs shook with unspent adrenaline. His wolf gave an anxious yip in the back of his mind. Something wasn't right.

"What's wrong?"

There was so much more that Owen wanted to say to Mia. He wanted to tell her that he was happy to see her, that he knew she'd keep her word, that simply having her by his side was enough to put his mind at ease. He wanted to compliment her wild beauty, to take her in his arms and put his mouth to hers. He wanted to strip her bare, run his nose along her skin as he inhaled her delicate, sweet river scent.

He wanted to show her just how much he missed her in such a short amount of time apart. All of that would have to wait, though. The coming conflict took precedence over Owen's love life. Gods, he hoped they got this matter with her father rectified soon.

"My father screwed me over, that's what's wrong!" Mia's infuriated tone threatened to coax a smile to Owen's lips. He certainly wouldn't want to be on the receiving end of that anger. "I should've known he'd go back on his word. Power-hungry bastard."

Owen had no idea what she was talking about but he made a mental note to get the full story as soon as possible. "Sounds like we have a lot to talk about." Owen took Mia by the hand and led her into the living room. "Were you able to find anything else out about his vendetta against the pack?"

Mia snorted. "He's delusional. And making a problem where there isn't one. He wouldn't tell me anything because that would mean he'd have to acknowledge I was capable of leadership. He's got something planned, though. For tonight. Maybe some sort of ambush."

"Shit." The timing couldn't be worse. "Tonight? You're sure?"

"Yeah." Mia fixed Owen with a curious stare. "Why?"

Owen dragged a hand through the strands of his hair and blew out a frustrated breath. "Because tonight's the full moon."

Mia's eyes widened a fraction of an inch. "Shit."

Exactly.

"It'll definitely make negotiating with him a little tough," Owen replied. "Plus, if your father's as threatened by us as he claims to be, coming face-to-face with a pack of wolves anxious for a hunt isn't exactly going to endear us to him."

"Yeah," Mia said on a breath. "That's definitely going to complicate things."

Understatement of the century. Liam wouldn't be happy with this development. "I take it your father isn't exactly a reasonable male?" From the sound of it, he was an unreasonable piece of shit. In the interest of keeping the peace, Owen decided it would be best to reserve judgment for now.

"What he is," Mia began, "is a lying, calculating, underhanded pile of crap."

Okay, so it looked like maybe Owen wouldn't have to reserve judgment. Mia's assertions about her father definitely indicated that dealing with him wouldn't be a picnic. No doubt they were about to step in it in the worst possible way.

"Do you know anything at all about his battle tactics?" Any tiny bit of information Mia could provide would be helpful. "Has your band ever gone to war before?"

"War?" Mia's incredulous tone was all the answer Owen needed. "I don't know if you realize this or not, Owen, but as supernatural creatures go, wood nymphs aren't exactly aggressive."

It was nearly impossible to realize anything about such a reclusive group. Especially when Mia was so tightlipped about her band and their culture. "So you don't tend to pick fights," Owen said. "That's good to know. But your father has to have some reason to believe that he'd win in a conflict. Otherwise, he wouldn't be doing what he's doing."

Mia worried her bottom lip between her teeth and it was all Owen could do not to kiss her. When this was all over, Owen vowed to do everything in his power to ensure Mia belonged fully to him. Mind, body, and soul.

"If you're suggesting he has an ace up his sleeve, I have absolutely no idea what it might be."

"Think, Mia." Surely she wasn't ignorant of her own

abilities. "You know what you are and what you're capable of. What would his advantages be in a fight?"

Mia stepped around him and took a seat on the couch. She settled back into the cushions and stared off into space. Owen forced away the agitation that crept up on him. She was his mate. There should be no secrets between them. And yet, she seemed to contemplate her forthcoming answer carefully, as though not sure how much to divulge. After a moment, she brought her gaze up to meet his, her brow furrowed.

"Honestly, Owen. I have no idea."

Her scent remained clean, which meant she hadn't tried to deceive him. Then again, Owen had let himself be misled by her before. He needed to be wary. He took a seat beside her but remained silent. He'd give her a few more minutes of reflection. It could be that her mind was simply scattered and she needed a moment to gather her thoughts.

"Wood nymphs aren't exactly powerful on the supernatural scale," Mia said with a sad laugh. She averted her gaze. "Our talents sort of lie in sex. Well, sex and influence. Our voices can bend certain creatures to our will."

Wasn't that the truth? They'd only been together once but it stood out as one of the best nights of Owen's existence. Her admission didn't surprise him. She'd tried, unsuccessfully, to influence him when he'd been in his wolf form. He wasn't bothered that for the most part the rumors and legends had turned out to be true. Owen supposed the world should count themselves lucky that wood nymphs chose to live isolated and deep in forested areas. If they ever decided to enter mainstream society, they could effectively rule the human world.

"Maybe your father thinks to control us with that power," Owen suggested. "He might think he can show up here, order Liam to leave, and expect him to obey with little to no conflict."

"No." Mia gave a slow shake of her head. "It can't be that simple."

"You can't think of any reason at all why your father wouldn't want werewolves in this territory?"

Mia contemplated Owen's question for a silent moment. "No." She brought her gaze up to meet his. "I mean, the chances of us even encountering one another are slim to none thanks to the vastness of the wilderness areas surrounding Stanley. And as far as trying to influence you to leave, it wouldn't work. It can't be done. I've tried with you and it doesn't even faze you. Our influence doesn't work on the dual-natured. Your minds are too strong."

Could it be that simple? Gods. The answer had been right in front of his face the entire time. "Come on." Owen grabbed Mia by the hand and hauled her up from the couch. "We need to go talk to Liam. Now."

Mia was surprised at the sheer size of the pack alpha's house in comparison to Owen's modest cabin. It was too big, too extravagant, and left too large a footprint for Mia's taste. It also seemed a mark of status. Another turnoff. Her father might have been a stubborn asshole who refused to share the privilege of ruling, but his yurt was no larger, no more extravagant than any other member of their band. For what seemed like the hundredth time since she'd met Owen, Mia wondered at their differences. How could his wolf possibly have chosen her as their mate when so many things seemed to divide them?

"Tonight? You're sure?"

Mia held in a snicker as Liam repeated Owen's earlier

words. Maybe they should have gathered the entire pack at once to eliminate anyone else asking for confirmation of the timeline.

"Nymphs can influence the wills of others," Owen said. "But according to Mia, the dual natured are immune to that power."

Liam fixed Mia with a scrutinizing stare. Power vibrated from him, much like the power she felt from Owen, only a little stronger. Gold flashed in his gaze, revealing a glimpse of the animal that lived beneath his skin. Cold dread stroked a finger down Mia's spine. Tonight was sure to end in disaster.

"Is that true?"

"Yes, it's true." There was no use mincing words with Owen's alpha. They were in their eleventh hour. The sun would be setting soon, and in its place a full moon would rise. The pack would have no choice but to succumb to its pull and Mia would be left virtually alone to face her father. It would've been nice if the pack had a non-werewolf spokesperson for times like these. In the space of a few days, she'd gone from wanting to rule her people to betraying them. All because of her own selfishness and a one-night stand.

"I think that's why he wants us out of here," Owen added. "Because he can't control us."

Mia's brow furrowed as she focused her attention to Owen. "What do you mean?"

"You said your father rarely left your encampment, but can you be sure? What if he's been venturing out for months, hell, years? What if he's been spending that time manipulating humans and other supernaturals? What if he's not content being the leader of a small band of wood nymphs? What if he wants more?"

Mia's jaw dropped. *Holy hell.* Owen's theory was as outlandish as it was believable. It's not like she kept tabs on her father. Mia tended to put as much distance between them as possible. She'd always just assumed he stayed close to home. He could've gone into town regularly and she probably wouldn't have known. "Stanley is a tiny community." If her father was interested in world domination, their small mountain town wasn't exactly an ideal place to start. "It's literally a stop on the way to somewhere else."

"Exactly!" Owen's eyes went wide with excitement. "Everywhere from Lowman to Sun Valley is a pit stop. Think about how much through traffic these tiny towns get. All it would take is for your father to plant a single thought in the mind of a passerby and they would carry it with them to wherever they went."

"Sort of like spreading a virus," Liam added with a derisive snort.

Gods. If Owen was right, her father could have amassed an army without anyone knowing. "He could bring a war to your front door and never even step foot across the threshold."

Owen and Liam exchanged a knowing look. Apparently, they'd come to the same conclusion.

"What are we going to do?"

Owen angled his body to face her. His grim expression sent a ripple of trepidation over her skin. "We wait for an attack and we fight back."

Mia couldn't remain neutral. She'd have to choose a side: her family, or the male who'd managed to worm his way under her skin over the course of a few short days. Either way, it was Mia who would be the loser. There was no turning back.

CHAPTER 12

Owen's skin crawled with the impending full moon shift. It would be a few hours before the moon was high enough in the sky to initiate the involuntary transition, and until then, he would have to suffer the mild discomfort that was a precursor to the event. Owen climbed the steps to his cabin, glad to have the meeting Liam had called with the pack concluded. They were as informed as they could be, and as prepared as they would get. All that was left to do now was wait.

He walked into the cabin to find Mia curled up on the couch asleep. Her beauty took his breath away. Living, breathing nature. Unpredictable and wild. His wolf gave an appreciative growl in the back of his mind. Owen still couldn't believe this extraordinary female belonged to him, no matter how tenuous their bond. The impending conflict didn't sit well with him. They hadn't talked about it, but they both knew Mia would need to make a choice: her mate, who she barely knew, or her father. Was it wrong that Owen desperately wanted her to choose him?

"Hey." Her lids cracked open with her groggy greeting. "How'd it go?"

"As well as can be expected," Owen said. "Considering we don't know what's coming."

Mia cringed. "I'm sorry, Owen. I really thought he'd let me in and tell me what he was planning."

Owen took a seat beside her. He lifted her legs and set them in his lap. "There's nothing for you to be sorry about. You gave us a heads-up, and that's enough."

"It sure doesn't feel like much. I always knew my father was ambitious, but if you're right, this surpasses even what I thought he was capable of."

"You should leave." Owen's wolf let out a low warning growl to express its displeasure with his words. *Tough shit.* Mia's safety was more important than their selfish need to have her by their side.

Mia braced herself on an elbow and brought her head up to study him. Her brow furrowed and her lips thinned. "You don't want me here?"

The hurt in her voice sliced through him. "I don't want you to leave," Owen said. "But I don't want you to get hurt and I don't want you caught in the middle of this."

Mia answered with a soft snort. "It's a little late for that."

"It doesn't have to be. Your father doesn't need to know you—"

"It's too late because I don't want to leave," Mia interrupted. "Gods." She let out a disdainful bark of laughter. "I can't believe I'm saying that."

Honestly, Owen was just as surprised. That's not to say he wasn't pleased as hell to hear it. "I can't have you here, Mia. We have no idea what to expect. There's bound to be chaos, confusion. If you get caught in the crossfire, I might not get to you in time." Owen's breath caught in his chest at the thought of losing her. They might have only known each other for a few days, but the intensity of the connection that bound them was undeniable.

"I can take care of myself, Owen," Mia replied. "You don't need to worry about me."

He laughed. "Obviously you have no idea how intense a werewolf's mate bond can be. Protecting you is tantamount. I would die to keep you safe."

Mia's lips parted, softening her beautiful mouth. "Owen, that's crazy." She sat up straight and scooted over until their thighs touched. "I would never ask you to sacrifice your life for me. I would never want you to."

Owen couldn't help himself. He reached up to cup her cheek in his palm. "I'd die anyway." It was the truth. Without his mate, Owen couldn't be allowed to live. "It would be worth the sacrifice to keep you safe."

Mia leaned in and put her mouth to his. Her petal-soft lips moved over his slowly, the kiss so deliberate and full of heat that it made Owen sweat. His arms went around her and he hauled Mia onto his lap. She leaned into his body as her arms went around his shoulders. One hand reached up to tease the hair that brushed the nape of his neck. His cock hardened behind his fly and Owen shifted. The timing couldn't be worse but he wasn't about to stop. Not when this might be the last time he'd ever hold his mate in his arms.

Mia broke their kiss. Her mouth brushed his jawline, his cheek, his ear. Her breath was like a cool breeze against his warmer flesh as she took the lobe between her teeth and bit down gently. Owen grunted as his hips gave an involuntary thrust. Her lips came to rest at the outer shell of his ear. "I want you, Owen. I've wanted you since the moment I laid eyes on you."

He couldn't have asked for sweeter words. He'd despaired that they'd ever be on the same page. Finally, it seemed like everything was beginning to fall into place. Too bad they might not survive the night.

Mia pushed away. Owen immediately missed the weight of her body against his as she stood, positioning herself between his legs. She reached for her shirt and stripped it from her body before discarding it to the floor. Her bra went next and Owen's breath caught as he took in the perfection of her high, upturned breasts. His gaze followed the path of her hands as they came to rest at her waist and remained there as he watched her slowly unfasten her pants and slide them down her thighs along with her underwear.

"Mia." He nearly choked on her name as his eyes wandered greedily over her naked body. "You're so gods-damned beautiful."

Her cheeks flushed as she averted her gaze. The compliment had been paltry in comparison to what he wanted to say to her. If they made it through this, he would shower her with compliments every day until she got tired of hearing them.

Mia leaned in close. She wrapped her fingers around the hem of Owen's shirt and stripped it from his body. Her gaze heated as she reached for his belt and unfastened it. Owen shifted on the couch, scooting his butt out to the edge of the cushion as she unfastened the button, dragged down the zipper, and pulled his jeans and underwear down to his ankles.

"You want to kick off your shoes or should I take care of it?"

The promise in her husky tone was all the encouragement Owen needed. He kicked his boots off with so much force, it was a wonder he didn't rip them. His feet fanned out like flippers as he kicked his jeans the rest of the way off. Mia's lips spread into a seductive smile that tightened Owen's gut. She kept her gaze locked with his as she climbed back onto the couch and straddled his hips.

He had no idea if they'd survive the night, but if not, she was about to give him one hell of a send-off to the afterlife.

Mia was tired of fighting her attraction to Owen. He'd occupied nearly every single one of her thoughts since the night they'd met, and as hard as she'd tried, she couldn't get him out of her head.

Every inch of her burned with need. Like the first time they were together, Mia couldn't be bothered with foreplay. The moon would be high in the sky soon enough and she didn't want to waste a single second.

Mia came up on her knees as she positioned herself over the rigid length of his erection. She reached behind her and took him in her hand as she guided him to her opening. She gasped at the shock of heat and let out an indulgent moan as she lowered herself fully on top of him. He filled her completely, stretching her inner walls. She began to move, gentle rolls of her hips that created the perfect amount of friction as he slid in and out of her.

"Oh gods, Owen. That feels so good."

His arms came around her and he pulled her down hard on top of him as his hips thrust upward. The sharp stab of pleasure caused Mia to gasp. He repeated the motion and she arched her back as her head rolled against her shoulders. "Yes." The word came out with all the forcefulness of a breath. "Just like that. Don't stop."

The pleasure was blinding in its intensity. It nearly paralyzed Mia's brain to the point that she couldn't form a coherent thought. She continued to roll her hips, meeting every one of Owen's desperate thrusts with equal fervor. She was out of her mind with want, wound so tight with the need for release that she could barely breathe. The only sound in the house was that of their racing breaths and low moans.

With every wild thrust of Owen's hips, power built and crested within Mia. The air sparked with magic and filled her with a sense of strength that she'd never felt before. Owen evoked something in her. Something primal and powerful. She felt as though she existed outside of her body, a being of infinite light that couldn't be contained by her physical form.

"Mia." Owen's voice filled with wonder as his hands came to rest at her hips. He continued to fuck her with wild abandon and she gripped him harder, letting her nails bite into his shoulders. "Can you feel that? The energy, it's amazing!"

She knew exactly what he felt and it was unreal. The foreign magic continued to build within Mia to the point that she didn't know how she'd be able to contain it. It was a force of nature. A summer storm, lightning, wind, and rain. It was a blizzard, blinding and fierce. It was the heat of the sun and the chill of ice, the crash of ocean waves and the rumble of the earth as it quaked. Mia felt its power in every cell that constructed her and her body went rigid as the deep pulsing shock waves of her orgasm overtook her.

Her cries of passion turned to deep wracking sobs of pleasure. Owen's fingers gripped her tight, biting into her hips as he thrust up once, hard, and went still. His head went back to rest on the cushions of the couch and a low, sultry growl rumbled in his chest. Tiny spasms shook his solidly built form and each little movement triggered another intense round of sensation that fired along Mia's nerve endings, leaving her feeling energized and exhausted at the same time.

She leaned forward and her head came to rest on Owen's

shoulder. "I've never . . . ," she began between panting breaths. "Wow. What in the hell was that?"

Owen gave a low chuckle. He sat up straighter and his mouth met her shoulder, her throat, and then her jaw. "I have no idea, but let's hope it happens again."

Mia laughed. "Don't worry. If I have my way it'll definitely happen again."

"Good." Owen smiled against her skin. "Because that was amazing."

Mia had never experienced anything like it and she'd thought the last time they were together had been amazing. It was nothing compared to what they'd just shared. Maybe there was more to their mate bond than she'd thought.

She lost track of time as they remained on the couch, bodies entwined, skin to skin. Owen groaned but it spoke more of pain than anything pleasant. Mia pulled back to look at him. Concern tightened her chest. "Are you okay?"

"Moon's almost up." Owen forced the words out and another wave of crippling fear stole over her. "I need to meet Liam and the others at the back of the property. Stay here. Lock the door. Don't leave. Promise me."

Mia didn't want Owen to leave. She didn't want him to step a foot out the door. Her own worry nearly crippled her. Owen lifted her as though she was the most precious of cargo and set her down gently beside him. His gaze delved into hers, deathly serious.

"Promise me, Mia."

"Okay." She couldn't say the exact words he wanted to hear because she knew if he got into trouble there was no way she could sit here and do nothing. "Be careful though, all right?"

Owen pushed himself up from the couch. He gave her a reassuring smile as he headed for the door. "I plan on picking up where we left off in the morning. I'll be more than careful."

The response coaxed a smile to Mia's lips. "Just gonna run out there in your birthday suit, huh?"

"Yup. Werewolves don't have a lot of use for clothes during a full moon. Be back soon. Lock the door when I leave."

Mia nodded. Locking the door wouldn't do a damn bit of good and he knew it. "See you soon."

He gave her a wink in parting before opening the door and stepping out into the cold winter air.

Mia didn't bother to lock the door. Instead, she hurried to dress and pulled on her boots. Unspent energy cycled through her body, causing her limbs to shake. She didn't know what it was that had happened to her, but she swore she'd find a way to put it to good use. Whatever her father was up to, he wasn't going to get away with it.

Five minutes passed, and then twenty. Twenty turned to forty and then fifty. The first howls pierced the quiet night and coaxed chills to the surface of Mia's skin. She waited for something, anything, that might signal danger. She hoped her father had come to his senses and given up on his quest to run the werewolves out of the territory. Mia's anxiety crested and she paced the confines of Owen's cabin. Around the living room, through the kitchen, up the stairs, and into his bedroom. She leaned against the doorjamb as she gazed at the bed they'd shared for one intense night. There was a lot that Mia didn't know, but one thing was certain. She belonged to Owen and he belonged to her.

She started at the sound of an angry snarl in the distance. Others joined in to create a cacophony of sound and Mia's heart leaped up into her throat. She rushed down the stairs and threw open the door. Under the light of the full moon Mia watched in horror at the ensuing attack. The wolves were outnumbered at least three to one. She didn't know who they fought but she damn well knew who commanded them. In the distance, she spotted her father watching the chaos from a safe distance away.

It was a good thing she hadn't outwardly promised to stay put. Because Mia was about to enter the fray.

CHAPTER 13

Owen cast a nervous glance back toward his cabin. His worry for Mia surpassed his own instincts of self-preservation. The animal part of his nature occupied too much of Owen's mind. The wolf cared only for its mate and nothing else. All the worry in the world wouldn't matter if they couldn't manage to stay alive. He needed to keep his head in the game. He needed to focus on the danger in front of him. He needed to eliminate the threat to his pack so he could turn his attention to his mate.

He hoped she'd done as he'd asked and locked herself in the damned house.

Apparently, Mia's father wasn't so interested in asking nicely before using force to evict the pack from the Sawtooth territory. Owen wasn't surprised. This wasn't about them encroaching on anyone's turf. This was about their inability to succumb to the wood nymph's influence. He couldn't control the werewolves and that made them dangerous to whatever he had planned. Owen wished it didn't have to go down this way. The last thing he wanted was to start a relationship with Mia amid so much strife.

The report of a gunshot rang out and Owen took off at a sprint, zigging and zagging to avoid being hit. From what he could tell, the army that had been sent to drive them away was primarily human, which meant the chance of them firing silver bullets was slim. That didn't mean Owen was interested in getting plugged. He let the wolf take charge. The animal part of him was stronger, faster, more intuitive. Magic resided in that part of him and Owen let it be a guiding force in the fight.

"There's one! Get it!"

The angry shout sent Owen darting to his right. The sound of the bullet's passage whizzed by his ear. What the hell sort of night-vision scopes were these guys using, anyway? This far from town, no one would pay any attention to the sounds of a few errant shots. If all Mia's father had brought with him were a handful of humans with rifles, the conflict would likely be over before it began. Liam had given strict orders that no one was to be harmed since they were likely being influenced to act. But if any member of the pack was mortally threatened, all bets were off.

Owen glanced back at the danger behind him, only to miss the one right in front of him. He might as well have run into a brick wall, and the cartilage in his snout crunched from the impact. *What . . . the . . .* Owen gave his head a rough shake to clear the haze from his rattled brain as he looked up to see what had knocked him on his ass. *Fuck.*

Since moving into the remote Sawtooth territory, Owen could safely say he'd seen his fair share of rare supernaturals. Like he had wood nymphs, Owen had always doubted the existence of the creature that loomed above him now, teeth bared and giant hands clutched into boulder-sized fists. But like Mia, the troll that swung its massive fist toward Owen was flesh and blood.

He let out a yip of surprise as he narrowly avoided the blow. The troll's fist pounded into the ground, leaving a three-foot-deep divot in the crusty snow that went all the way to the frozen ground. Owen's four-legged status gave him an edge in the balance and weight-distribution departments. The snow didn't slow him down like it did the cumbersome troll. He wished he could say it slowed down the humans, but thanks to their snowmobiles, they navigated the snowy landscape just fine. As the troll swung around with its left fist to deliver a second blow, another round of shots rang out. Owen couldn't avoid them both and he yelped at the burn of the bullet as it struck his right shoulder blade. The crunch of bone as it shattered echoed in his preternatural ears and the scent of blood permeated the air. The pack was scattered, each of them fighting their own battles within the building war. Owen was on his own.

He took a stumbling step as he waited for the bullet wound to heal. Had it been a silver slug, he'd be down for the count. Luckily, he just needed a few minutes for his body to push out the bullet and heal itself. On the downside, he had precious few minutes to spare.

"Oh my gods, Owen!"

Owen turned at the sound of his mate's voice. If he had a palm right now, he would've planted his face in it. What part of lock the door and don't come out hadn't Mia understood? He'd yet to learn his mate's strengths and weaknesses. Owen didn't think she was as impervious to a stray bullet as he was. Through his worry, a sense of smug satisfaction puffed his chest. She'd seen him in his wolf form only once and yet had managed to identify him in the dark and chaos of the fight. Their bond was strong.

Mia appeared to float on top of the snow as she ran toward him. Owen put the humans, who continued to fire their rifles at him, and the troll who tried to smash him, to the back of his mind as he changed course and sprinted toward his mate. Mia didn't pay any attention to the battle that raged around them. Her sole focus was Owen and he wanted to give her a solid shake for not paying better attention to her surroundings. A twinge of pain tugged at his shoulder but he shook it off as he noticed a dark form headed straight toward Mia from her left. He let out several warning barks but she paid his warning no mind. Damn it. He wasn't going to get to her in time.

Her pursuer overtook her in a few long strides. Owen gave a mournful howl as she was jerked backward and held immobile. With every ounce of strength he had, Owen pushed himself faster until he noticed the wink of metal under the moonlight. A dagger was held just below her chin, the point poised at her throat. Owen came to a tumbling stop as the snow gave way beneath him. He regained his footing and his fur stood on end along his spine as he bared his teeth and issued a menacing growl at the male who held his mate captive.

"My daughter seems quite concerned for you, wolf. Curious, wouldn't you agree?"

Daughter? Fuck. Owen's breath fogged the air as he took a tentative step backward. Looked like his first encounter with the old father-in-law wasn't going to be a pleasant one.

Mia didn't show an ounce of fear. Her forest-green eyes sparked with an angry fire and her jaw squared. Owen's inability to communicate with her frustrated him to the point of pain. His stomach knotted and his muscles ached with tension.

"Tell me, Mia, is this the male you thought would buy you your birthright?"

Mia's eyes darted to Owen's and her scent soured with anxiety. What in the hell was her father talking about? How could he have possibly helped to secure her birthright and what exactly did that entail? Never had he wanted so badly for the full moon to set. He needed this business with her father over and done with. And he and Mia needed to have a long talk.

"You and I both know you were never going to let that happen." The rage that simmered in Mia's tone could've melted the polar ice caps.

"True. I'd planned to pair you off with someone weak and easy to manipulate. Instead, you spread your legs for a werewolf, and look at the trouble it's caused you."

Owen snarled. One more insult and he'd tear the male's throat out.

"More to the point," Mia said. "Look at the trouble it's caused *you*."

Owen let out a chuff of breath at Mia's snarky comeback. The rest of the pack were holding their own. Liam had everyone organized and on task and as far as Owen could tell, there hadn't been any casualties. The issue wasn't the band of attackers, but rather the single force that controlled them. Owen could end this. Right now. All he had to do was kill his mate's father.

Easier said than done when that very male had a dagger pressed to Mia's throat. He could attack. Throw his body slightly to the left in the hopes of knocking the dagger away. It was a risk Owen wasn't sure he wanted to take, but the alternative was to leave Mia where she was. Owen didn't doubt for a second that the bastard would kill his own daughter to further his agenda.

Owen made the decision in an instant. If they were going to die here tonight he'd rather they died taking a stand than on their knees. He dug his back legs into the snow and pushed off, careful to aim for Mia's father's left shoulder. His reaction time was faster than Owen thought it would be and he swung the dagger away from Mia's throat at the exact moment Owen crashed into him. Pain ignited along his nerve endings as the blade sank into his gut. Not steel.

Silver.

Owen's snarl ended on a low whine as he collapsed to the ground. He should've known the son of a bitch would come prepared to fight werewolves. The annoyance of the bullet wound in his shoulder was a surface scratch in comparison to the large gash that had been opened in his stomach. Blood scented the air, so intense that it made Owen's snout wrinkle. His strength flagged as every bit of energy he had funneled to the wound that refused to heal thanks to the silver that burned through him.

He looked up and his eyes met Mia's. She stared, aghast, her hands covering her mouth. Her shivering form blurred in his vision and a single thought formed in Owen's mind: *Run.*

A scream lodged in Mia's throat. She watched, helpless, as Owen lay bleeding on the snow. She knew of only one thing that could effectively disable a werewolf. Silver. Her father had gutted Owen with the silver blade.

Anger and sorrow unlike anything she'd ever felt welled up inside of Mia to the point that it could no longer be contained. The power that her intimate moments with Owen had manifested swirled and built, adding to the storm that raged inside of her. Her skin tightened on her frame and a sharp stab of pain caused her to double over.

"You've only made matters worse." Mia's eyes went wide as she looked at her father. "I wanted the werewolves gone, but dead is just as good."

Mia looked up. Her father shifted the dagger in his grasp as he stepped up to Owen. Mia's heart clenched in her chest as her father brought up his arm for the killing blow. The power that she didn't know how to contain exploded through her with a violent shout. "Stop!"

Everything around her stilled. Not a single body moved. Power radiated around her, flowed through her, and thickened the air. Mia's teeth chattered from the force of it. Her breath raced from the effort it took to control it. She imposed her will on every living thing around her, including her father, who was the most powerful nymph she'd ever known. Her bond with Owen had given Mia unimaginable strength. She felt the connection arc between them as she forced herself to straighten.

She put her back to her father and Owen and turned to face the bulk of the conflict. She'd never used her powers of influence on so many at once and she wasn't quite sure how to do it. "Those of you who stand against the werewolves, leave this place and never return!"

A fair amount of pent-up energy drained from her with the command and Mia released a shuddering breath. She turned to face her father. He met her gaze, his eyes narrowed to hateful slits. She approached him slowly, the only sound that of her feet crunching on the snow. She plucked the dagger from his grip and pointed it at his face. "Father." Her entire body trembled from the force of magic that swirled within her. "Leave this territory, go far from here to the other end of the world, and never return."

The influence she exerted over her father's will drained Mia in an instant. She collapsed to her knees and let out quick panting breaths as she tried to stabilize her careening world. She watched as her father slowly turned and walked away. His shadowed form became harder to make out in the backdrop of night the farther away he moved and finally, it disappeared altogether in the darkness.

Mia barely had enough strength to cover the few feet of space that separated her from Owen. She crawled through the snow on her hands and knees, exhausted, shivering, barely able to support her own weight. She collapsed beside him in the snow and let out a sob as her fingers dove into his thick fur. He watched her with wary eyes, feral and bright gold.

"I don't know about you, but I could use a nap."

Owen's tongue lolled out and he lapped at her cheek. Mia let out a weak laugh. At least they were on the same page.

Mia felt as though she'd been run over by a truck. Every inch of her hurt, even her eyeballs. A dull, orange glow reflected in the back of her mind. She cracked a lid and shielded her eyes against the sudden brightness. Someone seriously needed to turn down the lights.

"Good morning."

Owen's gorgeous face came into focus and Mia came fully awake. Sunlight filtered in through the window of his bedroom and he reached out to smooth her hair away from her face.

"Hey." Her voice rasped in her raw throat. "We're not dead."

Owen chuckled at the revelation. "No," he said. "We're not."

"How is that possible?" As she'd lain in the snow last night, Mia had been certain that they were both done for. That they were both alive now seemed a miracle.

"Believe me, it's going to take a hell of a lot more than a silver dagger to my gut to take me away from you. I'll be laid up for a few days. Silver wounds take a little longer to heal, but I'm going to be fine."

Warm emotion bloomed in Mia's chest. She reached out

and put her fingertips to Owen's cheek. "I thought I was going to lose you."

His bright smile caused her stomach to do a back flip. "Never. Sorry to say, Mia, but you're never getting rid of me."

Thank the gods. Because Mia didn't know what she'd do without him. In such a short amount of time Owen had become the most important thing in her life. So much had changed so quickly, she still had a hard time wrapping her mind around it.

"What happened last night?" The details were a little hazy in her mind and she found it difficult to grasp onto any detail.

Owen chuckled. "What happened? For starters, you went completely badass, powerful wood nymph on everyone and shut down the conflict before it got out of hand and anyone got hurt."

Wow. Tiny bits and pieces began to fall back into place as Mia remembered the power that had exploded through her. "That's not exactly true," she said. "You got hurt."

"Okay." Owen leaned in and put his lips to her forehead. "No one got seriously hurt."

She supposed that was a little better. "My father . . . ?"

"Gone. You told him to leave and never come back. I've never seen anything like it. He just . . . obeyed as though he had no other choice. Liam sent out trackers early this morning to find him and there isn't even a trace. Whatever influence you exercised over him, it worked well."

Mia let out a slow breath. She still couldn't believe she possessed the strength to do what she'd done last night. "That influence might fade. He might come back . . ."

"If he does, we'll deal with it. But until then, I don't want you to worry about it. We're safe now and that's all that matters."

Anxiety tightened her stomach but Mia knew Owen was right. It wouldn't do them any good to worry about it. "I wouldn't have been able to do it without you."

Owen's brow furrowed. "What do you mean?"

Mia met his gaze. "Being with you . . . It's like . . . magic. I can't explain it, but it's amazing."

"The mate bond." Mia might not have been able to explain it, but Owen had no problem. "Do you doubt it now?"

"No," Mia said with a laugh. "Not at all."

Owen wrapped his arms around her and pulled Mia against him. The heat of his body permeated her skin and left her more relaxed and content than she'd ever thought she could feel. She couldn't believe she'd once thought it would be so easy to walk away from such an extraordinary male. Owen had no comparison. He was *hers*.

"What did your father mean when he said you used me to buy your birthright?"

Mia cringed. She supposed they'd have to talk about it eventually but she was ashamed for having used Owen in the way that she had. "My father refused me a position of leadership within our band. He gave me an ultimatum. Produce an heir or he would find me a suitable partner to get the job done. I refused to live my life on his terms. And so . . ." She found it difficult to finish the sentence.

"And so . . . you went out looking for someone to give you what you needed with no strings attached."

He spoke the words softly without an ounce of anger or hurt and it only endeared him to her more. "Yeah. That's exactly what I did." The admission burned a path up her throat, but speaking the truth lifted the weight of guilt from Mia's chest. "I'm sorry, Owen. I shouldn't have behaved so carelessly with you."

"There's nothing for you to apologize for." Owen held

her tighter and Mia hoped he'd never let her go. "You did what you thought you had to do and I admire your strength and conviction."

"Even if I went into it just wanting to use you?"

Amusement rumbled in his chest. "Baby, you can use me anytime you want. Just promise you'll never leave me again."

"Never." It was the easiest promise Mia had ever had to make. "But there is one small issue. With my father gone there's no one to lead our band. I don't expect you to leave your pack but I can't leave my people either."

"I would never ask you to. We're in this together. I'm not ever going to give you an ultimatum and you'll never have to choose between your family or me. You won't have to choose between anything that's important to you or me. We'll find a way to make it work. I'm not worried."

Owen certainly was one of a kind. "Thank you," she said. "And for the record, I'm not worried either."

"Good. Now that that's settled, let's discuss this issue of an heir . . ."

Mia smiled at the humor in Owen's voice. She sensed his excitement and was happy that she wouldn't disappoint him. "How do you feel about babies, Owen?"

"I absolutely love them."

"Good. Because I think you're going to be changing diapers soon."

Owen put his lips to her temple. "A new adventure." He pulled back and graced her with a brilliant smile. "I can't wait."

Owen was everything she could ask for and more and Mia wouldn't change how any of this had gone down for the world. After so many years of going without, she'd finally gotten everything she'd ever wanted. And the best part?

Owen would never make her choose, or make a sacrifice, and in return, she'd never make him sacrifice or choose. They would be partners. Equals. She returned his smile, her heart so full of tender emotion she thought it would burst. "Neither can I."